Farewell to the Flesh

FAREWELL TO THE FLESH

Gemma O'Connor

BANTAM BOOKS
TORONTO • NEW YORK • LONDON • SYDNEY • AUCKLAND

FAREWELL TO THE FLESH
A BANTAM BOOK: 0 553 50586 6

First publication in Great Britain

PRINTING HISTORY
Bantam edition published 1998

Set in 11/12pt Sabon by Deltatype Ltd, Birkenhead, Merseyside

Bantam Books are published by Transworld Publishers Ltd,
61–63 Uxbridge Road, London W5 5SA,
in Australia by Transworld Publishers (Australia) Pty Ltd,
15–25 Helles Avenue, Moorebank, NSW 2170,
and in New Zealand by Transworld Publishers (NZ) Ltd,
3 William Pickering Drive, Albany, Auckland.

Reproduced, printed and bound in Great Britain by
Cox & Wyman Ltd, Reading, Berks.

For my dear sons, Simon and Oscar, with my love

AUTHOR'S NOTE

All the characters in this book are fictitious, and any resemblance to actual persons, living or dead, is purely coincidental. There is no order of nuns nor convent of Holy Retreat. Both the foundation and its members are entirely imagined, as is their wonderful house. Making the great John Rothery its architect was by way of tribute to a magnificent artist. I am not sure to whom I should apologize for altering (beyond recognition) the coastline of Killiney Bay to make room for Holy Retreat and Glenadams School.

ACKNOWLEDGEMENTS

This story is based on two utterly unrelated encounters: a chance conversation with a nun in Dublin and a tour of the Putti Library of the Instituti Ortopedici Rizzoli in Bologna. I should like to thank my dear friend in Dublin for firing my imagination and Dr Anna Viganò for disclosing the secrets of that magnificent library. I am also greatly indebted to my friends the Leardini family: Dr Alberto and his wife, Maria-Luisa, in Bologna (and Oxford) and Signora Maria Teresa Toroni in Riccione, under whose hospitable roof I wrote the opening chapters of *Farewell to the Flesh*. To all of these, *ringraziamenti*.

The army of helpers and advisers grows longer with each book. I am astonished by the generosity of my friends who, between them, command a dazzling range of expertise which I plunder mercilessly. I thank them all without restraint and at the same time stress that any mistakes in religious, legal, medical, mortuary, bibliographical and other matters are mine alone. This time I had particular need of legal advice from Shelly Cranshaw, Brian Pattinson, Jane-Marie Harris, Marie O'Dwyer and Emily Taylor. Pauline Fitzpatrick for constant and generous help with the research in Dublin; Revd Bernard O'Connor OSA; Ruth McCarthy; Ritchie Gill; John King of Blackwells Antiquarian Books for introducing me to *The Private Case* by P.T. Kearney; Orla Murphy, Lucia Moffett and Ann Cadogan in West Cork; Oliver Doyle of Iarnod Eireann; the staff of the Cemeteries Division of Dublin Corporation. Finally, my little grandchildren, Eleanor, Joseph, Thomas and Alice deserve a grateful mention, not just for their glorious presence, but for providing me with perfect (if composite) models for my tinier characters.

Come pensive nun, devout and pure,
   Sober, steadfast, and demure,
   All in a robe of darkest grain,
   Flowing with majestic train,
   And sable stole of cypress lawn,
Over thy decent shoulders drawn,
Come, but keep thy wonted state,
With even step, and musing gait . . .

Il Penseroso, John Milton

KILLINEY BAY, CO. DUBLIN

IRELAND

29 October 1996

PROLOGUE

The undertaker was late. By the time he arrived dawn was well advanced. The weather, which had been mild for weeks, had turned unseasonably cold overnight. The ground was covered with a light frost and the two nuns were shivering with cold. Or perhaps fear. They huddled on either side of an erect young woman and clutched their black mantles around them with blue-tinged fingers. The peace of their cloistered world was shattered. The sisters stared in dismay as the JCB trundled up *their* driveway, leaving great snaking gouges along its edges. Never in their lives had they seen a more monstrous, more deafening, more *yellow* machine. They and their poor, dear, crumbling convent trembled at its approach. It was as if at that moment both the building and its inhabitants fully understood for the first time how soon an army of workmen would pull and tear at its foundations, its beetled-timbers. Renovating, restoring, *altering* the ruined fabric of their history, disturbing the peaceful serenity of their enclave.

The undertaker's car bumped and heaved in the JCB's wake, turning off to park by the side wall of the old house. Three men got out, pulling up their coat-collars against the sharp sea-breeze, as Tess Callaway hurried over to meet them.

'We're just waiting for the people from the

Health Board and the County Council—' she started.

'They're on their way,' the undertaker interrupted. 'They were just after me coming in but they must have parked by the lodge.' He bobbed his head at her. 'I suppose you're Miss Callaway?' He looked about him pointedly. 'What about the solicitor? Mr Murphy-Dunne?'

'I'm here in his place, I'm also a solicitor,' Tess replied briskly. 'I thought I mentioned that on the phone, Mr Dwyer?' They had spoken several times over the past few weeks. 'The nuns are anxious that we get started at once.'

One of the men drew in his breath sharply and delved into the boot of the car. When he straightened up he held a pickaxe, a couple of narrow, flat spades and a coil of strapping which he looped over his shoulder. He handed one of the spades to his mate and without exchanging a word, they plodded after the JCB.

'They don't like digging up graves. They're a bit superstitious,' the undertaker murmured and crossed himself. 'They're not the only ones.' He looked at Tess and shivered. 'I'm not that hot on it myself,' he added as they trudged across the dewy grass. The little graveyard was located by the southern boundary wall of the convent and though it was set in beautifully landscaped parkland, it still managed to look dismal.

'Thirty-one graves, Mother?'

'Thirty-one, Mr Dwyer.' The nun kept her eyes firmly on the ground. She sounded like the other sisters Tess had met over the past six or seven weeks, as if her voice-box had tightened or shrunk from too little use.

'Got the list, Mother?'

'Yes, Mr Dwyer.' She drew a sheaf of papers from beneath her cloak and passed them around. Tess ran her eye down the list of the convent dead which started from February 1867 and ran to January 1996. Name, age, date and cause of death were listed in four neat columns: heart disease, respiratory problems but TB for the most part; some of the younger recruits to the order had died pathetically young. She thought about the damp chill of the convent building and marvelled that any of the sisters survived the winters without heating or insulation.

The convent of Holy Retreat was in urgent need of renovation and in order to pay for it the sisters had agreed to sell a plot of land to the neighbouring school. Unfortunately the desired site which lay along the boundary of the next property, contained the nuns' cemetery. The decision to move it had taken over two years to reach. Recent trouble, when vandals had burned the memorial crosses, had finally swung the balance.

'How long will it take, Mr Dwyer?'

The group assembled: the two nuns – the superior and an elderly, nameless companion; Tess Callaway, solicitor; J.J. Dwyer, the undertaker; Mike Flood from the County Council (Cemeteries division) and Mrs Joan Fermoy from the Eastern Health Board. There was a moment's hesitation about whether to start digging up the oldest or the newest graves until the Mother Guardian raised her eyes to Mr Dwyer's and read his silent message.

'Start at the most recent,' she said firmly and began to pray.

At first all went smoothly. Because the first few coffins they lifted were still complete, progress was swift. The hours passed. There were no headstones to be removed, just a simple wooden cross over each grave. Some were original, faded and broken, others had recently been vandalized and had been temporarily replaced with small wooden stakes. Soon they got into an easy routine, the name plate on each was matched to the list, checked first by the nuns then by the officials. At first, Tess took little part; she wasn't even entirely sure why she'd offered to be there. Some instinct that she might be needed? A growing affection for the sisters and their plight? Or simply to witness this rare and curious ritual? Unique, according to the Council official.

Afterwards, when Tess Callaway looked back on those terrible few days, what she remembered most vividly were not the strange happenings at the convent or the dreadful isolation of her own recent bereavement, but the kindness of the Mother Guardian who, even while she was oppressed by the sinister events within the cloister, had embraced her loss and turned her from anger and despair.

As the day progressed the task became grimmer and a good deal slower. Many of the older coffins had long since fallen apart. By the early afternoon they were beginning to flag. There was little talk as they gathered and labelled the contents of each grave. By now everyone was helping, silently passing the body bags from hand to hand, checking and rechecking each label against the list. All the time the nuns paced up and down the sidelines, praying silently. It was almost as if they weren't there, the all-elaborate, all-enveloping hood of their black cloaks completely hiding their faces. They looked like black ghosts.

Work was almost finished for the day when one of the gravediggers suddenly waved his arm violently at the undertaker. 'Mr Dwyer,' he shouted, 'come quick.'

'What's up? What's up?' The Mother Guardian's voice cracked in alarm as she clutched hold of Tess Callaway's sleeve. Dwyer ran over to where the men had been digging. The others watched him bend down then shake his head as if in disbelief. The diggers leaned on their spades and looked on with interest. As the undertaker straightened up, the rest of them crowded around. He spoke directly to the Mother Guardian. His voice was full of foreboding.

'It's a lead coffin,' he said with ominous quiet.

The old nun gawped at Dwyer in disbelief. 'But it can't be,' she choked. 'There was no mention of a lead coffin in the convent records.' She looked around wildly for support. 'Such . . . such . . . extravagance would not be in keeping with our holy rule. We always . . . *have always* used simple wooden . . .' Her voice trailed away.

The undertaker straightened up and studiously dusted off the knees of his trousers. 'Well then,' he said heavily, 'in that case, we seem to have an extra body.' He paused and sucked in his cheeks. 'Or perhaps somebody has made a mistake?' His eyes met hers. 'You're going to have to check the convent records again. Aren't you, Reverend Mother?'

OXFORD

Late August – Early September 1996

My beloved is mine and I am his. He said to me:
Set me as a seal on your heart,
As a seal upon your arm;
For love is strong as death.

The Song of Songs 11:6–7

1

There was a large brass clock on the kitchen wall. It almost filled the space between the top of the door and the picture rail above. In the weeks before the baby was born Tess Callaway began to fancy she could hear its heavy, hesitant tick-tock yet she knew that could not be. Although the heavy brass case looked like an old ship's timepiece, the clock was a modern fake, quartz, and therefore silent.

Sometimes, in the last weeks of her pregnancy, when she looked up quickly she fancied she saw the shrouded figure of death leaning nonchalantly against the dresser, with a small, Soviet-style scythe hooked debonairly over his bony shoulder. His unseen skeleton legs crossed, his fleshless backside hitched on the edge of the lower cupboard. Marcus but not Marcus. The same self-deprecating shrug of the shoulders as if to say, 'I didn't mean to go.' He held a lighted cigarette in a long, elegant, ebony holder. As the imagined, intoxicatingly perfumed smoke wafted deliciously across the room, she would reach into the drawer of the kitchen table and feel for his packet of fags and lighter. Often, she came to at dawn, cold and stiff, still sprawled across the table.

Then, after the baby was born, fear of her own mortality consumed her thoughts and drove her actions. Fear for what would happen to Claire if she too were snatched away in some terrible accident. The nights were the worst. Having slept almost twenty-four hours a day while they were in hospital, once home, the baby hardly stopped crying. Or so it seemed. During the day, when friends or neighbours came to lend a hand, the infant behaved impeccably and slept like an angel – which gave the impression that Tess was coping with the situation. Nothing could have been further from the truth. Almost from the moment she carried her baby daughter over the threshold, the sleeping angel turned into a screaming dervish and acted as though she was being deliberately starved.

Night became day. At first Tess hadn't the energy to react, or to do anything the midwife suggested. Instead of letting the infant exhaust herself with crying, she took her into bed and dozed fitfully with Claire grazing and squirming restlessly beside her. Within days, any pretence of putting her into her cradle at night was abandoned. They slept together in the double bed which had once seemed perfectly adequate for a couple but now seemed much too small for one tiny scrap, still less her weepy and exhausted mother.

Mrs Blount, the health visitor, continually warned that by giving in to the little bully, she'd made a rod for her own back. 'Start as you mean to go on. Show her who's boss or she'll run you ragged,' she admonished, but Tess hadn't enough energy to care. And having lost that battle there was no respite. Every squeak, snuffle and shriek was rewarded with a rush of her anxious mother's milk. It was soon clear that it was the baby who had started as she meant to continue, Claire ruled the bed, the mother and the night. Within a couple of weeks she had her entire universe firmly within her control. Including Daisy Blount, Tess was somewhat relieved to note.

After the first flush of daily visitors thinned, it became possible for Tess to lie down when the baby napped during the day. As soon as Claire dropped off, Tess would fling herself down on the bed or sofa, and sink into immediate unconsciousness, which, instead of refreshing, made her more desperate. She became greedy for normal, dreaming sleep and the greedier she became, the more unattainable it seemed. She'd close her eyes and moments later, would find herself sitting bolt upright with pounding heart. Eventually there came a point when sheer, mind-numbing exhaustion turned into a kind of uncontrolled elation. Sometimes she felt as though the back of her head had separated from the front. A strange fluttering sensation tickled at the roots of her hair as if a colony of ants had taken up their busy residence between skin and bone. It was then that Tess began to comprehend the finality of her partner's death. The terrible moment when her grieving began and it became impossible for her to lie awake in their bed whose pillows and duvet seemed to retain his scent and shape. Their room was still scattered with his discarded clothes, which she could scarcely bear to look at, much less tidy away. Now, when the baby dropped off to sleep, she took to prowling the house, moving restlessly through the dark rooms, staring moodily out the windows.

Winchester Road, less than a mile from the very centre of Oxford, had a pleasing asymmetry, the houses having been built at different times and in different styles. It was a quiet road with only light passing traffic and few pedestrians since access was determined by a rather clever one-way system, presumably designed for that very purpose. Halfway down – or up – depending on the pedestrian's approach, a tree-lined walkway gave access into the Woodstock Road. Directly opposite, narrow, chic North Parade linked to the Banbury Road. Or from it, since it was too narrow to support more than one-way traffic.

Tess lived a couple of doors down from the corner in a charming nineteeth-century house built before gothic mania had properly taken hold of north Oxford. Only the windows gave a hint that its builders had been mildly influenced by the revival. But instead of the contorted shapes of later extravagances, in number, size and placement, the windows were still largely based on the Georgian model. Tess and Marcus had bought it five years before, shortly after the crash in house prices. But they still managed to pay well over the odds simply because they fell in love with the house at much the same time as they fell back into love with each other.

The road looked different by night. At eye-level, the mature trees which lined it merged with lesser garden trees and shrubs into an illusory woodland. The light cast by the old-fashioned street-lamps lent romance and mystery, specially in the walkway leading to the church of SS Philip and James which was diagonally opposite the house. It could almost have been in the countryside. Once the daytime comings and goings had stopped, the traffic on the main roads out of the town thinned and the lights in the houses were dowsed, nocturnal life began. The variety and number of creatures was startling. Sometimes the nights were hushed and still but more often they were filled with sound. Not just the ubiquitous and amorphous hum of traffic, but sounds which, even when they choused, retained their own shrill or harsh individuality. It was as if a corresponding society mimicked and mirrored its human equivalent. At first, the strange cries and sudden movements frightened her and made her twitch, feel vulnerable. But once she began to be able to match sound to living creature, the fear grew less.

Often, staring out of the window she distracted herself by matching her neighbours to an animal counterpart, real or imagined. There were more than enough to go round: feral cats, stray dogs, a couple of suburban foxes. Once, just once, she spotted a stout, shuffling hedgehog. Sometimes, if she sat still enough she saw a ghostly barn-owl return to his residence in the church tower. But she had to keep to his timetable, not hers, for he was a creature of the most precise habits. The degree of darkness had to be just right for his exits and returns. For such a big bird he was surprisingly difficult to spot even when flying and almost impossible when he perched in a tree. One night when she was staring into the middle distance, thinking of Marcus, she became aware of him sitting, like a piece of sculpture, on top of her own gatepost. As he turned his head slowly, the pale masked face glowed eerily in the moonlight and one eye opened as if he was winking at her.

It didn't take many night vigils for her to begin to observe that all was not entirely quiet on the human front either. Was it her imagination, or did the unexpected nocturnal activity lend a hint of romance to the comings and goings round the back of the student flats down at the Bevington Road end? Almost as if college curfews still applied. From where she sat in her darkened room, she viewed their unconstrained freedom with regret and more than a little envy.

She was most intrigued by the retired clergyman who, at about two in the morning, regularly crept across the street, from the alley, wearing only his dressing-gown. She strained to see where his bare and shapely old legs carried him but this she never discovered. His quarry was, unfortunately, out of her line of vision, in one of the three houses to her right. Speculating as to his choice gave her some amusement: a retired diplomat, a youngish divorcée or a middle-aged actor. Or perhaps all three? She smiled wryly as she recalled her startled reaction to the unspoken collusion between college porters and dons which had struck her forcefully when she first came to the city of dreaming spires. The invariable reply to her enquiries as to the whereabouts of her partner was, 'Oh, you've only just missed him. He passed the lodge a few seconds ago.' And she was either too proud or too slow to ask whether he was coming or going. The eternal position of the rambling don was, she soon decided, somewhere between his college and university department. Perhaps some of the same mobility applied to the old clergyman? She never knew when the old adventurer made his return journey, never caught sight of that pre-dawn sprint home. But at eight o'clock each morning he strode out of his own house with his nervy red setter prancing at his heels, as innocent and as bucolic as it was possible to be. Just like Hugo, she thought one morning as she watched the old rover set out. He bore a remarkable resemblance to the man she still thought of as her step-father. And at once she was overcome with a desperate longing for home.

By night on my bed I sought him whom my soul loveth:
I sought him, but I found him not.

The Song of Songs 11:28–29

2

'Hello! Tess, wait.' A breathless voice hailed her
from behind. 'Hang on. This hill is pretty steep.
Give a fellow a chance.'

Tess Callaway turned as a tall, somewhat
overweight, grey-haired man caught her up. Her
pale face was a mask of indifference as she turned
to face Marcus's brother.

'Hill? What hill?' She raised her eyebrows at
him in mock amazement. 'The Banbury Road is as
flat as a pancake. Owen Rogerson, you are
seriously out of condition.'

'Don't I know it. Anyway, who says it's flat? It
feels quite alpine to me,' he joked, trying not to
notice how very run-down she looked. And almost
skeletally thin. When he'd last seen her she'd been
heavily pregnant and utterly passive. Perhaps that
was how she'd survived those terrible weeks, by
switching herself off, not connecting, hardly
speaking. Yet he'd never seen her so serene or look
so utterly beautiful as she was then. Being so tall
and slim she had carried the great bump majestically before her, her shoulders thrown back to
retain some semblance of balance. Her face had

filled out and the pale skin had been almost luminous. Now it was muddy and the shadows around her eyes made her look as though she hadn't slept for months, which was probably true. Most disturbing of all, her clothes looked grubby. 'Anyone ever tell you you walk too fast?' he said lightly and put his arm around her shoulders.

'Frequently.' She ducked away from him. 'How did you know where to find me?' Her voice was brittle, challenging.

'I met Giorgio. He said he'd seen you striding past the restaurant. Very determined looking, he said.' He looked at her closely. 'It must be the new hairdo,' he quipped and could have bitten his tongue off for crass insensitivity. Tess had pulled her curly dark hair into an untidy bunch. It looked as though it urgently needed shampooing.

Tess glared at him. 'So what are you doing here?' she asked. She had not seen him since a week before the baby was born.

'I've come to see you both, of course. Don't be so spiky.'

'You took your time,' she started, then her face broke into a smile. 'I'm sorry. I'm absolutely knackered. It's lovely to see you.'

'Right then.' Owen looked pleased. To cover his embarrassment he leaned over the pram while Tess continued her march. 'Why, she's beautiful, isn't she?' He sounded surprised. Tess laughed.

'As long as she's asleep.' She looked him up and down. He was dressed casually in sand-coloured cords, blue check shirt and light blue cashmere sweater. But casual clothes don't make casual man: he looked terribly uncomfortable, unfamiliar. She tried to remember when she had ever seen

Owen in other than a flawlessly cut pinstripe. She chuckled softly to herself. Someone must be buying his clothes. Someone was trying to either jazz him up or relax him. Or possibly both.

'New girlfriend?' she asked casually and was rewarded with a sheepish grin.

'Like the duds?'

'More to the point, do you?'

'Sharp as ever.' He gave a short laugh. 'Not sure.' He touched her lightly on the cheek before turning his head away in embarrassment, afraid she might too quickly divine – and reject – the impulse for his new image. 'Enough of that. I'm sorry I couldn't get here sooner. The Hong Kong thing took much longer than I expected. I only got back on Tuesday. What a hell-hole. The heat was indescribable and I've had gippy tummy since I got back. Lord, but I'm out of condition.'

'Were you ever in?' chortled Tess. 'By the way, where's your car?'

'Back at the house. I've got some things for my little niece.'

'Thanks, Owen. And for ringing so often. It helped.' Both her voice and expression softened. He had telephoned five or six times from Hong Kong, usually late in the evening when she was at her lowest point, and talked her to sleep. It had been her lifeline. Perhaps all the more so because, until the shock of Marcus's death had drawn them together, they hadn't been particularly close. Feeling grateful also made her feel shy, and therefore, more than usually edgy.

'You coping?' The careless manner did nothing to disguise his concern.

She shrugged. 'Not sure about coping. More like existing. Trying to take it day to day.'

'How far are we walking?'

'I was heading towards Summertown. I thought I'd drop in on a friend. But it doesn't matter, I was going off the idea anyway. We can go back and have a cup of tea if you like.' She looked at his horrified expression and laughed. 'Or a drink. I was only trying to get her to sleep. Let's go back via the Woodstock Road, the traffic is a bit lighter.' They turned into Rawlinson Road and had walked a couple of hundred yards when a station-wagon drew up beside them and a woman stuck her head out the window.

'Hi, Owen,' she said. 'I thought I recognized you.' As she stepped out of the car Owen went scarlet but made no attempt to introduce her. She was of medium height, slender and good-looking. About fifty, with grey-streaked black hair and rather disconcerting pale grey-blue eyes. She smiled at Tess and peered in at Claire. 'How old?' she asked, cleverly avoiding gender.

'She's exactly five weeks. In an hour or two.'

'She's lovely. Doesn't she sleep well?' The woman smiled.

'No, she doesn't, she's perpetually hungry,' Tess said as the baby let out a piercing howl. 'Sorry, we have to keep moving.' She looked from Owen to the woman. 'Would you like to join us for tea?' she asked, hoping she'd refuse.

She did. 'I'd love to but I'm on my way to see one of my employees who's gone AWOL. I just hope she hasn't had an accident.'

'What?' Owen spoke sharply and put a protective

arm around Tess's shoulder. She shrugged him off, embarrassed. Her engorged breasts began to spurt as the baby's screams grew frantic.

'I'm sorry, I didn't mean to upset you.' The woman sounded mystified until she looked at Tess closely and took in the situation. 'Would you like to sit in the car while you feed the baby?' she asked kindly.

'Tess?' Owen's voice rose in horror. 'Tess, come back to the house. You can't do that in public.'

'Yes, I can,' she answered tersely. 'If you don't like it, go away. Oh, for heaven's sake wait,' she shouted as Owen bolted. Tess shrugged at the woman and they both laughed.

'New man, eh?'

'I'd better follow him. Thanks for the offer though.' Tess hurriedly waved goodbye and set off at a smart lick, trying to ignore Claire's screams. Owen, she noticed, had discovered a fine, uncharacteristic turn of speed. Watching him disappear into the distance she marvelled at how temperamentally unlike his brother he was. Which was odd because when she first met Marcus she'd thought the very opposite.

She'd been new to London, a recent recruit in Rogerson Midgeley, the law practice of which Owen was now the senior partner. He had introduced her to his younger brother at the dinner party he gave to welcome her. Her first impression of the brothers had been their formality. With apparently none of the *joie de vivre* of her erstwhile companions at home in Dublin. Beautiful manners but oh, so serious and oh, so boring. But as she got to know him, Marcus turned out to be anything but. Her heart had sunk on that first occasion when he told her that he was an engineer.

But that was before she learned how much excitement and pleasure he derived from his subject and from life in general. And that, in a sense, summed Marcus up: he didn't actually comprehend the word boredom. He reminded her of the more exciting type of interviewee she sometimes heard on 'Desert Island Discs' whom she'd always rather jeeringly categorized as the *Very Best Kind of Englishman*. His interests and knowledge ranged widely over music, theatre and literature as well as science but she had never, before or since, been so beguiled as by his eloquence on the subject of bridges. Bridges and Isambard Kingdom Brunel to be exact.

Socially, Marcus had always easily eclipsed his older brother. It would have infuriated a more generous man than Owen, she thought, as she watched him turn into Canterbury Road. They looked so alike. Tall, slightly heavy set and both had greyed prematurely. But Marcus had always been less stiff, less formal. She'd caught Owen's expression when the woman had said accident. Watched the carefully constructed mask crumble. Poor Owen, he was terrified she would break down, disgrace herself and cause him to break down as well. He was so buttoned up that he could hardly mention his younger brother's name, much less express his own terrible grief for his death. He'd been exactly the same when his wife Helen died of cancer five years before.

'Poor us,' she murmured.

By the time she got back home Claire was still wailing and Owen was nowhere in sight. She left the hall door on the latch and went to check that he wasn't waiting in the back garden but there was no sign of him. She wedged the kitchen door ajar, went through to the sitting-room and settled herself on the sofa. But Claire was in such a state of hunger that she fed too quickly, in furious gulps, and then immediately deposited a cascade of curdled milk down the shoulder of what had once been a very smart grey jacket. Tess groaned at her folly in wearing it as she carried the baby upstairs. She changed the jacket and Claire's entire outfit and went back down to the sofa to start the whole feeding process again. But by now the child was over-exhausted and kept falling asleep. Tess, willing herself to remain calm, began to doze off so that it was some time before she became aware of the sounds of clinking crockery from the kitchen. After about ten minutes Owen brought her a cup of tea but beat a hasty retreat at the sight of her suckling the baby.

She wondered if she'd misheard his murmured 'tidy up a bit' until she heard the vacuum cleaner being hauled across her bedroom floor. She waited until she heard him return to the kitchen before she tiptoed upstairs and put Claire into her cot. The bedroom was still a tip. Despite Owen's efforts, she could see no discernible difference except where the Hoover had actually passed over the gold-coloured carpet. A bit like the yellow brick road, she thought, looking at the piles of books and clothes he had carefully skirted.

He'd been more successful in the kitchen which he'd transformed into something approaching cleanliness. The piles of dishes had been cleared from the sink, the dishwasher was running and there was a huge bunch of irises in a clear glass vase on the table. Both were new. She wondered if it had been instinct or advice from the florist which had prompted his choice of her favourite flower. He looked extremely sheepish when she tried to thank him. 'I could murder a gin, though,' he said, plonking a bottle of Tanqueray on the table.

'I'm not sure there are any lemons.'

'There are. And a couple of limes. I got them when I nipped around to North Parade. There doesn't appear to be anything to eat in the fridge so I ordered a meal from the Luna Caprese. Giorgio said he'd send Luis around with it at about seven. That suit?'

She nodded. 'Amazing. Thanks, Owen.' She passed him his drink and they both sat down at table. 'By the way, who was that woman we met? She looked vaguely familiar.'

'Oh, don't you know her? She runs the antiquarian bookshop in Walton Street. I'm sorry I didn't introduce you but I just couldn't, for the life of me, remember her name.'

'Hartfield Magraw Rare Books?'

'That's it. Grace Hartfield.' He slapped his forehead. 'It went clean out of my head, so embarrassing. I often nip in there when I come up to see the parents.'

'Is she American?' she asked.

'I'm not sure, but her husband is, I think. He's the Magraw bit.'

'Was it the word accident that upset you? Or the thought of me feeding Claire?'

He laid his hand gently on hers. 'Both, I'm afraid. I can't bear to think about the accident and the baby is, well, the baby is utterly delicious but yes, I do find all that a little embarrassing. Hopeless, eh?' He shrugged and pulled a face.

'*All what?* Feeding a baby is perfectly natural,' Tess said crossly. 'Honestly, I wasn't going to strip off or anything. I'm not that indiscreet.'

'I know, I know. But I can't help it. I'm just not used to babies. Or the attendant bodily functions for that matter.'

'Bodily what?' she exploded. 'I don't believe what I'm hearing. For God's sake, Owen, what's the matter with you?'

'I know, I know. I'm the pits. Do you realize that she's the first infant in the Rogerson family for forty years? Since Marcus in fact.' He put his head in his hands. 'If she is in the Rogerson family,' he murmured. Tess tore his hands from his face.

'What the hell do you mean? That she's not Marcus's child? She is, you know. She bloody well, most definitely, is. How dare you!'

He looked at her appalled. 'Oh, Christ, Tess, of course, I didn't mean that. Oh, my dear, my dear.' He closed his eyes in despair. 'I meant, I simply meant to ask if she would be called Callaway or—'

'Claire Callaway?' she cut in harshly. 'Claire Callaway? CC? For heaven's sake give me some credit. She's called after your mother or didn't you notice?' She took the child's birth certificate from the table drawer and pushed it across to him. 'Check it yourself. She is Claire Marcia Rogerson.' She glared at him furiously.

'You registered her birth yourself?' It was typical of him that he should fix on the mechanics of the situation rather than the emotion, so that at first she didn't quite understand what byroad he was travelling. He looked as close to tears as someone so closed in could be.

'It wasn't a big deal. I got the taxi to take me to

the Register Office on the way home from the hospital. Claire was three days old.' She didn't add that superstition had driven her. Made her cling to the legal niceties. If Claire existed at all, in those first few days, her reality was described on that scrap of paper: Claire Rogerson, daughter of Tess Callaway and the late Marcus Rogerson. Tess didn't mention that she'd carried it in her pocket all the time for the first couple of weeks.

'You went off to register your baby's birth alone?' He shook his head from side to side, pityingly. 'You have to do all those things by yourself. So much. I wish I'd been here. Was there no one to help you?' She was grateful he didn't mention her family.

'I thought I could manage,' she said. 'I was wrong. Your mother mounted a rescue and came for a few days.'

Their eyes met. Marcia was in her late seventies and since she was almost crippled with arthritis, was more used to being helped than helper.

'Was that difficult?'

'No.' She swallowed. 'Not in the way you mean. I was glad she was here those first few days; she was magnificent. I could hardly hold the baby, I was so terrified. In a panic about everything. Somehow when you're reasonably competent you think looking after a baby will be a doddle. It's not. Your mother was surprisingly calm and very, very helpful.' She swallowed painfully. 'And kind. But it made her feel much worse about Marcus. I think as long as she was at home she could pretend that he was still alive, in Oxford, carrying on his life. Being here made the accident too real. Your father came to fetch her home. He couldn't hack it at all, poor Dudley. It took a huge effort for him even to step inside the house.' She looked at him ruefully. 'I know he minds dreadfully that we never got married.'

'Not in the way you mean, I think.' Owen took her hand again and this time would not release it. He spoke very earnestly, careful not to ruffle her raw feelings. 'But they are terrified that you will go back to live in Ireland and they'll lose contact with their only grandchild. They know as well as you and I that grandparents have no legal rights but . . .'

'. . . knowledge doesn't drive those feelings, does it?' she finished. She bit her lower lip. 'And even if we had been married, it wouldn't make any difference, would it?' she said bitterly. 'Show them the certificate. It may help.' She leaned forward. 'I will probably go to Ireland. But not permanently, just for a while, I promise. I've got to get out of Oxford. This house is getting me down.'

DUBLIN

Mid to Late September

Conveyancing: 1. *Deceitful contrivance* – 1690. 2. *The drawing of deeds and other instruments for the transference of property from one person to another; the branch of law which deals with titles and their transference* – 1714.

Oxford English Dictionary

3

It all happened so easily, so naturally, almost as if Hugo Boland had planned to get Tess Callaway involved with the business at Holy Retreat in advance. But that was absurd since he hadn't even known she was in Dublin until she turned up on his doorstep. But Hugo was a deep one, not given to explaining the unexplainable. All he said was, 'Come in, come in, darling, you have been much on my mind these past weeks.' As always he looked terribly pleased to see her.

Tess had started out on the journey in a moment of despair with no real plan and no thought of staying for longer than a couple of weeks. She certainly hadn't the least idea of working until Hugo took charge and changed everything with one sentence.

'Why not stay for a while,' he said, 'and give yourself time to recover?'

Tess was standing at the high, uncurtained window and at first appeared not to hear. She continued her absorbed study of the small paved garden. Below her a cat crouched, ready to spring on a plump little robin who held his head cheekily on one side.

She raised her eyes to the horizon. 'I didn't realize you could see the mountains from here,' she murmured, half to herself.

'Only on an exceptionally clear day. You should see the view from the top floor,' he replied, 'best in the house.'

She made an impatient little gesture and looked down at the garden again where the robin was pulling a fat wriggling worm from between the paving stones.

'It would be so nice to have you back, Tess,' he persisted. He was a little hard of hearing and spoke loudly. Out in the garden the cat sprang and the robin, still clinging to his quarry, hopped neatly onto the back of a wooden bench. At last, Tess turned to face Hugo.

'No.' The reply was uncompromising and emphatic. 'This isn't home any more. Oxford is. Anyway, it wouldn't work,' she said flatly, 'you know it wouldn't.' Her voice was tired, she looked depressed.

'I don't see why not.'

She crossed the room and joined him on the huge chesterfield. Burrowing comfortably into the opposite corner, she drew one leg up under her then reached out and took his hand. The parchment skin was mottled with huge liver-spots but the long slim fingers were still elegant. As were his clothes. He wore a dark blue linen suit which somehow contrived not to look rumpled.

'It would be impossible, Hugo, dear,' she said softly. 'My life is there, not here. In any case, I'm committed to go back to the Crown Prosecution Service.' She puffed out her lips and shrugged. 'The job is all I have to hang on to.' She gave him a watery little smile and raised an eyebrow. 'You were right all along – about court work – I like it a lot.'

'Well now—' he started but she cut him short.

'I couldn't stay. Mother would drive me spare,' she said.

'Surely not?' he mocked. But his rueful expression belied the words.

'Why do you think I've been away so long? A couple of weeks with Mother and you begin to believe that you have no right to a life that doesn't include dancing attendance on her. The great lesson I learned from you', Tess's eyes met his, 'is if you can't take it, run like hell.' She laughed mirthlessly.

'Oh dear. That just about sums me up, doesn't it? I wasn't much good to you, was I?'

'You were brilliant,' she said briskly. 'As you know. Anyway, Mother left you, don't forget. You lasted longer than most, including Dad. And,' she squeezed his hand, 'you were the only one who ever took the slightest notice of her gawky daughter.'

'Beauty,' he said and patted her arm fondly.

'Beast.' It was an old, private joke. She smiled. 'Susan's away I take it?'

'Yep. I haven't seen her since the funeral.' The careless words didn't quite hide the surprised hurt.

'But that's well over four months ago,' he expostulated. He sounded appalled. 'I thought . . . I hoped . . .'

'What? That she'd come over when the baby was born? That it would bring us closer together?' She looked sadly at the infant sleeping soundly in a Moses basket by the side of the sofa. 'Not Mother's scene, I'm afraid. She doesn't quite see herself as a grandmother.'

'No,' he said. 'I can quite appreciate that. So why are you here?'

'Showing my baby her – my – native land,' she shrugged. 'You know. The old emigrant thing; can't take it and can't quite leave it.' Her voice was neutral, disinterested as if she couldn't summon enough energy to talk. 'It seemed like as good a time as any – while I was off work, I mean.'

'Or while your mother was abroad?' he said, knowingly.

'I suppose. The tour was extended to Germany. Rave notices. She got some award it seems. She phoned to say they'd be taking a week's holiday to recover from the excitement,' she said laconically.

'They?' he asked lightly.

'She and Desmond, I suppose.'

'Er, no. I think not.' Hugo raised his eyebrows. 'I believe they've parted company.' He wondered if she knew Desmond had been traded in for a younger model but Tess said nothing to indicate she'd registered his remark. Nor that she'd seen any reference to the break-up in the newspapers. Susan Callaway was a well-known, successful actress who was not finding it easy to age gracefully. During the past year she'd had a couple of fairly public flings and the gossip columnists had given her a pretty bruising time of it. It was as well none of the Dublin papers had picked up on her daughter's tragedy. Which might have been one of the reasons, Hugo reflected charitably, that Susan had kept away from Oxford.

'Is anyone looking after you, Tess?' He looked at her anxiously.

'No, we have the place to ourselves. Thank goodness.'

'Nursing your grief in solitude,' he murmured, as if to himself.

She sniffed. 'Grief, anger, despair; I'm not sure which is worse.' Tess traced patterns on the leather armrest with her finger. She avoided his eye. 'It's strange, you know, I held together pretty well for the two months till Claire was born, then it was like a dam bursting.'

'Still angry?'

He waited a long time for her to reply, holding out the invitation until the tears she so valiantly tried to hide began to flow.

'Yes, I'm up to here with it,' she suddenly burst out. 'Fury, resentment . . .'

'Passion?' he said gently.

She cradled her head in her arms and began to cry. The old man got up creakily and shuffled to the door. He'd had a stroke some months before. He claimed it was very minor but his tall thin frame was stooped and his movements slower yet he navigated the fine furniture adroitly enough. When he returned some five minutes later he had his walking stick crooked over one arm and was holding a glass of whiskey in either hand. The ice made a tinkling sound against the cut glass. He busied himself arranging one of a nest of three small tables at Tess's elbow while he waited for her to look up. When at last she did, he held out one glass and drank deeply from his own.

'Not passion, rage,' she said shakily. 'How could he be so bloody stupid? Riding a motor bike at his age? Like a stupid teenager for God's sake. He was forty!' She held out her hand. 'How could he do it? I can't understand why he bought the blasted thing.'

'Can you talk about it? Tell me what happened?' He didn't resume his place on the sofa but sat directly opposite her in one of a pair of winged armchairs.

'He'd gone up to the BBC to do a programme. One of those late-night chat things. It was supposed to be a discussion on the lack of funding for scientific research. But what does it matter? All they were at was trying to be clever and sparking off each other – *Look at me Mommy, aren't I clever?* He couldn't resist. I sometimes thought he did it just to irritate the other Fellows in his college. They're not terribly keen on what they call *sprockety engineers* having a viewpoint. But he was good at it *and* he was a good teacher. He didn't see why he couldn't have both.'

'He was a good communicator, Tess. Unpompous, witty. Made sense of his subject and the wider issues of scientific research. I always watched him when I could.'

It was as if he hadn't spoken, as if she'd bottled everything up for so long that once started she couldn't stop talking. She looked frail, much too thin and pale, with that exhausted lethargy that comes from too many sleepless nights. She looked

46

her age, possibly older, and he wondered if thirty-seven wasn't just a little too old for single motherhood. He'd never before seen her so carelessly dressed. A long whitish, rather disgusting stain of baby-sick on the shoulder of her black jacket made her look vulnerable and, somehow, neglected and her beautiful dark hair was as unkempt as a rat's nest.

'The programme was pre-recorded,' Tess went on rapidly, unaware of his scrutiny. 'He must have been racing back from London to catch it. I assumed he was on the train. He always travelled by train.' She looked at him hopelessly. 'I thought it was a mistake, you know? When the policemen came to the door.

' "Mrs Rogerson?" they said. "Callaway," I started to argue – as usual – then something about their faces stopped me. I knew them both, I'd worked with them several times. They told me he'd only taken delivery of the bike that morning, that he'd been waiting for it for a couple of weeks. A huge BMW. They said it was much too powerful for an inexperienced biker. I think they meant for an old bloke like Marcus.' She gulped a mouthful of whiskey and made a sour face. 'They had to cut him out of those disgusting leathers . . .'

'Do you know how it happened?'

'Oh yes, I made them give me all the gory details. I couldn't stop asking questions.' She fell silent.

'Where did it happen?'

'On the M40 as he was coming down through the Chiltern escarpment. It was misty, it's some-times like that just there, particularly in the

47

morning or at night . . . It's not constant, it kind of swirls about. One minute you have complete visibility, the next you're in a white blanket.' She looked at him pitiably. 'And that's how the police described it as well.

'I was watching the bloody programme when they came to tell me. They usually see me in court, in control, so I suppose they thought I was a tough bitch and could take it. I don't think they're usually so brusque. They looked so young and frightened,' she added half to herself.

'They came back next day to see if I was all right.' She paused to take another sip from her glass. 'The motorist behind Marcus thought he must have forgotten the exit for Watlington and Princes Risborough at the bottom of the hill. The road divides and the motorway veers to the right. Apparently, he tried to pull the bike round too fast. It was his first time out so he can't have known how to control it properly. Hadn't a chance, really. White-line slip, they called it.'

'What's that?'

'You know the white markings on the edge of the motorway? Well, apparently they put glass shot in the paint to make it luminescent and when the road surface is wet, it becomes really, really slippy. He was travelling way too fast and couldn't hold the bike. The front tyre missed the white line but the back tyre caught it. It flipped on its side and skidded straight into the barrier marking the Watlington turn. Instead of letting go, Marcus held on. He was dragged along – at a hell of a lick.' There was a look of desperation on her face as she stared at him blindly. 'He was unrecognizable but I knew I had to see the body or I'd never believe he was . . . gone. Dead.' Tears flowed unchecked down her cheeks.

'It was such a cheat. We were together for nine years, but you know, the last three were the best – after I gave up the job in London. By then I desperately wanted a baby but I couldn't say anything. You see, I didn't think he'd want me to give up the job or the flat, but I was wrong about that as well.' She shrugged and tucked a loose strand of hair behind her ear. 'About everything, really. I was so sure he'd hate the thought of babies.'

'I hadn't realized, my dear . . .'

'It took me over two years to get pregnant,' she said dreamily. 'I was so surprised, up to then I always got what I wanted when I wanted it. Failure was such a shock. I thought any fool could have a baby. But not me. And then it happened, just when I'd given up hope.' She gave him a tense, bright little smile. 'And of course, Marcus was completely overjoyed. We both were. It was like a wonderful new beginning. We even talked about getting married then. I wish we had.' She took a deep slow breath and he was struck by how much effort it cost her.

'Poor little Claire. I wish, oh, Hugo, I wish . . .' She stared moodily at her glass but didn't say what she wished. The baby began to cry, but before Tess could move, Hugo picked her up. When he cradled her in his arms, she immediately went off to sleep again. Tess couldn't tell which amazed her more.

'Are you all right, holding her? She may need changing.'

'Don't look so surprised,' he laughed, 'I've

always liked babies. She's a delight. And quite dry. I promise I won't drop her.' As if to endorse his claim, Claire gave a contented little snore.

After a while he said casually, 'I never understood why you moved to Oxford. Couldn't Marcus have moved to London? If he was on the television so much?'

'Not that much. He liked it, and he liked the extra money. He was embarrassed that I earned so much more. University lecturers are appallingly paid, even in Oxford where there's the college stipend as well as the university salary. But he loved teaching, his research, the college. He never really outgrew Oxford. Some people don't. Marcus loved everything about it.'

'And you, Tess? Do you love Oxford?' He looked at her seriously.

'That's more difficult.' She smiled ruefully and shrugged. 'It's very beautiful but I suppose I can take it or leave it. College life doesn't exactly enchant me. I suppose, it's, well, a bit exclusive. Bitchy, even. But then I was never part of it.' She smiled wryly. 'As you know, I've never derived much strength from institutions.'

Which may be one of the reasons why you've avoided marriage so assiduously, he surmised to himself, avoiding the proffered red herring. 'If you feel excluded, why do you stay?' Now that Marcus is dead he wanted to add but couldn't. Tess considered for a long time before she answered, as if she was only just formulating her argument.

'I suppose for him, for Marcus and for Claire,' she whispered hoarsely. 'His parents live close by, only about twenty miles away. They're a nice family, close. Most of our friends are there. There's easy access to London and, of course the countryside is beautiful.'

'Most countryside is,' he replied laconically, 'if you like that sort of thing.' There was no mistaking his own preferences and he was pretty acute about hers. When he raised his eyebrows at her she smiled sheepishly.

'All right, it isn't exactly my bag but I didn't fancy bringing up a child in London. Neither did Marcus.' She shrugged. 'Besides, I'd had about enough of the rat race. I bought the whole Eighties consumer bit, you know. I had to have it all. The smart flat, the huge salary, the travel, the clothes, the fancy restaurants. I thought I had it sussed. That I could have a child when it was convenient for me. Actually at the time I'm not sure I wanted one at all.' She leaned forward and gently stroked the baby's face with the tip of her finger. 'I was so dismissive of my friends or women I worked with who had children. They bored me rigid. God, I feel so ashamed. I made absolutely no allowance for what they might be going through.' She laughed sourly. 'I know now, though.'

She shook her head sadly. 'The truth is I was afraid of losing control,' she said and he knew that what she was really saying was that she was afraid of repeating her mother's mistakes, fearful of rejection. How strange, he thought, how deeply insecurity buries itself . . .

'And then, and then, well, life caught up with me.' Tess shivered. 'I was ready for a change. I think we both knew we were in a rut. I wanted marriage but I couldn't quite bring myself to ask.'

He patted her hand. 'So, you'll stay in Oxford?'

'In the long term? Maybe. I just don't know.'

'You could come back and work here,' he said as if the thought had only just struck him. 'Tell you what. Why don't you both come and stay here with me for a bit?' He gave her a huge grin, delighted with his scheme. 'I had the top floor done up as a guest suite recently. It's empty and,' he paused triumphantly, 'and, it has a lift now. I get pretty lonely these days, it would be marvellous to have your company.'

All the things he's too kind to say, Tess thought, and felt a huge surge of relief knowing how much easier it would be to deal with her resentment of her mother at one remove. She recognized that Hugo, who liked them both, was offering them a chance to mend their fences on neutral territory. They could take it one step at a time and retreat when the tension rose.

'It's very nice of you, Hugo, but I don't know.' She took the child from his arms and held her close. 'She's quiet now but she cries a hell of a lot,' Tess started dubiously. 'Still . . .' She looked at him thoughtfully.

'Give Susan a chance, Tess, for both your sakes,' he begged earnestly.

'Give *her* a chance?' she flared.

'Yes. You can both dish the dirt. I do believe she's a little afraid of you.'

'That why she didn't make the effort to come and see Claire?'

'I dare say she had her reasons.' He kept his tone light. 'Perhaps she was afraid she wouldn't be welcome?'

'Mmm,' Tess growled, knowing he was right.

Bull's-eye. When she looked up she found him looking at her quizzically, his head to one side. She sighed. 'Perhaps. Somehow we just never seem to get it right, do we?'

'Apparently not,' he said briskly. 'Now then. You're not working at the moment, are you?'

'Not really. I've been offered the odd bit of conveyancing by my old firm in London. From home. Otherwise . . .'

'Pretty dull after your criminal work surely? Won't you miss the courts and prosecuting?' he asked shrewdly. She pulled a face but didn't answer.

'So what it amounts to is that you're not going back to the CPS for six months?'

'Bit over four. Claire's just over seven weeks now.' The baby began to make loud sucking noises and, as Tess held her close, she nuzzled her mother's neck enthusiastically.

'Well, then.' He beamed with pleasure. 'Well then, Beauty, I'll have Mary Mackie sort out the flat upstairs. You can move in tomorrow. We'll be delighted to have you both. And Susan can have visiting rights. Now there's . . .' He was rather like an eager schoolboy planning a bunk. He was in his element and would brook no protest. She was reminded of how thoughtfully he organized her adolescent leisure and smiled at the memory.

Hugo and her father had been partners in the same law firm and close friends. But he only properly entered her life when she was a neglected and sulky thirteen year old, a couple of years after her father's death. By the time her mother left him five years later (Susan had been upwardly mobile

at the time and had succumbed to the blandish-
ments of a judge) Hugo and Tess were devoted to
each other. He had provided more stability in her
life than had been possible during the years of her
parents on/off relationship. Even after he resumed
– with obvious relish – his bachelor life, he'd
remained firmly in the background as friend,
mentor and surrogate father. In a professional
sense Tess was Hugo's creature. He had given her
her first job, and had always appreciated her
exceptionally focused ambitions. He had
applauded when she chose commercial law and in
particular the roller-coaster world of property
development. In the end, of course, she had to go
away, find her independence. Her continued
success was a source of great pride to him and
they retained their mutual respect and affection.

'So, now then. What about doing a little work
for the old family firm?' Hugo was irrepressible
once he got going.

'Hugo! I can't. What about Claire?'

'But you said you wanted to keep your hand
in,' he laughed.

'But I couldn't practise here, how could I? I've
been away too long. I'd never manage to get back
in the swing. No network.'

'Network? Pshaw, I can soon fix that.' He
chuckled gleefully. 'You'd have a network in no
time.'

'Sounds more like patronage than networking,
old darling. I don't think I'd be too comfortable
with that.'

'Actually, I was thinking more of background
work,' he said, suddenly changing tack, 'advice,
that sort of thing. We have five or six trainees

these days,' he added vaguely. 'Flexible hours?' She could tell he was improvising but was incautious enough to show some interest which Hugo took to be complete capitulation. Then he waited in silence for her to make up her mind.

'I've left my car at Heathrow. I only planned to be here for a week.' Her brows knitted in concentration. 'Tell you what, I'll go home in a few days and sort things out in Oxford. It shouldn't take more than a week, then I'll come back for a couple of months. If that's all right with you.'

'Fine, fine,' he replied. 'That would be perfect.'

'What about a car though? I couldn't manage without one.'

'Don't worry about that. You can use one of the company cars. I'll fix it up for you.'

'Right then,' she grinned.

'Perfect, perfect.' He rubbed his hands in glee. 'It will be wonderful to have you back.' She was alarmed at how quickly his plan had become a *fait accompli*. 'Your father would have been so proud. We always thought Moore Boland and Callaway had quite a ring to it.'

'Oh? Moore Boland and Callaway, now, is it? What would poor Terence Murphy-Dunne have to say about you dropping his name so unceremoniously?' Tess laughed. Hugo looked at her closely for a moment. She obviously didn't know that her mother's name had been linked to 'poor Terence's' immediately after Desmond's demise though he'd apparently been replaced since. It was an awkward situation nonetheless and for someone of the old school, rather unsavoury. Hugo didn't enjoy the sight of his ageing ex-wife making a public spectacle of herself and he drew no comfort from her humiliation at the hands of one of his partners. Though in fairness, compared to her more recent (and younger) lover, M-D had behaved with comparative discretion. Nevertheless Hugo's loyalty to the Callaway women compelled him to try to spare Tess the sordid details.

'Wishful thinking,' he said and winked. 'But seriously, it would be lovely to have you back. The old firm's not the same without a Callaway, even a temporary one.' Tess smiled, pleased to have someone else making decisions that she no longer felt capable of. But why, oh why did she have the feeling that she was fitting in exactly with some long-laid plan?

'Now then, Hugo.' It was her turn to be brisk. 'Cut the acting. Tell me what you want me to do. I take it you have something specific in mind?' she said and raised her eyebrows at him.

'Well, oddly enough I do. Something I think you'd enjoy.'

'Oh?'

'It's a . . . Land. Convent land, as a matter of fact. Causing a few problems.'

'But Hugo,' she interrupted. 'You can't be serious. I haven't done any conveyancing for years. I'd be really worried about making a mess of it.'

'Don't worry my dear, you'll be fine,' he said airily. 'Besides, it's not really conveyancing, that's all been done. It's more . . . more management . . .'

'On what basis?' she asked.

Hugo rolled his eyes and laughed. 'Er, em, we won't be charging out your time, if that's what you mean. The work we do for the convent is *pro bono*, I'm afraid. But I'll see to it that you're not out of pocket.'

'I see,' she snorted. He grinned sheepishly as she continued thoughtfully, 'There have been some pretty extraordinary deals, haven't there? And some scandals I hear,' she added pointedly. 'So, which convent is it?'

He chewed at his thumb, brows knit in concentration. He might have been wrestling with confidentiality or, more likely, trying to remember the name of the convent, but Tess sensed he was prevaricating. As if he was considering how to frame his response. 'Strange place, odd goings on,' he said absently. 'Beautiful house. Cold as a morgue, needs heating. It's falling to rack and ruin which is why they need to sell the land. Built in the eighteenth century, name of the family escapes me. One of them founded this rather unique little community of contemplatives. Now then, what's it called again? Holy something.' He looked at her from beneath his eyebrows. 'Ah, I have it. Holy Retreat. Ever heard of it?'

'Why ye-es.' She dragged the word out to cover her surprise. 'Yes. It's the other side of Killiney, quite close to our old house, isn't it? I used to cycle past sometimes on my way home from school.' She grinned. 'When I was going through my religious phase.'

'Did you really? It was hardly on your way, was it? Bit off the beaten track.' He looked astonished that she should have remembered it. 'Actually I didn't realize you had a religious phase.' He sounded mildly surprised.

'There you go.' Tess grinned at him insouciantly. 'If you make a little detour you can pass by the gate. It was so mysterious, so exclusive, I used to long to know what went on there.'

'Well now, my dear, you can,' he said and chuckled. 'Isn't that the most extraordinary coincidence? We've been their solicitors for years and years. Not that they ever had much need of us but on the few occasions they did I usually dealt with them myself – until I retired. I became quite fond of one dear old thing. Sister Antonia-Maria. She's dead now.'

'Nice name, Antonia-Maria.'

'Yes, isn't it? Actually, many of them tag Maria to their name. Bit of a change from Sister Mary this and Sister Mary that or as my father used to say to my sister when she changed her mind about entering the Ursulines: *Sister-Mary-Never-Entered*. This lot are rather an individual bunch. The present superior is rather a fine woman. Never wise to underestimate any of them. Mind you, they have their little ways.' He chuckled. 'Their motto seems to be: *What is time to eternity?* As I know to my cost. Those charming old biddies expect their solicitor to be entirely at their beck and call. I passed them over to young Murphy-Dunne about three or four years back, but really, that boy . . .' He avoided her eye.

That boy, as Tess knew, because she'd had a schoolgirl passion for him, was well into his forties. But she could quite see that Terence Murphy-Dunne might find nuns rather a tough proposition.

'I always thought he was quite a go-getter.'

'Go-getter is right.' Hugo sounded disgusted. 'Gone and injured his back. He was carted off to hospital a couple of weeks ago. Which is what brought me out of my comfortable seclusion. The nuns are anxious to get the business finalized,' he continued. 'The sale has more or less gone through but there are loose ends to tie up, mainly administration, contracts, that sort of thing. Not M-D's strong points at the best of times. He's not a man for dull minutiae.'

'And I am, I suppose?' Tess laughed.

'I didn't mean it that way. You could help enormously and it wouldn't take up much of your time. To tell you the truth, darling, there's too much legwork for me.'

From which, Tess assumed, it was a small tract of land and therefore small potatoes for the likes of Murphy-Dunne or Hugo himself. She was less sanguine about how much of her own time it would take. Or why, since he had ascertained that she now preferred criminal to property law, it might hold her interest. With Hugo what he didn't say was sometimes a good deal more interesting than the information he let slip.

'Just one thing, Tess. I wonder if you'd nip out to see Mother Catherine before you go back to Oxford?'

'When?'

'Oh, tomorrow or the next day would do well enough,' Hugo answered.

'Why? Is there some problem?' she asked innocently.

It was his turn to look embarrassed. 'Well yes, as a matter of fact, there is, don't you know. But I think it may be right up your street. Or at least,' he added hastily, 'it would be in, er, other circumstances.' He chewed his lower lip. 'The problem,' he paused for full dramatic effect, 'the problem is, Tess dear, to get access to the most desirable site, they have to move their graveyard and I'm damned if any of us know quite how to go about it.'

4

Herbert Park, Dublin

Dear Marcus,
Not Dear, as in Dear So-and-so, or Dear Occupier or
Dear Sir. This is dear *as in precious, cherished, beloved.
Fugitive. It could have been Dearest or Darling or
Beloved. Just think of my warm breath on your right
ear-lobe;* Dear *Marcus. I had to write. I have to talk to
you.*

*I've been here for a couple of weeks. I thought it was
time to introduce Claire to her grandmother. And to her
Irish side. If I'm anything to go by she will worry at it
for the rest of her life so she may as well get to know
them at the beginning. No, I'm not sure that's really the
reason I'm here. The house was getting me down. Every
time I moved I tripped over some of your things. Have I
ever told you what an untidy sod you are, were? I
couldn't bear to put everything away. Or wash your
smell from your clothes. I left the same sheets on the bed
for nearly a month. But even then I couldn't bear to be in
it. Christ, Marcus, why didn't we get it together earlier?*

*So we bolted, Claire and me. As usual, my timing was
impeccable – I'm not sure if I mean that ironically –
Mother is away until next week. I suppose, if I'm
honest, that's partly why I chose to come now – to ease
our way in our own time. But it didn't work, I couldn't
get used to the flat. After three days I fell apart and went
off to see Hugo. I had almost forgotten how kind he is.
He is the same with Claire as he was with me when I was
a child. He has taken to her amazingly and sits for hours
with her asleep in his arms. The stroke seems to have left*

him quite frail and he claims her warmth is a great comfort to his weary old bones. I suppose he makes her feel useful because she just curls up and snores her little head off. Or perhaps she just finds him restful because she cries practically non-stop with me. I didn't realize how easily babies tune in to your moods. But then there is a lot I didn't realize. I was always odiously judgemental.

I took your daughter out to Powerscourt yesterday, to the waterfall. We sat and howled together on the flat rock with the water sloshing away behind us. Remember? I told her all about you, us, everything. Actually I talk to her all the time. One of these days she'll probably reply in fully formed and punctuated paragraphs. But now she just squidges up her muddy little eyes and stares at me. I don't yet know what colour they're going to be. At first I thought blue, then navy, then brown, now I don't know. Mud is nearest. She's just beginning to smile. Otherwise she is expert at only three things – eating, howling, and (occasionally) sleeping. Apart that is, from her frequent and considerable activities at the other end.

Something has come up which I'll tell you about as we go along. First, I'm going back to Oxford to sort out a few things, including getting a house-sitter. Then I'm coming back to stay with Hugo for a couple of months or so, until it's time for me to go back to the CPS. Hugo has roped me in to do a little work with the old firm. It's a put-up job really. I can see he hopes I'll stay permanently but perhaps I misjudge him and he simply and kindly wants me to feel useful, recover some confidence. Like Blanche Dubois, I depend on the kindness of – well, not strangers – honorary relations. Except for Susan and now Claire, they are the only kind I have. Strange, isn't it? Sometimes that thought almost kills me.

There are other reasons for staying, of course. In Oxford I keep being reminded of you. Everywhere I turn, every street I walk, everyone I meet. Strange what a relief it is to be with people who have no idea what happened. Not to have to cross the road to avoid talking about it. Meantime, Hugo and his housekeeper Mary Mackie – remember her? – completely appropriate the baby. She's had plenty of experience having six children of her own. As far as I can gather, the husband and two of them are in Mountjoy, one of them is doing a D. Phil. and the youngest is going to be Claire's nanny. She keeps surprisingly quiet about the others.

The work Hugo dug up is for a strange community of nuns. Quite a number of old convents in Ireland have been selling off land in the past few years. There have been some massive deals and not always to the benefit of the poor old nuns. This lot are a bit different, somehow. Quirky, inscrutable. It seems to fit that the land they're trying to sell is a graveyard. If anyone else but dear old Hugo had suggested I get involved, I'd have thought it a sick joke. But he knows them and he knows me. I hope I can help them. The thought of being useful is certainly helping me.

Dear Marcus, I've been doing some daft things. I had an extra telephone line installed before I left just so I could plug in your old answering machine. The one from college. I ring whenever I want to hear your voice. You sound, well, you sound like you. Do you remember?

'Hello. I can't answer just now. I'm either eating, drinking or, God help me, teaching. Whatever. Don't hang up. Leave a message. Please.'

And then there's a little pause. 'Tess? Tess? If that's you I'm either in the lab, at home or between the two, as the college porter said to the importunate wife. Try me in both.

I want to talk to you. Want you. Need you. So, use your initiative, my darling. Find me, find me, find me . . .'

Oh, Marcus, I wish I could, Tessie.

Retreat *Eccl. A period of seclusion or retirement from one's ordinary occupations devoted to religious exercises – 1756.*

Oxford English Dictionary

5

However it was managed, whether by abstinence or diet, those devotees of the convent of Holy Retreat who were not taken by disease or accident achieved considerable longevity. This was particularly so in the case of the superiors, or, as they were called at Holy Retreat: the Mother Guardian. In the hundred and forty-odd years since the convent was founded, only four women had ruled before the present incumbent. The foundress herself, Adelaide Maria Elderson Stebton, had reigned unchallenged for over forty years, her three successors averaged thirty apiece. The present superior, in contrast to those formidable women, had taken up office at an advanced age and, in consequence, could not hope to equal in length or strength of character any of her predecessors. She had only held office for nine years and was already in failing health. But then, she was over eighty.

The convent building was also showing signs of wear and tear. Time, the salt sea wind and persistent damp had taken a terrible toll on its elegant, classical structure. It was a large house, so even the convent endowment and its income together did not allow for proper and regular maintenance. A modern heating system was out of the question. Being so close to the sea made the interior chilly and draughty all year round, but in winter it was positively arctic. Yet the nuns did not seem to mind, or complain.

Little had changed in the century and a half since the foundation of Holy Retreat. Silence was observed except for a couple of hours' recreation each day. Latin plainchant was invariably sung in chapel in the thin, ethereal voices of the ageing sisters. Unusually for the time of founding, the community had never been divided into choir and lay members. Until recent times lay sisters were the domestics of most religious orders. At Holy Retreat, all were equal. One of the conditions of acceptance into the order was that postulants should be at least twenty-eight and of a sufficiently high standard of education – though precisely what that standard should be was unspecified. In fact many of the sisters did not enter until they were in their thirties and between them they covered a wide range of skills and professions.

Their day was long and strictly organized into periods of prayer, work, recreation and exercise. They rose at five-thirty each morning and retired at ten. Prayer was their *raison d'être* after which came the work of providing income for the convent. The balance and order of their lives was strictly maintained. Adelaide Elderson Stebton had been extraordinarily far-sighted in a period when women had few rights over the direction of their lives and none at all over their own property or income. However she had managed it, she had done her best to ensure her convent would, in perpetuity, maintain independence and that her nuns would live spiritually and intellectually fulfilling lives. But, alas, even one so far-sighted as Adelaide could not anticipate the soaring cost of living in the latter part of the twentieth century. Yet even that wasn't a complete disadvantage. Since the nuns were uniformly engaged in the skills required to earn the convent's income, they were individually well prepared if they ever needed to maintain their own living outside. They took simple vows, renewable year on year, and therefore they could leave at any time. Remarkably few did, but when they did they found provision had been made for that contingency also. Long before it was the norm, or even thought of by other religious institutions, Holy Retreat contributed to life insurance for the departing few.

The nuns' mode of dress had not altered an iota from the day Adelaide had devised their habit. It was simple and elegant, similar to many of the habits worn by nuns in the nineteenth century but it had individuality and a mild touch of eccentricity. It comprised a full-length dove-grey dress with a high, white detachable mandarin collar and a simple black woven belt. The rule did not demand shorn hair but the sisters' heads were covered with a finely woven full-length black veil over a neat white linen bonnet. In cold weather they wore the heavy, black, elaborately hooded cloak which had been traditionally worn by the women of West Cork. Their shoes were soft-soled black suede slippers with hand-knitted grey woollen stockings in winter. In summer they wore simple back leather sandals on their bare feet.

Manual labour was shared equally among the sisters. The founder's scheme for those under her care was simply based on the life of a well-run country house. Health, cleanliness and prayer were her watchwords. She was extremely specific about health and even rather visionary: she urged good, fresh, wholesome food and plenty of exercise. In providing her foundation with its beautiful, spacious house and a hundred and thirty acres of parkland with access to the sea, together with a handsome endowment, she had ensured that the sisters had all three.

The convent was largely self-sufficient. The nuns grew enough vegetables and fruit for their needs and extra income was derived from the sale of herbs, eggs and honey. The herb garden pre-dated the convent's foundation. It had always been exquisitely maintained and under the present gardener had been developed and enlarged until it completely filled the walled space which it had originally shared with the orchard. The harvesting and sale of herbs had become a major source of the convent income since the current Sister-Gardener had neatly anticipated, by some ten years, the burgeoning market in fresh herbs and the voracious appetite for daily supplies from the supermarkets.

Adelaide Elderson Stebton had permitted no divergence from her initial ambitions for those under her care, nor did her successors. Perhaps being so few helped enshrine, almost completely unchanged, the concept and aims of the foundress. There was another reason. Retreat was an apt description of both the convent and the order. Adelaide had started with twelve companions – the apostles as they came to be called – and within a few years they had risen to twenty. From that high point the numbers had slowly declined. This was not because of a particular rise in the death rate nor caused by the same exodus which afflicted other convents in the latter part of the twentieth century. However, even if almost none of the sisters left, fewer candidates came forward and in consequence the average age of the sisters rose steeply. By the 1990s the long-term future of Holy Retreat looked uncertain.

The foundation was an anachronism which existed in an apparently idyllic time-warp. Even as the boundaries of the city crept ever outwards and the relentless din of traffic grew ever more insistent, the nuns somehow appeared oblivious to the threat of encroachment. They were completely cut off from the world. They lived their cloistered life as they had always done, in peace, in prayer and in silence. The unit may have been small but it was strong and secure and, as far as the sisters were concerned, there seemed no reason, on earth or in heaven, why anything should change.

Her followers knew how carefully Adelaide had structured her foundation, how nimbly she had manoeuvred to ensure that she and her sisters retained their autonomy. In nineteenth-century Ireland there was a strong move to incorporate new (female) communities into the Church Universal. The contemplative way of life was deemed less appropriate to women than more practical occupations, such as the care of the sick and the poor. Schools, hospitals and orphanages had to be (wom)manned. Communities which had started with groups of women taking simple vows, often for a limited period, found themselves under increasing pressure to swap their cloisters for more useful work. While other of the recent foundations were being pressed by the ecclesiastical authorities into taking solemn vows, thus submitting to the pastoral – and more ominously financial – jurisdiction of their bishop, Adelaide alone, with the unshakeable confidence of her class and wealth, stood her ground.

For reasons which may have been clear then, but had been forgotten over time, she did not allow herself to be deflected from her plan. Hers, she claimed, was a limited ambition: one house, one rule, a handful of good and pious women who prayed, in reparation for – and this was quite specific – the sins of man and the innocent victims of promiscuity and disease. Had anyone in the 1990s read her little rule book they might have been struck at how prophetically she had anticipated Aids, but that would only be because modern man is often quite ignorant of the terrible social diseases of past times.

Time had stood still at Holy Retreat. Little changed from day to day, from decade to decade. The high granite walls kept the little community protected at once from the sights and sounds of the modern world. Set well back from a minor, little travelled cul-de-sac lane, only the arched name above the gateway gave any indication of what lay beyond. The nearest neighbour to the south was a school whose buildings were at least half a mile away from the convent enclosure. On the north side there was a small electrical substation and it too was well fenced off. The convent land ran right down to the cliff-edge, but along this boundary an ancient hedgerow of hebe and fuschia ran parallel to, and eventually replaced, the high wall. The enclosed land was extensive enough to provide the nuns' food and allow them to take the long daily walks recommended by their founder.

Canon Law: *A collection of ecclesiastical laws which serve as a rule of church government.*

Oxford English Dictionary

6

The heavy oak door silently swung open to reveal an eerily empty hall. Startled, Tess fell back a pace. After a moment's hesitation she leaned forward and peered anxiously into the gloom. There was nobody there, no sound from the house or garden save the pecking of a small white hen on the gravel behind her. She entered cautiously and almost went flying on the chocolate brown linoleum which gleamed as if no rough-shod foot had ever before touched its slippery surface. To her right a votive candle glimmered beneath a diamond-faceted red globe. A small vase of sweet-smelling stock did not quite mask the strange unworldly smell. Odour of Sanctity? More like damp, she concluded grimly.

'Welcome. Just push the door to, will you be so good?' An ancient, disembodied voice spoke creakily. It sounded reedy with disuse.

Tess jumped and stared around wildly. The hall was still empty. The only door, other than the entrance, stood to her right but it was firmly shut. I'm going mad she thought.

'Miss Callaway? It *is* Miss Callaway?' The

soft voice sounded amused. 'The door, could you . . . ?'

Obediently, and much against her instincts, Tess pushed the hall door closed and looked around again. No one. The hall was empty, the disembodied voice was still. She was alone. Alone and decidedly spooked since she could feel, if not see, that she was under close observation. It was as if some unknown power-game was being played for the purpose of keeping her at a disadvantage. Yet the voice was not powerful or sinister but seemingly gentle and amused. One hell of a ploy, she thought, as she revolved slowly trying to locate its source.

'I'm here. Right in front of you. Come forward, my dear.'

She followed the sound to the back wall of the dimly lit hall where there was a large grille, hung behind with a black drape. The sound appeared to be coming from somewhere behind it.

'See?' The curtain twitched for a fraction of a second. Too quick for her to actually see any-thing. 'I am Sister Joseph-Maria. You are Miss Callaway?' The voice was diffident now, almost nervous. 'The solicitor?'

'That's right.' Tess took possession of her-self. 'Tess Callaway from Moore, Boland and Murphy-Dunne.'

'You are much younger than I expected,' Sister Joseph-Maria said earnestly.

Tess gave a little laugh and realizing she was standing in deep shadow, stepped nearer the screen.

'There, Sister. Is that better? As you can see, I'm not all that young.'

'Mr Boland said you were very capable. I congratulate you, Miss Callaway,' the nun covered her confusion courteously.

'Thank you, that's kind. I have some papers for the Reverend Mother to sign.' Tess took a file from her briefcase and, feeling a complete fool, held it up.

'She's the Mother Guardian, but she prefers to be called by her name, Mother Catherine-Maria.'

'Oh? Not Reverend Mother?'

'No. Now, my dear, there's a revolving cupboard just to your left. If you would put the papers in there . . . ?'

As Tess put her hand out, the revolve spun silently open. She placed the buff file on the lower shelf as the drum began to spin closed. What a way to do business, Tess thought, remote, removed, impersonal. She felt distinctly put out. She didn't altogether relish being treated like a messenger, however courteously.

'And how is poor Mr Murphy-Dunne?'

'Getting a little better, I believe,' Tess improvised.

'*Deo gratias*. Now, my dear, will you come through?' The request was tentative, pleading.

Short of levitating through the grille, which started a good four feet from the floor, Tess could see no way of getting closer to the out-of-body voice.

'If you wouldn't mind telling me how, Sister Joseph-Maria,' she said dryly, 'I'd be delighted.' The nun chuckled softly.

'Is it your first time in an enclosed convent?'

'Yes. Do you always remain . . . er . . . hidden?'

'Always.' The nun sounded amused. 'But I can see you perfectly well.'

'But I may not see you?'

'No. It's one of our rules. We withdraw from the world,' she said, as if it made sense. Tess could think of no reasonable retort. Withdraw seemed too passive for those sinister grilles. Exclude seemed nearer the mark.

'You'll get used to our strange ways in time, Miss Callaway.' The nun's quiet voice broke in on her thoughts. She sounded as if she was enjoying herself hugely. 'Just step through the door on your right and wait in the parlour. There's some tea laid out for you. Mother Catherine will join you shortly.'

Join, Tess thought grimly, seems something of an exaggeration. She couldn't quite suppress a snort of derision. As if in reply there was another tiny chuckle followed by a faint swish of cloth, a light footfall, then silence. Feeling a little like Alice stepping through the looking-glass, Tess opened the parlour door.

Brown pervaded, overwhelmed, smothered her. Brown linoleum, heavy dark Victorian furniture gleaming and worn, a brown-clad statue of some saint or other. The windows were of opaque, engraved glass, the curtains an indeterminate floral pattern whose principal component was also brown. Yet the overall effect wasn't gloomy. The room was spotlessly clean, the wooden surfaces highly polished and the crisp linen cloth on a small circular table fairly dazzled with light and starch. On it were set one white china cup and saucer, one side plate with two coconut cream biscuits, a tiny bowl of sugar lumps, an even smaller jug and one small brown teapot. Tea for one. Having located another grille to the left of the door, Tess moved a chair around the table to face it, plonked herself down and poured her solitary cup of tea.

The tea was excellent. Slightly smoky and scalding hot, as if the unseen hand who had brought it had only done so seconds before she'd entered the parlour. Tess wondered if the ethereal Sister Joseph had been a-brewing even as she'd held her enthralled. She delicately nibbled the coconut off the sickly pink marshmallow then in a sudden burst of greed crammed the whole biscuit in her mouth. She hadn't tasted one since childhood when she would test herself as to how long she could take to finish. First nibbling the flecks of coconut, then sensuously licking and sucking at the marshmallow until the biscuit beneath lay nude and soggy enough to slowly disintegrate on her tongue. Once, she remembered, she'd held out for eight and a half minutes – she'd been a rather precise child. She picked up the second biscuit and ate it defiantly in two quick mouthfuls.

The minutes dragged by. Ten, fifteen. Somewhere, deep within the convent, a tinny-sounding bell began to peel. Three, pause, three, pause, three. The Angelus. Six o'clock already. Tess began to fret, the baby would soon need feeding. She was probably doing her nut by now. The declining evening sun shafted through the window. She moved edgily around the room, fingered the lamp, traced the swirling patterns of the etched window – *Ubi caritas et amor, Deus ibi est*

74

– the Latin words of some psalm? *Where charity and love are, God is there* – she translated moodily, blindly gazing into the light, wondering what it was an enclosed order got up to all day.

She began to wish she'd never got involved. Hugo had been very persuasive but her first perusal of the Holy Retreat file had left her with an impression of a jumble of loose ends. Which was as charitable as she could be. It looked as if Terence's mind had not been completely on the case even before he'd injured his back. Hugo had glossed it over but she was in no doubt that he knew perfectly well what he'd let her in for. One thing about Hugo, he had never underrated her capabilities nor stinted his appreciation of her professional talent. But perhaps, she thought sadly, he had completely overestimated her ability to switch off her present preoccupation with her baby.

She was not fooled for a second by the casual way he'd approached her about Holy Retreat. He would not insult her by dotting the i's or crossing the t's but she could tell he was troubled. Something was amiss. Ostensibly, he had canvassed her help because of her expertise in conveyancing. Yet ever since he first mentioned Holy Retreat, he'd been casually but persistently quizzing her about her criminal cases and points of criminal law. Though, infuriatingly, nothing specific. Never mind that he claimed to be intrigued as to how she managed her court appearances. His devious lawyer's mind was working on something. Whatever was troubling him, he kept to himself and at the same time tried to appear not to influence her. That was her best guess. Though as to what or why, was more difficult.

There was still no sign of the superior. Tess worried about her car, abandoned, hazard lights flashing, on the road outside since she'd not been able to discover any way of opening the main gates. The high stone walls of the convent were as formidable as she'd remembered. The ancient, elaborate, cast-iron gates were backed with rusting metal with the peeling banner *Holy Retreat* arched above them whose letters had long since lost their gilding. She'd pulled the bell-rope several times before she noticed that it was flapping loose. Then she followed the line to the top of the stone pillar and saw that it was disconnected. She noticed that the words *Elderson* and *Court* were still legible, barely, on the capital of either gatepost.

A narrow wooden doorway on one side had yielded smoothly to her touch. She'd half expected to be challenged at the lodge whose garden was well tended but whose windows were blank and curtainless, but nothing and no one stirred in the lazy autumn sunshine. She'd followed the long winding driveway without let or hindrance except for the curious glances of a couple of dewy-eyed cows chewing remorselessly with their heads lolling over the battered iron railings of their field.

The convent itself was a complete surprise. More surprise for its beauty than for its decay. The house was splendid, perfectly symmetrical, the pale rose brick almost silvery in the weak September light. Though on closer examination she saw a steadily dripping broken roof-gutter and several small but magnificently flowering buddleia growing out of the chimneys.

Tess shivered. It had been warmer outside than in. The sun went in and at once, as if a light had been switched off, the room became gloomy and dark. She rubbed her arms and sniffed at the pervasive smell of damp overriding the scent of the lavender beeswax. She turned at the sound of a light footfall but the dark drape behind the grille was impenetrable.

'Mother Catherine?'

'No, I am Benedicte-Maria, the bursar.' The voice was more educated, possibly younger than the sister-porter's but with the same strange quality of effort in forming the words. The accent was impossible to place.

The bursar? This must be the business manager of the convent. The very person she would, most likely, be dealing with. Tess suddenly and desperately needed to see this woman, judge her by her face and not that odd, strangulated speech. A moment before she would not have realized how much her judgement depended not on how or what people said but on their facial expression, their body language. In this room she was, to all intents and purposes, blind. The nun's next remark took her by surprise.

'Would you find it difficult to work for us, Miss Callaway?' It was as if she were reading her thoughts. But then, thought Tess, she has the advantage of me, she can see me. Everything I'm thinking must be written large on my face.

'I would find it a good deal easier if I could see you,' Tess replied flatly, suddenly feeling hostile.

There was a long low sigh and a considerable pause before the nun spoke again.

'Why? Surely you must conduct much of your business by telephone?'

'Not exclusively. I usually like to meet my clients at least once.'

'I'm sorry, but that is not possible without our Mother Guardian's permission. If you like I shall—'

'No. I don't suppose it matters,' Tess replied ungraciously. 'There isn't all that much to do, is there?'

'Oh? You've not spoken to Mr Murphy-Dunne?'

'I'm sorry, is there not some mistake? It was Hugo Boland who asked me to come. Mr Murphy-Dunne is in hospital. His back is injured, he's slipped a disc or something. He'll be laid up for several weeks. Mr Boland asked if I'd take over.'

'Oh.' The flat non-committal sound gave nothing away but Tess felt extremely uncomfortable as if she'd barged in where she was not wanted.

'I assumed you'd been told all that,' she said stiffly. 'Sister.'

'I knew he'd been taken ill but I wasn't told he was in hospital, that the injury was so severe. Do you know how it happened?'

'I understand he slipped in the shower.' Tess didn't add Hugo's embellishments about Terence being found by his charwoman as he crawled dripping and naked from the bathroom to call the doctor.

'Ah. I see.' After which baffling pronouncement the nun fell silent for a moment before adding, 'One of our sisters injured her spine some time ago. Our gardener. She tried to lift too heavy a load. She was laid up for weeks. Poor Mr Murphy-Dunne. The shower, you say?'

Tess couldn't make out if this last was a question she was meant to answer or an observation on the absurdity of the accident. There was another uncomfortable pause which eventually she felt compelled to fill.

'I quite understand if you would prefer to wait for Mr Murphy-Dunne to recover, Sister Benedicte. Though I understood from Mr Boland that you are anxious to get everything settled before winter.'

'Not I,' the nun corrected. Her voice sounded as if it came from a long way off. Preoccupied, distant. 'I just carry out the will of the community. The completion date is November the seventh, I believe.' Another interminable pause. What is bugging her? Tess thought irritably and was floored when the nun seemed to read her thoughts again.

'I'm sorry, Miss Callaway, there is much on my mind. This business has been rather protracted. And upsetting. Mother Guardian spoke to me about you but I wasn't aware you'd taken over completely from Mr Murphy-Dunne. But if Mother Guardian and Mr Boland recommend you, then that will be all right.'

'I came to help, not to apply for a job.' The words were out before Tess could stop herself. She was about to erupt into a diatribe on the superiority of both her training and her brain-power to that of the Blessed Murphy-Dunne, when the nun's tired voice cut in quickly.

'Forgive me, Miss Callaway, I did not intend a slight.'

'Tell me what it is you want me to do, Sister Benedicte, and I'll see if I can help speed things up.'

'Oh, you can help, Miss Callaway, I am quite sure of that,' the nun replied. Her voice was clearer now, more controlled. 'I have the signed papers for the Medical Officer of Health.'

'He is attached to Doctor Steven's Hospital?'

'That's correct. You *have* done your home-work,' the nun congratulated. Tess bristled but said nothing. 'Now, most urgent, there are the arrangements with the diocese. You deal with a Father Keane. That file is with the other papers. Sister Joseph will leave them in the hall for you to collect on the way out. One other thing. I've had the estimates for rebuilding the boundary wall and for moving the— and from the undertaker. The school had agreed to underwrite the work.' Her attention was fully engaged and sounded more friendly. 'Have the work contracts been drawn up yet?'

'Not yet, as far as I can see. But Mr Boland confirms that the funds have been lodged, so that's OK. Don't worry, if Murphy-Dunne hasn't already drawn up work contracts I'll do so next week.' She didn't feel it prudent to mention that she would be in Oxford in the interim. 'I'm right in thinking you've exchanged contracts for the sale of the land?'

'Yes, that's in order, we did so several weeks ago. Mr Murphy-Dunne has all the paperwork.'

'Fine. Now, just in case I need to, may I get in touch with you by phone, Sister?'

'Yes,' the nun spoke hesitantly, 'you can try by all means, but it isn't always convenient for me to answer. On the whole I prefer to call you. Between twelve and half past is best for me. I trust that will suit?'

Suit whom? Tess wondered and almost laughed aloud. No wonder it took so long to get anything done. She silently applauded Hugo's admirable footwork in getting her involved so adroitly. She was even beginning to view Terence Murphy-Dunne's sloppy work with a shade more sympathy.

'That will be fine, Sister. I'm staying with Mr Boland. You can leave a message with him or the housekeeper if I'm not available.'

'Of course. You're related to Mr Boland?' Sister Benedicte said in such a way that Tess wasn't sure whether she was asking a question or already knew the answer. The rusty voice was so unexpressive that it was hard to decide what exactly she meant, never mind how she meant it, without seeing her face. She wondered if she was making too much of this imposed blindness? After all she'd been sprung on Holy Retreat rather unceremoniously so it was hardly surprising that her arrival on the scene should provoke irritation if not suspicion.

Tess had a strong sense that the bursar had not been consulted about the change of solicitor. That it had been arranged over her head by Hugo and the – what did they insist on calling her? – the Mother Guardian. Reason enough for her spikiness, Tess conceded. Why shouldn't Sister Benedicte prefer to conduct the convent business with big, confident, handsome Murphy-Dunne? She was a woman after all, however removed. Yet it still niggled her that she could not see the Sister Bursar, read her, feel at ease with her. It was doubly unnerving because of course the nun wasn't so disadvantaged. Somewhere behind that opaque screen she was watching. Tess's hand snaked to her shoulder where she had hurriedly – and probably ineffectively – wiped away the baby's puke earlier. Every stitch she had was in the same condition. She became uncomfortably aware that the faint sour smell of milk lingered on her clothes.

'How old is the baby?' The nun softly confirmed Tess's speculation.

'Almost eight weeks. How did you . . . ?'

'There are traces of dried milk on the shoulder of your suit.' The nun sounded amused but not unkind. Eagle eyes. Tess was torn between surprise and affront.

'Occupational hazard, I'm afraid,' she said and laughed at her own absurdity in making a kind of bugbear of the nun. At once the tension in her neck eased and she relaxed a little.

'It must be hard to work and look after a baby.'

'It's just a temporary arrangement and only for a couple of hours a day while I'm in Dublin. I have a good babysitter.' Tess crossed her fingers. So far so good. Mary Mackie had lost no time in introducing her daughter, Sandra, as baby-minder. It was early days, but Claire didn't seem to object too violently.

There was a soft rustling movement and when the nun spoke again Tess realized she had stood up. Tess got to her feet and just stopped herself offering her hand to the blank screen.

'Thank you for your help, Miss Callaway.' The nun's voice had faded, as though something had upset her. Tess, musing on this, had not replied when she heard the soft click of a door and realized the bursar had left.

Tess opened the parlour door and let herself out into the hall. She had the uncomfortable feeling that the unseen woman had held something back. Something important. This thought filled her with disquiet.

The files were lying in the open drum. As Tess picked them up she heard a soft cough. It was enough to make her jump violently.

'What the . . .' She swirled around. God, she thought, this place is spooky.

'I'm sorry, Miss Callaway, I didn't mean to alarm you.' Another old, rusty voice. 'I am Mother Catherine. I'm sorry not to have come to welcome you sooner. Could you manage to stay for a few minutes? The exhumation of the graveyard troubles me a great deal. Mr Murphy-Dunne was anxious that it should be done in October. Before the winter sets in. I want to be certain I know exactly what is entailed before it begins.'

They made their separate ways to the parlour. Mother Catherine went to great pains to explain the reasoning which had led the nuns to their decision to sell the land. Afterwards she showed Tess the architect's plans for the phased refurbishment of their convent.

'Where will you live while the work is going on?' Tess asked.

'We've been preparing the lodge. It's almost ready.'

'Good heavens. Will it be big enough? Or warm enough?' Tess asked.

'Surprisingly yes. After this house, it wouldn't be hard.' The nun laughed, a surprisingly girlish little tinkle. 'Have you any idea how cold this house can be? The lodge is roomier than it looks and as to the warmth – well, after all, it's only for a short time. While the roof-timbers are being replaced.'

When Tess asked, Mother Catherine told her something of the history of the foundation of Holy Retreat. Then, for a few minutes, she spoke about their day-to-day life and their plans to expand the herb production on which they were increasingly dependent. The elderly superior was a less remote character than the bursar and, much to her own surprise, Tess found herself telling the nun about Marcus and the baby. And though she listened attentively to everything Tess said, the nun's interest seemed to quicken when she mentioned that she lived in Oxford.

'Our founder's ancestors came from Oxfordshire, on her father's side,' she said abruptly. 'Do you think you could find out a little about the family for me? I should be most grateful.'

'Do you know where in Oxfordshire?'

'Not precisely, but I believe both village and family had the same name. Stebton.'

For a moment Tess thought she had misheard. 'Did you say Stebton? I thought the Elderson family built this house.'

'Yes, they did. The founder's mother was an Elderson but her father was a Stebton.'

'Then, I have to tell you, Mother Catherine, that is a most amazing coincidence. Mar . . . My . . .' She swallowed. 'Claire's grandparents live in a village called Chipping Stebton. I shall be staying with them next weekend.'

It was only after she had promised to track down the Stebton family history that Tess realized that Mother Catherine hadn't shown the least surprise at the coincidence. But then perhaps the nuns were used to God's mysterious ways. Or Hugo's more like.

TWO YEARS EARLIER

OXFORDSHIRE

Spring 1994

Touche (de la), Gervase: *Histoire de Dom Bougre, Portier des Chartreux 1742. 8tvo A pocket reprint for ease of smuggling. Vellum binding, lavishly decorated. Finely printed with twenty bravura (anon) engravings.*

A d'A Cat. 2, item 8

7

A short history of Stebton Place by Jane-Edwina Stebton-Hillyard.

Some sixteen miles from the city of Oxford, on the borders of Oxfordshire and Gloucestershire, well off the A34 and about five miles from Burford, lies the village of Chipping Stebton. In common with all Cotswold villages with the name Chipping, it derived its wealth from the wool trade and its name from the sheep market which had long since evolved into the village green.

Like the surrounding villages, it was entirely built of the local pale and mellow stone and roofed in harmonious Stonesfield slate. The church dated from the twelfth century, the manor-house and vicarage close to it had originally been part of the same monastic settlement. The monastery itself had fallen early victim to that first great nationalization of land and property when Henry VIII had set about dismantling church holdings. In 1539, one William Ryland

Stebton, Gent., an obscure courtier who had made his fortune in disposing of treasure from the newly dissolved monasteries, was granted the right to buy the monastery and land in recognition of his services to his prince. In the deed of sale he was described starkly as a carrier.

A man with sharp political instincts, the first William Stebton quickly appointed a recently married clergyman of the new religion as priest of the renamed and de-effigied church which was in his gift. Whether this was out of piety or by way of eternal fire-insurance is not recorded. One week later, in the first wedding service of the new regime, William Ryland Stebton took one Thomasina Miller to wife and without further ado, moved into the new manor-house, lately converted from the chapterhouse of the old monastery. For the following three hundred and fifty years the property remained in the Stebton family, handed from one generation to the other through the male line, usually from father to son, sometimes through cousins. By the end of the nineteenth century, coincidental with the decline of the estate, male heirs not being forthcoming, the estate passed to Laura Stebton, daughter of the last male in the line, and from her to her daughter, Elfrida.

Over time, generations of Stebtons added some thirty cottages to the original eighteen shepherds' and labourers' dwellings which lined the two narrow lanes encircling the monastery and church. When viewed from a distance only the church steeple was visible, the rest of the buildings, poor and grand alike, simply merged into the undulating landscape. History contrived their preservation. Built during the flourishing of the wool trade, many of these prosperous villages stayed for centuries in their original state simply because the prosperity which built them did not last. They remained unchanged and unimproved after the wool trade declined. As its centre moved further north to Yorkshire and the craftsmen followed their trades, large numbers of villages were abandoned. Sometimes the craftsmen bore away the names of their native places with them. No more houses were built to destroy the beauty and symmetry of these peaceful villages. The cottages remained in the ownership of the lords of the manor whose houses, even if they appeared to be crumbling to extinction, often still housed the descendants of the original family. The churches, the jewels of the Cotswolds, listed their unchanging names, generations of them. In Burford: the Tanfields and Carys; in Great Barrington: the Brays and the Talbots. In Little Barrington: the Grayhursts. In Chipping Stebton: the Stebtons. And thus it remained for centuries until, strapped for cash, the family gradually sold off the village houses. This reversal of fortune, by an ironical twist of fate, meant that as the tiny cottages were enlarged and gentrified – in sympathetic style, of course – the grand house slipped into near ruin.

The last of the male Stebtons, Thomas, inherited the estate when he was nineteen. He shared Stebton Place with his mother until her death and did not marry until he was almost fifty. Thomas and Lucie were singularly unlucky in their attempts to raise a son and heir. Even for the time, their children were remarkably short-lived. Two of his three daughters succumbed to smallpox at the age of twelve and ten respectively. His youngest child was a boy who died at birth and took his mother with him. Nobody was surprised: childbirth was a risky business even by the end of the century. For a woman of forty-one it was considered suicidal. Of all his children only one little girl survived. Laura was only four when her mother died and her grandmother moved in to take charge of the widower and orphan. Thomas was sixty-four and in poor health.

Dorcas Toller, who was not much older than her son-in-law, was a handsome and overbearing woman who relished her position as chatelaine of Stebton Place but was less happy as substitute mother. As a result, Laura, already a shy and timid child, withdrew more and more into herself and into the company of her beloved father.

Thomas was a gentle and studious man and the prospect of placing himself or his tiny darling into his mother-in-law's charge was not one he cared to contemplate. His fears were well-placed; once installed, Dorcas Toller proved impossible to shift. Nonetheless, despite his failing health, the last years of Thomas's life were not unhappy. As the little girl grew, she became the inseparable companion of her beloved Papa and he adored her. He was her first and only teacher and she learned to read and write, in several languages, with a precocity which astonished and delighted him. They became a familiar sight around the village, the little dark-eyed child hand in hand with the old man.

Towards the end of his life, fears for the little girl's future preoccupied him. He did not entirely trust his mother-in-law so he fretted and connived as to how he might best protect his daughter's interests after his death. The family lawyers in London were consulted exhaustively and, by and large, successfully. Once he had secured Laura's inheritance of the manor and what remained of the property in Chipping Stebton for her lifetime, the old man's thoughts turned to his father's land in Ireland.

Aretino, Pietro di: *Sonnetti Lussuriosi. Venezia 1779. Exquisitely printed, on rectos only. Bound in full turkey, discreet gold lozenge decoration. Extremely rare.*

A d'A Cat. 3, item 12

8

Jane-Edwina Stebton-Hillyard laid down her pen and reread her manuscript before locking it away in the top drawer of her desk. She pushed her spectacles up on her forehead and rubbed her tired eyes, then stretched her arms lazily and pondered her next move. After a moment or two she began to pace the floor, stamping her feet to try to restore her circulation. The library was extremely chilly. As a result, her dress was somewhat individual for indoors on an early May morning. A long maroon velvet skirt reached right to the tops of her neat ankle-high leather boots. She wore a black polo-neck sweater under a velvet patchwork jacket which, though it was obviously home-made and well-worn, still contrived to look rather striking. Her dark curly hair peeped from under a woollen stocking hat in the garish royal blue and yellow colours of the Oxford United football team. She did not follow the team, the hat was merely a device used to irritate her sister who was apt to burst into the room without warning. In front of her on the desk a bust of her beloved grandmother,

Laura Stebton, known affectionately as Lal, sported a similar *chapeau* tilted rakishly to one side.

As long as her grandmother was alive, Jane-Edwina was content enough with life at Stebton Place. But after she died, when Jane-Edwina was twenty-five or so, everything changed and she could see no possibility of escape from the confines of her narrow life. Whereas Lal had shared and encouraged her bookishness, her mother, in charge at last, would have none of it. In the absence of servants, Jane-Edwina and her sister Felicity were required to 'pull their weight'. The huge house had an insatiable appetite for their energies and the family's dwindling income. Yet there was never any question of doing a deal and passing it on to their wealthier cousin next door at the vicarage who would have been only too willing to oblige. His branch of the Stebton family had lain in wait for years. After the twins, he was next in line and it looked increasingly likely that he would take over eventually. As far as Jane-Edwina was concerned, the sooner the better. Just so long as she could manage to fully exploit her grand-mother's inheritance before then. She knew she had better look sharp, of late she noticed a proprietorial glint in her cousin's eye whenever he entered the library. It was with considerable pleasure that she followed his vainly searching eyes. She gave him absolutely no indication that she had discovered its fabulous secrets.

She unlocked one of the bookcases and took a bulky file across to the desk. Before opening it, she leaned forward and absently stroked the statue's face. 'Now, darling Lal, enough teasing,' she murmured. But the blank eyes of the statue only stared back. She sighed in frustration, replaced her glasses and fingered the papers lying before her. The key to the riddle was here somewhere. Lal had been addicted to puzzles and conundrums, but her mind, even in old age, had worked precisely if a little eccentrically. Though she'd been dead fifteen years, every so often a large manila envelope arrived from beyond the grave, as it were. Conveniently, if mundanely, forwarded by the family solicitor. The first had arrived when Jane-Edwina was thirty and quite in despair of her dependent state. It was as if Lal had anticipated the rising arc of her frustration and at its apex had offered a means of escape. There had been three in all. She spread the contents of the most recent over the surface of the desk. The enclosed letter was in her grandmother's spidery hand.

My darling grand-daughter,
   We both love puzzles and this, I believe, is the best puzzle of all. By the time you receive it you will be forty and in need of independence, no matter what your marital state. I remember my own forties with deep unhappiness and frustration. This will be my very last letter to you. You see, my dearest one, I have always worried about your future with all those earnest divines clamouring for the Stebton inheritance. Though I secretly felt that the old monks who haunt this house would one day claim it for their own. For many reasons this would please me.
   By now you have discovered the secret of the library built by William Ryland Stebton in 1829, whose direct relationship to you is, to put it mildly, interesting. The librorum probitorum

must speak for itself. I assume you have found a good use for the books. Though they are extremely valuable I found them risible, or worse. My own taste was rather more like my dear father's. I cannot believe he knew of the secret shelves. Had I found them earlier I might have been able to save the village, but I did not. I can see you smile at the thought of such practicality from your poor old Lal.

My deepest regret is that I did not insist on a proper education for you. I was not wise enough to perceive until it was too late that it was the only real independence for a young woman in your circumstances. Forgive me, dear child, I sacrificed much for a quiet life and your dear companion-ship. Strangely, I never had the same fears for your sister. Though she is less clever than you she will find life easier I think. For one thing she is more conventional. Enough. If – and of course it is a preposterous notion of one so lively and amusing – you have not married, you will need a competence and even if you have, a little running-away money might come in useful. But I dis-semble, my dearest girl, because at the time I write, when you are almost twenty-five, I already know that, like me, you could not easily subjugate yourself to another's whim, you had too much of it from childhood. I suspect marriage is not for you. And because of that I am sending you my final gift which came to me from my dear father. The most unchanging, most valuable in my possession. I speak of literature and I speak of land. You may, in finding those, also find an unexpected way of life. Had I discovered it earlier myself, you might not be. It appealed to me powerfully. Perhaps it may also appeal to you?

Darling girl, I cannot imagine you as old as forty, but I have had fun trying. One thing I'm

*fairly sure of: if you haven't escaped Stebton Place
by now, it is time to do so or you will be caught
for ever. Solve my riddle as I have solved it and
you will, I believe, find it worthwhile. To help
you, I enclose my father's diary and his deed of
gift. But pray be careful, my child.*

Your loving grandmother, Laura Stebton.

Jane-Edwina held a large discoloured sheet of
paper to the light and compared the detail of a
precise little drawing with the room. There was a
neat caption in the bottom right hand corner:
*Adelaide Elderson Stebton fecit. June the twelfth,
1826, Papa's library.* The careful italic was childish, but if the drawing had been made by a child,
the draughtsmanship was exquisite. After a time
she sighed, laid down the sheet of paper and bit
her lip. The whole thing was wrong, not remotely
in scale. Which was strange, because the young
artist showed precocious talent. *Adelaide fecit.*
And who, pray, was Adelaide? What relation was
she? Jane-Edwina walked over to the window and
for a time stood staring down at the churchyard.
Was she out there perhaps? Under one of the
tombstones, listed amongst those many Stebton
names? The thought of trawling through the
generations made her feel tired.

She held the drawing up to the light again. The
room portrayed was similar to the Stebton Place
library in almost every detail except the windows
were shuttered and incorrectly placed. Surely even
a child, who had so accurately portrayed the
rather individual bookcases, might have got the
windows right? The colours were wrong as well,
though that was less important. She sat back and

looked around her. Family tradition had it that the library was based on the plans of a seventeenth-century Italian monastic library, built to her ancestor's specifications by craftsmen from Bath. Why did she doubt that the sketch was meant to be the Italian original?

She looked around her again. Tatty and faded though it was now, the room had once been decked out in rather sombre shades of blue. The rug, too, had a blue background which must once have looked rich and wonderful against the dark shelves but now, like everything else, was looking very definitely the worse for wear. All the furnishings in the drawing were in shades of red. *Adelaide fecit 1826.* She held the paper close to her eyes and reread the faded script. And then, as the solution began to dawn, she began to rock with silent laughter. How very slow she was becoming. She looked around, picked up her grandmother's last letter and checked the other date: 1829. But the Stebton Place library was said to have been installed around 1730. She looked about her, a smile still playing on her lips. The traditional estimate was out by a hundred years. Lal must have known all along. *Adelaide* had *fecit*-ed the blueprint. Was it a copy of an already existing library? And if so where was it? More important, who was Adelaide? She put the flimsy sheet of paper away and picked up a little sheaf of manuscript and read through it carefully. Then one by one she went through the rest of the contents of her grandmother's envelope. Last of all she studied a finely drawn map.

She laid her spectacles up on the desk and rubbed her eyes. Then she lay back in her chair, relishing the silence which she knew wouldn't last. Both her mother and sister had a passion for action – any action – even the most pointless. Strange then that neither of them had the slightest talent for the more useful, if mundane, household tasks. Nor, come to think of it, had she. Unfortunately, out of desperation when the last of their cook-housekeepers had departed, she had, after a fashion, taught herself the rudiments of cooking. A foolish move if ever there was one. In the twinkling of an eye responsibility for the kitchen had devolved on her – with the shopping, cleaning and the general household budget. Not income, not by any stretch of the imagination the remotest financial responsibility. Just small and inadequate sums grudgingly passed to her piecemeal first by Mama then by some arrangement which she still could not quite work out, by Felicity.

Rising forty-one years of age and still as utterly dependent as she'd been as a child. No private means and no formal education. Or only as much as a sporadic series of inadequate private tutors had managed to instil into her languid brain. Illogical, badly co-ordinated, (not quite) innumerate. Only her grandmother's love of books had saved her from illiteracy as well. Darling Lal was the only teacher with any real spark she'd ever had. Since her death she'd maundered along in her own dreamy fashion. Her grandmother's library was her secret place, her pleasure, her refuge from the rigours of Felicity's more active pursuits. In time, by dint of working her way through the library shelves, Jane-Edwina – or Jeddie, as she preferred to be called – taught herself to read in several languages. But it had taken a long time.

As a young girl her ambitions had been modest enough: marriage, home, children, loving husband. But that was long before she divined that though men attracted her, marriage did not. Even so she would have married to escape. But men were scarce in her isolated world. The twins did not mix with the village children, nor were they sent away to school where they might have made friends. Most of all, they were not equipped to earn a living. It was almost as if the twentieth century had not happened for them. They were in much the same plight as any Austen heroine, trapped by the promise of an income and inheritance which, like a mirage, withdrew further and further into the future. And of course they were twins. Which would inherit Stebton Place? And when?

Jeddie was almost thirty-five before she began to despair of a knight on a white charger. Her only suitor, a rather dim academic, had strung her along for a critical five years before he wed another whose income and prospects were more modest but a great deal more tangible. The relief she felt did not blind her to the realization that there would be no bail-outs, no possibility of anyone but herself seeing her safely into old age. It was then she turned her long years browsing in the library to advantage and got her first job – in a bookshop in Burford. With her modest earnings she began to frequent the local pub. Felicity had never forgiven her.

At much the same time, Timothy William Ryland Stebton, vicar of St Edwin's and their cousin, was widowed. He was a plump, good-natured, rather eager man. And he was, after the twins, next in line to inherit Stebton Place. Though they were slightly younger than he, the possibility of them having issue looked increasingly remote. Having made that assessment, the Revd Tim was happy enough to bide his time in the vicarage, secure in the knowledge that his line of the family would eventually come into their own. A most satisfactory outcome to anticipate, as Miss Austen might have concluded.

Within a year or two he and Felicity began to eye each other with interest. By then he'd worked out that Felicity was ostensibly the more powerful of the sisters. She had the ear of her mother and appeared to have charge of the family finances. A stately gavotte of courtship ensued during which Jeddie wondered how long it would take him to pluck up courage to marry Felicity. And whether she herself would have tired of his charms before then. One thing was quite clear, if they did get married, she would not remain at Stebton Place as gooseberry. Though how she would ever bear to leave the library she could not imagine. It was her favourite place, her refuge, her means of livelihood. And, since she first began trading its secret hoard, the source of a steady, and most satisfactory, increase in her assets. Her way to independence. If Lal's last scheme worked out she would have enough to live on for the remainder of her life. Even better she would be able to buy that little house she lusted for in Jericho. The delicious prospect of which made her head spin.

'J-E!' Felicity shrieked from the staircase. 'Come down at once. Now. This inst.' There was the sound of a furious stamping. 'I know exactly where you are, so will you please get down here?

At once! Mama wants her lunch and I'm going out, so you'd better get cracking. Jane? Do you hear me?' There was another thump.

Jeddie tiptoed to the library door, checked that it was firmly closed and turned the key silently in the lock. Her full lips curled in amusement. Mother was safely in bed and could wait for lunch. At the rate she was putting on weight, a few missed meals would benefit her, rather than the reverse. What Felicity did was up to her.

Jeddie swept the papers into a neat pile, slipped them back into their envelope and carried them across the room to one of the bookcases. The floor space of the library was about thirty foot square and, except for the chimney-breast, window and door, was completely lined with floor-to-ceiling bookcases. Here the ancient oak panelling of the rest of the old house gave way to the neo-classical. There were eight double-fronted mahogany bookcases. The doors on the lower part, to a height of some three feet, were wood-panelled, those on the upper part were brass-meshed and arched to a perfect semicircle. The bookcases were framed with fluted pilasters which rose from the lower cupboards and tapered gently to their exquisitely carved Corinthian capitals. The gracefully arched doors gave the bookcases an impression of height greater than the actual nine feet to the ceiling. From the outside the pilasters appeared to be merely decorative but inside were narrow, secret shelves whose whereabouts and means of access were, these days, known only to Jeddie. The knowledge of these, as with so much of the rest of the Stebton history, had been passed to her in those rewarding, infrequent increments by her adored grandmother.

Jeddie ran her hand along the base of one of the pilasters and as it swung back she placed her papers on the lower shelf of the secret cupboard which was otherwise empty. Then she took off her absurd cap and, chuckling softly, left the library and crept downstairs.

JEDDIE IN IRELAND

The First Visit – June 1994

Any attached plan must contain sufficient details of the surrounding roads and other features to enable the land to be identified satisfactorily on the Ordnance Survey Map.

Land Registry Application for an Official Search of the Index Map

9

All hovercraft crossings had been cancelled and the afternoon ferry from Holyhead was two hours delayed. Jeddie Stebton-Hillyard sat in the bar of the Innisfree and tried desperately to will her see-sawing stomach to settle down. Wind and sea-spray lashed the decks as the ferry rolled and plunged sickeningly. To make matters worse, by the time she thought of taking a cabin they had all been appropriated by more prescient souls so she was compelled to sit out the four-hour journey. She blearily eyed the crowd gathered around the bar who seemed bent on getting pie-eyed as quickly as possible. Normally Jeddie would have been tempted to join them but the smell of tobacco which, though she didn't smoke, she usually enjoyed, simply added to her nausea. She stared disconsolately at the melting ice in her vodka and wished them all to kingdom come.

The lounge was joyless, stale, shabby and unpleasant, as was the entire boat. She had, in a brief spirit of adventure, walked the length of it and several rounds of the deck before they'd set sail. At first the salt wind had been something of a relief after the stuffy train which had been crowded from the moment she set foot on it at Euston. She had never before made the crossing to Ireland and was somewhat put out that her five-hour journey from London was an hour longer and a good deal less comfortable than that described in her Victorian forbear's diary. She'd set out to replicate that early journey in a spirit of nostalgic adventure. Now she wondered why she hadn't simply taken the fifty-minute flight from Heathrow. Come what may, she vowed, she would not be making the return ferry crossing. A prolonged and deafening burst of singing from the bar merely strengthened her resolve.

Things began to look up the moment the boat docked. Almost the first thing she saw in the admittedly watery, early evening sunshine was a large sign directing her to the Royal Marine Hotel. She wondered vaguely why Royal was retained when Kingstown had become, unpronounceably for her, Dun Laoghaire. Murmuring 'Hang the cost,' Jeddie picked up her small holdall and made her weary and uncertain way through a formal garden which led from the pier straight up to the hotel entrance.

As it turned out, she could not have found a more convenient location for her stay had she planned it in advance. She skipped supper and went straight to bed armed with a bottle of duty-free vodka and a bundle of local maps kindly loaned to her by an obliging receptionist.

She slept heavily and awoke, as usual, at

precisely six-thirty. She sat up gingerly and reached for the Dublin telephone directory. There were nine entries under *Elder*, four *Elders*, one *Elderwood* but no *Elderson*. She heaved a sigh of relief. She had no desire for further complications to her already complicated scheme.

It was a complete fluke that the law firm whose name the Victorian diarist had so carefully noted, should be listed – albeit in somewhat modified form – in the same directory. Moore Stanhope Boland had become Moore Boland & Murphy-Dunne. One common name wouldn't have been enough – but surely two must mean something? She peered short-sightedly at some small print below the name but could not read it until she located – and rescued – her spectacles from beneath the bed, beside an upturned glass which she ignored. She perched them on her nose and found the name again. Moore Boland & Murphy-Dunne *formerly Moore Stanhope Boland & Callaway*. She let the directory slip off the bed and lay back with her eyes closed while she tried to work out what to do. After a few minutes she tore the page from the directory, folded it neatly and slipped it between the pages of her voluminous notebook. She would brood on it a while.

She spread the maps on the bed and pored over them but it became obvious at once that what she needed was a good Ordnance Survey map or at least something a good deal more detailed. Jeddie pushed off the bedclothes, padded to her *en suite* and ran a bath. The luxury of silence and privacy made her head swim. She moved about slowly, savouring the unusual pleasure of being mistress of her own fate and, even more precious, time. She had planned her getaway with precision and care and – luck holding – would not be missed. She emptied a little sachet of bubble bath into the steaming water then lay back, closed her eyes and planned her day.

The dining room was almost empty when eventually Jeddie went down to breakfast and to the discovery that in Ireland an admission or even a pose of helplessness elicited the most amazingly kindly response. A reference to literature, or a display of mild eccentricity even more so. By a combination of luck and instinct Jeddie managed to score on all points.

'Ar ya on holiday?' the waiter asked as he laid a huge plate of bacon and eggs before her which immediately made her stomach heave.

'Er, not exactly,' she replied hesitantly. 'I'm, er, I'm a writer, a kind of historian, actually.' She gave him a self-deprecating little smile. 'I'm here to do some research.' He was immediately interested. 'Would that be for the filums?' he asked eagerly.

'No,' she said, surprised. 'No, a rather dull book, I'm afraid.' She twinkled up at him. 'Are you interested in film?' She preferred his pronunciation – two syllables instead of one wherever possible – but, though tempted, didn't imitate his flat accent. She could easily have done; it was surprisingly like a Liverpool accent which, as it happened, she found particularly easy.

'Yeah. We get a lot of the filum people here, y'know. In and out the whole time.' To her amusement he gave time two syllables. 'They have a great time, d'you know that? Sure they've money to burn. What a life,' he added, admiringly. He leaned down until she could feel his hot breath on her ear. 'I'm a bit of an actor, meself, y'know. I was an extra, on the *Michael Collins* filum.' He winked conspiratorially and puffed out his chest. 'It was great crack altogether. The wife got the costume for me. There were thousands there but they picked me,' he said and waited for her to congratulate him. Jeddie obliged nicely since it seemed churlish to do otherwise; besides, she liked him. The fact that she had no idea what film he referred to was, in her view, neither here nor there. She warmed to his chatter which made a nice change from the barbed comments she usually had to endure over breakfast. Books or literature of any kind were not notably valued in the bosom of her immediate family.

'Did you have to travel far?'

'For wha'?' He poured her coffee at last. Jeddie buttered a thick slice of home-made brown bread and made an approximate stab at the bacon.

'To where they made the film,' she said with her mouth full. The bread was divine, the bacon mild and delicious. She pushed the congealing eggs aside.

'Sure aren't the studios only down the road,' he laughed, waving his right arm at the window. 'Along the coast there. In Bray. D'ya not know it? Other end of the bay. Beyond Killiney.'

'No, I'm afraid not,' she said thoughtfully. She spread some butter on another slice of bread and cut it into tiny squares. 'Killiney?' She looked up and gave him a dazzling smile and glanced at the name tag on his chest. 'Excuse me, Joe. Did you say Killiney?'

'Yeah,' he said carelessly. 'Ardmore Studios are a bit farther on, in Bray. They're famous.'

'Killiney Bay is close by, you say?' she persisted. 'Do you know it?'

'And why wouldn't I?' he said languidly. 'Don't I only live there?' He looked at her amiably as though she was just the tiniest bit soft in the head. Who wanted to talk about a seaside resort when there was his film career to discuss? He looked a little huffy as he began to clear the table. Jeddie touched his sleeve.

'Could you show me on the map? I think you might be able to help me. With my book,' she added shrewdly. His interest was immediately re-aroused.

'I'll just take this stuff to the kitchen, missis, then I'll be back to ya'.'

Jeddie moved to an empty table by the window, opened out the maps and consulted her notebook. When Joe returned a few minutes later he'd changed out of his black waistcoat into a tweed sports jacket which made him look both smaller and more careworn. Jeddie warmed to him again. She recognized an ally. He reminded her of one of her old cronies in the village and she knew in her bones that he would have a fund of local knowledge. And better still, just like Johnny Pittaway, he would be generous about sharing it. He had that same lonely, eager look. A bit like myself, she thought dryly, desperate for a friend to talk to, wild for adventure. She had found her serendipity.

'I'm looking for a house called Elderson Court,' she said quickly to cover her embarrassment and pointed to where Killiney Bay was marked on the map. Joe rubbed his chin with the flat of his palm. He looked puzzled.

'Never heard of it,' he said. 'You think it's somewhere around there? There's all sorts of hew-ege houses up that way. Y'know Bono lives there.'

'Bono?'

'Yeah. U2.' He waggled his beaming face from side to side waiting for her to gush.

'Me too?' She looked mystified. Joe gave up.

'Well, I'm scarlet for ya', missis!' He laughed down at her. 'Where have you been at all? U2. Sure isn't it only the most famous group in the whole world. Right on our own doorstep as well,' he added triumphantly.

'Sorry, I'm not much into groups.' She smiled up at him then bent over her notebook again. 'A short ride from Kingstown', she read, 'on the bay between Killiney and Bray.' She looked at him over her spectacles. 'I suppose he means on a horse.'

'Clippity-clop,' he said and grinned. 'What did you say the name was again?'

'Elderson Court.'

He shook his head slowly from side to side. He leaned over the map and followed the railway line with his finger. 'Somewhere about there you think?'

'Yes, though I believe it may have become a convent at some stage. That is only surmise, you understand . . .'

'A convent. Oh well now, that's different. Look,' he said, pointing to a tiny cross. 'I wonder what that is?' He half shut his eyes as if he was trying to picture the area. He reminded Jeddie of a sharp-nosed pointer sniffing the air. Or perhaps, she amended, giving him a sidelong glance, more like a Jack Russell.

'There's a big school somewhere about there, I think. Could that be it?'

'A church school?'

'A what? Oh, the cross. No, it's a boardin' school. For boys. Matter of fact I think it might be – what d'you call it? – non-denominational. Glenadams, it's called. I don't think it would have a cross on it.' He rubbed his chin and gave her a half-mocking, half-conspiratorial grin.

'Oh well,' Jeddie murmured and peered at the map again.

'Hey!' shouted Joe. 'What d'you know, look, it's marked. Just this side of the golf course.' She glanced up at him.

'Do crosses denote churches or convents?' she asked quietly.

Joe bit his lip and shrugged. 'Well,' he sighed, 'between them it is.' He laughed and glanced furtively at his watch. 'If I knew tha' you'd be home and dried, wouldn't ya?'

'Oh dear, I'm sorry. I'm taking up your time.'

'No problem, missis. Me bus doesn't go for another few minutes.'

'You're going home?' she asked and immediately she had what she later congratulated herself on as a brainwave. 'Are you off duty?'

'Yeah. I've the rest of the day off. I was on all nigh',' he laughed. 'I could do with a rest, me feet are only killin' me.'

'If,' Jeddie said slyly, 'if I hired a cab I could drop you off.'

He looked at her and laughed. 'Then I could

show you round a bit, y' mean?' He gave an amused little nod of the head. 'Game ball, missis, I'd be delighted. I'll get the girl in reception to call a car for you. You're ready to go now?'

'I'll just nip upstairs for a minute or two and get my coat. My friends call me Jeddie by the way.'

By the time Jeddie came downstairs again the car was waiting and Joe was looking dead pleased with himself.

'I just remembered, er, Jeddie,' he said shyly. 'I just remembered. There used to be an old convent near tha' school. I forgot about it because it's a bit off the beaten track. I can't remember what it's called. But it's in the right place.' He gave a funny little jerk of his head. 'I think so anyway. If it's still there, of course.'

'If you're right,' said Jeddie, 'we'll have a drink on it.'

'I'll hold you to tha',' he said and helped her into the car. 'I could murder a Guinness.'

They had some difficulty locating access to the convent from the Bray Road. The circuitous track which led to it had long since shrunk inwards from its grassy edges until it was barely wide enough for the car. A humped ridge of grass grew along the centre. They rumbled along at about five miles an hour. At regular intervals the driver turned around and asked pointedly if they knew where they were going until even the confident Joe began to doubt his instincts. Then quite suddenly the car jolted to a halt in front of a high stone wall and the driver said, 'Would you look at that? And I thought yiz were mad.'

'Wait here a few minutes, would you?' Jeddie

asked as she and Joe got out of the car. They followed the wall for a couple of hundred yards until they came to a high cast-iron gate backed with metal sheeting. They stepped back and looked up. Above it, set in a scrolled arch, were the words *Holy Retreat*.

Joe lit a cigarette and offered the package to Jeddie but she didn't notice. She was staring at the worn and barely legible lettering at the top of the high stone pillars on either side of the gate. *Elderson* on one side, *Court* on the other. The letters were almost weathered away. Joe followed her glance and whistled.

'Well now, would you look at tha',' he said. 'Bingo!' They grinned at each other.

'Are y'not goin' in?' He indicated the bell-pull attached to the wall.

Jeddie shook her head slowly and pointed to the discreet notice affixed to the gate just above the handle. It was explicit and to the point: *No entry without prior notice and written invitation.* It had been recently painted.

'That's that then. I'd better write for an appointment,' she said briskly, leading him away with a surprisingly firm hand. 'I believe I owe you a drink, Joe.' She smiled. 'Though on the whole, lunch might be better. If you'll remember, I didn't manage much breakfast.' They laughed.

Prestidigitateur *One who practises sleight of hand or legerdemain; a juggler, a conjuror, a trickster.*

Oxford English Dictionary

10

By four o'clock the same afternoon, Jeddie Stebton-Hillyard had removed herself and her baggage to a modest little guest house a mile or so closer to the city where the rates were low, the accommodation comfortable and the landlady was both obliging and talkative. In short, all the things Jeddie most liked. She left a bottle of Jameson at the hotel for Joe, with a note of thanks regretting that she had been so suddenly called away.

At precisely ten forty-five the following morning she presented herself at the plush Fitzwilliam Street offices of Moore Boland & Murphy-Dunne. She wore a hideous pair of rimless spectacles and had dressed with unusual care though few would have recognized it. The popular notion of Unworldly Academic was what she'd set out to achieve and, by and large, she succeeded. Besides her over-stuffed leather satchel she carried an umbrella and two large and well-filled plastic bags.

The offices were on the first floor of a glorious Georgian townhouse. She ignored the lift and gave herself the pleasure of climbing the splendid – and recently restored – staircase. A startlingly beautiful young girl with a long mop of shining red curls smiled at her from the reception desk. She had excellent manners; when she asked if she could help, she appeared to mean it.

'I hope you can.' Jeddie, fully aware of the impact of her rather eccentric appearance, smiled gamely and gave an embarrassed little cough. 'I hope you may be able to . . .' She let her voice drift off shyly. 'My name is Hillyard. *Miss* Hillyard. I'm a writer,' she whispered hoarsely and dropped both plastic bags.

'Yes?' The girl jumped up and began to gather Jeddie's scattered belongings.

'Yes. I'm working on some nineteenth-century ancestral papers.' Jeddie looked up vaguely. 'I am particularly interested in a large house, near Dublin.' She cleared her throat nervously. 'Well, actually, it's the family I'm really interested in. They had connections in both Ireland and England. Over a long period, don't you see?'

The girl looked up at her and tried vainly to stifle a laugh. 'Not really,' she said. 'But how can we help?'

'Well, you see, I'm trying to find the law firm involved with the business affairs of the estate. They were called, let me see, I have it here somewhere,' she said vaguely. She perched her over-stuffed satchel on the desk and began to rummage through it. Eventually she fished a large notebook from its depths and waved it triumphantly. Then she consulted it busily, though she didn't in the least need to do so. 'Moore Stanhope Boland. That strike a bell?' She looked up and blinked short-sightedly at the girl as an extremely well-dressed man strode into the room.

'Oh, Mr Murphy-Dunne,' the receptionist called. She was having trouble keeping a straight face. 'Perhaps you can help this lady? Miss, er, Hillier. She's a writer.'

'Hillyard,' Jeddie corrected gently. She looked up at him shyly. The first thing she noticed, and disliked, were his restless, bloodshot eyes. He was a big man, dark-haired, mid-forties with a slightly squashed nose. Rugger-player-running-to-seed was written all over him. He appeared to be having a little trouble controlling the flab around his middle though his excellent tailor had done his best to accommodate him. He wore a dark pinstripe suit with a bright and rather dashing pink silk tie. Probably Ferregamo, she thought since she took quite an interest in such things.

'Oh? A writer?' He swivelled around and looked Jeddie up and down, a complacent half-smile hovering at the corners of his full mouth. 'In what way may I help, Miss, er, Hillyard?' He put ironic emphasis on the Miss and raised his eyebrows at Jeddie who gave him one of her more baffled smiles and repeated her question.

'Yes,' he said. 'You have the right firm, though these days,' he drew himself up to his full six foot two, 'we are Moore Boland and Murphy-Dunne.' He held out his hand and at the same time gave a quick and obvious glance at his watch. 'Terence Murphy-Dunne at your service. I've got five minutes.' The receptionist looked at him with disgust knowing that he had no appointments for an hour. She half thought she should warn Miss Hillier, or whatever her name was, that Mr

Murphy-Dunne was not adverse to a little diversion. And making sport of hapless old ladies – Sinéad was only nineteen and to her Jeddie looked pretty ancient – was exactly up his street. Her mouth turned down in disapproval when she heard him say, 'Why don't you step into my office and tell me what you want to know?' *Said the spider to the fly*.

Jeddie preceded him fearlessly. 'I'm writing a history of my family,' she said, once she'd settled into the easy chair by the side of his desk. This time there was no hesitation, no dawdling. She was surprisingly businesslike. 'I'm specifically looking for a house called', she consulted the notebook again, 'Elderson Court?' She took off her spectacles and smiled innocently. Her face was immediately transformed. Not beautiful, not even very attractive, but somehow she contrived to convey more than a hint of raciness. She read her subject well.

There was a noticeable flicker of interest in Terence Murphy-Dunne's eyes as he leaned across the desk and considered her while he tried to work out what she was on about. Strange-looking woman. Mid-forties? Younger? Older? Probably not. When she smiled she looked younger. Early forties then. He spun his pencil on the polished surface of his desk while he gathered his thoughts.

'Do you mind if I smoke?' he asked politely and without waiting for her answer lit up. His antennae were gyrating wildly. Elderson Court, she'd said. How did she know that long-disused name? Christ, who was she? He'd better proceed cautiously, or everything would go haywire. Or was he imagining intrigue and threat where there was none? He shut his eyes against rising panic and when he opened them the woman was smiling expectantly, *knowingly*.

'I'm sorry.' He shook his head and gave her a regretful half-smile which didn't quite reach his eyes. 'Elderson rings no bells. Can you tell me why you think we may have had business there?' he added uneasily and flicked his cigarette against the ashtray on his desk.

'The name cropped up in some family papers,' she replied vaguely. 'Scraps. No real information. Just the name. I hoped you might be able to tell me if the house still exists. I really only want to go and look at it. Take a few pictures, fill in a few footnotes, so to speak.' She gave a nervous little titter. 'For my book.'

'Any idea where it was?'

'I hope it may still be,' she replied crisply.

'You say it was in Dublin?'

'Near, I think. According to my notes, a short journey by train from Kingstown.'

'Dun Laoghaire,' he laughed. 'The name was changed a very long time ago.'

Jeddie consulted the notebook again. Murphy-Dunne fidgeted from foot to foot while she rifled through the tatty pages. 'Killiney Bay?' She softened the second i to an e.

'Killiney,' he corrected absently but for the second time she noticed a glint of wariness in his eyes.

'You don't come from Ireland yourself, Miss Hillyard?' he prevaricated, oozing charm.

'No, indeed, I'm afraid not,' she said politely and looked at him under her lashes. 'My family is from Oxfordshire. But an ancestor of mine married into the Elderson family, so I have some little claim, connection.' The dark eyes were guileless and the emphasis on *claim* was so light as to be almost illusory. 'To Ireland, I mean.' She smiled at him.

'Of course.' He smiled back. Check.

'The family and the house were called Elderson, then?' He tilted his chair and sucked pleasurably at a back tooth. He looked completely disinterested but she noticed, as he leaned forward to stub out his cigarette, that the pulse in his temple had quickened.

'The original owners. The house may have become a convent at some stage.'

'A convent? In Killiney you say?' He smiled indulgently, as if to a particularly dim aunt. 'And what exactly is your connection? Or ours, I might ask?'

'When I was researching my family history I came across a couple of references to this, er, ancestor, who founded a convent in the family home. It was so intriguing – unusual – at least in England, that I just had to follow it up.'

'Somebody called Elderson?'

'Not quite. Of the Elderson family.'

'Miss Hillyard, could you come to the point? I cannot see the connection you're trying to make.'

'Certainly.' Jeddie smiled sweetly. 'The person who founded the convent was, I believe, called Stebton,' she said patiently. 'Her father's name. Her mother was an Elderson.' She smiled pleasantly. 'My family is also called Stebton. Actually my name is really *Stebton*-Hillyard.' Her speech became so rapid he was not able to interrupt even had he wanted. 'Jane-Edwina *Stebton*-Hillyard.'

She blinked up at him guilelessly. He thought, as she intended, that she looked both batty and confused. Jane-Edwina Stebton-Hillyard. What a moniker. She was all of a piece, the very picture of an eccentric, upper-class English lady. No, woman. Englishwoman. Woman suited her better. She reminded him suddenly of the actress who played the wife in *Fawlty Towers*. And the Queen for that matter. What was her name? Something equally absurd. Scales. Prunella Scales. His lips curled in amusement and then he suddenly sat up. Her name . . . hell's bells.

'I would prefer,' Jeddie cut in, as if she was tuned precisely to his thought-waves, 'I would prefer if you'd call me Hillyard, or Stebton if you prefer,' she burbled rapidly. 'I don't much care for *Stebton-Hillyard* and *Jane-Edwina* is utterly absurd. Two double-barrelled names seem excessive, don't you think?' She raised an eyebrow and they both laughed, though in truth he was unsettled by how deftly she revealed Murphy-Dunne for the affectation it was. There was something strange about how her expression kept changing. She was both knowing and amused. At him? At herself? At the situation? It was hard to guess. Her sharp black eyes blinked rapidly under his scrutiny. When she blushed slightly and looked away, he had the curious feeling that it was not his scrutiny which had embarrassed her but her own thoughts. And perhaps his. He lit another cigarette.

'I think, it's only the vaguest hunch, mind, this firm may have acted for them. The family lawyer, so to speak,' she said slowly and deliberately, looking straight at him.

'Yes?' At first he did not grasp what she meant. She changed pace and subject so confusingly it was hard to follow any one line of thought.

'And if that is the case, then you would certainly have a record of where the house was situated, don't you see?'

'Just its situation? Surely you could find that on a map? If not a modern one, then a contemporary edition?' He looked at her suspiciously. 'Have you not been to the Public Records office, Miss Stebton, em Hillyard?'

She smiled disarmingly. 'Actually I am more interested in the people. Which is why I hoped you might be able to help me.' She leaned back the better to hold his gaze. 'I am most particularly interested in a great nineteenth-century book-collector called Ryland Stebton. As a matter of fact, I believe he was my direct ancestor.'

Murphy-Dunne pushed his chair back abruptly, stood up and held out his hand. 'Heavens, is that the time? I'm sorry, Miss Hillyard.' He paused like Hamlet deciding whether to be or not to be. He touched his forehead theatrically as if a thought had suddenly struck him and began to tap his fingers impatiently on the desk. 'You did say Elderson, did you? Well now, that does begin to ring a little bell. I think.' He frowned. 'But alas, I have another appointment.' He beamed at her as if a wonderful idea had just occurred to him. 'I shall get Sinéad to look up the records and see what we can find. Will that do?'

'Wonderfully, Mr Murphy-Dunne.'

'So. Why don't you come back in a week or two?'

'Could it be sooner? I am only here for a couple more days. I would consider it a great favour.'

'Of course, of course. When would suit? Tomorrow afternoon? About five, say?'

Jeddie picked up her huge battered satchel and put on her shapeless beige overcoat. He was amused to notice, as she walked to the door, that she wore sheer, black, seamed stockings and beautiful black suede shoes. Italian and expensive by the look of them and at complete variance to the rest of her gear. He chuckled quietly to himself. She had surprisingly good legs. And the seams were straight.

'Till tomorrow then.' Her eyes met his. She smiled conspiratorially, slowly put on her glasses again and bumbled out of the room. It was then, while he watched her, that he felt the first cold blast of fear. He wasn't convinced by her shambling other-worldliness but he couldn't, for the life of him, work out what she wanted. Was his imagination playing tricks? Was she exactly what she seemed? A dim, bumbling academic? Or perhaps she fancied herself as some sort of amateur genealogist? All the same, the old bag unnerved him. He just needed a little time to check one or two things. And gather his thoughts. The mention of book-collecting had thrown him for a minute.

She came back at precisely five o'clock the next afternoon. Murphy-Dunne kept her waiting a statutory fifteen minutes before he allowed Sinéad to usher her into his office. He eyed her warily and was surprised at how small she seemed after all. Small and scruffy. Beguiling smile, though. Almost alluring for some reason. Her clothes were still a fright. No Irishwoman worth her salt would ever allow herself to appear in public like that, he thought. Schoolmarm was written all over her. She looked as if she'd ransacked the wardrobes of her ancestors and dressed in whatever had happened her way, randomly and without any attention to period, colour or style. A mess. Too plump, he thought, and was amused to notice that her hands dimpled in exactly the way a baby's did. She even had a soft bracelet of flesh at her wrists on which was slung – the strap loose – a bright blue Swatch watch, the Mickey Mouse figure on the dial clearly visible. He wondered if he'd imagined the elegant shoes of the day before, for beneath her long shapeless skirt, she was wearing shiny green wellingtons. Four distinctly muddy imprints traced her trajectory from the door to his desk. On his new pale-grey carpet. He closed his eyes and snorted. When he opened them, their eyes met.

'Is there some reason why you're asking all these questions? Some particular reason? Er, em, Miss Stebton-Hillyard? Other than for the book you say you're writing, of course? Your method of research seems, well, to be honest, a little haphazard.'

'Excuse me, I'm not sure I quite understand. You said you'd look up some records. That is why I'm here,' she said briskly. 'At your invitation, Mr Murphy-Dunne. If it's not convenient, of course . . .' She began to gather herself to leave. He waved her back in her seat.

'Well, you know one must be sure . . .'

'I quite understand your reluctance. One cannot be too careful, can one? Or so I find. One has to protect one's interests.' She smiled disarmingly. 'If you wish to verify my credentials,' she said, 'then by all means ring my family solicitor in London. It is a well-established firm which you may know: Churchman Goodall in Cheapside.'

'That won't be necessary,' Murphy-Dunne said decisively and drew a sheet of paper from his desk drawer. 'Elderson Court', he read, 'became the convent of Holy Retreat in the early eighteen-fifties or thereabouts. I'm afraid I didn't make the connection yesterday,' he added, making no attempt to sound convincing.

'Of course not,' Jeddie murmured. She bent over and picked an imaginary thread off her skirt. In spite of his protests, she assumed he'd check up on her. In his position she certainly would. She gave him the benefit of her most engaging smile which he responded to instantly.

'My secretary has made a copy of a map for you. If you wish to meet the nuns then I'm afraid you'll have to write for an appointment, even though I expect they'll be all excited about meeting a member of their founder's family.' He raised his eyebrows. She realized he didn't believe a word of her story when he added politely, 'However remote.' He gave her a bland open smile.

'Well, thank you so much, Mr Murphy-Dunne, for all your help.' Jeddie wiped a tear, rather touchingly, from the corner of her eye. 'Not all that remote, you know. In fact, pretty direct. Adelaide Elderson Stebton, I believe she was called. Would that be right?' She looked up at him hopefully. He was relieved to find her back in bumbling mode.

'I have no idea, but I expect the nuns will be able to help with the family history.' He stifled a yawn.

'There hasn't been a biography of Adelaide

already, has there?' She sounded faintly alarmed. 'One is always so afraid of being, er, pre-empted.' He smiled indulgently.

She was what she seemed after all. The hack author guarding her sources, jealous of her subject. He chortled silently. Not a subject likely to attract large sales. He'd overreacted to her yesterday.

'I've no means of knowing that,' he laughed. 'Religious biography is hardly my bedtime reading.'

'Will I be able to see over the house?' she asked eagerly.

'Oh no, I shouldn't think so. It is an enclosed order, you know. You won't actually see the nuns. They stay hidden behind screens.'

'Really? Like an eastern harem?' she asked innocently. 'How very exotic.' Her tongue lingered on the word. He let out a guffaw of relieved laughter.

'Not a bit like an eastern harem, I'm sorry to say. I find it a bit off-putting, to tell you the truth,' he added cosily, looking mightily relieved. 'You never actually see the nuns. It takes some getting used to.'

'I'll do my best to behave decorously, if they invite me to call,' she replied mockingly. 'You've been a great help. Thank you.' She gathered herself together and smiled up at him.

'Would you care to have lunch with me, Miss Hillyard? Perhaps when next you're in Dublin?' he asked though, with his reservations about her mode of dress, he had no intention of giving her lunch. Unless in some out of the way place where he would be spared the derision of his pals. All he wanted was to keep an eye on her movements. Find out if she had some ulterior motive in coming to Dublin.

Jeddie came over all flustered. 'Oh, that would be wonderful,' she replied, her eyes shining flirtatiously. 'But alas, I don't really know when that will be. Probably September? May I give you a ring and let you know?' She didn't, as he hoped she might, refer to her diary. He nodded and handed her his card which she tucked fussily in her enormous leather satchel.

He chuckled as he came around the desk to see her out. She would be so easy to keep track of. Pathetic really, how the old bag was flattered by his invitation. Did she really imagine he fancied her? Oh well. Let her keep her illusions. He bade her goodbye and closed the door gently after her.

But Jeddie Hillyard was quite aware that she was neither young nor beautiful. It was just that she had her own agenda and having lunch with Terence Murphy-Dunne would serve her purpose nicely.

He settled back in his chair with a self-satisfied grin on his face and was lighting a cigarette when she put her head back around the door.

'Oh, one last thing, Mr Murphy-Dunne,' she said apologetically. 'I may need to pick your brains about zoning laws in this country. Just a little something I've been researching.' She didn't wait to watch his jaw drop, but closed the door oh, so gently.

Superiors are to exercise a vigilant care to admit only those who beside being of required age, are healthy, have a suitable disposition, and have sufficient maturity to undertake the life which is proper to the institute.

Canon Law 642. Article 1: Admission of candidates and the formation of members

11

The driveway, which was badly rutted, was something over half a mile with a hairpin bend midway. Narrow tracks had been worn through the grassy banks on either side to make a much more direct path to the house. But the banks were steep and muddy and Jeddie, mindful of her expensive shoes, kept to the main track.

She felt nervous, aware that she might not get another chance to make a good and lasting impression on the nuns. She had sat up most of the night trying to put order on the material she'd cobbled together before she'd left home. Now she mentally flicked through the file: photographs, letters, drawings, her monograph on Stebton Place and a pamphlet history of the old monastery of St Edwin at Chipping Stebton which she'd slipped in at the last minute in the vague hope that it would engender a fellow feeling with the nuns. After all, she rehearsed, we both live in monasteries. And I bet, she muttered under her breath, your conditions are a hell of a lot better than mine. Not to mention prospects. She wondered just how much the nuns knew about the circumstances surrounding the foundation of their safe and beautiful cloister.

What exactly was she expecting of the nuns, she asked herself. A bunch of embittered crazies? Dried up, disappointed, unfulfilled? Withdrawn from the world and the sins of the flesh. Sins of the flesh were something Jeddie thought about quite a lot. And indulged in, when she got a chance. Even with not-so-distant relatives. And others too of course, since her line of business naturally brought her in contact with people as avid as herself for adventure. Poor old Hartfield Magraw had no idea what they'd taken on when she walked into their bookshop. Jeddie hugged herself with secret pleasure. What a lark it all was. She wondered, not for the first time, if her taste in literature was made more or less pleasurable by the odd types who shared it. Or had it something to do with their invariable surprise that such erudition and appreciation should come wrapped in such a cosy bundle? Jeddie Hillyard arranged precisely, and variably, the sort of impression she wished to make.

Today, for instance, she was dressed to inspire confidence. A severely cut dress in bitter chocolate, a single row of pearls. Her beige coat was miraculously restored to something of its classic shape by dint of emptying its voluminous pockets. Dark tights, brown court shoes. No tatty plastic bags. All in all she looked like a well-turned-out teacher or nurse perhaps. Or bookseller, if you thought upmarket like Blackwells or

Hatchards. She had brushed her greying, unruly dark hair into a neat bunch and tied it at the nape of her neck with a brown chiffon scarf. Her skin was perhaps her only really beautiful feature, pale olive and quite flawless. She wore no make-up except a light coat of dark lipstick. Her sharp, dark, merry eyes were hidden behind thin-rimmed tortoise-shell glasses. Murphy-Dunne would have been amazed at the chameleon change. But then, he hadn't quite appreciated her acting skills.

As she stepped lightly along the convent drive, she had but one purpose in mind: somehow or other she must gain access to the library. Preferably on a continual basis or at least for a reasonable duration. Perhaps it was as well that she did not fully understand the meaning of enclosed, particularly when it was applied to the convent of Holy Retreat. Nor understand that outsiders were forbidden access to the interior of the convent. Or that, under normal circumstances, the chances of gaining admittance to her ancestor's library were practically nil. But these were not normal circumstances. And she was not a casual stranger knocking at their door. She was, after all, related to the Holy Founder. In the event the nuns fell over themselves to accommodate her. What she did not bargain for was how deeply their simple trust in her would affect her self-image and, ultimately, her behaviour.

She came upon the house suddenly and was at once reminded of the astonished pleasure she always felt when she emerged from the Turl and came slap up against the Radcliffe Camera in Oxford. It was a *trompe l'œil* of the same spectacular kind and it made her laugh with sheer pleasure. The house was hidden by a copse of tall stately trees until the very last moment. She walked out of an archway of majestic copper beech and there it was. Pale, almost silvery pink in the afternoon sunshine. Jeddie gulped. It was undoubtedly in a parlous state of disrepair but it was magnificently, astonishingly beautiful. Once, just once in her life, she had seen a picture of a similar house. She had looked it up again when she learned that the architect of Elderson Court was John Rothery. The book, strangely enough, claimed only a couple of extant examples of the particular style. But if you ignored the crude two-storey bow addition on one side, here was another, smaller certainly, and in desperate and urgent need of tender loving care. She studied it carefully and for many minutes. Perhaps after all she had found the key to the library. The convent was evidently running out of funds, and if they were to save the house a large dollop of cash would be needed. Soon, if not before. What a beautiful, magical building it was. Jeddie Hillyard leaned against the trunk of one of the beeches, drank in the sight and fell disastrously in love.

The house had three windows on either side of the central door with the bow addition on the right, matched by a large and partially ruined conservatory on the left. Eight- or nine-foot-high brick walls undulated away from either side of the house with young yew trees filling in gaps where the brickwork had crumbled. The entrance to the house was through a central porch – a late and gimcrack addition by the look of it.

Jeddie stopped for a moment in front of the house, checked that her papers were in order, freshened her lipstick, took a deep breath and mounted the seven steps to the porch. There was an old-fashioned bell-pull on the right of the front doorway. Her first timid jangle went unanswered as did a second. She was about to try for a third time when she heard a soft mechanical clunk and noticed the door juddering slightly as if someone or something was tugging at it. She pushed against it experimentally and it swung open as if on gliders. She stared around the empty hall, blinded after the sunshine.

'Come in, Miss Stebton, we are overjoyed that you have come.'

Jeddie slithered across the shiny surface of the hall towards the sound, trying her best not to look surprised.

'I am Sister Joseph-Maria. Welcome, welcome. The Mother Guardian is delighted that you have come to us.'

This time Jeddie found the screen and spoke directly at it with a good deal more aplomb than she actually felt. 'Sister Joseph-Maria? You live in a beautiful place.'

'Blessed. Beautiful and blessed,' she rejoined solemnly, then in a more down-to-earth tone added, 'but falling to bits, and very, very cold.' They both laughed.

'It would take a lot of money to repair, I think?'

'Oh yes, a very great deal, but God is good. When we sell the bit of land, we might even be able to install central heating.' She laughed again.

'You're thinking of selling the land?' Jeddie's shock was genuine. Her first line of attack had been, it seemed, pre-empted.

'Ah no, no, no, God love us, only the smallest little bit. To help out the school next door. We just had an offer, right out of the blue. What would you think of that, Miss Stebton?'

'I would think it a very great shame,' Jeddie replied provocatively, hoping the nun was indiscreet enough to answer her next question. 'Of course, it would rather depend on how much land and where. Wouldn't it?'

Somewhere behind the screen there was a faint rustling sound, like dried leaves running before a gentle breeze. Jeddie could not identify it but Sister Joseph-Maria apparently did. Indiscreet she might be but her reactions were extraordinarily quick. They were, it seemed, being overheard.

'Mostly from the herbs,' she said rather bafflingly. 'The herbs have been a God-send.' She gave a little cough. 'And are you a gardener yourself, Miss Stebton?'

'Oh, in a rather amateurish sort of way.' Jeddie played along. 'I do what has to be done, from necessity rather than pleasure. I am more interested in books.'

'Oh, indeed? Oh? We have a lovely old library here.' There was genuine interest now but unfortunately they were interrupted again. This time Jeddie heard a murmured 'Mother Guardian ... waiting ...'

'There now, Miss Stebton, Mother Catherine is ready to see you.' She directed Jeddie to the parlour door and asked her to step inside.

'I hope we shall meet again,' Jeddie said, battening down her curiosity and ignoring her uneasiness at the strange procedures of the convent. Doors opened unaided, unseen people talked, no means of entrance to the interior. 'Thank you for your welcome, Sister Joseph-Maria. Oh, and by the way,' she said before she stepped lightly to the parlour door, 'I have a very great interest in old books. I work in a, er, library. Books are my great hobby and passion.' She hoped the nun could see her earnestly blinking eyes, and the unworldly shine of amateur enthusiasm on her face. Would she bite? Even though she had already demonstrated how quick-witted she was, Jeddie gambled that her own relationship to the exalted founder would allay the nun's suspicion. 'I would be so interested to talk to your librarian. Would that be possible?'

She was answered by a whispered, 'I sometimes help out in the library, Miss Stebton. I shall ask, but I am certain Sister Mary Rose would be pleased. Come tomorrow morning at about ten. I'm sure she will see you for half an hour or so, if you're free?'

'Oh yes, please. That would be wonderful.'

'Have you a special interest?' Sister Joseph asked. Jeddie turned and stared at the blank grille. Was that innocence or was the voice strangely alert?

'Oh, my tastes are rather catholic.' She hesitated and gave an embarrassed little titter. 'No, not Catholic. Small c. Oh dear. Amongst other things, I'm interested in early printed literature and, em, illustrated books.'

'I'm afraid,' the nun replied humorously, 'I'm very much afraid *most* of ours are in the, er, large C category. So there would be little enough to interest you, I'm afraid. But we have some nice old bindings.' She was interrupted again, this time by the sound of the doorbell. Jeddie turned to see who would come in but the nun ignored it.

'Now if you will just go through, Miss Stebton,' she said, 'Mother Guardian will join you in a moment or two. Till tomorrow, then,' she whispered, as Jeddie pushed open the parlour door.

Jeddie hesitated on the threshold wondering if she had imagined that light little emphasis on *most*. She pushed the door to, until it clunked shut.

'Miss Stebton-Hillyard?'

'Yes.' Jeddie looked around until she located the grille which was in an alcove beside a blocked-up chimney-breast on the left side of the room. A rather uncomfortable-looking upright chair had been placed directly in front of it. To one side of the chair, a little table was laden with a tea tray. Jeddie hovered awkwardly behind it.

'This is a very special occasion for us, Miss Stebton.' She spoke the name with reverence. 'Thank you for coming to see us at Holy Retreat.'

'It is a privilege for me. I am delighted to be here.'

'You say in your letter that you are a writer.'

Jeddie blushed. 'Hardly that,' she protested. 'But I am interested in the history of my family. I have been doing a lot of research but I could find very little about the Elderson side until I happened on a reference to the convent. Now of course that seems to be much more interesting. I've brought bits and pieces of writing to show you what I've been doing.'

'How are you connected to our founder, my child?' the nun asked gently.

'To be perfectly honest, I don't know precisely. I believe, though I am not entirely sure, that my grandmother was her niece. Or great niece. Her name was Laura Stebton. My grandmother is dead many years now but we were very close. She was very scholarly. Everything I know about the family I learned from her, Mother, er, Guardian . . .' She stumbled over the unfamiliar mode of address.

'Call me Mother Catherine, if it will make it easier for you,' the nun laughed. 'Guardian is simply my title. I am the head of house.' There was a slight movement behind the grille and without warning the curtain was pulled dramatically aside. Jeddie found herself staring into the dark eyes of an upright, elderly nun. She sat down abruptly.

'Oh. I'm sorry, I'm a little confused, I did not think you allowed . . . I did not think you could be seen?' Jeddie said in surprise.

Was this usual? Somehow the act of opening the curtain was a great deal more disconcerting than the blank screen had been. Jeddie felt as if she had violated a revered code. But even more, she felt personally exposed, shabby. On top of it all, she was confused, uncertain how to react to this new unexpected circumstance. She had carefully prepared herself. She would not be able to judge the nuns by their faces, their body-language; she would therefore have to tune into the tiniest inflection of voice and tone, as she would for an important telephone deal. Now came the realization that she had been, was, unable to arrange her mind around the fact that out in the hall the nun behind her screen had been one step ahead of her all the time. With all her rehearsal she had not fully grasped the difference between being seen but not seeing.

'This is a very special occasion, Miss Stebton, a very special occasion indeed. I believe God has sent you to us. I want you to feel comfortable with us. I would like you to feel at home in Holy Retreat. We have much to talk about.'

Jane-Edwina Stebton-Hillyard adjusted her face and smiled into the Mother Guardian's eyes.

OXFORDSHIRE

Early October 1996

That hallo I should know, what are you? speak;
Come not too near, you fall on iron stakes else.

Comus, *John Milton*

12

'That's Stebton Place.' Owen Rogerson pointed to
an imposing gateway about a hundred feet
beyond the churchyard. 'We can go in and take a
look if you like.'

'Could we? Wouldn't the owners mind?' Tess
asked. She had flown over from Dublin on the
Wednesday before and had driven out to Chipping Stebton on Friday afternoon, ostensibly to
visit the Rogerson parents but also to gather the
information Mother Catherine had asked for. She
was surprised when Owen showed up for lunch
on Saturday. Afterwards they'd left Claire with
her doting grandparents while they strolled
around the village.

'I don't see why they should since they're away.
We can prowl around the outside at least.'

'Actually now that I think of it, your mother
mentioned that when I tried to quiz her last
night.' She gave a little snort of laughter. 'I didn't
get very far, she couldn't tear herself away from
the baby.' She looked pleased.

Owen was relieved the visit was so obviously a

success. He smiled at her. 'Snap,' he said. 'So did I, but earlier. As a matter of fact I rang her immediately after you phoned the other night. She's been calling me back almost every day with extra little bits of information.'

'So she mentioned when she got tired of my questions. Apply to Owen she said.' She laughed. 'Did she know much about them?'

'Yes, when you put it all together, quite a bit. It was interesting because I'm ashamed that I knew so little myself. Specially since I've been coming here since I was a child. But then of course I was away at school most of the time.' There was a faint trace of bitterness in his voice and for a moment he sounded remarkably like Marcus. Or perhaps it was just that he echoed Marcus's dislike of public schools. This surprised her since Owen had always been a vociferous supporter of the status quo. It had been the source of much lively debate between the brothers. Verging on the acrimonious, she remembered wryly.

'Strange how death alters perspective,' she murmured almost inconsequentially. Owen responded by taking her hand clumsily in his.

'Not just perspective,' he murmured enigmatically.

'Let's walk up to the wood for a bit,' she said. 'I love it at this time of year. The leaves will all have fallen in another couple of weeks.' She led the way, her long legs making short work of the hill. Owen was hard pressed to keep up with her. She turned and as she waited for him she did a little dance in the dry crunchy leaves. 'Don't you love the sound,' she laughed, briefly carefree. She was looking a lot better, he thought, though she still seemed quite uninterested in her appearance. She wore not a trace of make-up on her pale, almost white face and there were dark circles around her grey-green eyes. Her vulnerability moved him deeply.

'I loathe autumn in London even on dry days, but when it's wet, as it has been all week, ugh! Why is it that wet leaves look slimy and disgusting on pavements but wonderful on country lanes? When we were children we loved charging through the piles of leaves. Marcus doing his damnedest to keep up, silly bugger . . .' His voice broke and they walked in silence up towards the wood which bordered the grounds of Stebton Place. 'It's the little things that really get to you, don't you find?' he asked glumly.

'Yes.' Her agreement was heartfelt. 'Just when you think it's all under control – wham . . .' She shivered and after a while said, 'Aren't the colours stunning?'

The trees were resplendent, a riot of orange, brown, red and gold. There had been an unusually cold snap the week before which had hurried the process of change while the trees were still in full leaf. Now it was mild again and the October sun gave almost an illusion of warmth. They sat on an old and favoured tree stump from where they could look down the hill over the village which was spread out in front of them. Owen drew her attention to the old manor house, but because it was tucked neatly into the side of the hill, little more than the roof line was visible.

'Looks like an old monastery,' Tess said.

'That's precisely what it was. Clever chaps the way they built, don't you think? The whole village looks like a natural part of the landscape from here, doesn't it?'

'Yes, yes it does. I remember standing here once when there was a fine mist. The whole thing just disappeared.' They fell silent for a moment, content in each other's company.

'Are you staying over tomorrow?' Tess deliberately broke the spell.

'No, alas. I'll have to drive back to town later tonight, after supper. I'm going to New York tomorrow. One of your old accounts – Pierponts,' he added lightly. She suppressed a tinge of jealousy. His life sounded so carefree suddenly, so full of possibility.

'How long will you be there?' she forced herself to ask.

'Oh, about a week. I thought I'd stay over next weekend and take in a show or two,' he said and immediately changed the subject. 'Did your nun tell you what, precisely, she's interested in?'

'No, not exactly. In fact not at all. But since I am a nosy solicitor and therefore rather suspicious, and given that we are dealing with land and property, I would guess – it's only a guess, mind – that it's the descendants she's interested in.'

'You think she might be worried about – what exactly? Claims on their property?'

'Well, you know, that might just work both ways, wouldn't you say? That's quite a desirable spread down there,' she said, describing it with her outstretched arm. Owen whistled softly.

'Indeed. Can you remember what it was your holy nun said?'

'Let me think. As far as I remember, only that

their founder's ancestors came from Oxfordshire, that she believed the village and the family had the same name and that she'd be interested in learning something about them. I almost fell over when she told me the family was called Stebton. I mean, it was something of a coincidence that your parents should live here.'

'There must be other villages called Stebton, surely? It needn't necessarily be this one, need it?'

'Not in Oxfordshire there aren't. At least none that I could find. I did a quick trot around the County Museum on Thursday. Chipping Stebton it seems to be. So tell me more about the people who live in the manor.'

'Two middle-aged maiden ladies and their termagant of a mother. Or at least that's how Mother described her. Elfrida is her name. She was an absolute tyrant in her time. Ruled the girls with a rod of iron for years but is now rather seriously gaga apparently. She's been completely out of it for some time; they put her in a home a couple of months ago. And one of the daughters, who's called Felicity, is presently in hospital in Oxford – the Acland, I believe. Mother can't remember when she last saw the other daughter so she thinks she must be away. Or perhaps she's moved into Oxford to be nearer the hospitals? I was delighted to learn,' he intoned portentously, 'that the lady's name is Jane-Edwina.' He chuckled. 'Called after St Edwin's, I presume.' He pointed at the church steeple sticking out of the trees. 'Jane-Edwina Stebton-Hillyard. Now, don't you think that's a name to conjure with?'

'Bit of a mouthful, isn't it? Did I hear two hyphens there?'

'You did indeed. But it seems the lady eschews both,' he said primly. 'She prefers to be known simply as Hillyard.'

'Do you know them?'

'Not really. The parents do, of course, at least socially – sherry once a year, that sort of thing. Oddly enough it seems I *have* met one of the Miss Hillyards a couple of times, though I didn't realize the Stebton connection or that she came from the village. I do hope she's Jane-Edwina.'

'Oh? Where was that?'

'In a bookshop in Oxford. She seems to work there sporadically.'

'In Blackwells?'

'No, in that small antiquarian place on Walton Street. You remember we met the woman who owns it the last time I saw you?'

'Hartfield?'

'That's right. Grace Hartfield. I think perhaps you should go and talk to her.'

'About Miss Hillyard? Maybe she wouldn't want to discuss her employee?'

'If you remember, my dear, Mrs Hartfield mentioned that her employee had gone AWOL?'

'Yes?' Tess remembered the remark, though she was surprised Owen had, he'd been in such a tizzy that day.

'Well, don't you see? I don't think she has more than one employee. So if Jane-Edwina is away and the employee has gone AWOL, then I rest my case, m'lud,' he finished triumphantly.

'You are an ass,' Tess laughed. 'That's almost a month ago. Isn't it more likely she's the one in hospital.'

'True, but Mother said, and I quote, "One of

them is rather tweedy. The booky one looks rather like Mrs Tiggy-Winkle," he ended triumphantly with a satisfied smirk.

'Oh? really?' Tess pulled up short. 'I've been in that shop several times. In which case I must have seen her as well.' She frowned. 'She wasn't that small rumpled-looking woman with', she giggled, 'the extraordinary wardrobe?'

'Mrs Tiggy-Winkle?' he laughed. 'Exactly so. You might ask Mrs Hartfield', he added carefully, 'what precisely Miss Tiggy's bibliographical interest are. Curious little woman.'

'Right, good idea. I'll nip in on Monday, see what I can dig up.'

'Oh? So when are you going back to Dublin?'

'Round about Thursday, I hope, if I can get everything sorted out by then,' she said but did not elaborate on what 'things' might be. 'Otherwise as soon as I can.'

'I shall be there myself at the end of the month, about the twenty-fifth or sixth. Or at least I'll be travelling through Dublin on my way to the Wexford Opera Festival,' he said sheepishly. 'Could we have lunch or something?'

'I'd like that. Come and meet Hugo. Oh, and my mother, if she's around.' When she asked, with a smile, if he'd be 'on his Owen?' he fished his diary out of his pocket and, avoiding her eye, studied it laboriously, sucking his lower lip as he did so. Finally he looked up. 'On second thoughts probably best on the way back. I could stay over on the twenty-eighth. How would that be? Slap up lunch on me, eh?'

'Fine,' she said. 'That would be fine. I know just the place. Oh, oh . . .' She stopped short and grimaced as her fingers tapped a little tattoo on her chin. 'Provided of course that the exhumation doesn't interfere. I hope it will all be over by then but the way things go . . .' She shrugged. 'Everything takes so long . . .'

He consulted his diary again and said impatiently, 'But it's a bank holiday. Surely they don't expect you to attend, do they? In the circumstances?' He looked horrified. 'That's positively ghoulish.'

'I don't think I'd find it as ghoulish as cremation,' she flared, her face flushed and angry. He turned away from her. It was obviously still a sore point. After Marcus's inquest she'd gone into false labour and was admitted to hospital. She was not yet seven months gone and it had been touch and go as to whether she'd lose the baby. Not knowing how long she'd be retained, he'd tried to be helpful and without consulting her had arranged for Marcus to be cremated. She had made no bones about how officious he'd been. Before and during the ceremony she had studiously avoided him, wouldn't speak to him.

'He should have had a proper funeral,' she'd hissed furiously when they got back to the house. She was deeply upset at how few people turned up. 'We know how to do funerals,' she cried, as if she was describing a party. He assumed, miserably, that she meant 'we Irish'. And she was right, of course. The impersonal cremation was both dismal and anti-climactic. The memorial service a month later in Marcus's college was even grimmer, though the chapel was packed.

'Antiseptic mourning', she'd called that. A phrase he couldn't get out of his head. He wished like hell he hadn't been so bumptious, so insensitive to her – officially at least – irregular position. With her and Marcus's friends it had been fine, but with elderly relations and colleagues it had been peculiarly difficult. It was extraordinary how words became such stumbling blocks, simple words were suddenly off-limits – like daughter-in-law, parents-in-law, husband. *Partner* was totally inadequate. People, overwhelmed with pity at her plight, were only too aware of that bulging stomach thrust out before her like a chest of drawers. The older generation specially didn't seem to quite know precisely what her position was or how to address her. Many of them had simply avoided the issue by presenting their condolences to his parents and ignoring the tall, obviously pregnant woman. 'Not the wife, not the widow,' she'd muttered bitterly afterwards and stalked away. It had caused a temporary coolness between her and his parents whom, up to then, she'd always referred to as *the hon-laws*. In the same way she had called him her brother-hon-law. Now, as she redefined her position, she had become awkward about doing so. As, to some extent, were they all. He did not yet admit to himself that he was relieved not to be constantly reminded of her relationship to his brother.

'I'm sorry,' Tess said. She pulled at his arm and turned him around to face her. 'I'm really, really sorry.' She rocked back and forth on the balls of her feet. He tipped her head up to him. The sea-green eyes were brimming with tears. Owen put his arms around her and held her close.

'I am so very sorry, Tess,' he whispered in her

ear, wanting to hold her tight, protect her, smother her with tenderness. Shower her with kisses. But he had learned to be circumspect. Her mood swings had become unpredictable since his brother's death. She had distanced herself not just from the family but from everyone except her child, as if she could not bear to lose her thin hold on self-control. 'I can't tell you how much I regret all that. How often I think of it. With deep, deep shame. Friends?' he pleaded softly.

She shook herself away from him. 'I'm a pig,' she said. She rubbed her eyes vigorously. 'Of course we're friends.'

'That's all right, then.'

'We'll have a wonderful lunch,' she said, over-brightly. 'I know just the place, great food.' They linked arms awkwardly and walked a little way in silence.

'You were saying Miss Hillyard was strange. Did you mean mad or unfriendly?' Tess broke into his thoughts. Owen considered her question some time before replying. If she was who he thought she might be, then very strange indeed, according to a rather dubious book-collector acquaintance in London. But he was loath to repeat vague gossip so he backed off.

'She is just rather . . . louche might be a better word, I suppose. Amusing but just a tiny bit eccentric. Probably runs in the family. They say the mother is as mad as a march hare. Last seen prancing gaily around the village green wrapped up in a chintz curtain declaring she was off to a ball. Who says village life is dull?'

'When was this?'

'Oh, it happened quite often, it seems. Almost

nightly, before they carried her off to the loony-bin in August.'

'Perhaps the bookshop Stebton inherited her taste in clothes,' Tess giggled. 'What about the other daughter?'

'Ah now. Felicity is said to be rather stiff and grand and much involved with the church – flower arranging and that kind of thing. And this will interest you,' he said in the manner of a conjuror pulling a rabbit from his hat. 'Mother opines that she's rather smitten with the vicar. Who is a remote cousin.' Looking remarkably pleased with himself he began to whistle nonchalantly under his breath.

'Of yours?'

'No,' he laughed. '*Of hers*. Actually he's the only *real* Stebton among them.'

'What? Come again. Aren't they all called Stebton?'

'Stebton-Hillyard. The Stebton is courtesy or maybe deed poll. Their grandmother was a Stebton. I'm not sure whether her husband, if she had one, took her name but she was always known as Laura Stebton. Rather beautiful but remote. She was still here when my parents bought the cottage. Indeed it was because of her bad management they were able to afford to buy it in the first place. The estate went to rack and ruin during her reign. Many of the village houses were sold off for half nothing. When Mother first came here she used to see old Laura walking around the village with one of her little grandchildren, who would have been either Felicity or Jane-Edwina. Mother couldn't say which of them it was, but she insisted that it was always the same child. I don't suppose it matters, it could have been either or both. You wouldn't think they were twins to look at them. Felicity is taller and rather horsy looking. Handsome gel,' he joked. 'According to Mother.'

'Did you know them? As children, I mean? You must be around the same age.'

'They're younger than me, about Marcus's age I think. But as a matter of fact we didn't get to know them as children. In those days, the parents only used the cottage at weekends and then, of course, I was already in prep school so we only came in the holidays. And not all of those. When we were at public school we hardly came at all; we boys preferred London. Now then, shall we descend to the manor-house?' He stood for a moment with his hands on her shoulders, before leading her down the hill. He looked as if his thoughts were miles away.

'And you didn't play with them, even in the holidays?' she said with a mischievous glint in her eyes.

Owen stopped and drew himself up to his full six feet. 'What can you be thinking of?' he said in mock horror. 'Play with *girls*? I was far too old for that kind of thing.'

'Perish the thought,' she chuckled. She ran her finger along the sleeve of his new-looking cashmere sweater. 'But not too old now, I deduce? You *are* going to town with the wardrobe these days,' she teased as he fell into step beside her.

Owen's mother had mentioned that he was seeing quite a lot of a new partner who had joined his law practice a few months before. Stephanie

Wrighton's name had featured rather prominently in Marcia's conversation that morning. Owen had also dropped her name once or twice over lunch, but more shyly. Tess noticed, with a faint but unmistakable proprietorial pang, that he did so with a tenderness and pleasure that could only mean one thing. Since Marcus's death he'd been a constant, if unobtrusive, support on which, she now admitted to herself with surprise, she rather counted. She was relieved she was going back to Dublin the following week, because as things stood he made her feel like a spectre at his feast.

'Glad you approve, ma'am.' He smiled down at her affectionately. Tess impulsively linked his arm again. 'Of course I'm pleased,' she said gently. 'Now then, Owen, let me get this straight – Elfrida Stebton married a Hillyard? That right?' Tess asked as he held open the gate of Stebton Place.

'Correct,' he answered as they walked up the overgrown drive. 'Huntin', shootin', fishin' type but quite good at business. Anthony Hillyard – or Stebton-Hillyard as he became. He was happy enough to take the name. He stopped the rot temporarily, got the farm up and running again. It didn't last long, he died young, in his mid-forties when the girls were kids. Killed in a hunting accident. Fell off his horse and broke his neck, poor chap.'

As they rounded a bend and came in full view of the house they stopped short.

'Looks as though they need a hell of a lot of money now,' Tess said thoughtfully.

Stebton Place's monastic origins were immediately obvious. It was built of pale Cotswold stone. Many of the windows retained their gothic mullions and the heavy studded front door looked as though a cardinal, at the very least, was about to issue from it. Full canonical regalia would not have been inappropriate at that. Yet though the house retained its majesty, it was in a sad state of decay. The stonework was in urgent need of repointing and the window frames renewal. It looked morose and gloomy and, in the dying light, abandoned and utterly still. The giant overhanging chestnut trees crowded too close for either safety or light. Tess shuddered.

'What?' Owen asked

'Nothing. A goose on my grave,' she said. 'I don't like this place. It looks ... it looks haunted.' She turned away.

'So they say in the Levellers – according to Dad.'

'Dudley in on the act too?'

'Oh yes. He suggested we might like to join him for a pint on the way back. He promised to introduce you to what he calls *the good ole boys*, who'll fill you in on anything you want to know.'

'You kept that to yourself,' she laughed.

'Oh yes,' he answered lightly. 'But then, I can only let you have one bit of information at a time. After all, I have to keep your interest, somehow.'

'What?' She twirled around violently, thinking she had misheard. Owen smiled at her blandly. 'They say old Laura Stebton haunts the house. Johnny Pittaway swears that she walks along the corridors every night with a candle in one hand and a book in the other.'

'What, no bell?'

'Bell?' He looked at her blankly.

'Bell, book and candle. A witch, is it? He's having you on. You didn't believe him, did you?' Tess scoffed.

'Not exactly,' he answered carefully, 'but I thought you would because he claims to have it on the best authority. He and Miss Jane-Edwina Stebton-Hillyard are boon drinking companions and soul mates. And somehow, I bet she's the one your holy nuns are interested in, don't you?'

St Edwin's Church, Chipping Stebton, Oxfordshire: *Unusually, the Parish Records and Registers date back to 1540, two years after Thomas Cromwell, secretary to Henry VIII, issued a decree that these should be kept in every parish in the Kingdom.*

Chipping Stebton Local History Record

13

There was, on the face of it, absolutely no reason in the world why Tess should have chased the Hillyard trail so avidly, except perhaps instinct. On Sunday morning, when she announced that she would like to accompany them to church, Marcia and Dudley Rogerson looked at her in such open-mouthed astonishment she had a hard time controlling her face.

'That'll be nice, dear,' Marcia recovered quickly. 'But I'm afraid it'll just be me. Our vicar is away and Dudley doesn't care for the relief curate.' She raised a conspiratorial eyebrow at Tess.

'Bloody women priests!' Dudley exploded. He looked more like an apoplectic general than a retired solicitor.

'Mr Stebton on holiday then?' Tess enquired, ignoring another look of surprise.

'He does his Swan Hellenic at this time every year. Around the Ionian coast.'

'Isn't that fiendishly expensive for him?'

'Oh, my dear, he's paid to go. He's a wonderful lecturer. We did it once with him, you know; such a scholarly man.'

'Scholarly my foot,' Dudley said irritably. 'He knows the bloody stuff by heart. Dull as ditchwater. He's been doing the same tour for years. Same damn lectures too, I don't doubt.'

'Now, Dudley darling, you know that's not fair. He doesn't go away just to inconvenience you,' Marcia said severely and turned to Tess. 'He's a very hardworking priest. He has to take care of five other parishes besides this one and since his wife died he's been quite a lonely man, so it's wonderful for him to have a treat to look forward to each year.'

'Lonely? Not sure about that,' Dudley muttered under his breath and picked up the Sunday paper. 'Man's a bloody teetotaller,' he added inconsequentially.

In the end none of them went to church. Encouraged by Tess, Claire took too long over her feed and Marcia, having defended the locum, showed little inclination to support her in church. They had an early lunch and while the Rogersons were having an afternoon nap, Tess took the baby out for a walk and had another snoop around the village.

The Reverend Timothy Ryland Stebton, MA (Cantab) D.Phil. (Oxon) was listed on the notice board outside St Edwin's Church. Tess walked up the stone-flagged path, pushed open the door and dragged the pushchair into the church. Inside, she paused at the dusty bookstand and fished out a photocopied leaflet giving a potted history of the church and, by happy chance, a list of the incumbents back to 1540. With few exceptions, members (presumably lesser) of the Stebton clan held the living. They were a prolific lot and indeed profligate with their off-spring, an uncomfortable number of whom died in infancy and, if not then, in their prime.

The interior of the beautiful little church was almost overwhelmed with memorials to the families of the lords of the manor. The oldest and most imposing monument was to William Ryland Stebton 1504–1567 and his lady Thomasina (née Miller). Five of their children who died in childhood were shown, touchingly out of scale, kneeling at their feet. The memorial to William's son Thomas and *his* lady was less spectacular and so it went on, down the centuries until the early part of the nineteenth century when the Stebtons took their places outside in the churchyard, to mingle with the lesser folk of the village.

Since there seemed to be several distinct lines of the family, Tess searched for headstones which listed *of Stebton Place* and worked backwards from the name she had heard the day before. It took some time to track down Laura Miranda Stebton (*d. 1979*) but she eventually found her among a number of her forbears in a huge angel-strewn mausoleum behind the church. Laura's father, Thomas Ryland Stebton (*d. 1903*), was also there with his wife Lucie Jane (née Toller), her grandfather Ryland William (*d. 1850*), his wife Sarah (née Mulholland) and three infant girls. The principal name was also the oldest: William Theophilus Ryland Stebton (*d. 1837*) and his memorial tablet obligingly informed that

Ryland William was his nephew and heir. But by then Tess' head was spinning with Rylands and Williams in whichever order. The repetition appeared endless.

Moving around the oldest part of the graveyard was almost impossible with the pushchair. Tess quickly tired of trying to decipher the script on the severely weathered tombstones. In any case she had no idea what, if anything, she was looking for. Some mention of an Elderson? Something to mark the connection with Elderson Court? But she found nothing. It was, she decided, a rum omission in a family who seemed so keen on their possessions that they practically listed their address and telephone number for posterity.

Seen one dead Stebton, seen a thousand, she concluded, as she walked away from the church and headed towards the vicarage. She found it was as shut up and empty as the big house. Somehow it was this universal absence that proved a powerful stimulus to her imagination and made her all the more determined to scour Oxford for the missing Stebtons.

It was almost noon on Monday by the time Tess got to the Walton Street bookshop. Hartfield Magraw Rare Books was in an end-of-century terrace directly opposite the Phoenix cinema. It was situated between an antique dealer and Saratoga – a shop whose lingerie, in her opinion, was to die for – or at least worth going into debt for.

Her first port of call was to the near-by Jericho Health Centre. Determined to kill two birds with one stone, she had taken Claire for her shots. This proved a huge mistake. Outraged by the offered insult, the baby had turned blue in the face and screamed the place down. Afterwards, it had taken an hour of feeding, cajoling and pounding the pavements before she went off to sleep again. By the time Tess made it to the bookshop she was thoroughly flustered.

The only member of staff was a rather preoccupied-looking American who identified himself as Murray Magraw and told her his wife would not be around until the next morning. Tess was about to enquire after Miss Hillyard when a couple of rather demanding customers stepped into the shop and immediately appropriated him. She wasn't even sure he heard her murmured, 'I'll come back tomorrow,' until he followed her to the door and whispered: 'If you've come about the job, around four o'clock is best. Will you leave your name?' He had a warm, lopsided smile.

'Tess Callaway,' she started and before she could disclaim herself as applicant – for Miss Hillyard's job presumably, since there was no sign of her – he returned to his impatient customers. Feeling somewhat at a loose end, Tess wandered further up the street and picked up a sandwich and a carton of soup at the delicatessen before turning for home. It was only a short distance – along Observatory Street, a short way up the Woodstock Road and through the tree-lined church walkway into Winchester Road. She was reluctant to go back to the house so she took her time, feeling it wiser to let sleeping babies lie. The day was chilly but unusually bright with a gusting breeze which brought down a steady dancing shower of leaves. She had just turned into Winchester Road when it occurred to her to go to Marcus' old department to see if one of his graduate students, who in the past had been a reliable house-sitter for them, was around.

As it happened, he was coming down the steep metal stairway from the Engineering Science building when she arrived. 'Hi! Tess!' He looked delighted to see her and made suitable flattering remarks about Claire. 'I'm just on my way to the pub for lunch.' Richard Stevens was the son of an out-of-work miner from South Derbyshire. He was short, stocky, and extremely good-natured. At thirty-three he was older than most of the other graduates. Marcus always claimed he was the most gifted student he had ever had and easily the most reliable.

'Why don't you come along? To the Bird and Baby.' He grinned. 'Pretty apt, eh?' The Bird and Baby was the local name for the Eagle and Child in St Giles once frequented by C. S. Lewis and his pals.

'As long as you don't mind if I have to feed this baby. She's apt to create.'

He laughed. 'She's lovely, Tess, just like her ma.' He leaned over the pram and gave her arm a quick squeeze. 'Though she's a bit like Marcus as well, isn't she? So she must have your brains, lucky girl.' He included Marcus naturally, as if he was still around. Tess felt almost weak with gratitude.

'Are you well?' he asked shyly.

'Well-ish. Tired. She's a bit of a night owl. To put it mildly.' She made a face and laughed. 'I'm lying. Most of the time she's the baby from hell. But that might have something to do with me being so uptight.'

'Are you surprised? You're not alone in the house, are you? Vanessa was asking if you'd like her, us, to come around some evening to give you a hand? We called around last night but you weren't home.'

'Well, actually that's one of the reasons I'm here.' She stopped short outside the Old Parsonage Hotel. 'Look Richard, why don't we have lunch here? It's quieter and easier to talk. I'm not really feeling up to a pub, do you mind?'

They walked through the stone arch into the little hotel whose dining room was, perversely but comfortably, arranged as a drawing room with clusters of easy chairs around a small number of polished tables. They found a quiet spot in a corner by the window with space for the push-chair beside them. Claire miraculously slept on.

'Richard, I have a proposition for you and Vanessa. I'm going to Dublin for a couple of months or so,' Tess said when the waiter had taken their order and brought them a glass of wine apiece. 'I was hoping you'd both come and house-sit for me while I'm away?' She didn't mention that she suspected his grant had run out. She didn't need to, he looked quite stunned with gratitude.

'Two months? Oh, Tess, you're not serious? Oh heck. Yes, please.'

'Really? Terrific. Great. Great.'

'When?' He asked so eagerly she wondered if he was sleeping rough.

'Anytime from now. I hope to go on Thursday,

but you could move in straightaway, the sooner the better. I hate being alone there.'

He thought for a second or two before he replied. 'Would tomorrow evening do? We could bring around a take-out and then move our stuff in when you've gone. That OK?'

'Perfect. That's a terrific relief.' She beamed at him then got all businesslike. 'Now tell me, when do you submit your thesis? And has your grant run out?' And with that the baby stirred and demanded a plug-in. The couple at the next table managed to look both disgusted and amazed that Tess could manage to feed the child and sip her wine at the same time. They clearly thought she was beyond the pale both politically and aesthetically. She ignored them defiantly and concentrated on what Richard was saying.

'Yes, afraid so. But not just me: there are three others at the writing stage, we've all run out. The department helped out a bit and our various colleges. Some more than others,' he added dryly. 'It's been tight but the worst is accommodation. At least it is for me. The lease on our flat ran out at the end of last month. After a lot of grovelling, the landlord gave us two weeks' grace.' He held his head on one side and grinned with delight. 'Which runs out at the end of this week, would you believe? After that it was going to be friends' floors, I'm afraid. So you can see how welcome your offer is. Two months. You've saved my life. I still can't quite believe it.'

'Maybe more, but I'll give you plenty of notice of when I'm getting back. Now listen to me, Richard.' Her face became serious. 'There's a quid pro quo.'

'Yes?' he asked.

'I had a letter from the BMW garage the other day. They've had an offer for the bike. I didn't realize the damn thing was worth so much. Could you deal with it?'

'Yes, of course. Where is it exactly?'

'It's out in a garage off the M40 near Thame but there's no need to go there. I can drop them a note and tell them to go ahead and sell. What I want you to do, Richard, is this. Find out exactly how much the delay has cost each of the four of you whose grants have run out. Eight and a half thousand may not cover it all, but it should go a fair way.'

Richard's jaw dropped. 'Are you certain, Tess? That's much too generous. It's a hell of a lot of money. Excuse me asking, but can you afford it?'

'Yes, I can afford it.' Her mouth tightened. 'I don't want anything from the sale of the wretched thing. I can hardly bear to think of it. If Marcus hadn't bought it . . .' Her shoulder hunched and immediately Claire began to whimper. Tess held her up to her shoulder and patted her back gently. 'I couldn't do anything until probate was granted.' Which it had been, without a hitch, at the end of the previous week. At least, she thought, they'd got that right. She and Marcus had made mutually beneficial wills a couple of years before.

'If you could gather the information from the others I can issue the cheques immediately. Just keep careful accounts, will you Richard? For the executors. It's a lot to ask but there's no one I . . . oh well. Just tell the others it was a bequest from Marcus, will you? They don't really need to know any more than that.'

They walked out into the afternoon sunshine and turned left at the gate. As they stood and chatted while Richard waited for a lull in the traffic to cross over to his lab, it occurred to Tess that she could easily drop into the Acland and see if the sick member of the Stebton-Hillyard family was there. The hospital was less than a hundred yards from the Old Parsonage and Richard was perfectly willing to push Claire up and down while Tess made her enquiries.

'I've come to see my cousin,' she whispered to the middle-aged receptionist. 'I wonder if you could tell me which room she's in? Her name is Stebton.' Tess had no idea what impulse guided her to leave out the hyphenated Hillyard, but it turned out to be fortunate.

'Felicity Stebton? Oh, she was discharged at the end of last week.' The receptionist paused and looked up suspiciously but before she had a chance to say anything further Tess cut in quickly.

'Oh damn, I can't believe it,' she sighed and put her hand to her forehead. 'I've been abroad, I didn't know she was ill until I got back this morning. Of course, nobody thought of letting me know. Poor darling, I would have come back sooner to look after her. Poor Felicity, she had no one to visit her with Auntie Elfrida ill as well.' As Tess warmed to the role of dutiful relative, the receptionist tutted in sympathy.

'Yes, I know. In Wisharts, isn't she? Your poor cousin was so anxious about her. But you mustn't worry about her having no visitors. Mr Stebton was in every other day. Such a nice man. I wish he was our vicar.' She smiled conspiratorially. 'So considerate too. He collected her himself,' she lowered her voice, 'in a hired *limousine*. They were so sweet. Off on their honeymoon, he told me. They'd had to delay it because of her illness. But hark at me telling you!' she tittered nervously.

'Oh yes,' said Tess, picking up the theme and crossing her fingers. 'Such a shame after they waited so long. I haven't seen her since then. Oh, poor Felicity, such a shame. I absolutely couldn't believe it when I heard. Never mind, I'll go out to the house and get it looking nice for when they get back.' Overwhelmed by her own sense of duty, she gave a martyred little smile. 'Thank you so much for your help,' she said and turned away.

Tess happened to look back as she reached the hall and noticed that the receptionist was being relieved by a younger model. On a hunch, she hung around unobtrusively until the older woman had disappeared before making her way back to the desk.

'Oh, excuse me. My cousin, Felicity Stebton, was discharged last week. She's lost her appointment card and she's too embarrassed to ring you about it herself. I'm sure she's fretting unnecessarily, but she asked if I could find out when her follow-up clinic is?'

'No problem.' The girl looked down at the desk-diary and grinned up at Tess. 'Well, what do you know? It's open at the right page. That must be a first.' She giggled and ran her finger down the page. 'Mrs Felicity Stebton, here it is, the twenty-ninth of October, 4 p.m.'

Mrs, thought Tess. The vicar's bride. She wondered what bearing Felicity's changed status had, or would have, on the case in hand. Nothing for it but to drive out to Wisharts and see the old lady. As far as she could remember the nursing home was somewhere near the Farmoor reservoir. Which meant an eight-mile car journey. Which, with any luck, also meant a sleeping baby since Claire adored being chauffeured about. She hurried outside.

14

Dear Owen,

Your guess was entirely right. The Stebton-Hillyard
who works in the bookshop is Jane-Edwina though I
didn't find her or Mrs Hartfield in the shop when I
called on Monday morning. Then when I nipped into
the Acland to try to find the sick sister, I found she
was gone as well. And you'll never guess, the cousin-
vicar has carried her off! They're married, or at least
so I gathered from the rather garrulous receptionist.
Having drawn such a complete succession of blanks, I
felt compelled to try my luck with the mother. The
receptionist in the Acland kindly let slip that she was
in Wisharts nursing home. And before you condemn
her for indiscretion let me tell you that she didn't stand
a chance with my virtuoso sleuthing. Well actually, to
be more exact, bare-faced lying.

My encounter with Elfrida Stebton-Hillyard was
entirely surreal. She is vast. At least two hundred
pounds of putty-coloured blubber, with not a wrinkle
on her face. I would guess she's over eighty but she'll
probably live for ever since she is careful not to exert
herself in any way. She must have been about my
height in her day, she's still rather imposing. Even
with her mind mostly gone, she has startling moments
of lucidity which I found quite unnerving. Her manner
is very much that of the grande dame. And how! One
of those women who must be hell to live with but
highly diverting for an hour or so. I felt quite refreshed
by her. The nuns have nothing to fear from this

particular Stebton-Hillyard, she thinks of no one but herself.

Claire was fast asleep in her sling. It was so cold, I tucked her under my massive old black overcoat which turned out to be an inspired move. I looked about nine months gone but I suspect old Elfrida must have thought I was another barrel and as a result warmed to me as a fellow fatso. Or more likely the old thing was lonely. I quizzed the nurse on duty who told me that no one has been to see her for weeks.

I can't vouch for the accuracy of my reportage but I'll try to give you a fair idea of what Elfrida was like. I'm really sorry you didn't know these people, I think they would have kept you amused.

'Have you brought my bananas?' was the first thing she said, well, shouted actually. 'I told that girl – what's her name? Claimed to be my daughter. I can't think where she got such an idea. But whoever she is, I hope she remembers the bananas. She's been so forgetful lately. Every time I tell her something . . .' She glared at me. 'Have you brought the bananas?' And on and on she went until her room-mate, Mrs Finstock, told her to shut up. That started an exchange of such acrimony I didn't quite know where to put myself. I let them battle it out since there was nothing I could do to stop them. Elfrida won hands down. She is undoubtedly used to getting her own way and doesn't yield an inch.

'Have you come to take me home? I wish to go home. How could those cruel and heartless girls put me in a place like this? After I told them I wanted to go to Cheltenham. The cab has been waiting all morning. What is the time? I don't think that clock can be right.'

'No. It seems to have stopped.'

'Aha. That's why. They're trying to keep me locked up, you know. Be careful what you say, because there are spies everywhere. So keep your voice down.' She

was maundering on, getting increasingly incoherent until her next remark which gave me the opening I was looking for. 'Did the girls send you to serve tea?'

'No,' I said. 'I couldn't find them.'

'That's because Felicity has been wed,' she said and stuck out her tongue. Not a pretty sight.

'No, not Felicity, the other one.'

'Other one? Which other one?'

'Jane-Edwina.' I chanced my arm.

'Silly bitch. If you haven't a banana what about a Pimm's?' And she was off again. I don't know if it was me or J-E who was the silly bitch. Her, I think. Through Elfrida's ramblings I gathered that Felicity is the one she respects and J-E the one who is most likely to do her bidding. She doesn't seem to care much for either of them, though interestingly she seemed more bewildered that J-E hadn't come to see her. That, I may say, caused Mrs Finstock much merriment.

Old age is truly terrible. That pair of old children were quite terrifying, their emotions so raw, so immediate. At any moment I felt old Elfrida would throw herself on top of me and crush me to death without any reason and less malice, like a bored kid in a playground, just for something to do. Something to relieve the tedium. I was about to leave when she suddenly said, 'I hope you don't waste your time on old books. My mother has a lot to answer for. Filling the silly child's head with such nonsense. It's mine by right. How dare she leave it to that silly girl. She was too old, ha, ha, ha. Thinks I know nothing. Thirty-five, forty, forty, forty-one, forty-three . . . Money is what we wanted. Useless scraps. Bits and bobs. Bits and bobs. Bits, bobs and bloody books. Useless, useless, useless, useless, useless, useless. Filling the place with rubbish is what she's good at.' She made my head spin.

Then before I could think of anything to say she was off again. 'Fetch my dress. She's coming to tea you know and then we're going to a thé dansant *at the Ritz. Going by train. Just get the gown, will you?'* It took me some time to figure out whether she was talking about her mother or J-E, but eventually I got there. I think.

If I'm right, then the situation is something like this. The sisters don't get on. The mother, being a bully, rather despises their lack of spirit. I would guess there's a battle going on between the daughters as to which of them is responsible for their mama. Which may be why J-E made herself so scarce. Who can blame her? It is interesting that once Elfrida was dispatched to Wisharts, Felicity and her vicar eloped and J-E took off, more or less permanently. Your mother was agog when I told her. No doubt it's all around the village by now. I gather Elfrida has been considerably inconvenienced in the past by J-E going off from time to time 'to grub around in musty old bookshops'. Yet at the same time, for some reason, these escapades seemed to fill the old woman with glee. She cackled like mad when she said it and then went off on a complete tangent about filthy old books and libraries.

I couldn't quite figure out what she meant about 'old papers'. Some sort of inheritance? Perhaps Johnny Pittaway's old ghost rescued J-E by leaving her an inheritance? But why wait until now? Always assuming Elfrida's ramblings aren't complete rubbish. Which, come to think of it, is assuming rather a lot. I've only given you the drift. If I tried to report everything she said, I'd end up as dotty as she is. My mind was doing acrobatics for the rest of the evening.

I'm going back to see Grace Hartfield in Walton Street tomorrow and then to Dublin on Thursday or Friday. One of Marcus's research students and his girlfriend will look after the house while I'm away. They've done so before and are utterly reliable. I was glad to have stayed with your parents this weekend,

*they were so welcoming and marvellous with Claire. A
bit of a lifeline for us both.*

*I'll write and let you know how I get on with my
hunt. I don't suppose any of it will be of the slightest
interest to Mother Catherine but the Hillyard woman
is beginning to intrigue me. I can't get her out of my
mind and to be truthful she's a welcome diversion. As
Johnny Pittaway said on Sunday, 'She bin a lively 'un.'
I bet she's fun. I imagine her in a Travels with my
Aunt scenario with her own special Wordsworth.
Wherever she is, I hope she's enjoying herself. Looking
after Elfrida can't have been much cop. And it sounds
as if the sister will take over Stebton Place by default.
Or maybe she'll move into the vicarage and abandon
the old house to the ghostly monks. I hope you're
enjoying New York. Claire sends a (nearly) smile.
She's been practising like mad and has almost got it
right. We look forward to seeing you in Dublin.*

Yours, Tess.

*P.S. Just before I left Elfrida, Claire woke up and let
out a little yelp. Without batting an eyelid Elfrida told
me to go and evacuate myself. Which somehow makes
me wonder if she was as gaga as she seemed. It might
have been a euphemism, don't you think, for piss-off?*

Aretino, *Pietro di*: *Capricciosi & Piacevoli Ragionamenti: Il Veritiere e'l divino, cognominato il flagello de'principi. Nuova Editione. Stampati in Cosmopoli 1660.*

A d'A Cet. 7, item 7

15

The Walton Street bookshop had an old-fashioned bell at the top of the door which tinkled merrily when Tess entered the shop. She dragged the pushchair awkwardly over the uneven threshold and looked around as the woman she'd met with Owen in north Oxford came towards her. She was elegantly dressed in a severely cut navy-blue suit which flattered her eyes and her greying hair.

'Are you the person who came about the job yesterday?' she asked hopefully. She looked a little harassed.

'Afraid not. I mean, I'm not after a job but I was in the shop yesterday and the man – your husband? – seemed to think I was.'

'Ah well,' the bookseller sounded disappointed, 'never mind. Sorry about that. Clearly wishful thinking on Murray's part,' she said resignedly. 'Look, there's more space for the stroller at the back, if you want to browse,' she added, then looked more closely at Tess. 'Haven't we met somewhere? Oh, I know, you're Owen Rogerson's wife, aren't you? Don't you remember, we met in North Oxford a few weeks ago?'

'Yes.' Tess coughed. 'But he's not my husband. I was . . . His brother was . . .' She pointed at the baby. 'Owen's her uncle,' she finished in a rush and blushed furiously. 'His brother was my partner.' Now why the hell couldn't she say husband? In every way, except for a stupid bit of legal paper, he was. Why did the lawyer in her always get in the way? Complicate things. She looked up at the other woman whose pale blue eyes were wide open and whose mouth formed a perfect O of horror.

'Oh my goodness, I am so sorry,' she said. She looked on the verge of tears. 'You're Marcus Rogerson's wife, aren't you? I just didn't recognize you. I saw you at the memorial service. I'm sorry, we didn't get a chance to talk to you. I'm sorry about Marcus. It was a terrible accident. He was such a lovely man . . .'

'We weren't married,' Tess burst out. She was grateful to the woman for mentioning Marcus's name but she was completely unable to handle her sympathy. Grace Hartfield laid her hand on Tess's sleeve.

'What does that matter? Aren't the legalities a matter for the two people involved? Didn't you feel married?'

'Yes, of course.'

'Well then, my dear.' She smiled. 'I am really pleased to meet you again.'

Tess held out her hand. 'My name is Tess Callaway,' she said.

'I'm Grace. Grace Hartfield.' She took Tess's hand in hers. 'Your husband was a good customer of mine. It was he who introduced Owen to the shop as I'm sure you know. Murray and I were very upset that we couldn't go to his funeral but we were in America when he died. I'm so sorry. It must have been a dreadful shock for you.'

'I almost lost Claire.' Tess found herself babbling incoherently. 'I think that's when I lost my nerve, control. I don't know why this marriage thing bugs me so much.' She chewed her lower lip. The last thing she would have expected was that verbal courtesies should be so important. She was flummoxed that a terminology had not been worked out to cover her situation. It was almost as if her right to mourn was in question. By herself most of all.

'Perhaps it's grief? It takes us in different ways.' Grace's quiet voice broke in on her thoughts. 'Something to get angry about, talk about? Don't you find the mere mention of death upsets some people? Embarrasses them? They won't let you talk? They just don't want to know. Walk across the street to avoid you?' She sounded as if she was speaking from bitter experience. 'Look, I've just made a cup of coffee. Come into the back and have one with me while I admire your gorgeous baby. I'm very envious.'

The storeroom was small, cluttered, and shelf-lined with extra piles of books on every surface. There were also four or five large, unopened packages about the size of wine cartons on the floor. Mrs Hartfield cleared a space for the baby and drew up a swivel-chair while Tess looked around.

'Did Marcus buy his poetry here? I didn't know.' So many little things I missed, she thought regretfully. It was as if they'd lived parallel lives all those years while she was in London. Touching and not touching. Not always making contact.

'Yes, he used to pop in quite often. Actually I recently managed to get hold of something he wanted for ages. I think he said it was for you. It's an early Percy French comic poem which wasn't copyrighted and then plagiarized. I'd like you to have it.' She rifled though a stack of books behind her until she found a slim pamphlet.

'Not Abdallah Bubbul Ameer?' Tess laughed, suddenly feeling her gloom lift.

'Precisely. It's a first edition signed by the man himself. Extremely rare.' The bookseller looked delighted with herself.

'I thought you were American, but you're Irish, aren't you?' Tess asked in surprise. 'I can just about hear it in your voice, now.'

'Yes, I was born there but I came to live here as a child. I didn't go back for a long time though in the past few years I've been doing a lot of buying trips in Ireland so maybe, after forty years, the accent is coming back.' She looked amused at the idea, and pleased. 'You, as well, I take it?' she asked. 'Now tell me, what it is you came in for and I'll see if I have it.'

'Actually, I came to see if Miss Hillyard was here.'

'Jeddie?' she sounded surprised. 'You know her?'

'No-o,' Tess replied slowly. 'No. A friend of mine asked me to pass on a message,' she improvised, then added with more accuracy, 'Actually, I just wanted to see her.'

'Hmm. Chance would be a fine thing.' Grace

Hartfield threw up her hands in mock despair. 'Honestly. I've just about reached the end of my tether with her. She took a fortnight's holiday over three weeks ago and apart from one postcard from Wales, I've not heard a word since. Actually, it's over a month. I went out to her house the other day but the place was utterly deserted.'

'Her mother had to go into a home and her sister was ill. Perhaps . . .'

'Sister? Did you say sister? You mean there are two of them?' Grace's voice teetered on the edge of laughter. 'I always thought that Jeddie was an absolute one-off. Though now, come to think of it, I believe I have heard her mention a sister once or twice, but it always seemed a little unlikely somehow. I do miss her. She can be extremely amusing and she's an amazing mimic. She does wonderful take-offs of our more, er, eccentric customers.' She laughed at some private memory. 'But I expect you know that?'

'Not at all. I've never met her. Except for catching a glimpse of her here, once or twice, but not really to talk to. Was she with you long?'

'Since we opened. About three years. But only part-time. She has her own little business as well. *Amici d'Aretino* is her trade name. She sells by catalogue.' Her lips twitched in amusement. 'She writes the best catalogue entries I've ever read. She's a brilliant bookseller. Absolutely encyclopaedic. Besides being an extremely witty woman. Well, bordering on the eccentric actually.' She giggled.

'Does she specialize?'

'Ye-es, she does.' Grace Hartfield answered hesitantly. 'Foreign language editions are her speciality. She reads several languages. Most of them dead, as she says herself.' Grace laughed. 'But she particularly likes early illustrated books.'

'Would that make a lot of money for her?' For some reason, Tess's question elicited a guffaw of laughter from Mrs Hartfield though she didn't share the source of her amusement.

'I'll say it does.'

'Then why does she work here?'

'Well, now, that, as they say, is a good question. She *says* because she likes to get out of the house. Meet people.'

'You mean snaffle your customers?' Tess asked.

Grace gave a little laugh. 'Oh no. I hope not. No. Jeddie isn't like that.'

'Oh?' Tess raised her eyebrows. 'Would that be because her speciality and yours, er, don't coincide?' she asked carefully. The bookseller looked uncomfortable but avoided the question.

'As I said, she is a fantastic linguist which is of enormous help to us,' she said blandly.

'Is it possible to get hold of one of her catalogues?'

'Well, I don't have any. But I'm sure if you wrote to her . . .' She left the words hanging in the air.

'Is there something dubious about her book-selling activities? Illegal?' Tess asked and waited for several moments while Mrs Hartfield considered her reply.

'I assume you must have your reasons for asking, Miss Callaway? But besides working for us, Jeddie is a friend. I like her very much. What she does in her own time is really not my business.'

'Nor is it mine. I'm sorry I shouldn't have asked. It doesn't matter.' Nor did it. The question had been more or less answered. Besides, she thought suddenly, Owen knows. It was he who had used the euphemism *curious* to describe Jeddie Hillyard.

'Perhaps *clandestine* might have been a better word?' Tess asked slyly and the bookseller's eyes met hers. They both broke out laughing.

'I wouldn't like to say. Write to Jeddie for a catalogue and make up your own mind.'

'But where is she?' Tess asked and for some unknown reason a tiny shiver of foreboding ran through her.

'Oh, Jeddie is sure to turn up. She often goes missing. Not for so long though. She'll be back,' she added confidently. 'She's probably on a book-buying trip. I expect we'll hold on for another week or two before we take on someone else.' She looked at Tess and wrinkled up her nose. 'Unless, of course . . . You don't, by any chance, want a part-time job with lousy pay and flexible hours, do you? Baby included?'

'I'm afraid she's too young and I've had another offer. Same basis except for the pay, which is quite generous.' Tess grinned. 'I'm going back to Dublin for a couple of months.' She stood as the baby began to stir. 'I've taken up enough of your time, Mrs Hartfield.'

'Oh, Grace, please,' she smiled.

'Tess, then.' They shook hands.

'Come and see me again, will you?'

'Of course. Thank you. And,' Tess took a deep breath, 'thank you for coming to the memorial service. You've made me feel better about it. To know, well . . .' She hunched her thin shoulders. 'Well, you know,' she added awkwardly.

'Anything I can do to help.' Grace touched her arm. 'Can I give Jeddie a message when I see her?'

'I don't think so. In fact, I'd prefer if you didn't say anything, if you don't mind. But I *will* call again. To see you.'

'Good, I'd like that.' She held the shop door open while Tess struggled with the pushchair. 'On the other hand,' Grace said, 'if you happen to run into Jeddie first, could you tell her some packages have come for her. They're cluttering up the storeroom. Ask her what she wants me to do with them. Or better still, tell her to come and deal with them herself.' She laughed and shook her head. 'That woman is the living end.'

Tess walked away thoughtfully. She wondered if Grace was referring to the packages in the storeroom. Because she'd happened to notice, while they were talking, that those packages all had Irish stamps on them.

DUBLIN

Mid to Late October 1996

Controversy over proposed sale of convent teacher training college. *Report criticizes use of taxpayers' millions. Nuns and officials urged to talk.*

Irish Newsheet

16

There was a definite feeling of autumn in the air when Tess and the baby got back to Dublin. The weather was mild and sunny but the trees were shedding their leaves like mad. She arrived in the early afternoon and the car Hugo promised was waiting for her, and so, fortunately, was a driver. The amount of baggage necessary for one tiny not-quite-three-month-old baby was amazing. As they tried to squeeze it all into the boot the driver remarked with typical Dublin dead-pan humour, 'D'you know, I have a feeling you can buy disposable nappies here. But then of course I could be wrong.'

During the first weekend her mother at last came to make the acquaintance of her baby grand-daughter. After an awkward and wary start the first visit went reasonably well and was, to their mutual amazement, closely followed by a second. Susan had always been a rather glamorous figure, successful, charming, but also rather distant. And though Tess would have died rather than admit it, very like her daughter. Susan did not, or perhaps could not, speak of Marcus' death but it was clear that mortality, if only her own, was much on her mind. Almost as if she feared death was a contagious disease she might catch from contact with Tess.

It was plain to see that Susan was frightened of the baby and at the same time fascinated by her. Consummate actress that she was, she strove gallantly to appear at ease. But watching her mother hold Claire awkwardly in her arms, Tess felt she was seeing her for the first time as a woman for whom motherhood had always been a trial and she was shamed by a sudden surge of fellow-feeling. She was also rather shocked to notice how her mother had aged. For the first time she looked every one of her sixty-six years. She seemed to have grown smaller, more frail, more uncertain. In the months since they'd last met, she'd become a faded version of her former self. But then as Tess caught sight of her own reflection in the window she hardly recognized the strained, almost middle-aged face staring back at her. It was a sobering moment. Her mother had been only twenty-six when she was born, eleven years younger than she was now. One day, very much sooner than she thought, Claire would look at Tess with the same terrible, insulting pity. Susan looked worn out, tired of the quest for eternal youth. Perhaps, Tess thought, we should allow ourselves to grow plump and comfortable and learn to inhabit our years. Then she laughed aloud at the sentimentality. 'Can the leopard change its spots?' she heard herself say aloud. Her mother threw her a startled look, suspecting hidden insult, and waited a little before she answered, 'With difficulty, but if you can, I can. Try at least.' It was a truce of sorts.

A couple of weeks later Tess at last got to the final stage of preparation for the exhumation. She left Claire with the baby-minder and spent a frustrating couple of hours in the Diocesan Office sorting out arrangements for the reburial ceremony. Father Keane was elderly, hard of hearing and highly suspicious. Tess disliked him on sight. Despite his unctuous, over-smiling manner, he clearly thought she was out of her depth. Burke and Hare hovered on the air, if not on his lips. He was a countryman to whom the selling of land, any land, was totally anathema. And worse if it was church property. Small matter that Holy Retreat was nothing of the sort. In his robustly stated view, the nuns were both feckless and incompetent. Tess grew impatient of his repeated questions until eventually she divined the source of his problem stemmed from the independent way Holy Retreat had originally been set up. He was outraged that the nuns were not beholden to the bishop. And the unnatural way they persisted in their foolishness. As he explained over and over, they had uniquely retained the ownership of their land from the time of the convent's foundation. And their autonomy. Something which clearly rankled with the elderly priest. Independence in women was a dangerous precedent but in nuns it was outrageous and not to be borne.

'But they have never made any demands on church resources, have they?' she had finally said in exasperation.

'Nor contributed anything either,' he retorted succinctly. But he had the grace to laugh when she began to mount a spirited defence. 'Well now and haven't they got you well trained?' he remarked slyly and congratulated her on her loyalty which rather stuck in her throat. She didn't take kindly to his avuncular pats on her hand either.

'I might come out with the bishop for the consecration,' he promised chummily, as she took her leave. 'I've never seen the place. I'd like to have a look. They say it was a fine house. Once.' He sounded alarmingly like a prospective buyer. Or worse, a debt collector.

'It still is, though it needs a lot of work.'

'And they'll be able to afford it now, will they?' He was all smiles and nods but Tess didn't tell him what he clearly wanted to know – the precise sum the nuns had got for the parcel of land. She just drew herself up to her full height, smiled sweetly down at him, and bid him goodbye.

But all the same, he triggered a vague germ of disquiet in her own mind which wouldn't go away. It was nothing specific, just a nebulous little bubble of doubt. Self-doubt or just plain old doubt? She couldn't tell, but then, she told herself, that was the way she was these days. All the old wives' tales about the brain shrinking in pregnancy surfaced. Hers had definitely gone soft, slowed up. The lightning fast connections she was once capable of were a thing of the past. Was it just lack of sleep?

Claire was sleeping less and less, specially at night, and more than ever she was perpetually hungry. Each day Tess thought she'd reached the zenith of exhaustion and every day it got worse.

She muddled through with a kind of wild uncontrolled nervous energy which had become a substitute for thought. She set up little routines like so many obstacles over which she had to leap and then neatly tick off. Traipsing in and out of Holy Retreat every few days was just one of those routines. Almost everything she was required to do could have been done in half the time by phone, fax or with a few, well-planned meetings. But in her present state such an approach seemed to be impossible. Doing was easier than thinking. She was honest enough to recognize that *feeling* useful was infinitely preferable to *being* efficient. And, bless their hearts, the nuns were experts at making her feel useful. If only by giving her a seemingly endless variety of errands to run.

She left the Diocesan Offices in Drumcondra, turned into Clonliffe Road and headed for the toll-bridge south across the Liffey. As always, the traffic was heavy and the journey took much longer than she had either anticipated or allowed for. The line of cars out of the city centre edged along at a pace comfortable enough to read the advertising hoarding, and even work out what the new Guinness ads meant, but progress was slow. Her patience was running out by the time she got to a long hold-up at the Merrion level-crossing.

It was while she was idly watching the train rush by that she began to wonder when the line had been built. The present day DART (*Dublin Area Rapid Transport*) ran along the coast, from Howth at the north end of Dublin Bay, through Killiney, to Bray on the south tip. Had the railway track been newly laid for the DART? Or was it run on the original Dublin–Wicklow railway line? She could remember going in and out of Killiney by train as a child but not often, since her parents preferred to travel by car. And then, all of a sudden, as she thought back, she remembered that the journeys of her childhood had terminated at the now defunct Harcourt Street Station. Therefore the train must have taken a more inland route. So it couldn't have run around the bay. She shrugged impatiently as her thoughts scattered without resolution and, for the time being at least, she missed the thread she had tried to follow.

The couple in the car in front, taking advantage of the delay, began to kiss passionately, taking so long to come up for air that she wondered if they'd suffocate. She started a countdown as a furious cacophony of car horns broke into her reverie. The couple turned, grinned and waved at her cheekily. They looked about sixteen. I shall never kiss like that again, she thought sadly and felt devastated. I shall probably never fall in love again either. A wild hot rush of energy coursed through her, unexpected, uncontrollable. Her mouth opened in a silent scream. *I want you. Fuck me, fuck me, me, me.* She leaned back languidly and closed her eyes. The car stalled as the engine cut out.

A large male hand went splat on her windscreen and a contorted face leered down at her. 'Feckin' women drivers. Would ye get out of the feckin' way, missis. You're a feckin' menace on the road, d'you know that?' She could barely make out the words against the rush of blood in her ears. After two false starts and a good deal more swearing both inside and out, she finally managed to get the engine firing again. Ignoring her persecutor, she rolled onto the pavement and rested her throbbing head on the steering wheel.

The hell with love, what she wanted was sex. Now. This instant. Immediate, wild, brutal, exciting, continuous. All day, all night, every day, every night. She wanted a great wonderful, throbbing male shaft inside her, filling her, fucking her senseless. *Like a virgin.* Another train rolled by – *celibate, celibate, celibate* – mocking her with its refrain, bringing her down to earth. Tess looked at herself wearily in the mirror and brushed damp tendrils of hair off her face.

Still shaking, she eased out into the Merrion Road and gradually managed to get herself under a semblance of control by concentrating on the list of things to be completed before the exhumations could start. Now that the bishop had fixed Sunday the twenty-seventh for the consecration of the new cemetery they were all set. Dwyer, the undertaker, reckoned it would take two days to lift and store the coffins. Say three to be on the safe side. Reburials only another day or so, since the new graves prepared beforehand would be open and waiting. The local parish priest had pencilled in Thursday and Friday. Final dates and times should be co-ordinated with the Health Board and the County Council. Both were insisting on sending observers, presumably to make sure everything was in order. The nuns had undertaken to provide a list of the dead and a notated site plan. What else? Labour contracts to be sorted. A temporary shelter for the coffins while they were awaiting reburial. Arrange payments for that and for extra coffins in case some had disintegrated. Dwyer suggested fifteen extra and didn't demur when Tess, with tongue in cheek, suggested sale or return. But he didn't laugh either. Perhaps it was unrealistic to expect humour from an undertaker?

The nuns wanted work on the new boundary wall to start the day after the reburial. So far this small item was proving the most irritating to arrange. The builder had given a very low estimate in the reasonable expectation that he would also be contracted to work on the house. But he was either unwilling or unable to start so soon. Somewhere along the line he had been given to understand that he would be able to do both jobs at the same time. Which meant that either the bursar or the architect had made a pig's ear of the arrangement and now all three were refusing to budge. Tess's suggestion of someone from the architect's office – a kind of clerk-of-works – to oversee and co-ordinate the restoration had been met with fury by the architect who refused responsibility for paying such a person and by the builder who didn't want (his words) 'some stuck-up young pup alienating his workmen'. Then the Mother Guardian blithely suggested that Tess herself might help out and to her surprise Hugo had stuck his oar in and backed her up. Tess didn't particularly want to be piggy-in-the-middle, but she didn't want to let the nuns down either, so she reluctantly agreed.

She assumed, wrongly, that the Guardian and Hugo, who were old friends, had devised this cunning ruse just to keep her occupied. A sort of bereavement therapy. And because it was therapy and because even manufactured business was better than mournful idleness, she did not object.

It was some time before she fully comprehended how subtle they were. Though, had she known it, the process of understanding had already begun that day as she sat in the queue by the railway track.

She finally made it to Holy Retreat at twenty past four. Since she had promised to be back to relieve the baby-minder at six, she kept her eye firmly on her watch. Experience had taught her that time had a habit of slipping by at the convent. Speed was not one of the nuns' most notable attributes. She spoke to Sister Benedicte first, for the few minutes it took to report on her visit to the Diocesan Office. The date for the exhumations to begin was now definitely set for Tuesday the twenty-ninth of October.

'Perhaps you'd be good enough to work out a schedule with the undertaker?' Sister Benedicte asked. 'He could move in the extra coffins the day before.'

'What about the pre-fab to hold them? It will take at least one day to erect, I should think. Do you want me to get that sorted as well?'

'If you would, I'd be grateful. So, is that all today, Miss Callaway?'

'I think so, unless Mother Catherine wants to see me.'

'I believe she does. Will you wait? And, Miss Callaway, thank you for all your excellent work.' It was the nearest the Bursar ever got to warmth and Tess was unaccountably pleased. She was about to say so when she heard the faintest swish of the nun's habit and realized she was alone. Of all the nuns, Benedicte moved most quietly. Yet her entrances and exits were curiously dramatic.

Often Tess had no idea she was behind the screen until she spoke. It did not endear the Bursar to her.

The Mother Guardian's arrival did not have quite the same unsettling quality. She always gave a characteristic little cough of warning as she entered. That day, the cough was harsher than usual and she sounded short of breath when she spoke.

'The surveyor thinks we should get another estimate.' Mother Catherine brought Tess up to date. She sounded hoarse, as if her tired voice had run out of lubrication. There was a scraping sound behind the screen, as she pulled forward her chair.

'He's worried that the costs will go up. He also said something about fixed-price contracts. Does that phrase mean anything to you, Tess?' The nun's voice was softer, nearer the curtain.

'Good idea. I'll draw something up if you like. The builders won't like it though. They'll argue that it's difficult to know what'll show up on a job like this.'

'Yes, that's what Mr Byrne thought. But he said they must understand that our resources are strictly limited.' The Guardian coughed and in the ensuing silence Tess had an uncomfortable feeling that there was someone else nearby, listening. Why, she could not say, it was no more than the very vaguest doubt.

'I'll try to devise something to cover you,' Tess promised. She pulled her chair nearer the screen. 'Do you mind if I ask a question, Mother Catherine?' she asked diffidently.

'How can I tell until you do?' The nun sounded amused.

'When did you decide to sell the land?' she

asked. There was so long a silence that Tess thought she had either overstepped the mark or the nun had dropped off to sleep, but eventually the Mother Catherine cleared her throat.

'That particular site, you mean?' She sounded far, far away.

'Yes, I think I do. Moving the cemetery is going to be, well, traumatic. I just wondered if another solution could have been found.'

'Not for the amount of money we needed. We went into the matter very thoroughly. First, we thought we might sell the lodge and its garden. But that would have meant strangers living almost within our enclosure. Then, out of the blue, the headmaster of Glenadams School made a generous offer. It was like an answer to prayer.'

'Out of the blue?'

'Yes. There was a serious road accident outside their gate. A couple of the pupils were knocked down and very badly injured. The parents were naturally very angry and demanded that the governors make a new entrance away from the main road. We were glad to be able to help after such a terrible tragedy.'

'Ah.' Tess was bemused that the answer to prayer should have come neatly disguised as an act of God but then chided herself for putting such a blasphemous gloss on remarks which were obviously innocently intended.

'When was that?' she asked, more to fill her embarrassment than a quest for information.

'Two and a half years ago, nineteen ninety-four. The offer came to us about a month after the accident.' She sighed. 'I shall be glad when the work is concluded. It's been very disrupting for our community life. We seem to have thought of little else for such a long time.'

There was another long lapse. Somewhere a little way off a door squeaked and there was the sound of rustling cloth. Tess, who was getting anxious about the time, was on the point of leaving when Mother Catherine cleared her throat again.

'Did you find out anything about our founder's family?' Her voice was barely audible and sounded as if she were holding a handkerchief against her mouth. At first Tess thought she was afraid of being overheard but it seemed she was trying to suppress a coughing fit.

'Well, I'm not sure. There *is* a family called Stebton in Chipping Stebton. Two branches, actually. But for various reasons I didn't meet any of them except one elderly lady whose name is Elfrida. She's in an old people's home. I'm afraid she's very confused and hardly coherent. The house is really beautiful – at least from the outside. It was once a monastery. Isn't that a strange coincidence?'

'In what way?' The nun spoke in measured tones, soft, wary.

'Well, I suppose I thought it interesting that over there a monastery became a manor house and this manor house became a monastery. And both in the same family,' Tess finished lamely. A chill seemed to have descended.

'Who else beside the old lady lives there?' the nun whispered.

'Her twin daughters. But neither of them were about. One has just been in hospital and is now abroad. The other one seems to have completely disappeared. Jane-Edwina she's called. She went on holiday about a month ago and hasn't returned yet. Nobody seems to know where she's got to. I didn't . . .' She broke off as something or someone crashed to the floor. 'Mother Catherine, are you all right?' she called anxiously but there was no reply. 'Mother Catherine?'

Tess tore into the hall and looked around for a bell or some means of raising the alarm. She held open the hall door and pressed her finger to the electric bell which was all she could think of. She could hear it echo through the house but for what seemed eternity there was no reply.

'Tess?' Sister Joseph sounded breathless. 'My goodness me, we were in chapel. What's wrong?'

'Mother Catherine, I think she's fainted or something,' Tess started but was interrupted by a disturbance within the enclosure. She heard the sound of running feet slapping against a bare floor. A door creaked. After a few seconds it creaked again and then, barely audible this time, more soft padding of feet. She could almost envisage the nun being carried along by her sisters. The strangest thing was that they were soundless; there were no shouted instructions not even whispers. She hesitated, not knowing whether to go or stay. Should she call a doctor? What did they do in such circumstances? As the minutes ticked by she wondered if Mother Catherine was dead.

'She'll be fine now.' Sister Joseph was back. 'You've had a shock, my dear. I've brought you a cup of camomile tea. It's in the drum. Drink it up, you'll feel better.'

'What happened?'

'Mother fainted. She hasn't been feeling at all

well, she's had a bad cough for a few weeks. She just had one of her turns. She's a bit anaemic.'

'Shall I fetch a doctor?' Tess asked.

Sister Joseph-Maria gave a characteristic little chuckle. 'We have a doctor. Sister Benedicte is a doctor. She looks after our health as well as our finances.' She laughed again. 'You haven't taken your tea.'

'Do you mind if I don't, Sister Joseph? I don't really like the taste of camomile.'

'I don't blame you. I'll take it away. I have something else for you, if you'll just wait another moment.'

The moment stretched into five minutes before she bustled back. Bustled? Tess spent what she called her blind time imagining the nuns' movements and facial expressions. Since it was unlikely that she would ever get the opportunity of checking her fantasies with reality, she could give her imagination full rein. Sister Joseph was therefore a large, plump, comfortable countrywoman who *bustled*.

'There now,' Sister Joseph said as she revolved the drum. 'We made a little gift for you.' As Tess opened the cupboard the hall was filled with the scent of basil and thyme. The herbs were arranged in neatly tied bunches in a wicker basket on the lower shelf. A dozen speckled eggs and a small pot of honey nestled amongst them. Tess buried her face in the fresh damp leaves.

'Oh, how lovely. Thank you. But can't I pay you? Please?'

'Oh, my goodness no. On no account. Best use the herbs at once, while they're fresh. Sister

Benedicte said you must eat well while you're feeding the baby.'

Tess laughed. 'Did she indeed?' She was amazed. She was still a little wary of Sister Benedicte who struck her as cold and remote. She had certainly never offered maternal advice before.

'How is the baby?'

'I'm afraid she's not at all happy with me just now. I've almost weaned her onto a bottle and she hates it. She was much too hungry. I'm going to try her on solids as well, I think.' She was amused to find herself so earnestly discussing her baby with an invisible nun. But Sister Joseph responded enthusiastically, as if she were an expert. Which, as it turned out, she was.

'I was a midwife for ten years before I entered,' she said and Tess could almost see the eyes crinkling in amusement. The nuns were full of surprises. She wondered what other experts lay within?

'So you could trust me to mind her for you when you see Mother Guardian. You don't always have to be paying babysitters.'

'Are you sure?'

'Of course I'm sure. We're all dying to see her. You didn't think we'd like babies, is that it?' Sister Joseph asked gently when Tess demurred. 'Why wouldn't we? We're normal women, you know. Just like you, Tess dear. Same doubts, same fears, same longings too, I dare say. You're finding it hard, aren't you?'

'Yes. At least . . . Yes, I am. I couldn't get the hang of it at first, liking her, getting used to the mess and the terrible smallness of her. The helplessness. I never wanted anyone to be so dependent on me. It terrified me. But now, it's strange, but I feel she's growing to be part of me – not my body, she was already that. She's like a troublesome conscience.' She gave a short embarrassed laugh. 'She's there and there's no shifting her. But, oddly enough, I find myself weak with love for her.' She sniffed. 'Stupid, isn't it? A woman of my age. Pathetic.'

'Pathetic? No, indeed,' Sister Joseph said softly. 'I think it's pretty normal. Motherhood, I believe it's called. Comes with the package, don't you know? If you don't mind my saying, Tess, you're a little hard on yourself. You have a lot to cope with, my dear. You must miss your partner. A woman shouldn't have to face all that alone.'

'Do you miss . . .' Tess started awkwardly then couldn't continue.

'Do I miss the possibility of having children? Do we, as nuns, think of children, relationships, sex, all that? Is that what you're asking? Of course we miss all of it.'

'Then why?'

'Why incarcerate ourselves? That's more difficult to answer if you don't have faith. Don't believe in the power of prayer. I suspect you don't, is that right?'

'Yes. I can see your life is a good life. I don't mean just for yourselves, but good *qua* good. But I can't imagine what would make me give up everything, my life, my work, and take vows to serve some impossible ideal.'

'We at Holy Retreat don't take solemn vows, Tess. We can leave at any time if the ideal proves impossible. We choose to stay. It is a good life both spiritually and intellectually and really in every way. Few women, even in these modern times, are as lucky. Our founder was an extremely far-seeing woman.' She was just warming to her theme when a bell began to peel. 'Five minutes to prayers. I'm afraid I must go. Tess, could you do a small message for me?'

'Yes, if I can.'

'There are two boxes, over there, under the hall table. Could you drop them off at Donnybrook church on your way home? I believe you pass it?'

Tess slid two large, brown cardboard boxes from under the table. They were surprisingly light. 'The church, you say? On the main road? Who shall I give them to?'

'The sacristan if he's there, otherwise drop them at the priest's house. I believe it's next door. They're altar breads. Communion hosts, you know. It's an emergency order. They've a couple of big funerals tomorrow and they're afraid they'll run out.'

'Do you make them?' Tess was surprised. She'd never really thought about where or how communion hosts were made unless it was that they dropped like manna from heaven. The nuns clearly had other lines of business besides the herbs.

'A small number, we're not properly equipped. The Carmelite sisters have the real monopoly. We only make about twenty thousand a week, they make more like two hundred thousand.' She spoke like a captain of industry being threatened by a take over.

'What? A quarter of a million?'

'Oh, yes a lot of people *still* go to Mass.' Sister

Joseph did nothing to disguise the hint of mockery. How much more do they know about me? Tess wondered, and then gave up. Probably everything.

'How do you make your deliveries?' Did a baker's van roll up and gather the hosts? Or an old-fashioned horse and dray? Or did they simply lasso stray solicitors whenever they wanted a messenger? The nun had a more practical solution.

'We have an arrangement with the post office, a monthly account. The postman collects the boxes every Thursday morning at ten, for next-day delivery. The boxes are left for him in the porch. Like clockwork he is. But these are an emergency. The sacristan rang early this afternoon. They need them for early Mass tomorrow. You don't mind, do you?'

'Not at all.' Tess picked up the boxes by the string, one in each hand, and brought them out to the car. She sat the bigger one on the front passenger seat and placed the second beneath it on the floor. She was still getting her mind around a business with such an esoteric product by the time she got to the dual carriageway at Stillorgan. But something was niggling at the back of her mind. Each time she pulled up at a traffic-light she absently drummed her fingers on the box top. The shiny brown paper crackled satisfactorily. The third time she stopped she began to flick the coarse twine with her fingernail. Suddenly she glanced sideways at the boxes. *Brown ... paper ... packag ...*

'Aaah.' She let out a long slow breath as she remembered the stack of parcels in the little storeroom at the back of the bookshop in Walton Street.

Solomon: Song of Songs: *Officina Massagna, Verona 1789. At time of printing, absurdly, a prohibited book like so many great poetic works. Edition limited to one hundred copies, elaborately printed and decorated (no attribution). Bound in full vellum, with delicately painted panels on covers and spine.*

A d'A Cat. 4, item 16

17

Tess met Hugo in the hall. He was standing at the bottom of the stairs with his head thrown back listening, as was all too obvious, to the pitiful screams coming from the flat. 'Come down and see me later,' he said, as Tess tore past him. Even though she'd more or less given up feeding Claire, the sound of her baby crying made her breasts feel engorged and sore again. She took the stairs three at a time and found Sandra the babysitter with her ear pressed to the bedroom door, consternation written all over her face.

'Honest to God, Tess, she was fine until half an hour ago. Then she got the hump. I can't do anything with her. I thought she'd burst a blood-vessel.'

'Thanks a bundle.' Tess felt like braining her. She dropped the basket on the floor, grabbed the bottle from the distraught girl and ran into the bedroom. As she bent down to pick Claire up, the baby abruptly stopped crying, opened her eyes and beamed up at her mother. Sandra, who had run in behind her, said, 'Janey, would you look at tha'.' She did a mock faint on the floor and groaned.

'You should be on the stage,' Tess said dryly. 'You wouldn't like to pour us both a glass of wine, would you? There's some in the fridge. I don't think either of our nerves are up to this, do you?'

She picked the now gurgling Claire and carried her into the little sitting-room where someone, Sandra presumably, had lit a fire. Mother and daughter settled on the sofa and both hit the bottle. For once the baby didn't protest about breast-deprivation. The ounces disappeared into her little gullet in a smooth and steady stream. Then she burped loudly, filled her nappy and fell fast asleep.

Tess looked at Sandra and rolled her eyes to heaven. 'Un-bloody-predictable, wouldn't you say?' They laughed.

'I'm really sorry for the fright I gave you,' Sandra said. 'I kinda lost my nerve.'

'Are you able to manage? Is she too much for you?'

'She's fine, honest, she's grand most of the time. She gets cross around sixish, but you're usually home by then. Yeah, I can manage.'

'Sure?'

'Sure. But maybe we could sort out a better timetable? She doesn't seem to like being without you for more than a couple of hours.'

'Right. From now on six is the limit. Except in emergencies and I don't anticipate many of those.

I'm sorry for being late today. Something came up.'

They chatted for half an hour or so until Sandra's boyfriend came roaring up the road on his motor bike. Since it appeared to have no silencer, its roar could be heard long before it was seen. It was a sound which etched itself painfully into Tess's brain every time she heard it.

'Here, I'd better go quick before Mr Boland goes on the warpath.' Sandra jumped up and grabbed her bomber jacket. 'Do you want me tomorrow, Tess?'

'No, I don't think so. But Friday afternoon, if you can. I'll give you a ring if I need you before then. By the way, did Mr Boland say if there were any phone calls?' The only real disadvantage of the little flat was that it hadn't its own phone line. Tess made yet another mental note to buy a mobile.

'Oh, yeah, I forgot to say. I couldn't find a pen. Owen somebody. That's all. Oh and ah, Richard. Sure you're beating the fellas off with your cap, Tess,' she said encouragingly and waved good-bye.

Tess lay back on the sofa and closed her eyes. Beating them off with her cap, was she? Chance would be a fine thing. Were her thoughts and longings unnatural? Adolescent? Could it be normal for a grieving non-widow of her advanced age to pant for sex when she should, more properly, weep from grief? Would she ever have sex again? Enjoy it the way she had with Marcus? Feel filled, fulfilled. The words seemed crude, cold. The comfort of him was what she missed. Missed? Her body screamed for his, spooned around hers, screamed for the touch of his sensual fingers. Tess poured a second glass of wine and waited for anger to hit her. It usually came in predictable waves. First the longing, the randiness, the maudlin self-pity, then total, furious, incapacitating anger. This time it stopped short of the final stage.

She looked down at the sleeping child whose tiny pink fingers were curled around the ribbons of her knitted jacket. She touched them gently and at once Claire opened her muddy eyes and smiled. Tess's heart turned over. It wasn't a fluke then, or wind, she really could smile. Learning to use the charm offensive, manipulating the carer. They come equipped, Tess thought with surprise. They come with their own built-in little protection system. She knows how to make me love her.

'I am your mother and you are mine. Hi, Claire, we'd better make the most of this. We're stuck with each other. But I'll look after you, I give you my word.' She picked up the baby and carried her to the bathroom to change and wash her. She felt warm and soft and utterly comforting.

An hour or so later, the baby was temporarily back in bed, stuffed full of four teaspoons of baby-rice, another half-bottle, a third clean nappy and a second fresh Babygro. Tess was about to make supper when she remembered Hugo's earlier invitation. She ran a wash-rag over her face, a comb through her hair and switched on the listening device. It was nine fifteen and Hugo was watching the RTE news.

'I've left a note of your phone calls on the hall

table, if you want to return them,' he smiled and clicked the TV off.

'I'll wait until the morning. I think I might get myself a mobile. It would be a lot handier,' Tess replied.

'Oh, glory be.' Hugo touched his forehead with the flat of his hand. 'I knew there was something. The office sent one for you yesterday. I plugged it in out there beside the phone. The battery should be well charged by now. Have you eaten, by the way?'

'Not yet. I'll make an omelette a little later. The nuns gave me some wonderful herbs and brown speckled eggs.' She wrinkled her nose at him and laughed. 'I think they've decided to fatten me up.'

'They'll have a job,' he chuckled. 'But their eggs are excellent. I always say hen's eggs are good, but nun's eggs are better.' He smirked at his well-rehearsed little quip. 'I take it the baby survived her hysterics?'

'Just. I'm not sure about poor Sandra.'

'Don't worry about her, she's a tough one. What about you? And even more to the point, what about a drink?'

'I'm awash with wine, Hugo, I'll leave it, thanks. I just wanted to ask you how Terence Murphy-Dunne is? Would he like a visitor? I'm not doing anything tomorrow and I thought, since I'm at a bit of a loose end, I'd go and cheer him up.' *Or give him the third degree more like.* 'I take it he's still in hospital?'

'Well, do you know, I'm not sure. Would he be in this long?' Hugo was off-hand, uninterested, but she noticed his eyes had narrowed.

'Have you not heard from him?'

'No, should I?'

'Oh, I just thought . . .'

'I'm not all that fond of him, you know. In fact, I find him a bit of a boor. The man's a pouncer. No woman is safe in his company. I find all that very unpleasant. Strutting about, cock-sure of himself,' he added sarcastically. 'Ring Ms Reilly tomorrow. She'll know where he is, I'll be bound. He's probably living with her,' he said surprisingly. Hugo wasn't often malicious. Or vulgar. 'He usually is. Runs through his juniors like a dose of salts. Then boasts of his conquests.' He snorted derisively as he stared her down. 'Unsavoury.'

Tess blushed furiously, her defences rising. She turned her face away from his baleful stare. Was Hugo afraid she would get involved with Terence again? Afraid she'd succumb to his charms as she had when she was barely seventeen, out for experience and he, a lusty, handsome, twenty-eight, eager to oblige. At least that was how it started but she hadn't been quite so sophisticated as she thought. Nor yet learned to tell the difference between love and lust. Terence was not remotely romantic, and romance was really, in the end, what she craved. At the time, she tried to pretend she wasn't hurt. Tried to ignore the pleasure he took from humiliating her. She grew hot with shame at the memory. It was a total shock to hear Hugo describe him as callous and disloyal because it meant that Hugo must have known about it all along. He was laying it on rather too thick, warning her off as if she were a child. Protecting her in her sad state? Had he some other reason for keeping some distance between her and Terence? Or was she just being neurotic? Losing trust in everyone else because she had so little in herself?

'Any reason you want to see him? Other than being a good Samaritan?' Hugo enquired too casually.

'No, not really. I thought he might like to know I'm enjoying Holy Retreat and that everything is pretty well on track.' *Well, it was more or less true.* 'But it doesn't matter. Maybe I'll go and get my hair cut instead. I need to clean up my act a bit. I look a mess.'

'Right then. Tell you what, you do that and I'll give you dinner,' he said encouragingly, eager to persuade her back into good humour. 'I've some people coming. Get your glad rags on and be here at eight sharp. You can bring Her Loudness with you. Specially if you can get her to sleep first. What about it?'

Tess accepted and slowly climbed the stairs to the flat. She wondered if Hugo had intended asking her to dinner or whether it was a small diversionary tactic he'd dreamed up on the spur of the moment. Was she being too fanciful? Did he suspect she might allow the priapic Murphy-Dunne to take advantage of her again? Or, God forbid, might even invite him to do so? Well, he could be right at that. She had made a fool of herself with him before, and not just when she was an inexperienced teenager. Beggars couldn't always be choosers, she thought sourly and felt humiliated all over again.

The baby was still fast asleep. Tess brought the herb basket into the kitchen and set it down on the table. She poured another glass of wine, put a

209

plate to heat in the oven and chopped a mixed bunch of the herbs. The perfume was intoxicating and the hunger pangs, which had worn off, returned. When she found two little brown scones among the eggs she popped them to warm in the oven as well. Then she heated the frying pan with a little olive oil and a knob of butter and beat up four of the eggs.

The omelette was perfection and though she'd intended to eat it comfortably by the fire once she'd tasted it she couldn't stop. She ate it standing in the kitchen in four minutes flat and even contemplated making another. Hugo was right about the eggs and the herbs were the freshest and best she'd ever had. If this was a taste of the Holy Retreat cuisine then the nuns did all right for themselves. She sipped her wine slowly as she washed up and cleared away. There was a Schubert string quintet on the radio, aptly enough *Death and the Maiden*. But identifying it didn't distress her in the way it might have done a month or two before.

The basket was too big for the fridge. She stored the remaining eggs in a bowl, divided the herbs into two bags and put them into the vegetable drawer. The leaves were still quite damp. She concluded that they must have been picked immediately after the shower of rain which had fallen while she was in the convent, because the paper which had been used to line the basket was soaked. As she eased it out to discard it she noticed it was a centre-fold from an A5 notebook. Three of the four sides were covered with neat writing. More out of idle curiosity than anything else she spread it open on the table but the ink had run on the damp paper and it was difficult to read. She laid it on the radiator and went off to have a bath.

By the time she'd bathed and made Claire's supply of bottles for the night, the paper was almost dry. Tess brought it through to the sitting-room where there was an Anglepoise lamp but even with the more powerful light she found it no easier to read. Where the ink had run, whole patches of script had been obliterated and even where words or lines were legible they didn't make much sense. *Curious* was repeated several times. *Clandestine. Rare.* She ran her finger idly up and down the pages trying to make sense of single words: *Romano, Cleland; Sedici modi; Chorier; dialogo.* It was a list of some kind, both in English and in several other languages. French being the only one with which she was familiar enough to work out that *—ole des fill—* might be *L'école des filles* perhaps. *L'académie des dames divisée en sept entités—* Some sort of school prospectus? Or convent since the next words she made out were in English. *—n the Cloister.* A little further down *Rochester*, then part of an address *Rue de Tribune Bru—*.

'I am completely barking.' She spoke aloud. A habit which seemed to be growing on her. 'I'm dead on my feet and what am I doing? Messing about, trying to solve puzzles on bits of waste-paper. What a fool I am. And that would have been that had she not turned the sheet over as she began crumpling it up. There were a couple of incomplete entries on the fourth page of the fold which caught her eye: *Da Andrea Vesalio, De Humani corporis— 1–43. Sonetti Lussuriosi di*

Aretino. 1534. —*Giulio Romano*. The word *Aretino* pulsated at her. Hello, she thought, have I seen that before somewhere? She sat down at the table with a bump.

Not seen, *heard*. It was a moment or two before she worked out why it was familiar. She smoothed out the damp wrinkles of the paper, slowly, soothingly, while her mind tiptoed back over the seemingly unconnected little coincidences of the past week. Or was that too strong a word? Too exact? *Amici d'Aretino*, Mrs Hartfield had said. And here, seemingly quite by chance, it was again, albeit in modified form. Who or what was *Aretino*? A place? A name? Tess thought about it for a long time but her mind simply went round and round in frustrating circles, getting nowhere. In the end it seemed absurd to assume that a sheet of wastepaper, thrust under some bunches of damp herbs, was meant for anything more than to absorb their moisture.

Tess folded the paper carefully and left it on the table. She felt as though she was looking at herself in slow motion, as if something of tremendous importance had or was about to happen. It was not an unfamiliar feeling, though it came more usually when she was on the brink of making a breakthrough in a difficult case. The quiet instant just before irritating uncertainties become clear, make sense. But why should it happen now? At this moment, in this place, when what she was involved in was simply a matter of organization, most of which was already done?

But just as a grain of sand can grow into a pearl by the steady accretion of layer upon layer, so it was with that tiny seed of doubt which had assailed her earlier. It grew and grew until it finally evolved into a full-blown and serious worry.

A stranger was missing. A train rolled by. An awkward question had been asked. A nun fainted. And now a ciphered message in a basket of herbs.

Was something sinister going on? Were her nuns in danger? Or were they being duped? Information had been withheld. Deliberately? Or was she suspecting malice where none was intended? And then, from nowhere, she felt a sense of personal danger so sharp and immediate that she ran to the bedroom to check on the sleeping child. Claire was oblivious to her fear but as Tess bent low to ease her swimming head, she sensed that her ever-present fear for her baby's safety had somehow become linked to a recognition of hidden evil – all the more threatening because she could not see where it was coming from. But the one thing she didn't doubt was its existence. If her long-time association with criminals had done anything, it had taught her to respect her instincts. When she recovered, she touched the baby's warm cheek lightly with her palm, drew up the covers and tiptoed back to the kitchen. Her eyes glided uneasily over the soggy sheet of paper. And, very gradually, the sleeping intelligence awoke.

Venus dans le Cloître *ou la Religieuse en Chemise. Entretiens curieux. 1692. Translated from the French by a person of honour.*

A d'A Cat. 9, item 23

18

On Thursday morning Tess overslept and had barely time to swallow a cup of coffee and get the baby fed and dressed before driving out to Holy Retreat. The post was due to be collected at ten and she wanted to talk to the postman. She was also keen to find out which of the nuns had packed the herbs. When she got there, she was relieved to notice several large boxes lying in the porch of the same variety as she'd taken to Donnybrook church the evening before. She glanced at her watch as she rang the doorbell. It was nine thirty-two.

'My goodness, Tess, you're early this morning. We didn't expect you till this afternoon. No baby today?' Sister Joseph asked.

'She's asleep outside in the car. I'm only here for a minute to thank you and return your basket.' Tess put the empty basket in the drum and rotated it. If she hoped the nun would remark on the missing lining paper, she was disappointed.

'Ah, there was no need to make a special journey, my dear, but thank you. Did you enjoy the produce?'

'I'd say divine, if you wouldn't think it blasphemous,' Tess replied with a grin. 'The eggs were delicious. So fresh and with such lovely yellow yolks. You must report to Dr Benedicte that I took her advice. I made a most delicious omelette,' she laughed, 'and ate it all up.'

'We feed the chickens with maize for the colour and they're always picking at the herbs when they get a chance, which gives them the flavour.'

'Ah, the herbs! I've never smelt such perfumed basil. And the thyme was just wonderful. Did you pick them yourself, Sister Joseph?' Tess asked, getting to the point of her rhapsody.

'Oh, heavens no. Sister Albertine would never allow an amateur to touch her secateurs,' the nun giggled, 'much less her beloved plants. No, Sister Albertine picked them.'

'It's a great name for a gardener,' Tess laughed. She glanced at her watch and kept an ear out for the post van.

'Isn't it? Actually it's not, strictly speaking, her name at all. She took the name Agatha when she entered. But none of us ever call her that.' She came nearer the screen. 'When you come in the summer, in June particularly, you will see why. The garden walls are covered with Albertine roses. The perfume is quite wonderful. She grows other varieties, of course, but those are her favourites. She's a great gardener.'

'Does she run the business side as well?'

'No, just the actual gardening. Sister Benedicte is in charge of that. It was she who really developed that end of things, which made the expansion of the gardens possible.'

'I forgot to mention that the scones were

delicious too, I had quite a feast.'

'In that case, I hope you had a nice glass of wine to round it off. I should have put in a bottle of our elderflower wine for you to taste.'

'You did beautifully, Sister Joseph. I knew I had you to thank for packing it so generously.' Tess laughed. 'Is there anything you don't make?'

'I don't make sense, very often,' Sister Joseph responded elliptically. 'By the way, did you manage to deliver the hosts?'

'I did. The sacristan was very grateful.' Tess consulted her watch. It was seven minutes to ten. 'Sister Joseph, could you tell Mother Catherine that I won't be out until early next week and that I'll talk to Mr Dwyer before I come.'

'I will. And is there anything else?'

'I don't think so,' Tess replied slowly, 'unless of course there is anything she wants me to do. Or perhaps *you* need some errands . . .' She let her voice trail off. There was a moment's silence before Sister Joseph replied.

'No I don't think so, my dear. But thank you.' Tess wasn't sure whether it was disappointment or relief she felt that Sister Joseph was offering no follow-up to the missive in the basket. But it was fairly clear that either she hadn't packed the goodies or if she had, the paper had no significance. More than disappointment, the whole absurdity of linking dubious books with the convent hit Tess rather forcefully as she went outside. She felt vaguely ashamed of her suspicions.

A small green post van was, at that moment, driving in to the forecourt. She was rather touched to notice that the driver had switched off his engine, allowing the van to roll quietly to a stop. The only sound was the muffled crunch of the gravel under its wheels. She picked up the four boxes as best she could, and brought them to him as he got out of the van. He was a friendly young man with red hair and bad skin.

'That's very nice of you, miss. You saved me the walk,' he said as he took the boxes from her.

'Not much of a walk,' Tess smiled back and muttered something about Sister Joseph-Maria wanting to check that the account had been paid. The postman opened the back of the van and pushed the boxes inside.

'Oh well, I wouldn't know.' He sounded slightly surprised. 'The office franks the boxes and deals with the account.' He looked at Tess ruefully and shrugged his shoulders. 'But she knows all that. She must be getting a bit confused. She'll have to ring the accounts people. Will you tell her?'

'Yes, of course,' Tess broke in but was immediately interrupted.

'Is she old? The nun?'

'Who? Sister Joseph? I've no idea. I've never seen her. But she doesn't sound all that old.' It was Tess's turn to shrug. 'You've never been inside the convent?'

'No, there's no need. They just leave the stuff outside in the porch for me,' he grimaced. 'I wouldn't want to go in and talk to a blank wall, though. Gi' me the creeps, it would. But don't get me wrong, they're very good. They're always leaving me things, like a few eggs or bunches of parsley and thyme, the odd chicken. The wife does be delighted with them.'

'Have you been coming out long?'

'Three or four years. I took over from a fellow who'd been making the deliveries for donkey's years. Twenty at least. He was a great pal of one of them. Sister Porter, he used to call her.'

He handed Tess a bundle of mail. A normal sort of bundle except that there were no circulars.

'No junk mail, I see.' She smiled.

'No, I don't bother them with any of that stuff. Not that there's much sure, hardly anyone knows about this place at all. As a matter of fact, you're one of the few people I ever saw out here. And I never saw a car before either.' He laughed. 'Isn't that a good one? It's like going back into the past. Sometimes I sit on the drive and have a smoke and just look around. Gives me time to catch up with myself. I like comin' out. Very peaceful it is.' He stepped close to Tess and whispered conspiratorially, 'D'you know what's in the boxes?' She knew by his expression that he was dying to tell her. She could have hugged him. He'd given her exactly the opening she wanted. She slowly shook her head.

'What?'

'Communion hosts. Isn't that a strange thing? Until I started this job I never thought about where they came from. Did you?'

'Heaven?' she said archly and he grinned.

'Well they're certainly light enough,' he said. 'Angel food, eh?'

'Always the same? Just the three or four boxes?'

'Yes,' he started. 'Eh,' he frowned. 'Pretty well. Sometimes a few more. The weight varies a bit. But yeah, always the same.'

'Communion hosts by post,' Tess quipped

saucily and when he laughed she said, 'I suppose they're always for the same churches?'

'Usually. Mostly to city churches. Oh and Donnybrook and that. But sometimes they go further afield. England even. Must be special orders. But that's only a few times. When the old nun brought them out herself. Strange old thing. Never came near me. Just waited till she saw the van and then legged it back inside. To tell you the truth she gave me the creeps. She had a terrible old black cloak up over her head.'

'When was that?' Tess asked shakily.

The postman scratched the back of his head. 'I only saw her a few times. To be honest I was dying to get closer, have a good look at her. It makes you curious, doesn't it? That they never show themselves? The first time I saw her was about . . . oh, must be nearly a couple of years ago,' he started slowly and then his voice livened. 'It was the summer. That's why I remember . . . well, I mean, the old cloak looked dead heavy . . . I suppose I saw her three or four times in all.' He grinned at Tess. 'I must say, you're a bit of an improvement. Here, you're not thinkin' of entering, are you?'

'No, not me, but I'm dead curious. I'd love to have a look at one of them.' She grinned conspiratorially. 'When was the last time you saw her?'

'Not so long ago. The days fly by, don't they? Could have been a couple of weeks or might be longer. A month? God alone knows . . .' He scratched his head again and looked as if he was about to add something, but at that moment the baby gave a blood-curdling scream. 'God between us and all harm, what's that?' he cried. Tess made a dash for the car with the postman following on her heels. Claire's little knitted hat had fallen down over her eyes and she was blue with fury.

'Yours, missis?' he asked as Tess opened the car and took Claire in her arms.

'Yes,' she said. 'All mine.'

'Well, I can see you won't be entering. Though you might want a bit a peace. That child has a powerful pair of lungs. I'll leave you to it,' he said and laughed. 'I get enough of them at home. We've four, under six.' He waved goodbye. 'Don't forget to tell the nun to ring the office.'

Tess held the baby close until she quietened sufficiently to allow herself to be strapped into her seat again. But once they got home Claire exacted a heavy price for being abandoned to the malign intent of her knitted cap. The twenty-minute respite in the car had merely given her time to catch her breath. She screamed blue murder and refused to feed until her distraught mother practically poured the formula down her throat. She then grizzled for a further twenty-five minutes before she finally dropped into a deep sleep. By which time Tess had become so uptight, she was practically in rigor mortis. She had to tell herself very firmly that physical abuse was not an option. But for the first time in her life she felt she might be beginning to understand how easily a person could be driven to it. The person being herself. Her hands were shaking too much for her to contemplate making even a cup of coffee. She closed her eyes for a few minutes before it occurred to her that a long gin and tonic might be a useful substitute. Even at eleven-thirty in the morning.

The appellations attached to censored libraries – Librorum Probitorum – *bear inspection if only for the amusement of the reader: The* Enfer *or* Hell *of the Bibliothèque Nationale in Paris; The Private Case of the British Museum; New York's Public Library's* ***** *Collection; The Delta Collection of The Library of Congress. The Bodleian Library in Oxford goes one better with* Ø *(punning on Fie!). Best of all, perhaps, is the German* Schund und Schmutz.

19

Not just useful, the gin wrought a near-miracle of restored energy. While the baby napped Tess set about mending her familial fences. She rang her mother and arranged to go to her for Sunday lunch. She tried Terence Murphy-Dunne's home number but it was persistently engaged. She worked for an hour or so on Holy Retreat business before allowing herself to turn to her immediate preoccupations of boxes, Aretino and Miss Jane-Edwina Stebton-Hillyard.

'Could I speak to Miss Hillyard, please?' Tess asked when she finally made contact with Hartfield Magraw.

'Miss Hillyard no longer works here. May I help? This is Murray Magraw.'

'Ah. Could I speak to Mrs Hartfield then?'

'Sure, if I can find her, she's under a pile of

books somewhere. Hang on a second. Here she is.'

'Grace? It's Tess Callaway. I hear Miss Hillyard hasn't returned to work.'

'No.' Grace lowered her voice. 'Nor is she going to. We had a letter of resignation a couple of days after you were here. I tried to ring you, but of course I only had your home number and whoever answered said he would pass on the message.'

'What message?' Tess asked croakily. Her mouth felt dry.

'That we'd heard from Jeddie.'

'Mind telling me what she said?'

'Just that she decided it would be too difficult to continue on a regular basis because of her mother being ill. To tell you the truth we were a bit annoyed with her. Which probably isn't fair, because it wasn't her fault. The letter took ages to come. I mean it mightn't have seemed too bad if we'd got it earlier but it was delayed ten days in the post. She wrote it on the twenty-third of September but, as I say, it didn't arrive until early October, the fifth, I think. But even allowing for that, it was a bit off-hand.'

'How?'

'Well, nothing about sorry for the inconvenience or anything like that. Just over and out as it were.' She laughed.

'You don't sound very annoyed.'

'Oh, well. I'm rather fond of her. She's been very helpful to us in the past so I owe her one or two favours. What about you? And the baby?'

'Both fine, thanks. Grace?' Tess was about to

ask her about Amici d'Aretino when Grace cut in again.

'What really made me steam is that she added a PS asking would I very much mind storing her property until she came to collect it. In person. Underlined. Cheek,' she snorted.

'And has she come in?'

'No, not yet. Her stuff is still here. Coats, shoes, hats, all sorts of stuff. Not very tidy, is Jeddie. Oh well, she'll turn up one of these days. Expect me when you see me, sort of thing. We've taken someone else on, by the way.'

'So where is she? Do you know?'

'Looking after her mad old mother I expect, poor love. And that mausoleum of a house. Oh hell, Tess, I've got to go. Customers. Can you ring again? I'd love a chat. I'll give you my home number.' After which she hung up too quickly for Tess to ask the other questions that were clogging up her brain.

Tess looked around the kitchen disconsolately and after a few minutes' reflection padded downstairs, snaffled Hugo's Dublin Yellow Pages directory from the hall and carted it back up to the flat. Somewhere in Dublin a rather precious, old college friend of hers had set himself up in an antiquarian book business. She eventually found him under *Zosimus Broadsheets*. She hoped the obscure literary reference didn't lose him too many potential customers. She dialled the number.

'Roderick, mind if I run something past you?' she asked when they'd gone through the usual preliminaries.

'Fire away.'

'If I said the word *Aretino* would it mean anything to you?' Tess asked and was surprised by a loud guffaw of laughter.

'Oooh,' he chuckled, 'certainly it would. And may I ask where you came across it?'

'Never mind that for a moment. Just tell me what it means, will you?'

'In the book sense, it means nothing, *qua* meaning, if you understand me,' Roderick started in his pedantic way. Tess rolled her eyes to heaven knowing that he would eventually, if left to himself, get to the point. 'It's a name actually. Pietro di Aretino, sixteenth-century. Known as Venetian because he worked there, but by birth and family probably Tuscan, from Arezzo most likely. Rather eclectic, very collectible but not my field, alas. That any help?'

'Depends on what you mean by eclectic,' Tess replied dryly and was rewarded by a half-suppressed titter but little else.

'Well then, let me try something else. Ever heard of Amici d'Aretino?'

'Very nice, but can't say I have. Care to explain?'

'I believe it's the name of a bookseller.' This time Roderick laughed outright. 'He sounds like something of a wag,' he said. 'I wouldn't mind meeting him.'

'Not him, her. Why wag? Or am I being dense?'

'No, not at all, Tess. I'm sorry, I'm just amused, that's all. No reason why you should ever have heard of Aretino. Though I dare say you will know others like him. Boccacio, for instance? Casanova? Rather high-class erotica. That is an extremely informative and witty name to give yourself if you deal in that sort of thing. Very. A woman, you say?' He sounded as if he didn't quite believe a woman would be capable of it. Tess took immediate umbrage.

'Yes, Roderick, imagine that. A woman. And blow me down but she seems to have dreamed it up all by herself,' Tess said crabbily and immediately doubted her claim. What, after all, did she know about it?

'Well, hats off to her whoever she is. Does she do catalogues?' He laughed again. Tess began to get a little tired of his nudge, nudge, wink, wink. But she had one other question she was burning to ask.

'Roderick? This is a serious question so no tittering, just a straight answer. Would she be likely to deal in, em, pornography?'

'Modern pornography, you mean? Dirty books? Paedophile material, that sort of thing?' He sucked in his breath with distaste.

'Yes. I think I do,' she answered slowly and waited while he considered his answer.

'Well now, that's a bit difficult. But no, I doubt it very much. A name like that would only make sense to the cognoscenti. In every sense. Scholars aren't all dull, y'know. And another thing, these are fine, in the trade sense *fine*, books we're talking about.'

'What does that mean exactly? Expensive?' she cut in quickly. 'Valuable?'

'Very. Books from the Aretino period are exquisitely printed, illustrated, bound. Many of them are beautiful and some are also, well, witty and clever. But to get back to your previous question. Remember that many books which were proscribed in the past, are no longer. I mean Victor Hugo was banned in his time. First person to use the expletive *merde* I believe. Then there are others you'll have heard of, probably read if you've any sense. Catullus, Cleland? Beardsley? Even some of Byron, would you believe? I could go on. I really don't know where you draw the line.'

'I see. Tell me, what is Aretino like?'

'I've never actually seen an Aretino or an original Bocaccio but I guess I would find them rare and beautiful. Some of the others I'm more doubtful about. Modern stuff disgusts me and Lady Chatterley bores me rigid. But compared to what you can buy on news-stands ... Well, need I go on? Maybe I'm partisan but anyone who calls herself Amici d'Aretino would be worth meeting. Whoever she is.'

'Hillyard is her name. She lives in Oxford,' Tess said and Roderick burst out laughing.

'Well, well,' he said. 'She would, wouldn't she?'

Absolute Title: *In the case of freeholds, this guarantees that the estate registered is vested in the proprietor of the land, subject only to the entries in the register and such overriding interests as may affect it.*

Registered land – General Information

20

Tess slowly sank the plunger in the cafetière and watched the amber-brown grains sink sensuously to the bottom of the glass jar. It was a pity, she thought, that the smell of freshly ground coffee beans was so infinitely better than the taste of the liquid. Perhaps sniffing would be a better option than drinking? She looked around the kitchen for a clean cup and found, to her disgust though not to her surprise, that the entire, unwashed stock of dishes was mouldering in the sink. Had been since the day before. Unless she was willing to forego her urgently required cup of coffee – and she was not – there was nothing for it but to tackle the lot while Claire was still asleep. She wondered suddenly how she was going to manage once she went back to work full time. Or if. There was beginning to be an *if* in her mind about the viability of the scheme. She was alarmed at just how many hours of the day were spent servicing her minuscule daughter, whose wants and demands seemed to grow exponentially to exceed the time available.

'Time to stop drifting,' she murmured as she swirled her hands around the warm soapy water. To be or not to be – superwoman? she mused. That is the first question to address. Whether 'tis nobler in the mind to suffer supercilious disdain for lost ambition or to grab outrageous fortune and employ a full-time professional baby-minder? Or perhaps some happy combination of the two? Was there a happy combination of part-time parent/part-time professional? Not, she knew, for herself as a prosecutor: villains were not generally accommodating enough to settle for the part-time deployment of their peculiar talents. Some other avenues would have to be explored.

At once she was assailed with memories of her childhood resentment of her mother's stage career, her constant absences. 'I don't want you famous, I want you here,' she used shout. She had hoarded her grudges for years, accruing interest until the animosity could not be contained. Until they had passed the point of no return. Had Susan waited in hope all those years that perhaps Tess, finding herself in the same position, might understand and forgive? But even Susan, dramatic though she was, could not have wanted this? But I will survive, she thought, touching wood. I am as tough as she. As ambitious, God help me.

Claire was still asleep. Tess left the dishes draining and crawled into bed beside her for a nap. She drifted into half-sleep listening to the soft rise and fall of the infant's breath, wondering for the nth time what Aretino, that exotic diversion, had to do with anything?

It was just after two when Tess opened her eyes. She glanced at her watch and groaned. If she'd slept at all it had only been for about fifteen minutes. She felt lousy and her eyes seemed to be clogged with sand. She turned her head and, to her surprise, Claire gave her a gummy grin. Tess sat up and stared at her. Awake and not bawling? Not just that, she was as warm as toast and looked dead pleased with herself. As well she might, since she was taking up two thirds of the bed. As usual.

A tiny, newly formed personality was beginning to emerge. 'Hello again, Smudge,' Tess muttered as she picked her up and stuck the bottle in her mouth. 'Be nice to me, sweetie, we have a heavy afternoon ahead of us. Haircut, dry-cleaners and a small visit to Moore Boland and Murphy-Dunne.' The baby stopped sucking and stared up at her intently, trying to focus the unfathomable eyes but she quickly gave up and started to suck again. Tess lay back against the pillow and let her tangled strands of thought unwind lazily. She made no attempt to make order or reason or even link one strand of thought to another. She just let what was there emerge gradually.

Had the scrap of paper in the basket been there by intent or by accident? If intent, then who had put it there for her to find? The Mother Guardian? Benedicte or Joseph? All three had known she was in the convent. But why do so in a way she might easily overlook? Surely any one of them could put what they wished in the files which regularly passed between them? Could it have been one of the nuns she didn't yet know? The gardener? The improbably named Sister Albertine? Maybe, but even to herself, it seemed a little far-fetched to link a writer of erotic books to a convent.

As far as she could see, the paper's only significance – if it had one at all – was the single word: *Aretino*. Was it, by some remote chance, a connection to Jeddie Hillyard's trade name, Amici d'Aretino? Surely it could not be mere chance that the scrap of paper had turned up *after* Mother Catherine asked about the Stebtons? Why had she asked about them? Why then? And why ask Tess? Was it idle curiosity or was something specific worrying her? She asked because she knew I lived in Oxford, and because she trusts me, Tess concluded. But that immediately begged another question: who then did the Guardian not trust?

It was of course true that Tess had hared off to the bookshop of her own volition and not at the nun's behest at all. And it was there the word had first cropped up. Why had she gone to the shop in the first place? She could not say whether she was intrigued by the sound of Jeddie or following some other obscure hunch. Or simply keeping herself busy? Leisure had become her enemy, filled with fear and regret and self-indulgent self-pity. She forced her drifting thoughts back to the case in hand. What of the other connections between Holy Retreat and Stebton Place? Were there any? Why was the nun so vague?

More to the point why was she, Tess Callaway, convinced, if only in the vaguest possible way, that Stebton Place or its inhabitants had some connection with the Mother Guardian's unspecified anxiety about moving the graves? Tess knew that, deep down, her own worry was less anxiety about the graveyard than about something being amiss with the land deal the nuns had made. And that being the case, why on earth was she wasting time haring around looking for Aretino's eccentric pal, when, more properly, she should be having a heart to heart with Terence Murphy-Dunne about the business in hand?

She was furious with herself. Her brain had turned to porridge. Where was her curiosity, for pity's sake? She did not know, for instance, the precise details of the agreement. Or who was driving it. Why had she not thought of looking at the conveyancing file sooner? Because there had been no need, she told herself sternly, and because she had not been invited to do so. The nuns were satisfied, nay delighted, with the deal Terence had done for them. It gave them more than enough to carry out repairs on the convent which was their objective. From the first they had spoken of him in glowing terms. All of them? Tess turned the thought over and over in her mind. No, not all of them: Mother Catherine hardly mentioned him. Nor did Hugo. Except to make sly personal comments.

Which brought her to another point. Why was Hugo so antagonistic towards Terence? Had he always disliked him or was it simply a case of querulous old age watching youth step into his shoes? Strange that Tess had not seen him though. Not once. Not even a phone call. Everything had been passed to her by the nuns, Elizabeth Reilly, his junior, Sinéad the receptionist, or Hugo. Which was pretty rum since Hugo had only been helping out since Murphy-Dunne got sick. He had been pretty well retired for more than three years. He himself called it semi-retirement but her mother told her he was just trying to save face, that it was the real thing. Doctor's orders, as a matter of fact; the stroke had been more incapacitating than he admitted.

There was yet another dimension to all this. The railway. What sequence of thought led her to the railway? Watching the DART go by had, she remembered, prompted some link to the priest's remark, though what exactly that link was eluded her. The land? The train used the old railway line which ran directly along the coast to Killiney then made an inland loop through Ballybrack and Shankill almost until it got to Bray. It gave the convent and the neighbouring school grounds a wide berth. As it did the golf course further along the coast. Tess sat up suddenly. She was concentrating on the wrong things. Forget Aretino, forget Jeddie. As from now she had two priorities. One, look at the contract and two, look at the Glenadams land. She got out of bed, smoothed her rumpled clothes and splashed water on her face.

It was just past three o'clock when she popped Claire in the pram and set off at a brisk pace for town. The afternoon was bright and chilly and for the first time in months Tess felt properly alive, as if she was at last taking hold of her life as well as the situation (if there was one) at the convent. It was true that she had no answers to her list of questions. Nor was she at all certain where she was headed in the future. Yet she was heartened by the thought that she had asked the questions and, for the first time, accepted that there might be a future.

It dawned on her, as she glanced down at Claire, that an important shift had taken place in her thinking; almost surreptitiously, certainly without conscious effort: she would never be alone again, never again quite free. Her prized independence was mortgaged to her daughter's dependence. She had planned the child as a shared venture, with her usual precision and confidence. And fate had mocked her hubris.

'You're my responsibility, mine alone,' she warbled to the infant who stared back at her with old-young disdain. She was luckier than most single mothers after all: she had means and she had a profession. She knew very well from her job just what the poverty trap meant for most single mothers. She could sum it up in one word: humiliation. Every mealy-mouthed state hand-out came with the same price tag. Not just lucky, damn lucky. Though she wondered how, in the future, she was going to react when she heard government ministers sounding off about feckless single mothers draining the state coffers. Tell them to sod off most likely. But then she could, couldn't she? She had the privilege of relative wealth.

'Oh, hi Tess. I didn't expect you today.' Sinéad greeted her with her usual warmth when she finally arrived at the Fitzwilliam Street offices just before four thirty.

'I won't delay you. Just a few things I wanted to check. Is Elizabeth Reilly in?' Tess asked and was relieved to be told Elizabeth was in court.

'All day?'

'She's been there all week,' Sinéad replied. 'She won't be back in the office till next week. Anything I can help with, Tess?'

'Yes, if you would. I want to take a look at some contracts. They'll probably be in the deeds cupboard. Do you have the key?'

'I do, but I don't think you'll be able to manage with the baby. They're way up at the top of the house. I can get them for you if you like.'

'Great. The Holy Retreat file. Oh, and Glen-adams if you can put your hand on it. Mr Murphy-Dunne was handling them.'

'It won't take long,' Sinéad promised, but ten minutes passed before she came back empty-handed and complaining. 'I couldn't find anything under those names. But I'm not surprised, that section is in a terrible muddle. I'm sorry, Tess, it'll take longer than I thought. Would tomorrow do? I'll find what you want, I promise, but if I'm off the switchboard too long I'll be in real trouble.'

'Fine, fine,' Tess soothed though she was utterly frustrated by the delay. 'I'll come in tomorrow morning. No actually I'll come in the evening, if that's all right? It's much easier for me. Do you think you could find it by then?'

'Sure. I'll leave it on Mr Murphy-Dunne's desk, if you like. Have you the keys to his office?' she asked, clearly assuming, wrongly, that as his replacement Tess had use of his room.

'I don't keep a set. I pick them up when I need then,' Tess murmured. 'Perhaps I should take them now and you can show me the keys for the outside doors at the same time. That OK?' She brushed aside a tinge of disquiet at taking advantage of the girl's inexperience and let Sinéad fuss over the baby for a few minutes while other members of staff stopped to chat. Just before she left Tess asked if there was any news of Terence Murphy-Dunne. The receptionist rolled her eyes to heaven.

'He's off to the Caribbean any day now, lucky devil. Rest cure he calls it,' she snorted.

'When did you speak to him?' Tess asked casually.

'I was talking to him a couple of weeks ago, while you were in England. He asked how things were going at the convent. He seemed to be in good form, joking away. You know what he's like.' She grinned.

'No,' said Tess with a smile she was having trouble maintaining, 'tell me?'

'Ah, you know, he was asking whether they'd moved the graves yet.' Her face broke into a grin then she shrugged and pulled a face. 'He was joking about Sean Penn in *Dead Man Walking* – the film, you know?' Tess knew. She'd seen it. She could guess what the joke was but she pressed Sinéad to repeat it.

'Something about "Dead Nuns Running",' the girl murmured and blushed scarlet.

'Two films in one, eh?' Tess asked lightly and raised her eyebrow. '*Nuns on the Run* as well? Isn't he the film buff. I expect he's seen more than his fair share of videos since he was laid low. Can't do much else, can he, lying flat on his back?'

'Oh well, who knows? But I wouldn't have

thought *that* would cramp his style, would you?'
Sinéad looked up at Tess, her expression was
amused. 'Did you need to talk to him?'

'It would be nice to have a word,' she said
lightly. 'Do you happen to know when he's
coming back to work?'

'No idea,' she started, then looked up at Tess.
'But I overheard Mr Moore say that he didn't
expect him until January at the earliest.'

'So long? Is he still in hospital?' she asked in
surprise. At least that would explain why her
attempts on Murphy-Dunne's home number had
yielded the same terse message of unavailability.

'No, he's been out of there for some time. At
least I think so.'

'But you haven't actually seen him?'

'No, he hasn't been in the office. He says he
can't manage the front steps yet.'

'Do you know when he's leaving? On the
Caribbean trip, I mean?'

'No, not really. I'm not sure he said. Soon. He's
probably waiting to get off the crutches.' She
giggled and blushed.

'Ah, right. I'll ring him at home, so.'

Sinéad coughed. 'He's not at home, actually.'
She wrinkled her nose and raised an eyebrow.
'He's staying with friends. But I've got a number
for him. It's a mobile I think.' She jotted a
number on a slip of paper and handed it over to
Tess.

'You'd better ring him soon, before he goes
flying off.' She gave an embarrassed little laugh.
'Mr Murphy-Dunne doesn't hang about, does
he?'

As she pushed the baby back to Herbert Park,

it occurred to Tess that a long plane journey was the very last thing she'd expect a man with a bad back to undertake. As soon as she got to the flat she dialled the number Sinéad had given her. But that line too was on a machine. A disembodied female voice announced that *one of us* would return the call. As soon as possible.

She waited for an hour or so but he didn't ring back. By which time her curiosity about his elusivity was fully aroused and her unfocused feeling of foreboding was gathering strength.

She'd completely forgotten Hugo's dinner party until he sent his housekeeper, Mary Mackie, to fetch her. By the time it was over she had one or two other little things to occupy her mind. And one of them was confirmation that Hugo was not being at all straight with her. Her reaction to that, for the following short while, was to keep her anxieties about Holy Retreat and everything else firmly to herself.

21

Herbert Park, Dublin

Dear Marcus,
The party's over. I stayed until eleven. I don't know
how I managed to get through it, but somehow I did. It
wasn't a roaring success. I just sat there drinking wine
until I was practically comatose.

Hugo had invited some actor friends so there was no
need to do any talking. One of them was very indiscreet
and let slip what Hugo had been trying to hide from
me. To be fair, the actor, Brian he was called, didn't
realize I was related to Susan when he started to regale
us with her latest. Hugo tried to shut him up. I just
froze.

It seems Mother was having an affair with Terence
Murphy-Dunne, the sod, at the time of your accident.
He must find the Callaway women irresistible or
perhaps we're just easy lays. I feel like throwing up.
Now I know why she didn't come when Claire was
born. Hugo got me in a huddle and tried to make out it
was because she was trying to protect me. That the
publicity was pretty rough. That they would have gone
to town on me and Claire and you. Not hard to imagine
the headlines, is it? Though I'd hardly describe M-D as
a toy-boy. The whole mess disgusts me. I feel sick at the
thought of it. I'm grateful to her and mad at her at the
same time. I think I preferred it when she brazened it
out. But oh God, I wish she'd pack it in.

Well, there you are, I feel like shit. Just when I
thought I was getting my act together. But at least it
explains why Mother is looking so rough and why

Hugo didn't want me to see M-D. But the hell with all that. I'm going to have to, I think. Something about the nuns' deal is awry though I'm not at all sure what. Not yet at any rate.

I'm writing this because I want to clarify things in my mind. At times I wonder if I'm not on a sort of witch-hunt by way of keeping my brain in working order. That or peevishness. Or, more likely, as a diversion from thoughts of you. You and me to be exact. And sex, if I'm honest. I even have some sympathy with Susan's desperation, since I'm constantly in the same state myself. Impotence is appalling but celibacy is worse. I could scream. I find myself in the one situation where nothing I can do will make the slightest difference. Nothing eases the constant, gnawing pain of loss which sits on my stomach like a badly digested meal. Something awful, like heavy, gooey, cheese fondue. Maybe it will turn out that there is nothing to worry about, that I am simply shifting my anger and frustration onto a mirage of my own devising. A conspiracy theory built out of nothing. Either that or I'm going loopy. I don't know which would be worse.

I drew a temporary blank on the contract. Sinéad has promised to find it for me but somehow in my bones I'm pretty sure it won't be of much help. If Terence was up to something he would hardly leave incriminating evidence around, would he? I don't believe he is either stupid or crooked – except in personal matters, of course. Nor Hugo either for that matter. I have a sort of hunch that something other than Mother's little adventure is going on between them. But what? Whatever it is, I wish Hugo would stop wrapping me in cotton wool.

As a matter of fact, Terence has done rather well by the nuns. Actually it's their neighbours, Glenadams School, I'm iffy about. And to be perfectly honest I'm a little dubious about the Bursar at Holy Retreat as well. But again, for no reason other than an unstated but *undeniable personal antipathy. Hormonal, I hear you snort. You're probably right. That child is making mincemeat of me.*

Now it is well past midnight and I'm waiting for Claire to wake up for her feast. I've decided I will follow my lines of disquiet as far as I can before I mention a word of this to anyone. Except you, of course. It's all so nebulous; it may mean absolutely nothing. I don't want to be branded hysterical at this stage of my life. It would be dreadful to be thought menopausal just when I've, at last, made it to mother-hood.

Aretino haunts me. I need some brains to pick. And the most desirable would be those of an antiquarian bookseller called Jeddie Stebton, whom I dearly want to get hold of, but so far she is proving hideously elusive. Her family is somehow connected with the convent, though precisely how I don't know. For whatever reason I can't get that woman out of my mind – or the feeling that something about the Stebton family connection deeply upsets the Mother Guardian. I shall have to closet her in her parlour and tease it out of her.

I've also become obsessed with railways. The Dublin to Bray railway line to be exact. It runs along the coast until it gets within a half mile or so of the convent. I believe part, or all of it, was built in the mid-nineteenth century, so I just wonder when the land was bought up. It probably has no bearing whatsoever on the present case – a complete red herring. Still, I can't get rid of the notion that I am missing something or, more likely, several things. My hunch is that sometime in the years leading up to the opening of the railway line, there must have been a lot of discussion about routes. There would be now, so there must have been then. Land would have been appropriated or bought. If you follow my line of thinking, a clever investor, who got it right, and got it early, could have pre-empted the railway.

On the other hand, there have been cliff falls along

the bay in the past and recently there has been considerable underpinning along Killiney beach, quite near the convent. Therefore the reasons for avoiding that patch are obvious. Does that sound like another dead end? Or is it, as I suspect, leading to Glenadams?

When I started this job it seemed a lifeline thrown to me by a kind and loving friend. The only thing I was dreading was the actual exhumation. I still do of course, but almost from the beginning I have felt a strong sense of foreboding about the business and no matter what I do, it doesn't leave me. There are strange currents rumbling away under the surface. If Hugo or the nuns share that feeling they do not admit it. I am almost sure that Hugo suspects Murphy-Dunne is up to something – specifically to do with the Holy Retreat deal – but has no corroborating evidence. And neither have I. The obvious thing would be that he is rooking the nuns, yet they are his firm champions. The first day I met her, Mother Catherine practically said he was a gift from God. Higher praise than which . . .

The strangest thing about all this is that the saint himself has not once contacted the poor sap (me) who is doing his work for him. No calls, no notes, no – how are you getting on, Tess? All right, now we know why. But no sign of the contract? There, you have it. That is what's really worrying me.

Tomorrow I shall take our cherubic daughter to walk along Killiney beach and perhaps a snoop around Glenadams. I am developing huge muscles in my upper arms from lifting her, small as she is, but I find her invaluable as a sounding board. Sometimes she is responsive. From which you will know that I am becoming more maternal than I ever would have expected. I find myself both shy and delighted to admit it. And greatly relieved. But it's probably only the hormones.

Love, Tessie.

Land value soars from two to nineteen million after RE-ZONE U-TURN. *County Councillors last night confirmed re-zonings covering 250 acres in Co Dublin.*

Irish Newsheet *report*

22

Sometimes, it appears, the unconscious solves problems more efficiently than an overworked and cluttered brain. Just as Tess thought the baby was at last settled for the night, she got herself well and truly steamed up again. It was well after two and Tess was utterly exhausted by the time she crawled into bed. Which put an effective stopper on any further attempt of making sense of her nagging disquiet. She still could not tell where it came from, nor for whose welfare she was more anxious. The nuns? Herself? *Claire?* As she closed her eyes she wondered if she might not be making enough allowance for the *bouleversement* that had taken place in her thinking since Marcus's death. The unexpected anguish of grief paralysed her. The world no longer seemed either as organized, as safe, or as under control, as once it had been.

She dreamt of trains. She was riding the DART along the coast watching the sunlight on the sea and counting off the familiar stations. Sandymount, Booterstown, Monkstown, Dun Laoghaire, Dalkey, Killiney. Suddenly she was in a long dark tunnel and the sea was gone. Then the train broke open like a great pod and released her. She was running along the tracks, leaping from sleeper to sleeper. Behind her she could hear the train's siren. It was getting closer, closer. Someone grabbed her hand and dragged her out of the way and, as the train swept past, she found herself following a line of black-clad women walking by the shore. They were carrying baskets on their heads.

Tess surfaced groggily. Her heart was pounding and the T-shirt she was wearing was soaked. *The priest*. Something he said had sent a tingle down her spine. The land. He'd asked what they'd got for the land. But that was in order, wasn't it? Murphy-Dunne had made an excellent deal for a narrow strip of five and half acres. Specially since it would have no value to any other purchaser but Glenadams. He'd managed to persuade the school trustees that the nuns should be compensated for the inconvenience of having to move the cemetery. It was strictly speaking an agricultural plot and being sold as such. There was no intention or permission to develop or re-zone the land for building purposes other than making a new entrance to the school. *As far as she knew*. Nevertheless Murphy-Dunne had craftily persuaded the school to pay over the odds and also to pay for moving the cemetery and rebuilding the boundary wall. Which was going to be an expensive exercise. A sum had been lodged in the bank and an account had been set up for the purpose.

Then why did the whole thing feel wrong all of a sudden? The deal had been thrashed out before she took over. Contracts had been exchanged. Hugo had been quite specific about her responsibilities. Her only job was to devise a plan of procedure, draw up the workmen's contracts and nursemaid the nuns through the red-tape involved in moving the graveyard. Nothing more, nothing less. Deep down, she'd acknowledged from day one that Hugo had got her involved simply as a means of keeping her occupied at a difficult time. Out of the kindness of his heart? Or was there another motive?

And then it crashed in on her. Hell, she thought, oh bloody hell. How could she be so damn stupid? The whole of Dublin was like a building site. Housing estates going up all over the place. The Euro-boom was on good and proper. Another single word hung in the air: *re-zoning*. A subject endlessly discussed in the newspapers. The value of land could increase almost exponentially if it was first sold as agricultural land or for restricted development, and was then *re-zoned* for denser use. A few hundred extra houses could make the difference of *millions*. But surely that couldn't apply here? It was, after all, only a small strip of rocky land wedged between an enclosed convent and a well-established school. *A rock and a hard place* – to put it mildly.

Tess got out of bed, dressed quickly, fed the baby, bundled her into the car and drove out to Glenadams School. There was a touch of frost in the air but even if it was cold it was, for the time being at least, sunny. Though she knew the entrance was on the old Bray Road close to Shanganagh, she still had difficulty finding it. She had driven past before she realized she'd missed it and then had to continue almost a mile along the busy road before there was a sufficient break in the traffic to make a U-turn. The reason for the school's proposed new entrance was so obvious that Tess felt a curious sense of relief.

The great, semi-circular gates of the school were obligingly open. A discreet brass plate on either gatepost simply read *Glenadams*. Otherwise there was nothing to show that she was entering the grounds of a large, expensive, boarding school. It could just as easily have been a private residence. Tess was surprised that it didn't have a more imposing name-board, then surmised that its discretion was probably in deference to the safety of its wealthy pupils. But as she drove through, she noticed that, indeed, a signboard had been taken down – presumably for re-painting, since its newly painted frame was standing just inside the gates with a ladder beside it.

The driveway was long and extremely well maintained though the grassy edges had not been cut for some time. The wooded parkland on either side of the drive was enclosed by a low, horizontal-barred fence which was painted dark blue. Surprisingly, there wasn't a soul about as Tess rolled up to the monstrous Victorian castellated pile which, with several more modest detached cubes on either side of it, comprised the school buildings.

Tess stepped hesitantly out of the car and was nearly swept off her feet by a gust of wind. The combination of that and the glare of sunlight made her squint. She didn't particularly want to go into the school. Her intention was to nose around the boundary between Glenadams and

Holy Retreat and to do so as discreetly as she could. She was trying to think of what approach to take with the school secretary when she noticed a short, dapper figure coming out the glass doorway. She almost burst out laughing. He was something of a sight, dressed for country pursuits circa 1910: green Norfolk jacket, plus-fours, over-sized tweed cap pulled low on his forehead. Only the dark, gold-rimmed sunglasses spoiled the effect. He had a walking stick in one hand and a gambolling spaniel at his heels. The very picture of a gent. Well, caricature, as it turned out. Because as *he* came closer she saw that it was a woman. Tess was so embarrassed that she could hardly look at her.

The woman walked straight up to her. 'How did you get in?' she asked sternly. She sounded annoyed and didn't identify herself.

'The gates were open,' Tess started.

'Damn workmen.' The mirrored sunglasses reflected blindingly in the sunlight as she asked Tess ungraciously if she had phoned for an appointment. When she admitted that she had not, the woman said in the same no-nonsense tone: 'The school is closed for half-term.'

'Oh, really? I didn't realize. How stupid of me.' Tess smiled vacantly at a point somewhere above the woman's head. She was uncomfortably aware of her height and the fact that she still hadn't taken her jacket to the cleaners. 'I'm terribly sorry but I've come such a long way. Would you mind if I look around the grounds? I can come back and talk to the headmaster in a few days.'

'He's away. Ring the school secretary next week for an appointment.' The woman replied so readily that Tess assumed she was herself the secretary determined to avoid being badgered on her time off. She didn't blame her.

'You have a boy you want to send here?' she asked Tess suspiciously. Perhaps she didn't look old enough to be a Glenadams parent? Even a prospective one? She certainly didn't look smart enough. She should have worn well-cut tweeds which, if the woman's outfit was anything to go by, were *de rigueur*.

'I'm thinking of it. My husband ... son ... We're thinking ...' Tess waffled blandly. 'I just wanted to have a chat.'

'You're not press, are you?'

'Press? No, certainly not.' Tess underlined her point by making a great play of checking that the baby was secure in her car seat. It seemed a rather peculiar question to ask until Tess remembered about the accident at the school gates. She smiled vaguely. 'Never mind, I'll come back some other day.'

'That would be best. But if you want to have a walk around, by all means do so. Avoid the school building though, we have security dogs during the break. They make a hell of a racket.' She smiled at Tess, called her small spaniel to heel and headed off down the drive. Tess noticed her looking back once or twice and didn't move until she was out of sight.

There was a paved pathway leading off to the left, just about wide enough to take the car. It appeared to be heading in the general direction of the boundary. Tess drove along it until it abruptly ended near a great outcrop of rock. Claire was fast asleep. She checked that there was no one about, opened all the windows a fraction and locked the doors. She didn't like the sound of guard dogs and had no wish to be ambushed by one of them with the child in her arms. Giving herself ten minutes maximum, she set off at a brisk pace and eventually came in sight of the sea.

She scrambled up one of the rocks which was more like a miniature mountain. The view was breath-taking. Fleecy white clouds were galloping across the deep blue sky, making ever-changing patches of light on the rolling waters. Off in the distance, to her left, she could see the ruin on Dalkey Island and a couple of little fishing boats running through the Sound. To her right, purple-blue Bray Head rose majestically from the sea, putting a spectacular full-stop to the bay. Behind it, the peak of the Sugar-loaf was wreathed in cloud – a Celtic Fujiyama. She turned away from the sea and turned in the direction of the convent, and found she was looking directly down onto the little graveyard. Since she had not yet been admitted to it by the nuns, it gave her quite a turn.

She slowly rotated through three hundred and sixty degrees and followed the boundaries of both properties as far as her eye could see. Glenadams appeared to be laid out as a parallelogram with its shortest side along the cliff – or so it seemed from her vantage point. She would have to check against an ordnance survey map. She rotated slowly again then stopped when she was facing due east, to the sea. There appeared to be a narrow strip of fallow or wasteland which ran to the cliff edge and straddled the boundaries of both properties. 'Oh, bloody, bloody hell,' she whispered as with her eyes she followed the nuns' boundary wall from the cliff edge back to the road. 'Oh, hell.'

As near as she could estimate, the waste ground was about a hundred feet wide, but she could not judge its length. While the Glenadams section was perfectly visible, it was harder to see the convent end because it lay beyond their high fence. She noticed that a low, make-shift fence of wooden stakes ran between the school and the waste-ground and that here and there it had collapsed.

Tess climbed thoughtfully down from her perch and walked quickly back to the car. As she came in sight of the school she saw there was a Land Rover parked by the steps and beside it a huge German Shepherd. A tall man was standing behind the dog, holding its short leash. When he saw her he bent down and fumbled with the dog-collar. Tess's heart flew into her mouth as she sprinted towards the car. She just managed to get inside as the dog came bounding up. She put her foot on the accelerator and, gears screaming, reversed back up the narrow path. She almost turned the car over as she spun around and roared off down the driveway. She didn't stop shaking until she got home. All the way, those terrible moments played over and over in her head, excluding every other thought. The tall security guard at the school. The alert dog. The slow, deliberate unleashing of the snarling animal.

It could have savaged her and mauled Claire to death, she thought fearfully. But as soon as she said it she knew that had the dog been released on time, nothing would have saved her. The security guard had held him back. The nasty, mean-minded, cruel bastard had been toying with her. He had judged the distance with sadistic precision. The dog was not sent to attack her. The dog was a warning not to go near the school. The school secretary had warned her earlier, she simply hadn't taken the warning seriously enough. But for all that, it seemed a rather extreme method of guarding an empty school. She concluded that they must have an awful lot of expensive equipment. It didn't, at that point, cross her mind that the dog-man had not been wearing the usual overalls of a security guard. Indeed he hadn't been wearing any sort of uniform at all but had been dressed casually in a sports jacket and grey slacks. But Tess didn't remember that until much, much later, when she saw Mrs Plus-fours for the second time.

By the time she got home her fright had turned to fury which subsided slightly when she found a card from Owen Rogerson to say that his plans had changed and he would be in Dublin on business the following Tuesday and, if she was free to have dinner, he would stay overnight at the Hibernian Hotel where she could contact him any time after four on the same afternoon.

She was just getting into the lift when Hugo popped his head round his sitting-room door. 'Sinéad rang to say that she was still trying to track the stuff down and would ring as soon as it turned up. That make any sense to you, Tess?' Tess ignored his raised eyebrow. She thanked him politely, if distantly, for dinner and said she had to get Claire fed. Fortunately, the baby colluded by opening her little mouth and letting out one of her blood-curdling yells. As the door of the lift closed on them Tess beamed down at her daughter who miraculously turned off the sound effects and beamed right back.

Until about fifty years ago, the category Erotica (also known variously as curious, clandestine, secret, rare, etc., etc.) in booksellers' catalogues included many diverse subjects such as: French literature, witchcraft, demonology, hauntings, alchemy, re-enlivening. Also books on medical subjects, costume, children's books and Technological Invention, especially the search for Perpetual Motion.

23

Early on Saturday morning a large padded envelope arrived in the first post, which for the time being effectively put all other thoughts out of Tess's head. She sat down at the kitchen table and examined the writing on the outside. It was printed in large well-formed letters. There was nothing to indicate who had written it and she didn't recognize the hand, which was surprising because only a small handful of people knew where she was staying. She examined the postmark minutely and saw that it had been posted in Bray. She assumed, therefore, that it was from Holy Retreat. She ripped it open and tipped the contents out on the table.

It was a motley collection of bits and pieces which included a small sheaf of single-sided, closely typed A4 sheets and what looked like a section torn from a small diary. There was a second wodge of handwritten notes though these were on much older, more tattered sheets of foolscap. Also, a white envelope containing scraps of both typed and handwritten notes stapled together and a couple of drawings, about eight inches by twelve, one of which appeared to be a photocopy but the second was a signed original with a piece torn off the corner. She picked this last up and held it close to the light as she tried to decipher the neat italic hand on the bottom right-hand corner. *Adelaide fecit*, she read *June the twe* . . . The rest had been torn off.

Tess laid the drawing carefully on the table. She felt as though she was looking at herself in slow motion. Her eyes swept over the scattered pages but for a moment she made no attempt to read any of them. They could wait for a moment. Who had the envelope come from? Mother Catherine? Sister Joseph? Or whoever had packed the basket of goodies the previous Wednesday. Tess fetched the Aretino waste sheet and laid it beside the latest instalment. The writing in the diary was close though not exactly similar. She stared into the middle distance, trying to do what she did best: make order out of chaos. She could not proceed with trying to interpret whatever message was contained in the papers until she at least attempted to work out why they'd been sent to her and from whom.

Sister Joseph never actually said she packed the basket, did she? She had muttered something about wine. 'I should have put in a bottle of elder-flower wine.' Not: 'Yes, I packed it.' It could have been anyone. Tess sighed, drew the papers to her and began to read. She did not attempt to make sense of them, or put order on them. She read them with an open mind, sequentially, as she might, in preparing for a trial, examine written evidence from a variety of witnesses. The papers turned out to be just as varied and just as baffling. But, she kept reminding herself, someone had given them to her for a purpose. It was up to her to find it.

* * *

The first paper: pages from an anonymous diary

I left it too late. How could I not have foreseen that he would take what he wanted? So cool and she so compliant. They make a singular pair. Like smiling vultures. I tried to seduce with desiderata. But he had already smelt the prey. He said he needed the library to write his sermons. So innocent, but I could see at once that he knew what it contained. And its value. Lal always said those books brought bad luck. She was not entirely right: they have been my salvation, my means of escape, my livelihood. But I should have moved the remainder long since. I should have realized. Still, there's little left. He will get a nasty surprise and I shall make sure I am not there when he does. Pity, we have so much in common.

I shall miss the house. Sometimes at night I wander through looking for Lal. I know every room, every creak in the floorboards, each twist and turn of the passageways. I know the feel of the silky ridges of the ancient elm against my bare feet. It is all falling apart. The window sashes are rotten and at night rattle so much I fear the undulating glass will burst out of its lead restraints. There is a faint and lingering smell of mould, or perhaps mice. Is it dust or are malignant microbes beavering away at the curtains and carpets? Sometimes I see the tiny flash of silverfish in the dusty beams of moonlight and I think she has come back. But when I turn she is gone.

The gutters need attention: the rain forms rivulets, dissolving the porous stone. When I touch an outside wall I can feel the damp ooze through my chilly fingers and I know the stone is turning to wet sand; returning to the earth. After five, six hundred years – who knows how old it is? – the house is weary of standing upright. It longs to lie down, to sink into itself, close its eyes and rest. It has seen too much.

The old monks are back. Sometimes, in my perambulations, I feel the swish of the rough cloth of their habits, hear the slapping of their cold bare feet on the stairs, smell their unwashed human, decayed smell. It reminds me of small, damp, furry animals. Sometimes at night I hear them chant their mournful dirge. *Dies irae, dies illa*. They have come to claim what is rightly theirs. They pervade every space, every nook and cranny. I feel their restless spirits flutter in the night.

Where are those ghosts of later generations? Except for Lal, the monks have seen them off. They've come back to claim their stolen, deconsecrated monastery, their secret oratory. Sometimes while I wander I disturb their penitential prayers.

There is no sound of laughter. This house has missed the sounds of childhood, the lightness happy children give. Too many sad and cruel people have lived in this house, too many babies died. In all those long centuries, more deaths than lives, as if those tiny souls turned in despair from this sacrilegious place. It has not prospered. Too many unhappy people locked in battle over sticks and stones. For what else is property? It is over a hundred years since the last real family lived here and even that was an illusion for that family brought about the destruction that is almost complete. One brave soul, even one not so brave, cannot put back time nor arrest decay.

* * *

The second paper: modern, typewritten, entitled 'A short history of Elderson Court'
Elderson Court was, by the grandiose standards of the time, of modest size. Completed in 1746, it was one of the few great houses of the period, built on the south coast of Dublin Bay. The larger and more important exemplars of that golden age were on the north side of the city which was, by the standards of the time, by far the more fashionable. Perhaps the seaside was not then as highly regarded as it later became. Powerscourt apart, which was fifteen years older and altogether more important, was built a few miles south but a good deal further inland. Mountains, it seems, provided both a more desirable ambience and better views than the cold sea. Which might explain why the reception and drawing rooms on the *piano nobile* of Elderson Court looked inland towards Wicklow and the Sugar-loaf. Of the other day rooms, only the library and the schoolroom had a view of glorious Killiney Bay. The best views of all, of both the sea and the mountains, were at the very top of the house, from the poky little bedrooms under the roof. But for the hundred odd years that the house was in the hands of the Elderson family, only the servants benefited from the beauty of the landscape.

The house was a minor jewel which rose to three stories from a basement beneath. It was built of mellow, rose-coloured brick with three string-courses of Dalkey granite and a granite frieze below the eaves. A flight of seven steps led up to the entrance, which was central, with two windows at either side, five matching windows above and five half-size on the top floor.

A narrow, formal rose garden was planted in front of the house with two walled gardens, some distance away, on either side: one for vegetables, the other an orchard. Beyond those stretched the parkland, with rolling lawns, a miniature woodland and several majestic stands of copper beech. A little brook flowed along its northern boundary into the sea and near its bank a narrow postern gate on the cliff-top led, down a steep flight of steps, to the stony beach below. There was space to ride ponies and a cinder-track for bouncing along in a little pony-trap. It should have been an idyllic playground for generations of children, yet the Elderson family was not noted for happy off-spring. This was especially true in the case of the children of Sophia (née Elderson) and Ryland William Stebton, the last family to occupy Elderson Court.

* * *

The third paper: a scrap, handwritten
They were a strange lot, by all accounts. Strong women with little education, weak men with too much. A muddle of generations with a repetition of names difficult to unravel. It might also have been useful? It was difficult to link one generation to the other.

* * *

The fourth paper: Two half-written pages, both with heavy pencil marks through them entitled 'Nuns: An endangered species?'

1. It is ironic and perhaps a little sad that more often than not contemporary accounts of the cloistered life should be offered to the reading public by ex-nuns. Those . . .

2. Many small informal groups of nuns, living together in slum areas or living with the most deprived and the most disadvantaged sections of contemporary society, have come full circle to the inspiration of their original founders. With their autonomy eroded . . .

* * *

The fifth paper: 'Carne Vale: Adelaide Elderson Stebton'. An attempt at an historical novel?

The shutters on the tall sash window were half-closed. A small brass oil lamp on the desk gave off the only light. A child stood quietly in the corridor, peering at her dim image in the obscure glass. She was a solemn, slim child of seven or eight, tall for her age, raven-haired and dark-eyed. She wore a long blue pinafore with matching ribbons in her hair and over the dress, a close-fitting grey jacket. Black kid-skin boots, white woollen stockings. The lace edging of her frilly white pantaloons peeped from beneath her dress. She walked slowly forward on tippy-toe, nearer and nearer her reflection which seemed to mesmerize her. She bobbed and curtsied grace-fully, turning this way and that without making a sound, as if she was keeping time to some rhythm in her head. When she got about halfway along the corridor she stopped and waited, trembling with excitement . . . She had no idea how it worked, she could not make it out, but somehow, when she reached this point, just beside the little painted rose, when she counted to eight, the magic would begin.

'Come in, come in, little one,' a voice called softly. The angle of the door gave him an excellent view, as was intended, of the mirror. He had been watching her antics with indulgence and amusement from the moment she had crept through the outer door.

The child turned around but she could not see her darling Pappy. Nor could she work out how or why he always knew when she was there. She peered at the dark mirror but it only filled with her own image. She edged closer to the library door.

'I'm waiting. I can see you,' he sang out and gave a little chuckle.

'Oh, Pappy! How do you know it is me? How can you tell?' She stamped her foot in frustration. Her voice was high-pitched and imperious.

'Oh, I can't tell you that, little one. That is a big important secret.'

'Oh, Pappy, you are such a tease!'

He laughed again, amused by the puzzled little image in the glass. Her intense face was full of wonder at his 'clever, clever magic'. He sighed. Soon enough she would work out how easily it was done. He watched her sidle slowly around the doorpost, one foot scratching at the back of her other leg. As soon as she saw him she put her finger to her lips.

'I promise to be very, very quiet,' she whispered.

He closed his book, but kept his place with one finger while he smiled at her over his half-moon spectacles. Neither spoke until, with supreme effort, the little girl entered the room and pushed the heavy door closed. Then she danced across to his desk, where she stood with her chin resting on its surface.

'I may stay with you, Pappy?'

'Tell me first where Mama is?' he asked.

'She is resting. She sent me away. She said she is not well, that I make her tired with my chatter.'

A flash of impatience crossed his face but he said nothing for a moment.

'Pappy? You are not listening.'

'Oh, I am, poppet.' He put his finger under her chin and looked into her dark eyes. 'And do you?'

'Chatter? No, Pappy, I just talk. Only magpies chatter. You told me so yourself. And blackbirds and starlings and . . .' She stopped as he held his hand up. 'Perhaps Mama has another headache?' she asked anxiously.

'Perhaps. Now quick, tell where is your little brother? And your sister?'

'Nurse has taken them for a walk. They're going to collect stones from the beach. When they come back I shall help William build a fort for his soldiers. Am I not a kind sister?'

'Good girl. But why did you not go with them?' He was saddened by her intensity. She was too solitary for an eight year old. Even her more gregarious twin sister could seldom penetrate her private world. They got on well, though they were as unlike as chalk and cheese. Augusta was full of high spirits and mischief, Adelaide, serious and over-responsible. A substitute mother for their baby brother.

'Oh, Pappy! You know you promised I could come and read with you. You said. You promised, yesterday. Do you not remember? Nurse did. She told me to cut along.' She unconsciously mimicked Nanny's thick brogue. He suppressed a laugh. There was little enough to laugh at, after all. The child looked up at him, her eyes round as saucers and welling with tears as the promised

260

treat seemed about to fade away. 'Oh, Pappy, do you not remember your promise?'

He laughed softly and held up his hand. 'Of course, little one, but you need to run and play also. You must be good to little William. You may stay but after a little while you must run away and find Nurse. Promise?'

'Upon my honour, Pappy,' she replied solemnly.

'So, you like to be here with me?'

'Oh yes, Pappy. Oh yes.' She looked up at him with shining eyes. 'I wish you would be here always. I hate it when you go away on your travels. I wish you would never go away at all. Or that I might go with you,' she added daringly. He brushed her hair lightly with his hand, and shook his head. His face was lined with regret. 'Next time, Pappy, may I come with you?' she persisted. 'I don't like it when you go away.'

He stretched past her, opened the centre drawer of the desk and took out a child's sketchbook and a box of pastel chalks. 'You may stay. But only if you're quiet as a little mouse,' he whispered. 'We must not disturb Mama. But listen, I have a very, very important task for you.'

'I may draw, Pappy? In my book, now?' She smiled at him eagerly. 'Oh, I shall be very quiet. I promise, Pappy.'

He stretched out his hand, led her to his side of the desk and settled her into his chair.

'I want you to make a beautiful picture, little one.' He threw out his arms to encompass the room. He crossed the room and opened one of the upper bookcases. He smiled back at her. 'With all my books. Will you do that for me? Your very best effort,' he instructed seriously. 'Make a beautiful picture for your Papa to keep with him always. Every detail, mind!'

The little girl, who did not understand the meaning of his words, glowed with self-importance and pleasure. 'Shall I put my name on top?' she asked.

'And the date. Do you know what year it is?'

'Of course I do, Pappy. It is 1826 and it is the twelfth day of June.' She looked at him triumphantly.

'Good girl. Write it all down, Addie, and don't forget to sign your name.'

Little Adelaide Elderson Stebton bent over her book, her tiny pink tongue stuck out in concentration, and began to draw.

*   *   *

Tess sifted through the papers on the table until she found the drawing. She studied it intently. After a long time she tilted her chair back and rocking gently to and fro stared blindly into space, thinking through, slowly and carefully, the implications of the drawing, what she'd read and the snippets of information which had been gathering like fluff in her brain. Who had given her the envelope wasn't important at this stage, but something the postman said pricked urgently at her memory. She went back over their conversation as nearly as she could remember it. After a while she picked up the phone and rang Grace Hartfeld.

It rang and rang, ten, twelve times with no answer until just as Tess was about to ring off Grace answered. She sounded breathless and cross and before Tess could get a word in edgeways said, 'I'm sorry we're not open yet. Ring again later.'

'Grace? Please don't hang up. It's Tess Callaway again.'

'Oh, Tess, sorry to have been so rude, I was trying to do some accounts. How are things going?' She sounded as if she was jumping up and down with impatience.

'I need your help, Grace. This is tricky. Probably unethical as well. It's about Jeddie Hillyard.' There was a short pause before Grace responded resignedly.

'Ye-es?'

'Grace, this is the awkward bit. Remember when I was in the shop? As I was leaving you mentioned some packages had come for her.'

'Blasted things! They're still under my feet. I'm going to have to store them at home, I keep tripping over them.'

'May I describe them?' Tess asked quietly and quickly added, 'About fifteen inches square, lid about two inches deep, tied with strong white twine. Posted in Ireland.'

'How did you know that?' Grace sounded as though her jaw had dropped.

'I noticed the stamps when I was in your office. Grace? I know where they came from,' Tess said slowly. 'I also think I know what's in them. How many are there?'

'Five, alto—' Grace started but was quickly interrupted by Tess.

'Could I persuade you to open one?' This was greeted by a long silence.

'I couldn't do that, I'm sorry. Not unless there was very good reason. Is there good reason?'

'Yes, I'm very much afraid there may be . . .'

'Did someone tell me you're a lawyer?' Grace asked guardedly.

'Yes, I'm a solicitor.'

'Then I can only assume we're talking criminal?'

'At least. But I can't be sure until I know what's in those boxes. Grace? You haven't seen her, have you? No? Well, I don't want to be alarmist but you may be holding stolen goods.' This was pure conjecture and Tess knew it. They might as easily be bartered goods. Tess closed her eyes and prayed that she wasn't maligning an innocent woman simply to protect her own clients.

'Why do you say that, Tess?' Grace Hartfield's voice was more distant, colder.

'I believe the packages contain extremely rare and valuable books which were smuggled out of a convent in Dublin.'

'A convent?' Grace chuckled. 'I think you must be barking up the wrong tree, my dear. A convent wouldn't be Jeddie's pitch at all,' she said flatly. 'A monastery, perhaps. Jeddie is very definitely a man's woman. She may not look it but she's quite the *femme fatale*. I don't know what she's got but there's always some man hovering about. Believe me a convent is the last place she'd be likely to fetch up.' Let's hope you're right, Tess thought as Grace continued. 'If there's some monkey business going on then *cherchez l'homme* is what I say. Now, do you mind telling me what this is about?'

'The boxes are normally used – you're not going to like this, specially if you're a Catholic – the boxes are normally used to hold communion breads.'

Grace stifled a laugh. 'And the books, since Jeddie is interested in them, are erotica? How am I doing?'

'Spot on.'

'Bit far-fetched, isn't it?' Grace asked dryly.

'Not if you consider that one of Jeddie's ancestors was the collector. She may well consider the books her property.'

'So what were they doing in a convent?'

'I wish I knew. I also wish I knew who, if anyone, knew they were there. It's easy to see why she was shifting them but why so surreptitiously?'

'No mystery about that.' Grace chortled. 'Typical Jeddie. She likes a little frisson of excitement but with her speciality she has to be discreet. I sometimes think she stokes up little mysteries just to keep herself interested. She should have been on the stage.'

There seemed no useful reply to that so Tess said nothing. Since it was obvious that Grace would not breach her friend's trust, she decided there was no point in prolonging the situation.

'Don't go for a minute,' Grace said when Tess thanked her, intending to put the phone down. 'There are three other similar boxes on Jeddie's shelf. Stuff she's been cataloguing over the past few months. As far as I know they were delivered sometime last summer. While she was still on holiday . . .'

'Where?' Tess interjected quickly.

'Where was she on holiday? Oh, North Wales I think. Somewhere around Bangor. She's been going there rather a lot in the past few years. She said she'd found a nice little retreat.'

It was Tess's turn to laugh. 'Did she so? Oh, my

goodness, Grace. And do you know what the convent in Dublin is called? *Holy Retreat*. I would guess your pal only lingered in North Wales long enough to write a few postcards before crossing to Dun Laoghaire.'

A moment's silence was followed by a minor explosion. 'Oh hell, I'm looking at one of the postcards she sent last summer. It's pinned to the noticeboard in front of me. Holyhead, as ever was. Right,' she said decisively, 'hold on. I'll have a look in one of the open ones.' She put the phone on the desk where it continued to pick up the sounds in the tiny office. For the next few minutes patches of silence were interrupted by spluttered expletives and when at last Grace picked up the phone again her voice was awestruck.

'I don't normally blaspheme,' she said, 'but I can think of a few ripe ones now. Those boxes have been sitting innocently on that shelf for the best part of six months. I've only looked in one. Her catalogue notes are sitting on top. It's a frigging treasure trove and we're not insured for anything remotely like the value of that one sodding box.'

'Calm down, Grace. Tell me, are there name plates in the books?'

'Name plates? Bugger the name plates, listen to the authors! Some of these books are so rare that ... My head is swimming. Get a load of this: Boccacio, Aretino, Romano, Chorier, Casanova de Seingalt ... I think I'm going to have a heart attack.'

'The names mean nothing to me, Grace. What are they worth?'

'Worth?' she exploded. 'I'll just add up the sum

of the first of five, no, seven pages . . . There are eight entries on each.' She began to count slowly under her breath then she gave a long low whistle. 'How does forty thousand grab you?'

'Multiply that by seven . . . Christ, over two hundred thousand.'

'That's only one box. Now multiply that by three plus five, though I can't believe they're all of this quality but even half that and you're talking a million,' Grace said. 'With no outlay, it's clear profit.'

But all Tess could think of was that compared to certain land values around her native town a million was probably small potatoes. 'What are we going to do?' Grace asked.

'If you wouldn't mind storing them in a safe place? Away from the shop, I should think. Nobody except me, and now you, knows anything about them. Oh, and Jeddie of course. I should like to talk to her before she spirits them away.' Tess paused and thought for a moment. 'By the way, how could she sell them without flooding the market or without the Internal Revenue people getting whiff of it?'

'Not easy if your business is upfront like ours,' Grace said bitterly. 'I don't know quite how she works, but in her line it might be easier. Ah God, do I feel a fool. Now I see why Jeddie was so willing to work for peanuts. Bloody woman was using us as a convenience address. We gave her respectability. As to flooding the market, believe me, Jeddie was far too canny for that. Do you know what I think? I bet she's planning her retirement. Now that the mad old mother is tucked away she's going to vamoose.'

If she hasn't already done so, Tess thought sourly, visions of gently waving palm trees and golden beaches entering her mind. And the fine tall figure of a man.

'One last thing, Grace. The name plates. Could you check a couple of the books?' Would name plates be enough to establish ownership? Would the nuns want anything to do with them?

'I've three of them open in front of me. There are two small name plates on a couple and a third on the other which is Italian – Lupini mean anything? No? The other names are Ryland William Stebton – quite an elaborate coat of arms – and beneath that a much smaller one, a single line, no frills: Adelaide Elderson Stebton.'

'Oh, Jesus wept,' is all Tess could say.

If you let time slip, like a neglected rose
It withers on the stalk with languished head.
Beauty is nature's brag, and must be shown
In courts, at feasts, and high solemnities . . .

Comus, *John Milton*

24

'Next Tuesday? So soon? Are you nervous about it?' Owen asked as he peered at her over the menu. He had lost some weight and looked tanned and healthy. He had arrived, unannounced ten minutes before she was due to leave for the restaurant, claiming that Marcia would have his guts for garters if he didn't give a full report on her granddaughter's progress.

Tess considered the question carefully and didn't answer until she'd ordered dinner. They were in a rather smart restaurant off Grafton Street where the style was terrific and the food superb. She had dressed carefully in a new dark blue silk crêpe suit, specially bought for the occasion. It was a complete change from her current uniform of jeans and sweatshirt. She had accentuated the lean lines of the suit and her own height with an additional two inches of high heel, which made her match Owen's six feet. She looked stunning. The moment they strolled into the restaurant he realized that if he didn't move fast he would lose her for ever. Heads turned as she took her place at the table. She had allowed her newly cut short, shiny black hair to curl naturally and a liberal application of make-up had scattered unaccustomed roses on her normally pale face.

'Not as anxious as I thought I might be. I've got used to the idea, though what the reality will be is anyone's guess. I think we've got it well organized and in different circumstances I would be quite, well, I suppose excited is not the word. An exhumation on this scale is an extraordinary procedure and it doesn't happen very often. So I shall be interested to witness it.' She did not have to explain what she meant by different circumstances. As always when she and Owen met, Marcus was never far from their thoughts and as a result, interaction between them was constrained. As if to compensate they both tried a little too hard to seem at ease.

'How was Wexford?' she asked as the waiter arrived with a bottle of Pouilly-Fumé. Owen waited until their glasses were filled before he replied.

'I don't know yet, I changed my plans. I'm going down tomorrow morning. I had to cut it short this year. I wish you'd come,' he said ambiguously and smiled sheepishly. Tess bit back a sharp retort along the lines of you didn't invite me, which was both untrue and petty. Even assuming she would have contemplated leaving Claire overnight, Owen knew perfectly well that she was fairly lukewarm about opera.

'Some other time,' she said. 'When I'm more together. What will you see?' The cool, crisp wine acted as balm, soothing and relaxing them. Tess smiled. It was the first meal she'd had in a restaurant since the baby was born and because of that, as much as the ambience, it felt like an occasion – a treat.

'I usually do all three, one each night. A sort of cultural pig-out. I'll just see one this time, *Sarka*. They say it's splendid. I'd never even heard of it before. Won't understand a word either of course, since it's in Czech. Ever heard of Fibich?' He grinned. 'But that's not the point. I just like going. Wexford is wonderful, I love it all. The singers are young and good-looking, the audience *en fête* and everyone in the town sets out to give you a good time. The pubs pulsate into the small hours. So even at that level it's terrific.' He stretched across the table and took her hand. 'Next year I hope you'll come. With me.'

Tess dropped her eyes and gave a deprecatory little snort. 'That would be nice. I'd love to, if you think . . .' She stopped herself going into a worried little diatribe about time permitting, or work, or babies or, or what? That she didn't know what she'd be doing next year, or where she would be living? Fortunately the arrival of their food saved her. A discreet helping of linguini with langoustine tails and sorrel for her; a warm scallop mousse for him. They ate in silence for a couple of appreciative minutes.

'You look much better, Tess. Can I say, less strained, without getting bopped on the head?'

Tess laughed. 'You can. You can say what you like when you feed me like this.'

'By the way, I've been doing a little sleuthing for you. I was down in Chipping Stebton last weekend and got myself invited to a party at Stebton Place.'

'Oh? How come? Was the bookseller sister there?' Tess sat up to attention. 'Did you meet the vicar? What's the sister like? What's the house like?'

Owen held up his hand which was adroitly filled with a wine list by the hovering waiter. They both laughed.

'Hold on, hold on. First things first. Let's get ourselves sorted. You're having pheasant, I'm having, what? Oh right, I'm having pheasant too. With Calvados and apple and onion confit – whatever that is. Julienas OK?'

'As long as you send me home by taxi with a knock-out drop for the child, fine.' She grinned. 'When did you get here?'

'Lunchtime.' He replied so evasively she couldn't resist a slight dig.

'The others gone ahead then?' she asked but he didn't answer. He just looked at her with a half-suppressed smile.

'Right then,' he said. 'Your questions, in order of asking. Miss Jane-Edwina is alleged to be abroad. Mother says that the word around the village is that she's taken the hump about her sister, the magisterial Felicity, marrying the widowed vicar, one Timothy Theophilus Stebton. It appears the only person she's contacted is her old pal Johnny Pittaway who has had a couple of postcards. He didn't say where from but Italy was mentioned as a possibility.' Owen sat back while their main course was presented, carved, flambéed, served, and tasted. He feigned a swoon of pleasure before he continued.

'The other ripe little titbit of gossip going around, well, whispered, is even more delicious than this exquisite pheasant: Jane-Edwina, the scamp, has been having a rather long-term relationship with the same cousin, the aforesaid Revd Tim. The real reason for her sudden bunk is that she was seriously put out when her sister carried him off. So what do you think of that?' He sat back and waited for her astonished reaction and Tess did her best to oblige him. But since her visit to the Acland Hospital in search of Felicity, she had already worked out the drift of things. It wasn't a surprise; nevertheless, she was pleased that at least one of her guesses had turned out right.

'She sounds like something of a goer, doesn't she? What's the sister like?'

'Medium height, very English counties type, horsey but handsome. Well dressed in what I call the Cirencester look – hacking jackets, pleated skirts, ubiquitous green wellies. You know the sort of thing I mean?'

'In a word: Jaeger?'

'Perhaps not quite that degree of dated elegance, but yes, more or less,' he replied seriously. Tess chuckled and leaned across at him.

'Tell me, Owen, how come you're such an expert in fashion all of a sudden? And, by the way, you're looking rather elegant yourself.' He was, though he'd reverted to his previous style of well-cut, dark formality which suited him better than his uncomfortable forays into country casuals.

'I'd better come clean – I'm quoting Mother. The village opinion is that it was a match made in heaven – no pun intended – she's the perfect vicar's lady. All are pleased. Except perhaps J-E. But the main thing is that no one is the least surprised at her flight. Now, do you want to hear about the house?'

'Yes please. Was the party there?'

'It was. Genteel glasses of sherry and Marks and Spencer party nibbles . . .'

'Marcia again?'

'The sharp-eyed Marcia as ever was. I'll tell you what, Tess, this business had shown me a quite unexpected side of Mother. Not just sharp-eyed, but surprisingly sharp-tongued. And all those years I thought it was Dad who was the wit.'

'Goes to show, doesn't it. Can't take anything for granted, can you?' Tess asked playfully but even as she spoke she realized she had stumbled. Owen's eyes caught and held hers and a surprised shock charged through her. More disconcertingly, her cheeks flushed. She made a great play of pushing her wine glass aside as if to indicate that it alone was responsible. But her thoughts were in turmoil.

'Nothing.' He picked up his glass but watched her carefully over the rim. Neither said anything while the waiter cleared their plates. The moment passed.

'We'll rest for a bit before we order dessert,' Owen instructed. 'That all right with you, Tess?'

'I'm not sure I want any. I think I'll just have coffee. Eventually. That was remarkably good, wasn't it?'

'First rate.' He spoke rather too jovially.

'You said you saw Stebton Place? Were you shown around?'

'I got the Revd Tim to give me the guided tour while my mother engaged the lady of the manor. It's stunningly beautiful but practically falling down, alas. It needs a vast injection of serious cash poured into it to make it properly habitable. I suppose in a way lack of funds has kept it from being messed about, so that there is an accretion rather than subtraction. None of the original features have been taken away. Vast medieval fireplaces, stone mullioned windows, even original undulating glass to catch whatever sunlight there is. Have you ever been to Haddon Hall in Derbyshire?' he interrupted himself, and when Tess nodded he continued. 'You know that wonderful gallery upstairs? Well, blow me down if there isn't a smaller version of it on the ground floor of Stebton Place. It hasn't got anything like the same aspect but in its own way, it is wonderful. Rather like a miniature Oxford college. But then, of course, it's much the same period as some of the older ones. It was apparently the chapter house of the original monastery. That's where we had the sherry though what we needed was mulled wine. Grrr.'

'Or hot whiskies?'

'Hot whiskies even better. There are two vast fireplaces, one at either end, but they can't light the fires very often because they made no impact at all. It was as cold as the fens. Absolutely perishing. You could see drips forming at the end of noses. There were about forty people there but the room could have taken two hundred. I don't think they use it very often.'

'Did you see any other rooms?'

'Oh yes, I got the whole VIP treatment,' he said

smugly and continued to describe the rest of the house. But it was when he began to describe the library that she really sat up and took notice. She had a very definite feeling of *déjà vu*.

'I don't know where the furnishings came from because they don't match anything else I saw, which for all its decayed grandeur is rather Spartan. You enter the library along a concealed corridor which has an ornately decorated barrel-vaulted ceiling. It is extraordinary. Revd Tim claims it was originally hidden behind a huge mirror. Now the archway is open though there is a floor to ceiling mirror at the far end. The silvering has faded so that the glass is very mottled. I think the Americans call it antique glass. Very disconcerting; you see yourself approaching through a glass darkly—'

'St Paul.'

'What about St Paul?'

'The quotation's from St Paul. *Through a glass darkly*. You hear it at weddings and funerals. The one that starts, "Now I am a man, etc., etc., etc., etc." I always thought the old misogynist had no business at weddings. I, for one, would never . . . Sorry. Go on, I interrupted you.' She muttered an apology and kicked herself for losing her grip. Owen didn't seem to notice, he was too well into his description of Stebton Place.

'The actual door of the library is set at an angle which, I soon discovered, gives anyone inside warning and indeed a full frontal of approaching intruders. It's a very elaborate set-up for what amounts to a private study, even if it is very grand. When I asked the vicar about it he said legend had it that the whole thing, corridor, doors and furnishings of the library were plundered from an Italian monastery. Which is not hard to believe. It's all very ornate and very splendid. Much better maintained than any other room in the house. It was in meticulous order.'

'Did he give you an exact date?'

'For what?'

'For the library,' she retorted impatiently. Owen stared at her for a moment. He rubbed his forefinger along his lower lip – an habitual gesture when he was racking his memory.

'Yes, I believe he did mention a date. Early eighteenth century? Let me think. Seventeen thirty?' he said hesitantly. 'I was surprised. I know the house is much earlier, but the library was clearly installed much later. At a guess, I'd have said around eighteen hundred.' Tess sat back. So the Revd Tim was in the dark, didn't know the real age of the library. His cousin wasn't into sharing then, was she?

'Almost right. Eighteen twenties,' Tess said softly and Owen's eyes almost popped out of his head.

'My goodness, how do you know that?'

'I found a contemporary description. At least I'm fairly sure it . . .' She leaned across the table earnestly. 'Could you describe the bookcases?' she asked quietly. Her hands were unaccountably clammy. She wiped them against her skirt.

'The room is lined with them. There must be ten, twelve? But they are all of a piece, as if the room was built around them rather than the reverse. Floor to ceiling, say about seven and a half, eight foot. Probably made of either mahogany or chestnut. Look European, Italian maybe. Beautiful patina. Each pair is divided by flat columns. Corinthian. Are they called pilasters? Anyway, the lower part has wood-panelled doors, the upper has a kind of metal mesh instead of glass. The doors are arched, by the way. That's about as much as I remember. Fantastic room.' He leaned back and grinned so expansively that Tess knew he was holding something back.

'What?' she obliged.

'Nothing really.' He examined the dregs of the bottle with some regret. 'Just that our reverend friend said it was Jane-Edwina's private domain and that she couldn't stand intruders.'

'That all?' she asked, studiously avoiding his eye.

'Not quite. He also said that tradition had it that there were secret bookshelves concealed somewhere in the room but that he had no idea where.'

'From which you gathered he'd been trying to find them?'

'That's right. In the same circumstances so would I – wouldn't you?' he asked. Tess nodded. 'I expect it's where Jane-Edwina keeps her stock,' he added. She grinned as he stuck his tongue in his jaw and raised his eyebrows at her.

'Ah, you've found out about that too, have you?' she asked.

'Amici d'Aretino? Yep. Not much, but enough.' He looked disappointed that it wasn't a surprise. Which made two of them. 'You?'

'Same. Probably less. I rang a bookseller friend, he confirmed my hunch.' She shrugged. 'I was feeling pretty pleased with myself. I should have known you'd get there first. So. Tell me about the vicar.'

'I quite liked the chap, actually. He seems an agreeable sort, unworldly and rather touchingly pleased at having carried off his bride. At the same time he managed to convey both affection and respect for her sister.'

'So if the village gossip is true, he's quite a juggler then. Nimble on the old feet?'

'Well, I suppose, but somehow he seemed more, I don't know, uncomplicated?' He looked at Tess and they both burst out laughing at the same thought. Who was taking who for a ride? Or was it whom?

'He could have been having me on, of course. Probably was, come to think of it.'

'Is he one of her customers, do you think?' she asked carefully, running her finger around the rim of her empty glass.

'Well now.' Owen gave a snort of laughter. 'Oh, ho, ho, ho. Oh my, oh my. You could well be right. It would fit, wouldn't it? It might not have been an affair at all. More a, er, book exchange? That would be funny.'

'I think I may have seen a drawing of that library,' Tess said slowly.

'You have? Where?' Owen spoke too loudly and as heads turned in their direction he lowered his voice.

'Tess? Do you mind telling me what, if anything, this Stebton woman has to do with your nuns?'

'I wouldn't mind at all, Owen,' she said, suddenly coming to the decision which had been brewing since he started describing Stebton Place. 'In fact it would be rather a relief.'

'Is something going on? Something illegal?' he asked quickly. He looked quite concerned.

'I don't know. It's only a hunch. Oh hell, something stinks but I'm not sure what. Look, would you like to come back to the flat for a chat? Rather a long one, I'm afraid. I need to talk to another solicitor and for various reasons I'd prefer it if it isn't Hugo.'

He didn't reply. He looked at his watch, asked to be excused, then trundled downstairs in the direction of the gents. And the telephones, she had no doubt. Tess ordered coffee and waited for his return.

I was asleep, but my heart waked:
It is the voice of my beloved that knocketh, saying,
Open to me, my sister, my love, my dove ...

The Song of Songs: 4:1–3

25

All was quiet when they got to the flat. Sandra was asleep on the sofa and the baby was tucked up snugly in her cot. Tess sent the babysitter home by taxi and made some coffee. Her head was splitting from the wine. She took a couple of paracetamol and went through to the little sitting-room where Owen was standing at the window. He turned around and smiled at her approach. For a moment he looked so like Marcus her heart skipped a beat. He looked more tired than he had in the soft light of the restaurant, she noticed. He was leaner but not necessarily better or younger looking. Now he wore an air of discouragement, as if he was weary of being depended upon. Weary of being regarded by her, as much as anybody, as an also-ran to his younger, more dazzling, more gifted, more selfish brother. The memory of their quarrel after Marcus's funeral still hung in the air between them.

After everyone else had gone, only kind, good, thoughtful Owen had stayed behind to help her. They had both drunk too much; she was weepy and self-pitying but Owen, for the first time since she had known him, was angry. It started as a dull rumble of invective against the fates that had cut down his brother in his prime but almost without her noticing, it had developed into a full-blown tirade against Marcus's predilection for hogging the limelight, being so opportunistic, so profligate of his talents and then, in a final furious burst, to the bloody bike. She listened aghast when the words crashed against her own dormant fear. 'Dicing with death, inviting it, with his child on the way.' And then he'd snarled, 'You made yourself a doormat for him, you stupid, stupid woman. Don't you realize just how he was using you? He was jealous of your talent, don't you know that? You gave up your career for him. Buried yourself in this self-regarding town. Did it never occur to you to ask him to do that for you?'

'Stop it. Stop trying to make me a victim. I was not forced or coerced, I chose my life. I chose Marcus. I chose to give up London. I'm not stupid. I knew exactly what he was like, I knew about the infidelities. But let me tell you something, he wanted the baby as much as me. The last three years were the happiest of my life.'

'Three?' he snarled. 'Don't make me laugh. You gave him ten.'

'Did you manage as much in fifteen years? Did you? Did you? Just tell me that,' she screamed. She remembered how he'd turned on her then, looking as if he wanted to box her ears. There was real venom in his voice.

'So why did he do that suicide run? If he wanted it all so much he wouldn't have thrown it away. The bike was shit. He couldn't grow up, that was his trouble. He didn't know what he had. You encouraged his idiocy. He didn't deserve you.'

'Get out,' she'd yelled. 'Get the hell out of my house.' But Owen had not responded. Instead, in slow motion and with infinite precision, he keeled over awkwardly onto the sofa, dead to the world. She'd left him there, perilously sprawled, fully clothed and shod. She expected, hoped, he'd be crippled with cramp the next morning but when she got up he had cleared the kitchen, the dishwasher was running and coffee was brewing. They ate their breakfast in silence. There were no apologies, no recriminations. If he remembered the fight he didn't refer to it, nor did she. They simply resumed their previous warm, but reserved relationship: she the cherished partner of the beloved little brother, he the dull dependable elder brother whose kindness she had always and would continue to take for granted.

Now, as he stood by the window in Hugo's flat, she recognized that she had scarcely ever given thought to what his private life might be like. Like Marcus, she too had thought of his existence only in relation to them. She had made no tender inquiries then, or indeed ever, about his girlfriends. About Stephanie. If it was Stephanie, if she was his girlfriend. Her face turned bright red with shame. She tried to form words of apology, but before she could say anything Owen spoke.

'I can see why you like it here. I can see why you might not be able to tear yourself away. Is that a park down there? The trees are marvellous in the moonlight,' he said sadly.

'Yes, Herbert Park. I know every inch of it. It's where I take Claire when she wants to let off steam. Which is less frequent than it was, thank God.' She tried to sound normal, put some lightness into her voice, but it didn't work. She felt like weeping though she could not have said why.

'Perhaps you're getting more accustomed to her little ways?' he said gently.

'Little? Nothing about that child is little, least of all her vocal chords,' she said gruffly.

He refused the coffee in favour of brandy and as she passed him the glass his fingers touched hers. Neither said anything until she went to the bedroom and fetched a bundle of papers which she plonked between them on the sofa.

'This may all be a storm in a teacup, Owen. And I'm probably imagining most of it. Hunches, instinct, what have you?'

'Bit fey for you, isn't it?' She could almost see him mentally shake himself, force himself to concentrate. 'Never mind the excuses. Tell me everything. From the beginning. I'd like to help if I can.'

'What I'm really kicking myself for is not asking questions at the beginning myself. I wasn't thinking straight . . .'

Owen held his hands in front of his face in a gesture of mock despair. 'Tess, Tess. For fuck's sake would you get on with it. If you weren't thinking straight, you had plenty of reason. As I understood it, you took on an undemanding little job that Hugo had set up to keep you occupied.

Right? You weren't supposed to be acting the hot shot. Give yourself a break,' he said tiredly. 'And me. Quit apologizing, it gets on my nerves and it doesn't suit you.'

'Sorry,' she said and they both laughed. 'OK, here goes, from the top. When I got here the nuns had agreed the sale of the land with a completion date for the seventh of November. I'm not sure how they arrived at the date and I don't suppose it matters. The whole business had been going on for a couple of years or more so I guess Terence Murphy-Dunne, who was doing the conveyancing, was desperate to wrap it up. The scenario I was presented with was that the graveyard would have to be moved before completion. The purchaser, Glenadams School, agreed to underwrite the costs and to rebuild the convent boundary wall.'

'Your job being to see that work was properly contracted?'

'Yes, but also to sort permissions with the council, public health, cemeteries and the church authorities. There was plenty to do – of the paper-pushing variety. Terence Murphy-Dunne had begun to make a stab at it then he fell and hurt his back and was carted off to hospital. Enter yours truly.'

'Hang on. Is Murphy-Dunne a one-man band? Was there no one else in the office to take over? Didn't he have an assistant?'

'Of course, and she would have taken over but then Hugo put his oar in and suggested me. Actually the partners were delighted. I agreed to work for a notional amount – probably paid by Hugo, if I know anything – so it was no skin off their collective nose. Elizabeth Reilly hadn't been working on the case – it was only a small matter after all. So I could as easily be briefed as she. Everyone was happy with the arrangement. Me, most of all, because Hugo was spot on, it did make me feel useful. He was right about something else too. He said I'd like the nuns, and I do. I suppose that's why I want everything to be in order for them.'

'So you took your instructions from Terence and—'

'No,' Tess interrupted. 'He was in hospital. I haven't talked to him at all.'

'You mean *he* hasn't spoken to you?' Owen's disbelief was almost comical. 'He didn't even ring you? Why ever not? He should have done, even out of courtesy. The man has no manners,' he spluttered indignantly. Tess made a wry face and shrugged.

'There really wasn't any need. Then,' she added pointedly.

'Is he still in hospital?'

'No, that's the killing thing. I haven't been able to raise him, though I've tried, God knows. I think he may have gone abroad. Slipped away when I wasn't looking. He was due to go soon anyway, for a rest cure in the sun, it seems. For three weeks. To the Caribbean,' she added thoughtfully. Owen took her hand in his.

'That's precisely what *you* need. How about it?' he asked lightly. Their eyes met and held but Tess said nothing as she gently disengaged her hand. He'd broken her concentration, confused her. She couldn't get her head around his feelings, much less her own. The intimacy of his gesture had, paradoxically, completely destroyed the easiness between them. They both knew it. After a few minutes' silence Owen dragged himself up off the sofa and poured himself another brandy.

'Sorry,' she said. He sighed deeply and gave her a long mock-despairing look.

'I wish you'd stop apologizing. It unnerves me,' he laughed. Then added over-heartily, 'So, you weren't particularly upset that you didn't see Terence?'

'Not at all,' she said, noting that he had hit the nail squarely on the head. 'As I say, my end of things had hardly started when I arrived so I could work away when and if I pleased. In my own way which, as you know, I prefer. It wasn't very demanding, you know. Actually I now believe Hugo was deliberately keeping me away from him.'

'Oh really? Why?'

'In case he'd tarnish my gleaming reputation. Hugo is rather over-protective and old-fashioned. Murphy-Dunne is something of a lad.' She blushed and turned her face away in case he read the hurt and humiliation.

'Ladies' man, you mean?' Owen asked primly.

'For Christ's sake, Owen, I'm thirty-seven, I can take care of myself.'

'Really? So you told Hugo, I expect.' He didn't sound convinced.

'Certainly I did.'

'So why, if that is the case, do you *now* feel you should have seen Murphy-Dunne?'

'Not Murphy-Dunne. *The contract*. I should have looked at the contract between the nuns and Glenadams.'

'But isn't it in the office?' he asked mildly. 'Haven't you asked for it?'

'Yes, of course,' she said patiently. 'But it's not there. Or at least I couldn't lay my hands on it.'

'Was there some particular reason why you wanted to see it, Tess?'

'Well, that's where instinct comes in.' She described her visit to the office and then her expedition to Glenadams when she caught sight of the wasteland and what she suspected it might imply.

'There was an accident on the road outside the school gate two and a half years ago. Two pupils were knocked down and badly injured. The school governors decided there was urgent need to make a new entrance off the main road. The lane that serves the convent was the obvious choice since it runs right up to Glenadams land and a little beyond. It might have been possible just to re-site the drive within their own boundaries but unfortunately the appropriate chunk is basically nothing but a long outcrop of rock. Buying the strip from the nuns means that they can have their main gates and arc the new driveway around the rocks. It will look really attractive. They don't have to make a new roadway either, since it's already there. A neat solution all round, you might say.'

'So it would seem. What's in it for the nuns?'

'A good deal. They get their boundary wall rebuilt and, with the proceeds of the sale, they can carry out essential repairs on the convent building. It's a beautiful Georgian house, by the way, I'd love you to see it.'

'I'd settle for you loving me,' he said so softly

and absently that she thought she was hearing things. She bit her lip but couldn't look at him. Her heart was in turmoil. His intensity made her afraid. She had already made too many mistakes.

'One of the things I most regret,' she said, after an awkward pause, 'is that until a couple of days ago, I never thought of looking at the route of the driveway from the Glenadams side. That's when I noticed that there was a long strip of land running between the boundaries of both properties and the cliff edge. I could clearly see all of the Glenadams end of it where it is definitely fallow. I couldn't quite see beyond the nuns' hedge to the other end. But . . .' She paused and pursed her mouth as if she mistrusted her own conclusion.

'But?'

'I thought I could make out an opening, an archway in the hedge from the enclosure, into the field. And whereas the field was overgrown at the school end, I am almost sure the other end is cultivated.'

'Is that a cause for alarm? Perhaps they bought it? Or if it was abandoned, put in a claim for adverse possession. That would be perfectly legal.' He looked at her closely, his expression perplexed. 'Is there something else? Or are we talking instinct?'

'Stink, anyway.' She wrinkled her nose and shook her head from side to side. 'I don't know, something doesn't smell quite right. But I can't start laying about me because of a hunch. I just feel . . . I don't know, I just feel something's out of kilter.'

'Could you tease out your reasoning?'

'I'll try. I don't know if you've noticed that

Ireland is considered something of an economic miracle in Europe at present? The emerald tiger, no less. There's a huge building boom here, specially in Dublin. Land, specially building land, is worth a fortune. Killiney is much sought after. That's one situation. Another is this: a lot of religious communities have died out or dispersed in the past twenty years, leaving many of the convents lying empty. There have been some very dubious deals in the past decade. Institutions are sold off and afterwards the land is, fortuitously, re-zoned for housing.' She held her head on one side. 'Do you get my drift?'

'I do indeed.' Owen nodded slowly. 'You think something like that may happen to Holy Retreat?'

'Yeah, I'm afraid I do.'

'But you have no evidence for such a claim?'

'No, not a shred, not even a whiff. But it is what I fear,' she cried passionately. 'Holy Retreat isn't dying out, it's viable, it's self-supporting and the nuns seem very content. There's still a community of fourteen and I don't want them taken advantage of. That plot beyond Glenadams is land-locked. I think that's what bothers me most. It's never been mentioned.'

'Any reason why it should have been?'

'None at all, that's the rub. But taken together with the school ground and the new access, it is very, very attractive. And extensive. Maybe the plot by the cliff edge is unsuitable for building, but just say the school was sold and re-zoned for housing, that land would make spectacular gardens. Overlooking one of the most beautiful bays in Europe? Gi'me a break,' she said in mock

American, 'but the way I look at it, you could fit a sizeable number of executive homes into that space. Selling at half a million apiece.'

'It would be worth a fortune.' He looked at her sourly. 'Tricky.'

'Very. It's all conjecture. I haven't an iota of evidence. The deal between the school and the nuns will be completed in two weeks and unless I come up with something in the meantime . . .' She held out her hands hopelessly. 'And there's another thing. There was something odd about the school when I went out. Everyone was away because it was half-term but the place was patrolled by a vicious-looking guard dog.'

'I'm not surprised. There's a fair old traffic in computers, you know. We had two stolen a couple of weeks ago,' he remarked and immediately Tess realized that she'd made a mountain out of a molehill. The security man had only been doing his job, after all.

'Nobody stopped you prowling around?' Owen asked. It was a pertinent question which Tess considered carefully.

'No, not really. I met the school secretary – at least that's who I think she was, a rather masculine type. She had no objection when I asked if I could look around. But then,' she added wryly, 'she thought I was a prospective parent.'

Owen laughed. 'Well now, I wonder how she got that idea?' Tess grinned at him and made a face.

'That must have eased your mind a bit,' Owen said. 'That you were allowed free access, I mean.'

'Yes,' Tess answered though she sounded

vaguely surprised. 'Yes, I suppose it did.' She didn't mention how threatened she'd felt by the brutes, both man and beast.

'Can't you stop the exhumations?'

'No. Oddly enough, I don't think that would help. The nuns have been wanting to move the graves for years. The present cemetery is slap up against the boundary wall and they'd much prefer if it was on the other side of the convent building, further into the enclosure. It's quite visible from Glenadams land, for instance; they've also been having trouble with vandals. Some of the graves were desecrated recently. Not seriously, it looked more like the work of mischievous kids or so they think, but they found it very shocking. And, you see, there's another advantage of the sale. That particular stretch of land is only enclosed by a huge hedge, not a wall. The vandals made them appreciate how vulnerable they are, so a new wall was one of their conditions for the sale.'

'I suppose it had occurred to you that there seems to have been quite a little accumulation of, er, arguments for selling?'

Tess beamed at him gratefully. 'Oh, Owen, you're such a comfort. I knew you'd see it, get my thoughts in order . . .'

'Reliable, ain't I?' He smiled disarmingly. 'You seem to be doing very well without me. But glad to be of service,' he added dryly. He looked depressed.

She turned to him earnestly. 'I can't start shooting my mouth off, can I? On the face of it the school made an honourable deal which the nuns are delighted with. Terence negotiated a handsome settlement. And on top of that, Hugo would certainly not involve me if there was any doubt about Murphy-Dunne's professional probity. He'd be outraged at the suggestion that his beloved law firm was involved in scandal.'

'True. And that's where you must be careful of your own reputation and not let emotion cloud your judgement. There may not be a scandal.' He stopped for a moment and stroked his chin. 'Still, there's no harm in doing a little discreet investigation, is there? For your own peace of mind. If it turns out your fears are groundless, then no harm done. You just forget it. The seventh of November? Less than two weeks? You haven't got long, have you? But I think,' he considered slowly, 'I think you should try to get the nuns to agree not to complete without giving you sight of the contract. Assuming it hasn't turned up before.' He pursed his lips and looked at her steadily. 'And do you know, Tess, I rather think it won't.' Their eyes met and he smiled. 'Nothing like a knotty little problem for getting the old adrenalin going is there?' he asked but Tess was too preoccupied to comment.

'I'll talk to Mother Catherine. If I make a plausible case, she'll listen. By the way, I've already applied to the land registry to do an index map search and local land searches. The lot. I also applied for an office copy of the convent deeds.'

'There must be trustees. Know anything about them?'

'Yes, I discovered from the diocesan office, but it doesn't help my case. The nuns have a rather unusual arrangement, devised by the founder who seems to have been a sharp cookie. They have a system of rotating trusteeships for periods of ten years unless terminated by death, and they're held by three nuns from within the community. No outsiders. At present they are my pal, the Mother Guardian, the Bursar and a Sister Mary-Rose whom I've not met. The priest who told me was outraged at their temerity.' She chuckled at the memory of his sour face. 'But the system has worked well for them over the years.'

'Heavens Tess, you sound so enthusiastic. You're not going to enlist, are you?' he joked, as a cry from the baby put an effective end to their conversation.

Owen stayed on for half an hour or so to keep her company while she was feeding Claire. 'I'll have to get on, Tess,' he said at last. He looked weary. 'If you point me in the right direction I'll stroll back to the Hibernian. It's not far, is it? I'll think over what you said and ring you when I get back to London. You can tell me the rest then. About the Hillyard woman, I mean.'

'Fine.' She kept her tone neutral. 'You seem to be getting as obsessed as I am about her.' She kissed his cheek and hugged him. 'You are such a dear, Owen. Thanks for a marvellous dinner and for listening so patiently.' She stood back and held him at arm's length. Her expression was suddenly serious. 'You don't think I'm off the wall about all this, do you?'

'I don't think you're off the wall about anything, my dearest Tess.' He dropped a kiss on Claire's forehead, touched Tess on the arm and left, leaving Tess to wonder childishly why she felt left out. He hadn't even responded to her good-bye kiss.

Adverse Possession: *(1) One of the main ways in which an estate or interest in land may be extinguished is under the doctrine of 'adverse possession', as it operates under modern Statutes of Limitations. This doctrine, however, has become one of the most controversial features of modern land law.*

Wylie: Irish Land Law 23.01

26

A couple of days later, early on Thursday morning, Sinéad rang Tess with the news that she thought she'd located the files. Tess said she'd drop by the office that evening. Though she was already tied up for most of the day, her chief reason for an evening visit was because she wanted a private snoop around Murphy-Dunne's office. By eight fifteen Claire was bathed and fed and tucked up snugly in her travelling chair. She was also, happily, sound asleep. Tess glanced out of the window and saw that it was already quite dark.

She carried the baby quietly downstairs. She let herself out of the house and walked swiftly to the car. The baby didn't stir during the whole procedure. The drive to the office took no more than seven or eight minutes. Tess parked immediately outside, locked the car and carried the baby up the steps. Sinéad had warned the night security guard to expect her. He was just finishing his hourly round and was on his way down to the basement when she let herself in.

'Miss Callaway.' He greeted her with a broad grin. 'Isn't it a bit late for the young one?'

'I thought I'd give her a treat, show her around,' Tess joked. 'But she's no appreciation of the finer things, she's gone and fallen asleep on me.' She smiled at him. 'I'm just collecting some files.'

'Sinéad said you'd be in. She said to tell you she left what you wanted on the desk. It's unusual to have people working so late of a Friday. Will you be long?'

'A few minutes is all. I'll just go up and pick them up.'

'Fair enough. Do you want me to hold on to her nibs while you're above?'

'No, that's OK, thanks. I'll take her with me. She'll start bawling if she wakes up. There's nobody else around I take it?'

'Not a soul. You don't mind being all alone?'

'No, not a bit. I'll see you on the way out, Steve.'

'I'll be down having a cup of tea. Just give me a shout before you leave.'

Murphy-Dunne's office was one of two, looking onto the street, on the first floor. Tess unlocked the door and eased the door open. The room was in darkness, the heavy brocade curtains on the tall window had already been drawn. She switched on the main light, carried Claire over to the desk and set her down on the floor between it and the window, where she could keep an eye on her while she worked. She turned on the desk light and found a slim file with her name on it lying on the writing pad. Tess sat down and opened it.

Dear Tess,
  I'm afraid I had to leave the files back in the deeds cupboard. Mr Moore caught me taking them out and said it wasn't company practice to leave files lying about. Even when I told him I was putting them in Mr Murphy-Dunne's office for you, he said to put them back, that it was safer for you to collect them yourself. I've left them in one of the black canvas bags for you (easier to carry!). It's at the top of the pile on the middle shelf in M-D's row so you'll be able to put your hand on it, no trouble. I hope you don't mind. I did my best. Mr Moore wasn't cross or anything. Just careful. He said you'd understand.
  Sorry about that. Can you put the key to the deeds cupboard in the top drawer of my desk when you've finished? By the way, Mr Murphy-Dunne said to tell you he was asking for you. I rang him on Wednesday when I couldn't find the files and he told me exactly where they were. He's gone on holiday. He was on his way to the airport when I caught him. He said sorry he missed you. He got your message and tried to ring you several times but kept missing you. He's off the crutches by the way but says the back's giving him terrible trouble. He'll be in touch when he gets back on the 6th. Not going for long, is he?
  Sinéad Ryan

Tess glanced at the baby who was still sleeping peacefully. It would take her only a few minutes to take the lift to the top floor. Best to do it while Claire was settled. She could do her snooping when she got back. She turned off the main light on her way out, left the door open and buzzed for the lift. It was twenty minutes to nine. She wedged the lift door open.

Exactly five minutes later she replaced the key and a scribbled note of thanks for Sinéad. It was only when she turned to go and collect Claire that she saw that the door to Murphy-Dunne's office was closed. Her heart stopped.

Tess stood stock still, hardly breathing, every nerve end in her body vibrating with anxiety. For two or three endless seconds she could not force her feet to move. Then as she released her pent-up breath, she hurled herself at the door. It gave way as she fell against it and she found herself rolling towards the desk before she could stop the momentum. The room was ablaze with light and the curtains were wide open. She heard herself sobbing as she crawled towards the desk. The baby was gone.

She squeezed her eyes shut in disbelief. She'd made a mistake, the baby was there, the baby was there. She opened them and looked around frantically, in utter terror, but the wide expanse of pale grey carpet was utterly empty, empty, empty. She locked her arms around her head and sank to the floor. 'Oh help me. Oh help me. God, oh Jesus, oh help me,' she whimpered. 'Somebody help me. My baby's gone. My baby. Somebody, somebody please help me.' It was as if her stomach had ripped open and her guts spilled on the floor. Her child was torn from her; she was paralysed with shock. She crouched on all fours, her breath coming in loud harsh gasps as a sudden commotion started up outside in the street. Tess shakily dragged herself up on the window frame. Outside on the street her car lights were flashing, the doors were wide open and the burglar alarm was screaming. She tore out of the room, down the stairs and out through the open door. Steve, the security guard, was standing by her car. He was holding Claire in his arms and she was screeching.

'What did you do to her? You took my baby! You bastard. Give her to me.' Tess pounded on his back and yanked the terrified infant from his arms. As he yielded his hold he slapped Tess sharply across the face.

'I didn't take your baby, Miss Callaway,' he said quietly. 'Your baby was in the car when I came out to see what the commotion was about. You shouldn't have left her there.'

Tess stared at him open-mouthed but couldn't speak. She began to hyperventilate. He took her handbag from the front seat and banged the car doors shut. Then he took Tess firmly by the shoulders and half walked, half dragged her back inside. Further down the street a Land Rover pulled away from the kerb, but neither of them noticed it.

Steve said nothing until he got them safely down to his warm cubby-hole in the basement. By now the child had stopped crying but Tess was sobbing miserably. Steve silently made a fresh cup of tea and stood over her while she drank it.

'Miss Callaway, that's a serious charge you made out there. I didn't take your baby. She was strapped in her little seat when I came out. The burglar alarm must have woken her up. She was terrified with the noise. I only picked her up to stop her having hysterics,' Steve said carefully as Tess sipped the hot sweet tea.

Tess looked up at him contritely. His face was ashen. He was clearly in a complete panic, terrified of what further charge she would level at him. He began pacing up and down the tiny room, as anger took the upper hand. Claire had miraculously gone back to sleep as if nothing had happened. Tess gulped down the remains of the tea. She was still trembling but she tried desperately to compose her thoughts.

'I know that, Steve. I know that.' She held out her shaking hand and touched his arm. 'I am completely overwrought. I cannot tell you how sorry I am. Please, please forgive me?' She swallowed. 'Thank you for looking after Claire. I was very, very stupid to leave her.'

'Can you please tell me what happened?' he asked calmly and Tess knew that she must make up something so plausible that he would stop worrying about charges of kidnapping, or abuse, or other dreadful, unanswerable horrors. Most of all she had to keep the police out of it because she knew for sure that they would rather believe any kind of hysterical accusation from her, a well-established solicitor, than reason from him, a lowly night-watchman. Sometimes women held cards too powerful to use. He knew, and she knew, that an unconsidered word from her could ruin his life for ever. So she had better wait until later to figure out exactly what had happened. She better tell it good.

'I collected the files and went to return the keys,' she whispered brokenly. 'While I was doing that I must have put the files down on Sinéad's desk. Then I went down to the car and put Claire in. That's when I realized that I'd left the files upstairs.' She looked straight at him. 'They're still there.' She waited for him to say something but he didn't. 'I must have left my bag strap hanging out. That or something else must have activated the alarm. When I dashed back upstairs I heard it going off. I don't remember coming down again.' She began to sob again. 'Oh, God, I got such a terrible fright. I thought someone had taken her. I couldn't bear it. That's when I attacked you. I'm sorry, I'm sorry, I'm sorry. I should never have left her, even for a second. It was completely irresponsible. Someone could have stolen the car with her in it. Anything could have happened. She might have been killed.' She bent over and howled inconsolably. He stood aside awkwardly, silently, until she'd calmed down; as if he was afraid even to stand near her. 'You saved her life, Steve and oh, God, I am so sorry for shouting at you, for saying what I did. You could sue me, you know.' She made a feeble effort to smile at him.

'You know I wouldn't do that, Miss Callaway.' The man spoke with dignity and a little disdain. 'I know what you've been through these past months. You got a fright, that's all. We both did. We'll say no more about it.'

Tess held out her hand shakily and after a fractional hesitation, he took it in his. 'Thank you,' she said.

'I'll go up and collect your files for you,' he said and quickly left the room. She didn't blame him for checking on her story but she hoped like hell that whoever was stalking her, whoever arranged the diabolical escapade, didn't do so for the purpose of swiping the files.

'Here you are, safe and sound.' Steve's voice

was stronger, less strained. 'Now, are you sure you're fit to drive home? I can call a taxi, if you like. And drive your car home when I finish my shift. If you like,' he repeated. He looked at her warily.

'Yes, please. I'd be very grateful. I'm staying with Mr Boland. In Herbert Park.'

And that seemed to finally alleviate his fears. While she waited for the taxi they drank another cup of tea.

She could hardly make it up the front steps. She knocked timidly on Hugo's door but there was no answer. She was too scared to step into the lift. As she dragged herself wearily up the long flights of stairs to the flat Claire began to whimper. Tess made up a fresh bottle and poured herself a stiff brandy. Then they huddled together on the bed until the baby went back to sleep.

Tess sat up all night, afraid if she closed her eyes someone would take her child again. She had experienced the worst a parent could; if only for a few endless life-shattering moments – the loss of her child – and she was terrified of being alone in the empty flat. Of more intruders. Her horror of someone being able to get in at will, walk around, shift the baby from one room to another scared her half to death. Now, more than ever, she didn't know who to trust. Or, more to the point, who was watching her movements, stalking her. Her confidence was shattered again. Just when she had begun to get it together. Emotionally speaking, she was in pieces. She knew that what she'd just experienced would leave a lasting, recurring mark that would never leave her.

27

Oh, Marcus, Marcus

I am frightened to death. It is past four in the morning and the flat is cold and dark. The baby is fed, changed and fast asleep again but I am too wired even to lie down. I don't know what I'd have done if anything had happened to my Claire. If she'd been really gone I think I would have lost my mind. I want to pull out, go home, get lost in some crowd somewhere. I do not know who carried my baby out into the car or why Steve didn't see them. Whoever it was must have been in the building waiting for me to arrive. There was no reason why Sinéad should have kept the information to herself. But I wish she hadn't rung him. If he's at the back of this, I'll bloody nail him.

That's the only reason I will cling on. I am ashamed to admit I always had a weakness for that sod. Defended him. I knew he was a chancer but I never, ever suspected he was cruel. Or crooked. Now I'm pretty sure he is both.

God help me, my mind is going around in circles too swift for me to figure out what is going on. I only know that he didn't want me to get hold of the contracts. They are, I have just discovered, missing from the files. In fact there is nothing to do with either Glenadams or Holy Retreat in either of them. All I found was a sheaf of ancient deeds stuffed into the wrong holders. Sod him. Because, you know, it's precisely the same sort of trick he used to play when I was doing my articles. The kind of warped joke that would ensure you didn't get finished in time, hold *everything and everybody up. Make himself look like the soul of efficiency by comparison. But until tonight I had no real doubt about his honesty.*

Deep in my bones I know that all this has something to do with the parcel of land running between both the old Elderson estate and its neighbour, Glenadams. It is land-locked. At the moment. And I do not know who, if anyone, owns that land. Or what bearing it has on the Holy Retreat sale. And that, I'm afraid, is my point. There is a lot more going on than I thought.

I swear to God I didn't leave her for more than a few minutes. For five at most. It never occurred to me there was anyone else in the building. Steve said there wasn't when I went in. Afterwards I couldn't bring myself to ask him. Not after I made up the story. I only did it to protect him. And myself. The social services take babies away from incompetent mothers, or unstable ones, and I have been both. I can look after her. I swear it. I love her. I love her more than my life. I didn't at the beginning. But I do, I do now. I swear.

In that terrible moment, as I stared at the empty space where I'd left her, I knew what it would be like if she died. I felt my body rip open and my blood spill over that empty space. I saw your mangled body and I thought she was gone for ever. I knew then, and I know now that if that happened, I could not live.

Adverse Possession: *(2) Since 1833,* 'adverse possession'
means simply possession of land which is inconsistent with
the title of the true owner . . .

Wylie: Irish Land Law 23.05

28

It began to rain at about eleven on Friday
morning and then came down in a steady drizzle
for much of the day. Tess passed the morning in a
frenzy of domestic and childminding activity.
Apart from Steve, who brought back the car at
eight in the morning, she saw nobody. She didn't
go out, she didn't answer the phone; she was still
too scared to do either. But gradually, over the
course of the day, as the first heart-stopping
horror left her, she forced herself to go over each
moment of the night before. Somehow she had to
make sense of it. Work out what was intended.
To scare her? Yes. To harm Claire? No. The point
was to warn her off interfering in the land sale.
She thought about that for a long time until it
dawned on her that it wasn't the sale itself which
was the problem. *It was to prevent her seeing
who the purchasers were.* But wouldn't the nuns
know? They had signed the contract after all, so
they must know exactly who they'd sold the land
to – Glenadams *School,* they said. Yes. And if the

name on the contract was different it could have been passed off as a holding company for the school. Which wouldn't have bothered them because it was a normal device for many businesses. In any case the deal appeared to be an excellent one from their point of view. So they would not have asked who owned the holding company. But Tess could. She didn't need the deed. She could start on the assumption that any holding company would have Glenadams in the name. She could do a little private nosing around. But not today. Today she was too scared that she was still being watched.

She was standing at the window in the early afternoon, looking out on the park, when another thought came to her. There wasn't just one land sale, *there were two*. Glenadams and the wasteland. And of the two the latter was the more important. Why? Why? Why? She stared out over the tree-tops, seeing in her mind's eye the long rough grass blowing in the breeze and it came to her at last. Because just when the deal with Glenadams had gone through the owner or owners of the previously unclaimed land had turned up and put a spanner in the works. Oh, glory be, she thought, and I bet I know exactly who.

She read and re-read what she called 'The Stebton papers' and sketched maps of the land around the convent. What she wanted most to do was to rehash the whole thing over and over with Owen. But since he was unavailable, she had only herself to argue the case against. This proved as frustrating as it was pointless. By the following morning she had argued herself to such a mental standstill that the whole scheme seemed but a figment of her imagination.

After lunch, when she couldn't stand being indoors another second, she bundled Claire into the car. After a moment's hesitation, she headed for the nearest DART station at Sydney Parade where she parked the car and bought a return train ticket to Bray. The rain died away and a weak, post-rain sun had edged its way through the clouds by the time the train rolled into Blackrock. Claire evidently thought it was all a great lark as long as the train was actually moving, though her tolerance of stopping and starting was more uncertain. Tess sat at the window, noting every change in the landscape as they skimmed the coast to Dun Laoghaire. From there the train went inland around Dalkey until they emerged at Sorrento Point with the full glory of the semi-circular bay spread before them, to Bray Head at the other end. As she sat in Killiney station she tried to estimate the distance to the convent and once again her mind turned to the wasteland and to speculating about its possible ownership.

The train slid out of the station and the sea briefly was gone from view. Ballybrack, Shankill, by Woodbrook Golf Course until they were back in sight of the sea and another, closer view of Bray Head. Within minutes they were at the terminus. Claire wasn't at all pleased at being taken out into the elements and set up a grizzle of protest against the gusting wind as Tess carried her across the pedestrian bridge. They just made it to the return train before the rain began again in earnest. Tess settled them in a forward-facing seat in the empty front carriage and wiped the misted window with the sleeve of her jacket. She peered out moodily and then sat bolt upright. A visual history of the railway was painted in panels all along the platform. The first was precisely opposite her: 1854 *Dublin–Wicklow Railway opened. Harcourt Street–Bray.* The legend hit her in the eye. She jumped up and almost crashed into an elderly man who was trying to settle himself in the opposite seat.

'Great, aren't they?' He nodded in the direction of the paintings. 'Liven the place up grand.' He gave her a gummy grin as the train slid silently out of the station. Tess sat back with a bump.

'Excuse me,' she said, 'do you happen to know the route that train took? Harcourt Street to Bray?'

'Certainly,' he said. 'I should, shouldn't I? I've been going in and out since I was a chizzler and I'm eighty-five next birthday.' He sat back with a pleased smirk waiting for her to congratulate him on his longevity. She wondered what the watershed was. When did you begin to boast about age instead of trying to reduce it? As far as she was concerned, forty was getting too close for comfort. The old man, who had been gabbling to himself softly, began to speak out. 'I think I have it,' he said. 'I can tell you the main stations anyway.' He closed his eyes and reeled the names off by rote like a child saying his times tables: 'Harcourt Street, Ranelagh, Dundrum, Stillorgan, Foxrock, Shankill, Bray.' His eyelids snapped open and he gave her a pleased grin. 'How's that for memory?' he asked proudly.

Tess beamed at him. 'You're a genius,' she said.

'D'you know that? Thanks very much. Now, I've got another question for you: does the DART use the same line from Shankill?'

He scratched his head. 'This is like one of them pub quizzes. Yeah, I think it does. No, no, don't say a word. I might be wrong. D'you know, I think it's a new line but it must be very close to the old one. If you wait a few seconds we'll be able to see. Look there,' he pointed excitedly, 'see that old hump-backed bridge? That's the old line. Shangannah Junction, it was called then,' he said, pulling the rabbit from the hat.

'Thanks a lot. I've been having an argument with a friend. I think I've won.'

'Game ball, so. That's a fine little baby, you have. How old is it?'

'Nearly four months. She's getting very heavy.'

'As long as she's healthy. That's all you want, isn't it?'

'Yes,' said Tess earnestly. 'She is.'

They chatted amiably until Tess got out at Killiney. She went to the ticket office and, more in hope than expectation, asked the cashier if he knew when the station was opened.

'Seven to midnight,' he said.

'No, sorry, I mean what year was it built?' He gave her a long look to make sure she wasn't codding him then moved aside so she could read a plaque set into the wall behind him. 'Kingstown–Killiney extension. Station opened 1854. Killiney & Ballybrack amalgamated 1882.'

'It's not still called Killiney and Ballybrack, is it?'

He looked her up and down before replying. 'No, the original Ballybrack station was a mile further down the line. That was closed in 1882 and the name was dropped altogether in 1922. Anything else you want to know?'

'Yes, do you happen to know when the Dublin–Kingstown line was built?'

The man scratched his head. 'Around the eighteen thirties, I think. Eighteen thirty-four rings a bell.' Tess thanked him and joined the straggled group of passengers boarding the next train. If it was confirmation she'd been seeking she'd got it in spades but it didn't seem to bring her any further. It now seemed more and more likely that the wasteland was acquired as a speculation against proposed railway routes sometime during those twenty years, before the convent was founded. *When the Stebtons were still at Elderson Court.* Alternative routes must have been publicly discussed as they would be, ad nauseam, nowadays. Or was she completely up the creek? Perhaps it was exactly what it seemed, just a tract of unused, unclaimed, forgotten land. For a wonderful light-hearted moment, she let her suspicions roll away. She held the baby close to her face and kissed her warm little cheeks and was thrilled to notice, in the reflected light off the sea, that the baby's eyes had changed colour and were now a kind of deep aquamarine. A happy mixture of her blue and Marcus's hazel. 'The sea's in your eyes,' she whispered and felt unaccountably pleased.

By the time they got back to Sydney Parade, the moment of euphoria has passed. There seemed nothing for it but to ring up the Mother Guardian and ask if she could pay her a visit the next day. At the very least she might be able to find out where the mysterious package had come from and if the nun could confirm her suspicions about the land. Though she was still unsure about how much she should say. All her lawyer's training urged her not to make wild, unsubstantiated statements. She was reluctant to set off false alarms especially since it was the bank holiday weekend and the exhumation of the graveyard was scheduled to start immediately after, at eight o'clock on Tuesday morning. Tess was trying not to think about having to leave Claire in the baby-sitter's charge all day. Mary Mackie had promised to keep an eye on things, but Tess vowed that on the morrow, over lunch with her mother, she would press-gang her into helping out. Hugo too, for that matter. She had to make sure there were people around the baby all the time. No matter how incompetent. Guardian angels didn't have to be efficient. They just had to *be*.

She bathed and fed Claire and put her into her cot. It was a pointless ritual she went through each evening. So far, the infant's record for staying put was seventy-five minutes. Tess could more or less guarantee that, by nine, Claire would be tucked up snugly, plum in the centre of the big bed with a smirk of satisfaction on her fat little face.

Tess crept out of the bedroom and made her call. She timed it to coincide with what she knew to be the nuns' recreation hour, seven-thirty. Even then, it took at least fifteen minutes for whoever answered the phone to pass on the message to her superior. Or at any rate it was that long before Tess heard the familiar clearing of her throat and the reedy, 'Ye-es?'

When Tess identified herself there was a long pause then, to her surprise, the nun said softly the line was bad and that she would call back. The line went dead and remained so until just before half past eight.

'I would like to talk to you for a few minutes, Mother Catherine, tomorrow, if that's convenient.'

'You haven't forgotten the bishop will be here in the afternoon to consecrate the new cemetery, have you?' she answered without preamble.

'Oh, Lord. I had for the moment. Never mind—'

'He won't be here till three,' Mother Catherine interrupted. 'Come at twelve-fifteen, I can see you for about half an hour,' she said and put down the phone abruptly.

Had it been anyone else Tess would have surmised that she was being, or was afraid of being, overheard. The few times they had made contact by phone she had not been so short. Tess mulled it over for a few minutes then, chiding herself for an overheated imagination, she opened a bottle of St Gimigniano and cooked herself pasta with an obscene amount of fresh Dublin Bay prawns, fresh tomatoes and the last of the basil.

Title: *Where a squatter bars the right of action and title of the dispossessed owner of the land, he acquires a title good against anyone other than a person with a better title to the land.*

Wylie: Irish Land Law 23.08

29

'Is everything all right for Tuesday? For the exhumation? You seemed quite anxious on the phone. Is there something worrying you?' Short of saying, yes, someone in your convent has dumped a load of papers on me which I can't make head or tail of, Tess didn't quite know where to start. Mother Catherine's voice was even quieter than usual so that she had to lean quite close to the grille to hear her.

'Fine,' she said brightly. 'I'm fine for Tuesday, honestly. I wanted to check everything has been delivered, then go over the final arrangements with you.' She paused, then came clean. 'Actually, Mother Catherine, I came about something else.' She took a breath as she conjured up a picture of herself poised on a diving board, nose held, plunging in. 'Do you remember asking me about the Stebton family in Oxfordshire? I just thought you'd like to know that I saw my, er, Marcus' brother the other day and he told me quite a lot about the house.'

'The house?' Mother Catherine sounded perplexed as if her thoughts were a million miles away. 'I'm not interested in the house.'

'Then why did you ask?'

'Oh, it hardly matters. I was interested in one of the family who comes to see us. We hadn't heard from her for some time but shortly afterwards I had a letter from her to say her mother was ill. I was a bit anxious about her at the time, that was all,' she said studiously, like a child making over-elaborate excuses for some misdemeanour. It sounded all wrong. For a woman of so few words, it was overcomplicated. One thing her job had taught Tess was how to sniff out unlikely stories.

'That will be Jane-Edwina Stebton-Hillyard?'

'Why, yes, do you know her?' Mother Catherine's interest livened.

'The bookseller? Owen does,' Tess answered. The reaction was remarkable.

'Bookseller?' For the nun it was tantamount to a shout. 'No, you're mistaken, she used to work as a librarian, but she's a writer now.'

'Miss Hillyard is a writer?'

'Oh yes. That's how she came to us. She was researching a book on women's religious foundations.' The nun chuckled softly. 'She was convinced we were an endangered species. Almost the first thing I said to her was that we didn't feel particularly endangered.'

'Did you say "*endangered species*"?' Tess said breathlessly.

'Yes.' The nun gave another little laugh. 'She has quite a sense of humour. It was what she was going to call her book.' Tess felt as though the hoard from the padded envelope was being scattered by a whirlwind. Why had the notes been sent to her if the nuns already knew about the book? If there was a book. The evidence seemed rather slight. Contrived, even?

'Was?'

'Yes, she's changed direction a little. She's concentrating on Holy Retreat now.'

'How did she happen on this particular convent?' Tess asked curiously.

'Oh, because in the course of her research, she discovered her ancestor had founded our little order. She was very excited about it and of course it further enlivened her interest in the general subject. But then, as she says herself, Adelaide took over and she gave up the idea of the nuns' book for the time being.' She started to laugh but it quickly turned into a hacking cough and took a minute or so for her to recover. 'She decided instead to write a life of Adelaide and the foundation of Holy Retreat.' She paused. 'Which pleased us a good deal.' Another amused little sniff. 'She had a name for that as well . . .'

Tess was about to chip in '*Carne Vale*' and tell her all about the padded envelope when Mother Catherine suddenly said, 'So of course she has to do her research here. She comes and stays with us a couple of times each year.'

'*Within* the cloister?' Tess couldn't keep the surprise from her voice. 'I thought it wasn't allowed.'

'In certain circumstances it is,' the nun said patiently. 'For instance, it's our practice to invite applicants to the order to stay with us for a couple of weeks. For two reasons: one, she gets to know just what is entailed; and two, we get to know if she will fit in with our way of life.'

'A sort of trial marriage,' Tess said thoughtfully. 'Not a bad idea. But did Miss Hillyard want to join you?'

'She toyed with the idea certainly, but no, not really. We invited her as a special privilege because of her connection with the founder and to help with her research. She can work in the library in perfect quiet. We like having her, she fits in very well. She loves it here. Perhaps one day she *may* even join us permanently.'

I'll bet. Tess found it hard to bite back the thought. Somewhere deep in her unconscious, something stirred. 'I'd like to meet her sometime,' she said.

'Oh, you'll be able to do so on Tuesday,' Mother Catherine said impassively. 'She's coming over for the exhumations.'

'Really? You're in touch?' Tess was flabbergasted. She was torn between scepticism and intrigue. Though she could not tell why she, who did not know the woman, should be so doubtful of her motives when the nun, who did know her, clearly was not. Mother Catherine was nobody's fool. *But being so honest herself, might she be too trusting?* One thing was sure, it was not Mother Catherine who had left the padded envelope in the hall. So it was pointless to ask her why someone was busily disposing of Jeddie Stebton-Hillyard's notes. And why they had chosen such a curious way of doing so.

'Oh yes. She was here in June. She was due again in late September but her mother was taken ill. She wrote to say that if she didn't make it earlier she would like to be here for the exhumation. To help in any way she can. I wrote to her a week or so ago to confirm the date.'

Well, that was that then. One mystery solved. All would be made plain in the next couple of days, yet for some reason that knowledge didn't make for any lessening of Tess's tension. She decided there was nothing for it but to come clean and get to the real point of her visit.

'Mother Catherine, I wonder if you have an outline map of the proposed changes? There's something I'd like to check,' she asked in a more business-like tone.

'But my dear, haven't you got one?' The nun sounded puzzled.

'Yes, but only of the enclosure. I was anxious to see how it is placed in the landscape. I wondered if you have a detail of the surrounding area, or at least the two properties?'

'Yes, I believe we do. If you just wait, I'll get it.' There was the sound of her chair being pushed back, click of a door, then silence for a couple of minutes. Claire, who had been sleeping in the car chair by her feet, began to stir. Tess bent down and held her bottle in her mouth until she dropped off to sleep again. She didn't hear the nun come back until she began to speak again. For some reason the whole charade got on Tess's nerves more than usual.

'Can you tell me why you want the map?' she asked, facing Tess with the dilemma of precisely how much to tell her.

'Em,' she started inauspiciously and sighed. No use beating about the bush any longer. Voicing her disquiet might just clear the air. 'I am a little worried about the possible implications of selling that particular plot.' She waited for what seemed an age for the nun to speak again.

'Is there any particular reason for your anxiety, my dear?'

'No, there really isn't. I'm just surprised I haven't seen a proper map, though I have to say I didn't think of asking for one before now. The seventh of November is very close. I would just like to make sure everything is in order. I haven't seen the contracts either, of course.' There it was out. In the ensuing silence she had the uncomfortable impression that there was more than one presence behind the screen. There was no particular reason why she should think so, no extra sound, no extra breathing and yet, somehow, the impression lingered.

'I think, Tess, you'd better explain yourself. This is surely Mr Murphy-Dunne's province. He is holding the contract. If something is troubling you, I would prefer to know. You need not fear it will go any further. I didn't think you would come today, when we're expecting the bishop, without good cause. Is the baby with you?'

'Yes, she's here beside me in her little car-chair. She's fast asleep.'

'Good. I'm afraid I shall have to go in a few minutes. So please, can you go on?'

'I went to Glenadams on Thursday to look around. I wanted to see your boundary wall from the other side, see how you would be affected by the sale. I take it you have never been in Glenadams?'

'No. We've worked from the maps.'

'And I see these maps have no contour lines?

Well then. There are two things which gave me pause for thought: the first is that there is a huge outcrop of rock marching along your boundary. Of course I realize that's why the school wanted the extra slice of land to go around it. What I didn't appreciate is just how high it is. Do you know your graveyard is completely overlooked?'

'Yes, of course. That is our most urgent reason for moving it. We got someone to go to the Glenadams side for us,' she said patiently and Tess felt mildly rebuked for underestimating her.

'Mr Murphy-Dunne?'

'No, Jane Stebton went and drew it all out for us. She's an excellent artist. But you say there's something else?'

Even fearing that it was probably another exercise in futility Tess felt compelled to go on. 'There is a tract of wasteland which edges the cliff and straddles both properties—'

And that was as far as she got. There was a short whispered discussion on the other side of the screen. Her instinct had been right then, there were at least two nuns there. She felt betrayed, angry.

'I thought we were speaking in confidence, Mother Catherine?' she said crossly.

'I'm sorry, my dear, I should have told you Sister Benedicte brought the map. We thought something had gone wrong about the exhumation and felt it would be better to deal with it together.'

'But I told—'

'I know, I know, but clearly something about this business is troubling you. Do you mind if she stays?'

'As long as the entire community isn't there watching me make a fool of myself.'

There was another whispered conversation before the black backing curtain behind the screen was drawn back – or at least one of them was. There still remained a thin black gauze drape through which she could make out the shadowy outlines of the nuns. There were only two.

'You wondered if perhaps we knew about that wasteland?' It was Sister Benedicte who spoke. She sounded relieved and something else – amused? Somehow she always managed to get up Tess's nose and this was no exception.

'Of course you know about the wasteland, you've appropriated some of it,' Tess accused bluntly and immediately felt like biting her tongue off. She had stupidly allowed herself to be goaded into indiscretion. She also felt sad. Until now she had been on excellent terms with the nuns. Now she could see their mutual trust draining away.

'We will have to tell her,' Mother Catherine said flatly. Tess could vaguely make out the other figure nodding agreement. 'In the strictest confidence, of course. My dear, that piece of land was bequeathed to us.'

'All of it? Right along the Glenadams fence? How long have you owned it?'

'Not all of it. Just the portion we've cultivated. A couple of years.'

Tess let the information sink in. If they had one piece of the property then they knew who owned the rest. And so did she, suddenly. The name was on the tip of her tongue as the nun pronounced it.

'Miss Stebton-Hillyard came over that first time

specifically to give it to us. She inherited it from her great-grandfather through her grandmother, so in a sense it came from Adelaide herself. Her father acquired it in 1828.'

Bingo, thought Tess, and I bet he intended to sell it to the railway company. She wasn't completely off-beam then. 'So it's been in the Stebton family a long time,' Tess said casually.

'Oh yes. But Jane only came into possession of it after her grandmother's death. It was not part of the family estate so she could dispose of it as she wished. Stray land, Jane called it. She said it was the only land she owned absolutely. Everything else was tied up with the Stebton inheritance. She was very proud that her grandmother had willed it to her. Very pleased she could pass it on to us.'

'You've seen the deeds? I don't suppose you've registered the gift, have you?'

'Yes,' the nun replied calmly. 'Jane showed us the deeds and she will register it herself. Indeed she probably has already done so.'

'With Miss Hillyard retaining the larger portion of the plot?' Tess said slowly, feeling her way. She hesitated for a second then blurted, 'The cultivation looks older than two years.'

In the ensuing silence, her heart had begun to pump and out of nowhere, she conjured up the ancient churchyard in Chipping Stebton. In the next few minutes she felt again that odd sense of _déjà vu_. It was as if she herself had written the scene they were playing out.

'We fenced it and put in an adverse claim for it almost five years ago. Had Jane not turned up we would have gained possession of it—'

'After seven years,' Tess finished. 'I see. Tell me, Sister Benedicte, who advised you then?'

'Mr Boland.'

'But how did he know about it? You can't see it unless you climb the rocks in Glenadams.'

'We took him through to see it, of course,' the nun countered in surprise, as if to imply that they were not quite so rigid about their rules as she, the outsider.

'And this was a long time before the Glenadams offer?' *Or the arrival of Jeddie Hillyard?*

'Two or three years. Mr Boland felt it likely that the school would put in a claim for it, indeed he was surprised they hadn't already. He suggested that we claim the whole thing but we didn't think that would be right. I expect the school has put in its own claim by now. They've been using it for a long time for nature studies and will, I believe, continue to do so.'

'Except that Miss Hillyard has the deeds and can pre-empt an adverse claim. She may have other ideas.'

'Oh no, Jane isn't in the least grasping. We are assured she prefers to keep the status quo. She has no interest in the land whatsoever. She says her family has already more than they can manage properly. We think she will probably gift it to the school, eventually.' *And I might win the lottery,* thought Tess rudely.

'I suppose you told Mr Murphy-Dunne the good news,' she asked blandly.

'Well, no. Jane wanted no fuss. She was adamant that the sale go through before we told anyone. It was her only condition. Which is why we said nothing to you either, Tess dear. You won't break our confidence, will you?'

'Of course not. You have my word. Just one thing more: have you put any restrictions on the sale?' Tess asked softly.

'Yes, it's all in order. Mr Murphy-Dunne saw to it that there is to be no extension of the school, or school sports buildings or the like, within a certain limit of our enclosure. He was quite specific.' Too specific, Tess discerned immediately. Much too specific. What if it was no longer a school? Now more than ever she needed to see the contract.

'Mother Catherine, Sister Benedicte.' Tess spoke clearly and confidently. As far as she was concerned it was time to stop shilly-shallying. Perhaps Jeddie Stebton-Hillyard was trying to protect the nuns. That could certainly be one interpretation of her antics. On the other hand it might not. Either way, Tess looked forward eagerly to meeting her. 'I'm glad Mr Murphy-Dunne has everything in order. He seems to have made a splendid deal for you. Just as a matter of professional interest, I'd be very keen to see how he managed it. It's pretty well a one-off situation but there's always something new to learn, isn't there? I'd really like to have sight of the contracts before you complete.' She wondered if she was piling it on too thick or if she'd managed to stay clear of maligning her colleague when it was Jeddie Hillyard who seemed to be calling the shots.

'Of course, we'd be delighted if you would. But all the papers are lodged at the bank. Perhaps you'd do it when the exhumation is complete?

Say Thursday or Friday? This is a very big moment for us.' Sister Benedicte appeared to mean every word. 'It's the first time we've had to make changes since our foundation and we are naturally very anxious to get everything right.'

'Of course. Thank you. One last thing I'm curious about. Was Miss Hillyard's gift in exchange for help with the book she was writing?' Tess posed her naïve question with as much humour as she could muster. 'Or was she interested in the library?'

'Yes, she simply loves the library. Of course it is very beautiful.' Mother Catherine sounded only mildly surprised. 'And being a librarian, she is a great help with the books. We have a great number from our founder's time. We always thought it was Mother Adelaide's personal collection. But we learned from Jane that it was Adelaide's father, Ryland Stebton, who was the great collector. Once we knew that, we decided to clear the open shelves. His volumes are mainly Italian literature and art which are not much use to us. Indeed they take up so much shelf-space we have very little room for our own books. We offered the collection to Jane but she wouldn't hear of taking them all, just those which interest her particularly, which she always sets aside for us to approve first. When she first saw the collection, before she knew about the Glenadams offer, she suggested we could sell the more valuable to help raise a maintenance fund for the convent. Even with the Glenadams deal, we thought it an excellent idea for the future. She has almost completed the cataloguing and has marked out the most valuable, to sell should the need arise.' *The most valuable? Wouldn't chance be a fine thing.* She couldn't help admiring the skill with which Jeddie Hillyard had dug herself in and diverted attention away from her real target.

'The librarian must be glad of her help,' Tess said coolly.

'Oh, our librarian is only concerned with our own little collection. We keep to our daily routine. Sister Mary-Rose spends at most a couple of hours a day in the library. So Jane, I'm afraid, mostly works alone.'

'Alone?' Tess asked too loudly, sounding like a disapproving dowager. 'Are you always so trusting? Is that safe? As a general rule, I mean,' she added hastily.

'Oh heavens no, we keep our safeguards, even with Jane. She lays the books she wants to one side. We put them in her little attaché case and she collects them from the hall. It would be too much to have her carrying a heavy case all the way downstairs. She has a bad heart, you know.'

'She didn't send them by post then,' Tess said faintly as Claire opened her eyes and began to look around. A sure prelude to attending to her bodily functions, which she usually did with quadraphonic sound and scent effects. Tess picked her up hurriedly.

'I'm afraid I must go, Mother. I shall see you early on Tuesday. I take it everything has been delivered?'

'Yes, everything. The hut was erected on Friday afternoon. We assumed you'd probably want to check. The cemetery gate is on the latch. You won't be disturbed.' She came nearer the screen. 'My goodness, the baby is growing well.'

'And heavy,' Tess laughed. 'She's become quite an armful. Noisy too. I'm not yet used to the fact she's awake more than she sleeps.'

'They don't be long growing up. She's a beautiful child. Tess?' There was anxiety in Mother Catherine's voice. 'I would like you to know that we're very grateful for all your help. You're so conscientious. We rely on you utterly. We'll see you early Tuesday morning.' She gave a little chuckle. 'And you'll see us.'

On the way out Tess looked in on the rather forlorn little cemetery. The little wooden crosses which marked the graves were being buffeted by a stiff wind coming in from the sea. Tess didn't linger. She made straight for the temporary shed which had been erected close to the boundary fence, some hundred feet from the graves. She was surprised at how large it was until she went inside. A note was pinned to the door which was unlocked. *I'll lock up after you've gone, Tess. The lists will be in the hall Tuesday morning. Mr Dwyer will be here at eight, + Joseph-Maria.* Although she was expecting to see the coffins, Tess got a shock when faced with the sheer numbers. There were five rows of three mounted on low trestles, which half filled the floor space. There was a further stack of folded trestles leaning neatly against the wall. It was as she checked that there were also plenty of body-bags and labels that, for the first time, she faced the reality of what was entailed in the whole enterprise. She felt quite numb as she stumbled out of the shed.

I opened to my beloved;
But my beloved had withdrawn himself, and was gone.
My soul had failed me when he spoke:
I sought him but could not find him;
I called him but he gave no answer.

The Song of Songs: 4:14–18

30

On the way to lunch at her mother's house, Tess parked along the Vico Road with all the other Sunday drivers. She opened wide the car window and let the wind blow through the car and her aching head. Below her, people walked along the beach, played with their dogs, flew their kites. One or two foolhardy souls plunged into the briny. Trains came and went at fifteen-minute intervals and each time the clickety-click of their wheels drummed the same message. The nuns were being shafted. Though specifically by whom and how would not become clear until she had received the documentation from the Land Registry. And perhaps not even then. Whichever, because of the bank holiday, for the next couple of days at least there was absolutely nothing she could do about it. Unless, of course, the nuns' darling, Jane-Edwina Stebton-Hillyard, could be persuaded to confide her agenda. On the whole, it seemed unlikely.

She went back over her latest visit to the convent, particularly the moment when the Guardian had drawn back the outer drape, leaving only the inner curtain between her and the two shadowy figures behind the screen. Cypress lawn, a line from Milton, popped into her head, learned by rote when she was just fourteen: *And sable stole of cypress lawn.* Black lawn, the stuff from which nuns' veiling was traditionally made. Strange, that instead of making her more comfortable, the nuns' almost ritual gesture had made her less so. She'd felt as if the opaque gauze was smothering and blinding her. Shifting her vision not from, but towards, whatever was really troubling the nuns. Away from the land and deep into the cloister.

She'd explained, as freely as she felt she could with no evidence, what she feared and to each point they had a rejoinder – soothing away her disquiet. Or was this only her imagination? Were they so totally concentrated on the bishop's visit and Tuesday's macabre proceedings that they could not, would not, think of anything else? She knew that they had gone into retreat – two days of prayer before the exhumations and would so continue for several days after. She had disturbed their meditations, which they took very seriously, and then had merely waffled when the seriousness of the occasion had called for decisiveness.

Tess sighed, wishing that she could sometimes not see each side of an argument. Nor be quite so practical. She decided on Friday that she had done everything she could until after the exhumation was out of the way. That there was nothing to be gained until she had some concrete evidence of malpractice. She should have stuck to her guns. Which would have been a deal better than throwing a badly aimed spanner into the convent and working herself into a lather. It wasn't as if she hadn't plenty of other things on her mind. Like that eternal, endless, heart-stopping moment when she looked for her baby and found her gone. She tried all sorts of devices to stop thinking about it, stop going over and over each terrible detail, tried to force herself to forget. The only sensible thing was to put it firmly behind her. But she might, as she acknowledged later, have been arguing sense with the wall.

She arrived at her mother's house expecting a small lunch party for three, plus infant; but besides Hugo, Susan had invited another half dozen. One couple, whom Tess had been talking to most of the afternoon, had to leave early because, they moaned, their teenage girls were home from school for the half-term and demanded entertaining. When Tess asked if all the schools took the half-term break at the same time, she was told that it was usually quite well co-ordinated. In reply to her next question she was told that happily the girls would be safely back in school the next evening by six o'clock. Their parents made no bones about their relief; the girls were, apparently, at an awkward stage.

It rained early on Monday, and for the rest of the day it was cold and overcast. Claire was out of sorts. And whether it was that Tess was nervous about the baby's safety or because she was in a bit of a lather about the morrow's proceedings, she spent the morning dawdling around the flat. By noon it was fairly clear that the only hope of getting the child to settle was to take her on a long drive. Tess headed for the Wicklow mountains and eventually fetched up in Avoca. On the way home, partly on whim and partly because it was much on her mind, she drove past Glenadams School. It was late afternoon and she fully expected to see large numbers of limos piling in through the gates, returning their offspring after the half-term. There were none. She pulled the car into the semi-circular forecourt in front of the gates. This time they were closed, locked, and chained, though thankfully there was no sign of the hound. She peered through the bars but apart from a single lamp halfway up the driveway, there was absolutely no sign of life. She got back into the car and racked her brains for someone she knew, reasonably local, with teenage children. After some thought she settled on a gossipy old pal who lived in Stillorgan which wasn't too far away. On the off chance of finding her at home she drove straight to the house. It was a singularly happy choice. Her friend came up with the goods as if she'd been primed.

'Odd question, Bernie,' she said after a cursory greeting and a few minutes' chat and baby worship. 'I'm trying to settle an argument. Do you know when Glenadams School finish their half-term break?'

'Yes, as a matter of fact I do. The kid next door goes there and since, when he's at home, he spends most of his time in a catatonic stupor in front of Feargal's PC, I know more about him than I want or need. I dread the holidays. Specially half-terms, which he's on at the moment. Of course all the other bloody boarding schools go back tonight. But not his nibs. Honest to God, Tess, his blasted parents keep ponning him off on me. Just because I don't go out to work.' She heaved a great sigh and looked at Tess balefully. 'Sorry for going on,' she said, then laughed nervously and Tess sensed that her friend was terrified that she would start talking about Marcus' death. It gave her a shock to realize how little she, herself, had thought about him for the past day or so.

She smiled at her friend. 'That's OK, Bernie. Better than baby talk, anyway. I'm up to here with nappies and bowel movements. Teenage angst seems quite interesting by comparison.'

'Ha, don't you believe it. They're like sloths; minimum effort, maximum confrontation. And don't even move a muscle doing it. Believe me, teenagers can slide from inactivity to complete inertia in one fluid movement. How old is Claire, did you say?'

'A little way off adolescence,' Tess laughed. 'What about the Glenadams half-term? When does it end?'

'They don't go back till Wednesday. Damn them.'

'You sure?'

'Sure. Why are you so interested? You're not thinking of recommending it to someone? If you are, I wouldn't bother.'

'Why not?' The air around Tess's head froze.

'Because it's winding down, is why not. They haven't taken on any new pupils this year. Or last, I think. Once the present lot are finished, they're closing down next summer.'

'You're joking.'

'No. That's the truth. Have you won?'

'Won what?'

'The argument,' her friend said impatiently.

'Yes, Bernie. I believe I have.'

As she drove slowly home Tess went over and over her previous visit to Glenadams School. Inch by inch, line by line. She had been hopelessly naïve. She had swallowed Mrs Plus-Four's pantomime act wholesale. What did they call it in the old days? Prestidigitation. There was no doubt about it. She was a formidable opponent. The question was, what on earth was she up to? Tomorrow might well be a rather interesting day. She began to chuckle softly until she remembered the other things that had happened to her, and Claire, in the past few days. Maybe interesting was too benign a word.

She had grown anxious and gloomy again by the time she got home. As she got out of the car she glanced up at the dark house and her heart turned over. A tall man uncoiled from a slouching position against the railing at the top of the steps and came down towards her. She stood staring up at him for a few minutes before she could propel her feet forward.

'Owen? You gave me the fright of my life. What are you doing here?'

'Whoa. Is that all the greeting I get?' He kissed her lightly on the cheek but she pulled away nervously. Claire responded more enthusiastically: when he dropped a kiss on her forehead she gurgled merrily at him. He took the carry-chair from Tess. 'Somebody loves me,' he said. The light had gone out of his face.

Tess didn't trust herself to answer. She was cross with herself for being cross with him. But unexpected visits had recently acquired an unpleasant connotation for her and she found it difficult to lower her defences enough to show any warmth. She wanted to; but she couldn't. He should have given her warning of his visit but how was he to know the reason for her overactive nerves since she had no intention of telling him? She gave him a wan smile and led the way up to the flat.

'Sorry for the frozen mitt,' she said contritely. 'I got a bit of a fright when I saw you standing there in the gloom. How was Wexford?'

'I gave it a miss. I didn't feel much like it,' he said in a I-don't-want-to-discuss-it-tone and changed the subject. 'You look tired, Tess love. Are you all right?' He tried to keep his tone light but as he looked at her strained features he radically revised his script. He had been fooled by her appearance last week. Thought she was recovering some of her vitality but now she looked half-dead again. Fragile. Vulnerable. He wished like anything she would jettison her plan to attend the grave-digging next day but he was too wise to broach the subject. He knew Tess well and avuncular advice was not something she particularly appreciated. Making contact with her was rather like treading on eggshells.

'I'm only passing through. I'm going back this evening. In fact,' he glanced at his watch, 'I must leave for the airport in half an hour.' He gave her a rueful smile and shrugged. 'Damp squib, eh?'

'I'll drive you, if you like. I'll just feed Claire first.'

'No. Thanks. I wouldn't hear of it. I've arranged for a taxi to pick me up in about half an hour.'

'Ah, Owen, I'm really sorry I wasn't here earlier. I didn't realize you were in Dublin.' *Or with whom.*

'I thought I'd surprise you for lunch. Silly me. I eventually gave up and had it solo in that place in Ballsbridge.'

'And I had lunch with my mother.' She grimaced. 'First time in a year, would you believe? I could spit.' She fibbed fluently for fear of hurting his feelings with the more truthful admission that she'd been driving around aimlessly all day. 'How long have you been here?'

'Hours. I got here early this morning. I had to meet a client.'

'On a bank holiday?'

'Well, yes. He was willing, so was I.' He raised his eyebrows at her, challenging her to question his claim. An anxious little smile played around his mouth as if he was trying to stop blurting something out. He's going to marry Stephanie, she thought suddenly. He came over specially to tell me and he's afraid to. Her heart bumped erratically down to her boots as she willed herself to be happy for him. Or if not that, then generous enough to feign it. She put the baby on a blanket on the floor where she flippered around happily.

'Have you time for a drink?'

'Just about.'

'This all right?' She opened a bottle of cheap Muscadet and when they were sitting at the kitchen table drinking it, she said quietly. 'You have some news.'

'Have I?' he laughed.

'I think so.' She got up from the table and went to the window. She stood with her back to him looking out into the park. 'So, tell me? Is it Stephanie?'

He didn't answer for a moment or two. Claire began to grizzle for her feed but Tess didn't turn around. All she could think of was that every fixed point in her life was falling away. She was more adrift than ever.

'What the hell has Stephanie to do with anything?'

She didn't notice he'd got up from the table until she felt his arms around her shoulders. Down in the street a taxi honked its horn. 'Oh, fuck,' Owen said. He pulled her around to face him and kissed her. Gently until she began to respond and then in an explosion of passion, hungrily, remorselessly and with gratifying expertise. Her lips were sore when she pulled away.

'Hmm.' She smiled at him shakily and laid her hand against his cheek. 'You have me confused, Owen. I'd put you down as the quiet and dependable one.'

'No, I'm the wild and passionate one. But they're not mutually exclusive, you know,' he said lightly and grinned at her discomfort. 'You've always been a lousy judge of character. Still,' he added thoughtfully, as they went downstairs, 'confusion will do for a start.'

She stood at the hall door holding Claire, while he ran down the steps towards the taxi. As he got in, he hesitated and came running back to her. He took a bottle of Veuve Cliquot from his battered old briefcase and thrust it into her free hand.

'What's this?'

'Another great scheme that didn't quite work out. Put it on ice.' He put his mouth to hers and played with her tongue for a tiny, tantalizing second. Then he pulled away and sprinted down the steps again. Still with his back to her and with his arms outstretched, he did a Zorba-like couple of little dance steps before he climbed into the taxi. 'Keep it for when I come,' he shouted out through the open window. 'I only drink champagne in bed. Or was that something else you didn't know about me?'

Tess walked slowly along the hall and sat down heavily at the bottom of the stairs. She touched her hand to her bruised lips. She could still taste him in her mouth, mixed with the fruity wine they'd been drinking. He had surprised her. Twice. By his ardour and by his remark: 'They are not mutually exclusive.' Passion and consideration? As far as her experience went, they were. *Passion and consideration?* A heady mixture. Was it what she wanted? Needed?

As a child, she had been a bystander, an unobserved witness of the wild roller-coaster of her parents' emotional life. Was it because they had externalized everything, she did the opposite? Persuaded herself that hers was a calm and tolerant nature? She had, she told herself, learned from that experience. She'd known how to cope with Marcus. She was his balance. Him like them. All the pyrotechnics she claimed to admire, the spewing of the cherished personal volcanoes, were really the profligate expenditure of the vast reservoir beneath. She had allowed herself to be swept along in his, as in their, wake. Casting herself as the quiet, reserved, reasonable one when really she was as turbulent as they. She laughed softly. Claire sucked her fingers contentedly and looked beyond her as the hall door opened and Hugo walked in.

'Tess? You startled me. What on earth are you doing in the dark?'

'Thinking,' she answered dreamily. 'Owen was here. He's just gone.'

Hugo paused at his door. He looked tired. 'Drink?' he asked gallantly but without much enthusiasm. They hadn't really spoken since the dinner party. Tess stood up and started up the stairs.

'Thanks, Hugo, but I've an early start in the morning. Big day. Night.'

'Owen, eh?' He spoke half to himself. 'I've always considered him the more . . .' He stopped and looked up at her. 'Good luck for tomorrow, Tess.' She turned at the landing and saw that he was still standing at the open door watching her. 'Worthwhile chap, Owen,' he said and went inside.

Was he? she wondered as she continued, heavyfooted, up the stairs. His ambivalence was baffling. He hadn't, after all, declared himself. One kiss wasn't much to go on, however passionate. On reflection, she didn't think she could cope with such restraint, even under the guise of consideration. Not in her present state of heightened carnal desire. Her emotional response to him was even more unpredictable. And confused.

They are all gone, and all with them is gone,
Nor aught to me remains but to lament
My long decay, which no man else doth moan,
And mourn my fall with doleful dreariment.

The Ruines of Time, *Edmund Spenser*

31

Tuesday, October the twenty-ninth, the day Tess had been dreading. It was still dark when she got up, too restless to sleep and much too agitated to eat more than a half slice of toast. Claire was still fast asleep when Sandra turned up, bleary-eyed, at six, and plonked herself down beside her in the big bed. They were still snoring their heads off when Tess left at half past.

It had turned unseasonably cold overnight and a thin layer of frost sparkled on the car windscreen. Traffic was light going south but there was already a build-up in the opposite direction, towards the city. She was surprised that it started so early. As she got nearer the convent she tried to concentrate on the radio and not think of the horrors ahead. Coffins and graves were still a raw subject. She tried not to think about Marcus and found herself speculating about Owen. Most of all she tried, desperately, not to think about Claire. Not to keep trying to imagine what exactly she might be doing from minute to minute. She felt as though part of her had been amputated.

After all her foreboding, it was calm and peaceful when she got to Holy Retreat. Apart from the arrival of the JCB, of course. But she was there before anyone else arrived.

'Have you got the list of the deceased and site-plans, Mother Catherine?' She found she couldn't quite manage to look the nuns in the face. For some reason they made her feel shy.

'Yes, Tess, I have them here.' The nun cleared her throat. She drew a sheaf of papers from beneath her cloak and handed several to Tess, one of which had her name written at the top. Tess ran her eye down the sheet. The first death was in 1867, ten years after the convent was founded, the most recent in January 1996. The pages were handwritten in fine italic and ruled neatly into four columns listing the religious names of the deceased, their age, the cause and date of death. Those who died in the past four decades or so were all quite old, but the further back she went the younger they seemed. Twenty-four, twenty-six, thirty, thirty-five. Three or four had died of heart disease, a similar number of pneumonia but until the nineteen fifties TB claimed, by far, the greater proportion of the lives.

Tess thought then of her first visit to the convent, almost two months before. Even on that mild and sunny September morning, the parlour had felt chill and damp. She wondered now, as she'd wondered then, how the sisters survived cold, wet Irish winters without heat or insulation. Under the pretence of reading she studied the nuns covertly. Without the all-enveloping security and mystery of the enclosure, the all-pervasive scent of lavender, the ubiquitous opaque screens, they looked diminished. A shiver ran through her. Suddenly she wanted to throw her arms around them and shelter them.

Tess turned away and looked across at the back of the convent building which was coated in crazed plaster. It was in an even worse state than the brickwork in front. Dripping gutters had left huge green slime marks up the grey and crumbling plaster, some of the wooden window-frames were rotting. An inhabited ruin. Looking at the house in the cold morning light, she had no doubt how desperately it needed renovation – indeed, almost rebuilding – but she also knew, from dear gossipy Sister Joseph-Maria, that at the beginning several of the sisters had been opposed to the deal and were unhappy about the resiting of the graveyard. In the end, of course, they had been persuaded. The porteress had innocently kept Tess well abreast of the debate within the cloister as well as much else.

'What time are you expecting Miss Hillyard, Mother Catherine?' Tess kept her voice neutral.

'About ten, I should think,' she replied calmly and Tess assumed Jeddie had confirmed her attendance.

While they were waiting the two nuns took Tess to see the newly sited and consecrated graveyard, on the far side of the convent building, which had been prepared over the previous few weeks. It followed a more formal plan than the old, which had grown, less by design than accident, into a rough semi-circle, at the centre of which had once stood an ancient Celtic cross. This had already

340

been re-erected on the new site where the new graves lay open, waiting to receive their incumbents. They radiated out in two rows from a circular raised bed in which the cross had been placed. There were several piles of coloured stones, about fist-size, lying inside the circle. Someone, the gardener presumably, had already planted tiny lavender clumps around the edge inside which *Magnificat Anima Mea* had been spelled out in pinkish stones against a background of mica-speckled granite. It was skilfully done and Tess was struck by what the artist – it was undoubtedly an artist – had managed to achieve with seaside pebbles. She recognized them as having come from nearby Killiney beach. But given that the beach was beyond the cloister she wondered who the good sisters had roped in to do their hauling. Having become, insidiously but rapidly, a kind of fetching and carrying supernumerary of Holy Retreat, she was faintly surprised not to have been asked to do a bit of the quarrying herself. Though perhaps she was being premature, she noted in some alarm that the granite stones had almost run out.

The undertaker and his men, closely followed by Mr Mike Flood from the County Council and Mrs Joan Fermoy from the Health Board, arrived soon after they got back to the convent forecourt. The two nuns stood to one side, in silence, while Tess greeted them and distributed the lists. Before the work began the undertaker huddled with his men and worked out a simple plan of procedure which he then announced to the rest of the assembly. The grass turf and topsoil to a depth of two or three feet would be removed and set to one side before the individual graves were opened. Once each coffin was raised, it would be identified, labelled, then stacked in the shed. Where the coffins had perished, the remains would be bagged and labelled at the graveside, taken to the shed and placed in one of the new coffins and labelled a second time. The gravediggers removed the crosses one at a time and when the JCB had cleared the topsoil, they took over again. They staked out each grave before they began to dig in reverse sequence.

The morning was chilly. Tess stamped her feet to keep the circulation going. Every hour or so, a plump middle-aged nun, agog with curiosity, darted from the convent bearing a thermos of hot tea which she shared around.

'You go inside and warm up, Mother, you look perished. Wouldn't you let me stay and relieve you?' Tess heard her murmur at least three times before the besieged superior sighed in resignation, dispatched her elderly and nameless companion inside and let the importunate nun replace her. Sister Julian-Maria was everywhere. She was somewhat younger than the other two nuns and from what Tess could gather from her excited whispers, she was hoping – nay, expecting – a miracle. A whiff of roses, an apparition, an intact body. Left to herself, Tess had little doubt that she'd have each and every coffin opened – 'just to make sure'.

Where the soil was driest, some of the older coffins had long since disintegrated – or fell apart as soon as the workmen tried to lift them. No one spoke very much as they gathered the contents of each – bones, scraps of fabric, rosary beads – into black plastic bags and labelled them. The frail and silent superior seemed to have more strength than even the grave-diggers. She stood her ground while they were replaced by a second shift, just after one. But she prayed the whole time, unobtrusively and silently.

They had worked their way through twelve graves when, at about one thirty, a couple of nuns came to whisper shyly that lunch was laid in the parlour. They fluttered anxiously when the new workmen said they'd brought their own sandwiches and that they'd prefer a cup in the hand where they were. The rest of the party trooped wearily inside. The two sisters showed them into the parlour then modestly excused themselves and disappeared.

There was little talk. And although none of them had shown much enthusiasm for food beforehand, now faced with piles of egg sandwiches and buttery scones, they fell to with an appetite which took them by surprise.

'There aren't many more. We should get through the best part of the job today. Finish tomorrow,' Dwyer calculated, wiping his mouth. 'Thank God,' he added grimly.

'Let's hope.' Mrs Fermoy spoke up for the first time. 'I find it all very gruesome.'

'You've never done anything like this before?' Tess asked the undertaker.

'I believe it's only the second or third time in this country. At the very most,' Mike Flood interjected, explaining that he was supervisor of the south city cemeteries but even in that capacity had not witnessed a mass exhumation before. He was a tall, rather stooped man of about fifty, with a quiet

343

voice and gentle manner. Over the hours, the colour had leeched from his face until it was almost as pale as his unruly hair.

'Are you from the west?' Tess asked, making conversation.

'County Clare.' He smiled and she was surprised how much more interesting he looked close-up. Outside, huddled up in a vile green anorak he'd looked like any old train-spotter. His blue-green Donegal tweed suited him better. She didn't quite know why, but she wondered if he was a musician and the question was out before she could stop herself.

'Why yes, how did you know?' He sounded surprised and pleased. 'I play the uilleann pipes. You?'

'I don't play the uillean pipes.' They laughed.

'You're the solicitor, aren't you?' he asked. 'Much red tape?' Outside, the JCB started up again.

'Oh, yes,' she replied, 'both from church and state. It's taken months to arrange.'

'Have you done it all?' he asked.

'The firm I work for did. I took over from one of the partners some weeks ago when he was taken ill.' She smiled. 'It's been very interesting. I've grown to like the nuns.' She moved a little closer and lowered her voice. 'By the way, did you notice those kids hanging around outside?'

'I thought I saw something. Was there more than one? I noticed something certainly. Though I'm not sure it was a kid. About eleven o'clock?'

'Yes. I wondered if I was dreaming. A head popped up near the boundary wall and then disappeared. I was too far away to see clearly.'

'I'm not sure I even saw a head – just some movement at the far corner.' He chuckled softly. 'They didn't stick around long, whoever they were. All those coffins probably gave them the fright of their lives.'

'Didn't someone say they'd had some trouble with vandals recently?' Mrs Fermoy interjected.

'Yes, a few of the memorial crosses were burnt, the rest were left lying around. They've been replaced,' Tess said. 'As far as I know they were only a bunch of youngsters.'

'I'll have a look around before I go home, if you like. See if the wall's been breached,' Mike Flood murmured.

'That would be good. I'll come along as well. No need to worry Mother Catherine.'

'No, hardly. Remarkable woman, isn't she?' he said.

'I thought she'd pass out a couple of times. I know I felt I might.' Mrs Fermoy from the Health Board did indeed look ill. 'What a business it is,' she continued as the door opened silently and the Mother Guardian beckoned. She looked much refreshed though her cheeks were flushed and her eyes over-bright. She fell in beside Tess as they walked towards the graveyard.

'You will be able to come back tomorrow, Tess?' she asked anxiously. 'The light will soon be gone and there seems such a lot to do still.'

'Yes, of course. If it could be a little later . . . the baby . . .'

'Of course, of course, my dear. I should have thought . . . I rather hoped Jane might be able to help out. She mustn't have been able to get away.' She sounded preoccupied.

'You've had no word from her then?' Tess asked but Mother Catherine didn't answer. She moved away, to the shelter of a stand of rowan trees, where she and her companion paced up and down reading from their breviaries. From time to time the sing-song sound of the psalms drifted over the graveyard. Eventually they finished and wandered back to where Tess was standing.

'Are you all right, Mother? Could you not get someone to take your place?' Tess began. She stopped abruptly as one of the workmen began to wave his arms violently at the undertaker.

'What's up? What's up?' The old nun's voice cracked in alarm. She clutched Tess's sleeve and held her back. Dwyer ran to where the JCB was clearing the earth and they saw him bend down and shake his head. The workmen leaned on their spades and watched as the shovel of the JCB poised in mid-air. Mr Dwyer straightened up as the rest of the party approached.

'It's a lead coffin.' He spoke directly to Mother Catherine.

'A lead coffin? But it can't be!' She sounded horrified, agitated. 'None of our religious would be buried in a lead coffin. It's not possible. How could it be so?' She looked from one to the other and compressed her lips. 'We have a vow of poverty,' she said stiffly, offering what she took to be a clincher. But her audience looked at her blankly. The nun turned away. Afterwards, Tess recalled with some amazement how quickly she had grasped the implication of this strange incident.

Mrs Fermoy nudged Tess. 'What's a lead coffin?' she whispered.

'I'm not sure.' Tess spoke tentatively and caught Mike Flood's eye. 'Do you know?'

'Yes. They are usually lead *lined* – for burial overseas, for instance. This one's rather more unusual: it seems to be wrapped in lead sheeting.'

'How weird. Why? Why would they do that?' Mrs Fermoy persisted. Tess shrugged and shook her head.

'There shouldn't be a coffin there at all. That's not a grave. At least, not according to this,' Mike Flood said as he held out the site-plan to the Mother Guardian.

'It can't be one of our sisters,' she said distractedly ignoring the paper. Her voice trembled and she shook her head in disbelief.

'Whoever it is, we can't lift it.' One of the workmen made a feeble attempt to lighten the situation. ''Tis way too heavy and it's forming a suction with the wet clay.'

Mr Dwyer was heard to mutter something about too many effing experts as he ordered them all to stand away. He gestured impatiently to the JCB driver who edged forward into position beside the open grave. There was a sickening thud as the teeth of the grab gashed the top end before it scooped the coffin up, swung it towards the hut and set it down. Dwyer hurried over and covered it with a tarpaulin sheet.

'We'll deal with it later, Mother,' he said firmly. 'That all right with the rest of ye?' His voice was surly. 'OK boys, let's get goin' again,' he called and hurried back to the grave.

'Why can't it be a nun?' Joan Fermoy's bafflement was almost comic.

'We have a vow of poverty, Mrs Fermoy,' the

nun repeated, as if that explained everything. She drew her lips together as if speaking was painful to her.

'Maybe one of the early sisters came from a wealthy family? A lady?' Mrs Fermoy persisted.

The Mother Guardian flicked the list of the deceased against her skirt impatiently and looked at her.

'Mrs Fermoy, we have a full history of all our sisters,' she said hopelessly. 'We have no lead coffins. What possible reason would there be for such a thing? It would not be in the spirit of our Holy Rule.'

'It was not so very unusual in the nineteenth century,' Mike Flood interjected *sotto voce*. None of them paid much attention.

'What about your foundress, Mother?' Tess asked.

'Our Foundress is over there. The first on the list, the last to be lifted. We planned to take her directly to the new site.' The nun swallowed. She looked threatened, cornered, as though she wanted to back away from their imperious enquiry, their demands for information she could not give.

'Did the early foundation not have any other benefactor or benefactress?' Tess asked quietly and kicked herself as Jeddie Hillyard's name popped into her head. She still hadn't turned up. Tess looked around as if by willing it, the woman might appear. But there was no sign of her.

'Not apart from our founder. The house, the land, everything came from her family,' the nun murmured and sighed deeply. She was lethargic, exhausted. Defeated. Tess looked at her thoughtfully but before she could say anything else the old nun turned away and walked over to where the lead coffin lay. She stood gazing down at it for a long time, the beads of her rosary slipping compulsively through her shaking fingers. After a few minutes she went to Dwyer and spoke to him briefly.

The next grave was cleared quickly and easily but because it was in a seam of dry and sandy soil, the coffin had long since crumbled to dust. The small brass tag with the name and date of the deceased was, thankfully, still there. The atmosphere lightened a little as the workmen moved a few yards and began work on the final group of graves. It was extraordinary how variable the soil was. It was almost as if there were alternate strands, wet, dry, wet, dry. This time the patch they'd hit was almost marshy and their feet quickly sank into the oozing peat. Mike Flood, still clutching his plan, wandered over to Tess's side.

'Six more, I think.' He ran his finger down the list. 'Unless of course the plan is wrong and by great good fortune,' he murmured, too quietly for the nun to hear, 'Sister Adelaide-Maria is in that lead coffin. In which case there will only be five.'

'Of course.' Tess smiled at him with relief. 'She was the foundress, after all. And her family was rich enough.' She glanced at the pencilled notes on her plan and thought her own thoughts. Perhaps they had intended to bury Sister Adelaide elsewhere. At home in Oxfordshire, for instance. Hence the *lead* coffin.

'You tell me. I haven't a clue. Trouble is, her grave is marked as the one they're digging now.'

'Oh, dear. I thought Mother Catherine said they'd leave it till tomorrow. That she wanted it taken up last. I wonder why she changed her mind?' She looked around for the nun and saw that she was beckoning them to join her and Dwyer at the graveside. He too was studying the plan. The labourers looked up at them and then at Dwyer.

'We've hit something,' they said. 'This one's intact, thank God.'

The men slipped lengths of the webbed strapping through the coffin handles and tried to heave it up but it took Herculean effort for almost half an hour before they managed to break the suction. When at last the coffin was hauled to the surface it was amazingly well-preserved. Its name-tag was still neatly screwed to the lid, inscribed in floric italic: Mother Adelaide-Maria, Founded Holy Retreat 1852, died 1908. Mike glanced at Tess. They both shrugged regretfully and looked at the Mother Catherine.

'I hoped,' she said mournfully, 'I hoped she might be in that.' She pointed to the lead coffin. 'Mr Dwyer, can you stop the work for the night, please?' Tears welled in her eyes. 'I'd so hoped . . .' She bit her lip and turned to Tess. 'Tess, dear, can you go into the convent and ask Sister Joseph-Maria to call the community together? We must take our Holy Founder to the chapel tonight. Tell them to light the candles. I will wait here.' Her sad eyes met Tess's. 'Will you come and wait with me?'

As Tess hurried off, the nun joined Dwyer and Flood who were talking earnestly together. 'We have one too many, haven't we?' She had a fit of coughing before she looked up into the undertaker's face. Her eyes were watering badly.

'Maybe not, maybe not. We must wait and see,' he soothed. 'Get someone to re-check your records tonight. We mustn't anticipate trouble. These things usually turn out to have very simple explanations.' He looked at her steadily. 'Don't you find, Reverend Mother? We must wait and see when all the graves are dug.' He patted her hand. 'We can hold on till tomorrow, can't we, Mr Flood?' It was more a challenge than a question and left Mike with little option but to agree.

'If the worst comes to the worst we'll have to call the coroner and open it up for identification,' Mr Dwyer said briskly, unemotionally, pointing towards the tarpaulin. 'But only if the worst comes to the worst. Maybe the solicitor can find something in the records?' He appealed to the nun but she had withdrawn into herself and did not reply.

'Perhaps if we could peel the lead back there may be an inscription underneath?' Mike Flood looked at the others but the light was fading fast and no one volunteered support. It was clear Mother Guardian wanted them to leave before the procession assembled to carry their founder into the chapel.

'I think it can wait until tomorrow,' Mr Dwyer said decisively. 'That lead coffin isn't going anywhere.'

Let's hope that one of the Elderson dynasty is in it, thought Tess, as she hurried back to join them. Otherwise it's going to be murder to sort out.

But let my due feet never fail
To walk the studious cloister's pale.
And love the high enbowèd roof,
With antique pillars' massy proof,
And storied windows richly dight,
Casting a dim religious light.

Il Penseroso, *John Milton*

32

It was strange how much the Mother Guardian managed to convey with so few words. She had been standing by the coffin of the foundress watching the little group leave the cemetery but when Tess went over to say goodbye, Mother Catherine took hold of her hand and, almost imperceptibly, shook her head.

Tess turned and waved good-bye to Mike Flood and Mrs Fermoy. Rather regretfully, it had to be said, since she was both tired and anxious and her legs ached. The strain of leaving Claire for the whole day had not been notably relieved by a couple of hurried checks on the mobile. Sandra was inclined to the laconic which tended to pall on an anxious mother who was looking for reassurance rather than smart-ass remarks. But at least her mother had come up trumps and promised to stay until it was time to go to the theatre.

It bore in on her that the *ad hoc* nature of her arrangements seemed very precarious. Doubts about the workability of her future plans had been rumbling at the back of her mind for weeks. The shock of the previous Friday evening had given them a severe jolt forward and now they were even stronger. Leaving Claire with a baby-minder would become a daily routine *if* she went back to work full-time and she knew she still wasn't nearly ready to cope. Not just with stroppy young Sandra; with anyone. She took wry note of that little *if* which increasingly featured in her thoughts.

Having waited so long for motherhood she was alarmed at how quickly the baby had taken over her life and at the same time relieved to find how deeply committed to Claire she'd become. In many ways she enjoyed motherhood. Strange how enjoyment could be so hedged about by almost perpetual anxiety. Stranger still, how deeply that tiny scrap had burrowed into her every thought; her demands filled every waking moment. Not just the present, but the future too had been comprehensively mortgaged as well. Tess nervously glanced at her watch and looked up to find Mother Catherine watching her. Seeing her face to face, Tess thought, was like meeting her for the first time.

As their eyes met and held, Tess felt as though a sudden, violent, electrical charge had passed between them. That was when she really became aware of the eloquence and power of the nun's silence. She was caught and held enraptured by this strange, fugitive glimpse of the force of the nun's confidence in her own way of life. Or was it faith? Belief? She could not have articulated then, nor at any other time before or after, the meaning or the usefulness of the contemplative life, but for that tiny fleeting moment, in that one instant, she felt its meaning surge into her. Wordless, mysterious but somehow *believed*. But rumbling beneath it was fear.

The undertaker's men brushed down the wooden bier they'd been using to shift the coffins. Then one of them fetched a soft rag and rubbed it clean. They wheeled it to the founder's grave and hoisted the simple box-like coffin onto it and stood for a moment with bowed heads. As they shuffled off, Mr Dwyer came over to where Tess and the nun were standing.

'What time do you want us tomorrow, Reverend Mother?'

The nun cleared her throat and rubbed her finger along her lower lips before replying.

'Half past nine?' She could barely get the words out her voice was so dry.

'Then we'll be off, Mother.' He bobbed his head at them both. 'You'll be here as well, miss?' It was more a statement than question. As Dwyer hurried off to catch up with his men, Mother Catherine and Tess moved closer together until the folds of the nun's voluminous cloak and Tess's long black coat intermingled. As the older woman drew herself up to her full height, Tess became aware how impressive she was. Mother Catherine looked no more than a couple of inches less than her own five foot ten, though the raised hood of her mantle may have added to the impression of height. Her face was lined and tired but the dark hooded eyes appeared more luminous in the half-light, reminding Tess of an El Greco saint. Strange how that austere face was never still, the eyes darted this way and that, noting everything, missing nothing. Hidden by the folds of cloth the old nun's dry cold fingers encircled Tess's wrist, signalling her to silence. They stood side by side, still as statues, watching until the heavy wooden gate was slammed shut.

'Tess, don't move, don't look up.' The nun's voice was low and urgent. 'Can you come tomorrow morning at half past seven? I know how hard it is for you to leave the baby, but please, please do this for me. I need to talk to you. Leave your car outside the main gate. I shall meet you at the lodge. Come to the back door. The nuns will be at prayer. I shall watch out for you.'

Even as Tess calmly nodded agreement she began to work out the logistics of getting to the convent so early: baby out of cot by six-thirty, fed, into car to collect sleepy, protesting Sandra, dump screaming child and crotchety minder, grab cup of coffee before facing twenty-minute drive to the convent. Baby-sitter would have a fit. As would baby. Tess groaned.

Mother Catherine released her hand, took her rosary from her pocket and stepped nimbly aside. As Tess turned away there was a sudden commotion from the convent. The shutters were pushed open and the rococo interior of the convent chapel was flooded with light. A harmonium played softly in the background.

'Stay,' the nun whispered as the nuns gathered at the open doorway. When the harmonium fell silent, they filed slowly from the chapel. There were thirteen of them and each held a lighted candle. They walked forward in stately procession, their eyes on the ground. They were not wearing their splendid cloaks but the long black veils which fell over their shoulders almost touched the ground. In the flickering light the simple grey habits looked a ghostly, shimmering silver. No white veils; no novices, Tess noted with some surprise, and wondered when they had last admitted a postulant to the enclosure. It was an ageing community, some indeed appeared both old and infirm.

As they walked, they sang the Magnificat. Their thin eerie voices were slightly off-key yet the sound they made was almost ethereally beautiful. Tess watched and listened in awed silence until she became aware that the old nun was talking again. At first she assumed she was repeating some sort of liturgical litany but her ears pricked up when she realized that Mother Catherine was identifying each of the nuns.

'. . . Maria . . . Our gardener Sister Albertine-Maria, Sister Ambrose-Maria, Sister Marie-Claire, who was here this morning. Sister Maria Magdalena, Sister Raphael-Maria, Sister Majella, Sister Julian-Maria, Sister Agatha-Louise, Sister Mary-Rose the librarian, Sister Anna-Maria, Sister St John, our musician, and Sister Joseph-Maria.' Almost as if she'd heard her name, the tiny woman at the rear momentarily looked up and Tess had a quick impression of a mischievous wrinkled apple of a face.

'Where is Sister Benedicte?' Tess whispered as the Mother Superior threw back the hood of her cloak and made to step forward to join her sisters.

'She came out first. There.' She hunched her shoulders impatiently and pointed to the head of the procession, but just an instant too late. The singing stopped as the nuns fanned out around the bier and it was impossible to distinguish one from the other. Even allowing for variations in height, the habit barred all individuality. After weeks of only hearing their voices Tess had formed her own images of the three nuns she'd talked to, which, if Mother Catherine was anything to go by, did not in the least tally with the reality. She had pictured Sister Joseph to be a big, merry countrywoman, yet she was tiny. She had expected the Superior herself to be small and comfortable and she was neither. She wondered in what particulars she had misconstrued Sister Benedicte, since she was, and it seemed would remain, the most mysterious of all.

Mother Catherine walked forward to join her community. As she reached the graveside, two of the nuns stepped to one side and allowed the Superior to slip into the centre of the semi-circle around the coffin. One of the sisters passed her a lighted candle and immediately a single quavering voice lifted to the *Te Deum Laudamus*. As the bier was pushed slowly forward, the choir fell into procession behind it and took up the response. From where Tess stood all that was visible was a phalanx of the long black veils billowing outward in the gentle breeze. They could have been Arab women in their timeless all-enveloping black robes or a scene from the Bible. The sight was at once exclusive and so primitive that she stood transfixed until they disappeared into the chapel.

As she let herself out of the cemetery, she turned to look back. Over on the other side, beyond the wooden shed, where the lead coffin lay under the tarpaulin, something moved. At first she thought it was the wind in the hedgerow but then she distinctly saw the unmistakable glow of a cigarette. The tiny bright spot burned brightly for a second, then as quickly disappeared. She waited for a few seconds but saw nothing more. But all her anxieties resurfaced.

She shut the gate and crossed the front of the convent towards her car. As soon as she reached it she pulled her mobile phone from the glove compartment and dialled Hugo's number. Please, oh please, let Claire be OK, Tess breathed, as she waited for an answer. Sandra picked it up on the third ring and listened in heavy silence to Tess's rush of apology for being late. Sandra wasn't big on charm, nor had she her mother's confident touch. Something Claire had latched onto very smartly. Although she was pretty good with the baby, Sandra had made it plain from the first that flexibility was not her best suit. Another problem was trying to read the girl's rather off-hand, take it or leave it manner.

'I'm sorry, there was a delay. Look, I'm going be to at least another half hour, maybe more, depending on the traffic,' Tess rushed nervously. God, she thought, why am I so craven?

'You're all right. Your mother has only just left and Mr Boland is coming up in a minute,' Sandra drawled. 'I don't think the pair of them trust me. They've been fussing in and out all day. The baby's fine. She's been fast asleep for hours.' Oh

358

help, oh rats, thought Tess, her heart sinking, she'll be awake all night.

'Sandra?'

'Yeah?' Sandra said in her flat dead-pan Dublin accent.

'There have been some problems here. It's going to take a bit longer than we expected. Another couple of days, maybe.'

'Oh, yeah?'

'Yeah,' Tess echoed irritably and plunged forth. 'Can you come very early again tomorrow morning?'

'How early?' Sandra asked suspiciously.

Tess swallowed hard. If this morning's effort was anything to go by, early mornings were not quite Sandra's thing either.

'I'll collect you at, er, seven.' Tess held the phone away from her ear and waited for a diatribe of protest.

'Why don't I just stay the night? You must be jaded. Me ma left us a casserole. I'll ask her to get a lend of a camp bed from Mr Boland.'

'What? You don't mind? Are you sure?' Tess asked. The prospect of a long hot leisurely bath rose tantalizingly in front of her.

There was a burst of laughter from the other end. 'Know somethin', Tess? You worry too much. I was only jokin' you about the kid being asleep. I'm just going to give her a bottle now. She was great today. She was awake most of the time. Sittin' up and takin' notice. And she's learnt to laugh. Honest. I think I'm gettin' to like her,' she added provocatively and laughed again. 'Take your time. Honest. Mr Boland warned us you'd be late. He said the old nuns would have you running around in circles for them. Was he right?'

'He was right,' Tess said and gave a little snort of relieved laughter.

She switched on the ignition, wiped away the condensation from the windscreen and gasped with pleasure. The front of the convent was bathed in the rose glow of the sunset and looked as the original builder must have intended and hoped. The scars and cracks and decay had vanished leaving only a fleeting vision of perfection. She stared out and thought about her very first visit to Holy Retreat a couple of months before. Then, as now, she had been thrilled by the beauty of the old house. Getting to know the strange, almost alien way of life of its inhabitants had merely added to her romantic perception of Holy Retreat. The name seemed to imply peace, tranquillity, other worldliness. A place apart. Fixed, immutable, uncluttered. All eyes raised to heaven. 'That was then,' she murmured and let out the clutch. 'And this is now.' She wondered, for the umpteenth time that day, why Jeddie Hillyard had not shown up as promised. She also noticed that she was not particularly surprised. Which was strange, because it had been perfectly obvious that Mother Catherine was feeling a little put out at the non-appearance, though she'd said nothing. Curiously, all Tess had felt was relief.

The element itself,
Shall not behold her face at ample view;
But, like a cloistress, she will veiled walk,
Twelfth Night I i 26, *Shakespeare*

33

All the other cars were gone. It took quite an effort for Tess to force the convent gates closed. The hinges had rusted from infrequent use, as a result the gates had dropped a fraction and resisted every inch of the way. Because the base of the gates had also rusted out, the rough and jagged edges scraped and screamed against the gravel and set Tess's teeth on edge.

The clouds had scattered as the wind died. The setting sun streaked the sky pale pink and golden; and though it would soon be dark, it was temporarily brighter than it had been earlier. Tess hopped back into her car and was about to turn right towards the city when, on a whim, she turned the other way and slowly followed the boundary wall to her left. She glanced at her watch as she drove along. It was twenty minutes to six and she had been at Holy Retreat since seven that morning. Eleven hours almost; the thought made her whole body ache and she longed for a large, iced, alcoholic drink.

She felt as though she'd been on hold for hours,

absorbing impressions but neither reacting nor drawing any conclusions. Her awareness that, lead coffin apart, something was terribly amiss within the enclosure continued to grow. As did her anxiety about Claire's – and her own – safety. About the nuns, her disquiet was of a more passive anxious nature, more . . . more what . . . ? Unsavoury? No, it was much more to do with the unsettling nature of inter-personal tension between the two nuns which had been so obvious on Sunday. Now she came to the conclusion that one of them, she wasn't sure which, had been trying to gag the other.

Was it only an extension of what she'd felt on her very first visit to the convent? When the strangeness of hearing but not seeing those she spoke to had so disturbed her. Yet today the Mother Guardian had been with her all the time. Aha, came the mocking thought – physically, but not spiritually. But surely that was more than a little fanciful? Could it be that the old woman had long since lost the knack of face-to-face confrontation? Had she simply become more skilled with the order's *modus operandi*? More comfortable protected by her screen?

But from the first Mother Catherine had recognized how difficult Tess found this aspect of their life. In fact both she and Sister Joseph had always appeared to be mildly amused by her discomfort. Not unkindly, but playfully. Like children playing peek-a-boo with their hands in front of their own faces. Tess had never been entirely easy with this idea and sometimes wondered if they ever literally played hide-and-seek? With their husky unused voices, could one nun substitute for another without her knowing? Why on earth would they? She laughed out loud at the absurdity of her fantasy. It might have been possible the first couple of times she'd visited Holy Retreat but not any more.

As the formidable bursar had been at pains to point out, talking through the screen wasn't any different to talking on the phone, was it? She had become used to their individual voices. And today she'd actually matched face to voice. Except in the case of the Sister Bursar, of course.

She came to the end of the road and pulled up beside a parked car which she recognized with relief as Mike Flood's. She got out and stood for a moment looking up at the sky. The light would barely hold for another half hour. After about a quarter of a mile the high stone wall curved to the left towards the sea and after another fifty yards merged into a high dense hedge. A narrow tractor-track had been dug out close to the hedge and wavered in and out of the huge stony outcrop boundary of the neighbouring boarding school.

She followed closely, trying to estimate the point where she would begin to border the cemetery. From her sighting the previous week she was able to count off two or three little telltale signs. A clump of fading red fuschia in the dark foliage of the hebe and a tall walnut tree just before the short stretch of the cemetery wall. She pulled up abruptly. Just before the wall started a portion of the hedge had been pulled aside exposing a huge boulder, like a mounting block, at the base of the wall. She could not remember seeing it before. A man stood on the stone with his back to her, peering over the wall. She let out a gasp of relief when she saw that it was Mike Flood. He must have watched her approach because he spoke her name softly without turning around. He was puffing contentedly on a long black cheroot.

'Miss Callaway. Climb up here a moment.' He turned to stretch out a helping hand.

'My God. You gave me a fright,' she said clambering up beside him.

'Sorry. I didn't mean to. I've been watching you since you turned the corner. I thought you'd probably seen me. Look over there.'

The stone was long and wide enough to hold them comfortably. They had a clear view into the cemetery and beyond that, over the whole south side of the enclosure, to the convent building. Below them and a little to their left was the temporary shed with its padlocked door. Directly in front of them lay the tarpaulin-covered coffin and beyond that again, the worked graves. Tess rested her elbows on the wall ledge and rubbed her chin.

'Not much of an enclosure, is it?' she asked ruefully. 'I wonder how long they've had snoopers? Poor old nuns, it's not very safe, is it?'

Mike jumped off the rock. 'Come over here.' He drew her into the hedgerow and pointed at the ground where four or five cigarette ends had been stubbed out.

'The kids we saw?' She bit her lip and hoped they weren't some knowing little gurriers who would try to make a few quid out of the story of the moving cemetery. They'd best get a security firm on patrol for the duration. She was so preoccupied with this idea that she had to ask Mike to repeat himself.

'No, not kids. A guy in a Land Rover,' he said and Tess's blood ran cold. 'It passed by as I drove out the gate. At first I thought it must be coming from the school but then I remembered the school entrance is on the Shangannah Road.' He looked at Tess. 'Do you think it was somebody from the newspapers?'

'I hope not. More likely the security man from the school. He has a Land Rover. I was in there last week. He has a vicious great hound as well.' She shivered. 'A newspaper man might be preferable.'

'Hardly a story though, is it?' he asked and their eyes met.

'Not until today.' Tess spoke half to herself. She sat down on the stone and began to chew thoughtfully at her thumb nail. 'I bet they could make some sort of story out of that lead coffin though. I'd better contact a security firm.' She wrinkled her nose. 'I'd better go home as well. The babysitter will . . .'

'How many children have you got?' he asked, falling into step beside her. Now that the sun had gone down a fine mist had begun to roll in from the sea.

'How many?' Tess laughed. 'One. You?'

'Five. From sixteen years to seventeen months,' he said as if he'd rehearsed his reply often. He was a relief to be with; so normal, so everyday. 'How old is yours?'

'Four months.'

'Your husband a lawyer as well?'

'I am alone,' Tess returned rather over-dramatically. 'I have no husband. My partner is dead,' she said and to her surprise and embarrassment found that tears were rolling down her cheeks.

These thoughts may startle well, but not astound
The virtuous mind, that ever walks attended
by a strong siding champion conscience . . .

Comus, *John Milton*

34

Next morning, Tess was up and dressed before six. She fed Claire and, crossing her fingers, laid her in the camp bed beside Sandra, who grinned up at her and took the baby in her arms. Tess beat back a wave of jealousy and made herself a quick cup of coffee. She gulped it down standing beside the kitchen stove. The heating had only just come on and the flat was cold. The only sound was a gentle duet of snores and snuffles from the sitting-room. She pulled her heavy winter coat tightly around her and crept downstairs holding her shoes in her hand.

There was a light frost, a sort of half-hearted affair which would quickly melt, but there was a distinct nip of winter in the air. As always in Dublin there was wind, light but searching. She scraped the windscreen and got into the freezing car. Like the day before, there was little traffic and she made it to the convent in record time. She drove a couple of hundred yards beyond the gate, parked the car as far into the bushes as she dared, then walked slowly back towards the convent.

When she turned at the gate to check, the car was no longer visible. Her heart was in her boots; she could not get rid of the feeling that she could no longer put off straightening things out with the Mother Guardian. What, she wondered, were the chances of the messenger being spared? The problem was, there were so many strands, each time she followed one, she lost temporary sight of another. And then of course, with her mind engaged with Claire's safety, and her own emotions, she kept feeling she must be overlooking vital bits of information. She glanced at her watch: it was ten minutes to seven and the sky was lightening visibly.

The gate was standing slightly ajar. She slipped inside, closed it carefully and headed for the lodge. No sign of lights or life. Her soft-soled shoes made no sound as she followed the little path around to the back door. It opened at her approach and Mother Catherine beckoned her in. She was wearing her great black mantle. Tess followed the nun into the front room where two chairs had been drawn up in front of an old-fashioned single bar electric fire which made little impression on the frigid temperature of the room. Tess pulled her coat more tightly around her as she sat down and waited for Mother Catherine to speak. The nun was deathly white. She coughed and nervously licked her parched lips.

'I'm worried about Jane,' she said. 'On Sunday you mentioned that you knew something about the Stebton house in Oxford.' It was about the last thing Tess expected her to say. 'Can you tell me about it, please?'

'What do you want to know?' Tess asked.

'Everything. Everything you can think of.'

'Owen, my . . . Marcus's brother, was shown around the house by the vicar of St Edwin's, Revd Tim Stebton. He's a widower and he's just married Jane-Edwina's sister. You did know she has a sister, did you?' Tess asked.

The nun shook her head. 'I understood she is the last of the family. She was quite specific about it. It was her reason for donating the land to us. "I am the last of the Stebtons and since I'm too old to have children, I shall be the very last," she said.'

'She and her sister are twins. At least, so I was told. The Revd Tim is next in line, but since he's older than the twins his children will probably inherit.'

'Are you saying the land isn't hers to give? She was very specific about that to us.'

'Not necessarily so. You said she inherited from her grandmother as a personal bequest. I'm sure there's nothing to worry about.' She avoided the nun's eye. 'But just in case, I'm running a search with the Land Registry.' To her surprise the nun didn't react to this little nugget. It didn't seem appropriate to press her about the contract, nor did Tess add that she was also investigating the ownership of Glenadams School. 'I should have it in a day or so. Perhaps even today. I'll let you know as soon as it comes. But I'm sure it'll be all right,' she added reassuringly. The nun held her gaze for some time. She seemed a million miles away. 'I'm more anxious about that lead coffin,' she whispered.

Tess took a deep breath. 'When I was in Oxford,' she said circumspectly, 'I visited the graveyard. I looked for mention of the Elderson connection.' The nun gave a gasp then leaned forward and looked up fearfully at Tess. 'You didn't find one, did you?' It was less a question than a demand for confirmation.

'No, I'm afraid I didn't. There may be something there but I didn't find it. Mind you, Mother, I only gave the graveyard a very quick once-over. Some of the graves are very hard to read.'

'Thank God.'

'What?'

'I said thank God. It means the lead coffin may contain Adelaide's mother, Sophia. It is what we hope.'

'Her mother? But wouldn't you have known she was there? Is it not in the records?'

'No. There are no records prior to the foundation of Holy Retreat. The Eldersons were all buried in Bray. But there's no grave for Sophia there, we checked with the parish. The Stebton side of the family went back to Oxford, that is, according to the scanty information handed down to us. We know that Adelaide's younger brother William Stebton's remains were shipped over to England. I think we all assumed that his mother, Sophia Elderson Stebton, was too.'

'In lead coffins? Of course,' Tess said softly and the nun inclined her head. 'Couldn't you ask your friend Jeddie?'

'Jeddie?'

'Short for Jane-Edwina. It seems to be what she usually calls herself.' Strange that Jeddie hadn't told the nuns her nickname but let them use the more staid, the more simple form of her cumbersome name. Perhaps she thought Jeddie was too rackety somehow? Tess took a deep breath. 'You know she's a bookseller, don't you, Mother Catherine?'

'Yes,' she answered vaguely. What was going on? On Sunday she seemed horrified at the idea. Tess studied her face closely but the nun did not flinch. And then Tess knew. She hadn't wanted to discuss Jeddie in front of Benedicte. God Almighty, she thought, wheels within wheels.

'She no longer works in the bookshop,' Tess said gently but didn't expand on how she knew. She was still trying to get her mind around Jeddie's connection with the lead coffin. If there was one as the nun seemed to imply. It was all so damn confused. 'Should we try ringing her at home?'

'It would do no good,' Mother Catherine said sadly. 'She's not at home. When she didn't turn up yesterday, I telephoned the contact number I have for her. A machine answers, as it has done for the past month or more.'

'That's what I was trying to tell you,' Tess said gently. 'Nobody seems to have seen her for at least a month. Though a friend of hers in the village has had a card. From Italy, I was told,' she finished lamely. She was absolutely dying for a cup of coffee. She looked around hopefully for a kettle but the room was bare. 'There isn't any coffee about, Mother? Or tea?' she asked optimistically.

'Yes, I forgot.' The nun left the room for a moment and returned bearing a flask and two cups. The tea was sweet and milky both of which

Tess normally detested. Surprisingly, it was very good and put the warmth into them that the fire had singularly failed to do.

'Mr Murphy-Dunne has gone away as well.' Tess didn't quite know why she said it except to reassure herself. He seemed the only possible candidate for getting into the offices unseen. The question of how he'd managed on crutches was more difficult. But then she wasn't entirely convinced about the entire back story.

'I thought he was in hospital.' The nun looked startled.

'I believe he's gone to the West Indies,' Tess said and immediately realized she believed nothing of the sort.

'Since when?'

'As soon as he got off the crutches. Thursday, I think. Why?'

'I saw him, I'm sure it was he, early on Friday morning, while I was waiting for the shed to be delivered. He didn't have crutches. He was standing on the rocks overlooking the graveyard with someone else. I thought I'd caught the vandals. I was looking at them through field glasses.' She smiled wanly at Tess's look of utter disbelief. 'Oh come Tess, we may be nuns, but we don't live in the stone age, you know. This is a splendid place for bird-watching.'

'But it poured all day. I remember.' She didn't say why.

'Not out here, it was quite sunny until nearly midday. A beautiful morning.'

'Who was with him? Did you see?' Tess could hardly get the words out. Mother Catherine's face was half-hidden by her hood so that it was impossible to read her features. 'It looked remarkably like Jane,' she said hoarsely. 'But I must be wrong.' She spoke like a sleepwalker. 'I was following a kittiwake. I didn't recognize her at first, she was so strangely dressed. He came up behind her and put his hands over her eyes. Like blind man's buff. They were larking about first on the outcrop and then along the waste patch, near the Glenadams end. I picked her up several times in the binoculars. I lost them while I trained back to the bird and when she next came into focus he was pulling her up from the grass. By then I'd lost the kittiwake and so I watched them for a while. I was a little upset that she hadn't come to see us.' She pulled back the hood and looked earnestly at Tess. 'I was surprised by who she was with. I didn't realize she knew Mr Murphy-Dunne.' She paused uncertainly. Tess could almost see her put uncharitable thoughts aside. 'You said he was ill,' she accused. 'So did Mr Boland. But he didn't seem in the least ill, or lame.' Tess drew in her breath sharply and bit back a cry as the nun continued dreamily, as if she were looking back into her memory and seeing again the picture she was painting.

'They began to play tag or something. Like children, pushing and shoving ... racing each other ... She was winning when I last saw her ... she was surprisingly fast but of course he was much taller and was catching up ...' She pursed her lips in distaste and because of that Tess assumed that the game had some sexual connotation. 'The builders came with the shed, so I had to go.' She looked at Tess. 'But I don't understand what she was doing there. I thought it was Jane.

That is why I was so sure she'd be here yesterday. Maybe I made a mistake. I feel uneasy. More than that, disturbed. But perhaps it is only my anxiety about the lead coffin?' But the way she said it made Tess doubt that the lead coffin was uppermost in her mind.

'Did he see you?' Tess asked slowly. She felt as though she was watching figures weave in and out of the mist, now singly, now in couples, dancing a slow pavane of death. She shivered. The nun touched her hand.

'You're cold?'

'That too.' Tess looked into the dark hooded eyes. 'I am more afraid than cold. You?'

'Yes, I am afraid. And I am afraid to speak my fear lest I make it real.' She gave a long low sigh and passed her trembling hand over her eyes. 'I must go or I shall be missed. Mass begins in five minutes.'

'Go then. I will ring Chipping Stebton and ask a friend to go look up the parish records for you. At least we can try to set your mind at rest about the coffin.'

'At this hour?'

'Yes. I'll try to be back by nine, before Mr Dwyer shows up.' She held out her hand. 'Mother Catherine? Trust me. I'll do my best.' She didn't say what, or why, or even how. The nun inclined her head.

'Tess? There's something . . .' She started, then stopped abruptly and without another word, she slipped out the back door.

Tess looked after her wondering what it was the nun hadn't the courage, or the will, to say. She sprinted to the car and drove at breakneck

374

speed to the nearest hotel, no more than a couple of miles away. Throwing caution to the winds she drove boldly up to the main entrance and abandoned the car directly outside. Being early in the week and out of season, the dining room was practically empty. Tess sat at a table by the window and ordered a large pot of coffee and toast and while she was waiting rang the Rogersons' number in Chipping Stebton on her mobile. Dudley picked up the phone and the urgency of her request with a surprising turn of speed. He silenced her apologies about the early hour and the difficulties of gaining access to the church records. Had she forgotten he was church warden? he asked. Then she remembered, joyously, that he and Marcia were also keen local historians.

'I'll go at once,' he boomed. 'Around the eighteen forties and fifties you say? Back in fifteen minutes, latest. Talk to Owen while you're waiting.' And before she could say another word he dropped the receiver with a loud clang. It sounded as though it had hit the old dinner gong which sat like a surreal symbol of MGM in the tiny hall. Owen picked it up as her breakfast arrived.

'Owen? You seem to be everywhere.' She felt unaccountably pleased.

'That's the general idea.' He laughed. 'The line is hopeless. I can hardly hear you.'

'Damn. I'm on a mobile and there's a lot of interference. Either that or it's running out of juice. I forgot to charge it last night. I'll find a regular phone and call you back in a few minutes, OK?' She switched it off and turned to find the waiter had brought a house phone to the table and plugged it in beside her. He waved aside her thanks as he ambled back towards the kitchen.

Tess gulped down her first cup of coffee and wished she'd ordered tea, which was usually the better option in her homeland's hostelries, something she regularly forgot. But because the coffee was hot it was welcome and the view out the window was beyond spectacular. The hotel sat on a hill overlooking the sea. Had the window been open she might have heard the sound of the waves crashing on the shingle. The sky was streaked with pink, the sea dark blue and across the horizon a monster catamaran was churning its way back to Holyhead. Which made her think of Jeddie Hillyard and her postcards. She dialled the Rogersons' number again.

'I thought you said you were going back to London?' she said when Owen answered.

'Mother's finally to have her hip replacement. She went into the Nuffield yesterday. Operation tomorrow. I only found out when I got back on Monday night.'

'Her hip? But I thought all her joints were affected?'

'Hips more than others, it seems. The surgeon predicts a good result. She's been in a lot of pain. I took a few days off, to keep Dad company. Is this nuns' business you've sent him on? He looked pleased as punch.'

'Really?' Tess glanced at her watch. Barely five minutes had passed but it seemed like eternity. 'Something came up that I needed him to check. I would have asked you but I didn't know you were there.'

'Literally?' He cut across her embarrassment. 'Come up I mean? The exhumation was yesterday, wasn't it?'

'Yes and yes,' she gave a nervous little giggle. 'A lead coffin to be precise. Nobody knows who the hell's in it.'

'Very Hammer House of Horrors. Sounds tricky. Hello, I see Dad has just come out of the church, he'll be with you in a couple of minutes. I'll give you a ring tonight, if that's all right?'

'Of course, and Owen?' She hesitated. 'You were a fantastic help on Wednesday. Absolutely marvellous. And, er, sorry your visit on Monday was such a drag. But thanks for coming.'

'Is that what you call it?' He chuckled softly. 'How's Baba? And Mama, come to that?'

'Surviving,' she said earnestly and crossed her fingers.

'I'll be interested to hear what transpires with your nuns. I feel as if I've half read a novel and want to know the ending.'

'Me too,' she said fervently. 'How long are you staying in Chipping?'

'Only a few days,' he answered. 'I'm going to have to sort something out. The old dears are getting a bit past living in such an isolated village. Shopping has become a real problem for them. Besides, I'm getting pissed off with all the travelling I do. It's beginning to get me down. Tess, I'm thinking of taking early retirement.'

'You're not? But you're only forty-six for God's sake.' But her mind wasn't on Owen's woes. 'Is Dudley back yet?' she asked impatiently.

'Hold your horses. He's just crossing the road, he'll be here in a tic. Tess?'

'Yes?'

'You coming back to Oxford or do I have to move to Dublin to get you to marry me?'

He spoke in a rush and when he heard her involuntary squawk he put the phone down gently. She was still catching her breath when Dudley's booming voice sounded in her ear.

'Sorry it took so long. Got a pencil at the ready? Here goes. Blasted family seem to have only a few names between them, generation after generation, which makes it difficult to trace anything. Pretty poor lot on the imagination front. However, here we go. Church records first. They practically run back to the Reformation. The first Stebton died in 1573, fancy that. The only Elderson I can find is William Ryland Elderson Stebton who was drowned when he was eight in May 1839. His father Ryland William Stebton died in April 1850, fall from a horse – in Chester it says here. Hunting it seems. Bit unfortunate, eh? No sign whatsoever of Sophia Elderson. I traced from 1860 back to 1820. That any help?'

Any help? Tess heaved a sigh of deep relief. Even if the nuns didn't come up with any corroborating evidence, the chances were that the lead coffin contained Sophia's remains. Tess began to thank Dudley when he cut her short.

'Hang on, my dear. There is something a little odd you may be interested in. You're sure about the name, Sophia? It couldn't have been Sarah, could it? Unless of course she was his first wife,' he added half to himself.

'First? No only.'

'No, you're wrong. I missed it at first, in the

378

records. There's so much gumph I couldn't wade through it all. I'll go back later, now you've got me hooked. It makes interesting reading. The modern entries are very dull by comparison. As I say, there are so many of them with variations of the same names. I would have missed it entirely if the cleaning lady hadn't shown up and rolled back the carpet in the centre aisle which normally covers the medieval brasses. And as it happens one or two memorials, besides. Got the pencil handy again? I'll read what it says verbatim, then you must make of it what you will: *Beloved son of Ryland William Stebton, William Ryland Elderson aged eight years drowned at sea 1839. Ryland William Stebton, killed while hunting, in April 1850, aged 59 years, dearly loved husband of Sarah Phoebe Stebton (née Mulholland) of Shrewsbury, died August 1876, aged 74 years.* Then we have mention of four nameless children who died in infancy. But the last line reads: *Erected by her grieving son, Thomas Ryland Stebton, as a just memorial to his beloved parents.* Have you got that?'

'I have,' Tess said faintly. 'Did you get Thomas' dates?'

'Of course. You don't miss much, do you, my girl? Eighteen thirty-three to nineteen hundred and six. I leave you to work out what it means.' He gave a satisfied hoot of laughter. Tess could see him begin to embroider the story for his wife's amusement. She cradled the phone, paid her bill, and went to the cloakroom to wash. She bent over the sink and dashed water on her overheated face then ran a comb through her hair which, as usual, had crinkled from the sea mist. She looked curiously excited, her eyes over-bright, her cheeks flushed. Like a sad clown, she thought, and was taken with a nervous fit of dry, humourless laughter at the realization that she had spent the previous ten minutes discussing what she suspected was bigamy, in the middle of which, if she wasn't dreaming, Owen Rogerson had proposed marriage. She stared at herself in the mirror. Her long black coat made her look like an ad for Sandeman's Port. Or an undertaker's mute.

Possessory: *In the case of either freeholds or leaseholds, registration with Possessory title does not affect or prejudice the enforcement of any estate right or interest adverse to the title of the first proprietor.*

Registered land – General Information

35

Tess hightailed it out of the hotel car park but after a few minutes she slowed down and almost immediately after that stopped altogether. It was quarter past nine and the undertaker was not due until nine thirty. If she hurried she could get there a few minutes before him. On the other hand, if she delayed, the decision about whether or not to open the coffin might have been already taken.

To call the coroner or not to call the coroner, that was the question exercising her mind. And the nuns' too, no doubt. Dudley's bombshell bore thinking about. She needed to get her head straight. She pulled into a small lay-by overlooking the sea and switched off the engine.

She stared at the notes she'd scribbled on the back of the cemetery list. When was Sophia supposed to have died? She could not remember anybody ever mentioning a date but presumed it must have been prior to the convent being set up in 1852. How long would that take? A year or two? She tapped her pen against the steering wheel and stared, sightlessly, at the sea. After a while, chiding herself for being melodramatic, she listed her queries, one under the other in order of priority. Almost at once she began to chuckle at how effortlessly she had reverted to rigid Catholic doctrine under the influence of the nuns. The thought of divorce, as a possibility, had simply not entered her head. The Eldersons were Catholic but the Stebtons were not. Even if Ryland had converted, he might have un-converted.

She'd been making a mountain out of a molehill. Why would Ryland take his abandoned wife to the family vault? Much more likely she was buried in the grounds of her home. It was not uncommon pre twentieth century. No mystery there. No foul play suspected, ergo, no coroner. 'Ooooh, what a relief,' she cried and drew a line under the notes. The chances were that the nuns would have found the lost records by the time she got back. The other implications of Dudley's findings could be addressed later. Including Chester which lodged itself at the back of her mind like a wart on the end of a nose – neither in vision nor out of it. She pulled her phone out and dialled the flat. Happily, the line was clear.

'The baby only just woke up. I think she might have a bit of a cold, did you know that?' Sandra announced in her usual off-hand way, plunging Tess into immediate crises. It was terrifying how rapidly her overvolatile emotions could swing from relative tranquillity to blind panic. She was instantly responsive to the slightest hint of threat. Or criticism. 'Oh my God, is she all right? Has she got a temperature? I'll come home at once. Call the doctor.'

'Tess? For heaven's sake, calm down.' Mary Mackie's calm voice arrested the fusillade.

'What are you doing there? Claire's really ill, I know it—'

'Tess! Stop it. I'll kill that Sandra for getting you in a panic over nothing. The child is probably teething, that's all. We'll get something from the chemist to rub on her gums. You calm down and stay where you are. I just came up to check how they were doing. The baby's grand. If I'm needed I'm downstairs all day. By the way, your mother rang to say she'd drop in later this afternoon. That baby has us all dancing attendance on her. She's fine. You get on with your job. We'll expect you at about six? I'll cook a chicken for you. OK?'

Six? The thought of a whole day in a lather of sweat over her baby was too much for Tess. She arranged to meet both babysitter-and-sat, for lunch, at the hotel between half past one and two. They could travel out by train. Killiney Station was only five minutes' walk away. Pleased with this solution, Tess was about to ring off when, without preamble, Hugo came on the line.

'Tess, Susan's just called in on her way to the airport, she's on her way to London – replacing someone in some Ibsen play. She sends her love.' I bet, thought Tess tiredly, wondering why Hugo thought her mother's comings and goings important enough to bring him scurrying up to the flat. Her immediate thought was that the baby was worse than they made out, but she bit back another outburst of anxiety. In three hours she would see for herself.

'OK. Look, I have to go . . .'

'*Ghosts* is the play, I just remembered,' Hugo said. Tess closed her eyes in disbelief and tried to cut him short. 'No, Tess, wait a minute.' She could barely make out the words. 'All that about your mother is bunk. I was just waiting for the others to leave the room. Look, Murphy-Dunne has resigned, I thought you should know,' he said in a rush. 'The nuns too, I suppose.'

'I thought he was on holiday?'

'Holiday, my arse,' Hugo exploded. 'I think we'd better talk tonight, you and I. Tess?' He waited for her to answer but she couldn't get the words out. She felt as though a heavy weight had landed on her head. A million thoughts bombarded her.

'One other thing, Sinéad says to tell you the stuff you were waiting for has arrived. She wants to know what she should do with it? Will I collect it for you?'

'Yes. No. I'll deal with that,' Tess cut in squeakily. 'Hugo? Is the Murphy-Dunne thing a surprise?' There was a sharp intake of breath before he replied.

'The extent of it, yes. Bloody bombshell, to put it as charitably as I can. I'll see you tonight. We'll talk about it over dinner. I should have done so sooner,' he added, half to himself.

'Hugo?' she arrested him sharply. 'Are you by any chance the author of his back problems?'

'What do you mean?'

'For God's sake, Hugo, stop messing. Was he ill or was it just something you made up?'

'I'm afraid I made it up. I wanted him out without raising too many eyebrows. Or arousing suspicion that something was wrong. Not until I knew the extent of it.'

'And do you?'

'I'm not sure I can tell yet. I'm sorry, Tess. How did you guess?'

She sighed. 'It's taken me long enough,' she said and cut the connection. She didn't feel like a post-mortem, even a figurative one. She could only try her best to plod on, taking each thing in turn. She lay back and closed her eyes for a minute or two. Just get one problem sorted, she thought, and another, much worse, hits you in the face. She made herself do three minutes deep breathing before she felt able to start the car.

She drove to the convent at a sedate speed only because she was not calm enough to do otherwise. But while she could control the pace of the car she could not control the turmoil in her head: Jeddie and the books, Jeddie and the land, Murphy-Dunne and Jeddie, Murphy-Dunne and the land. The pair of them playing in the grass. The dog. *Claire disparue*. Bigamy. Plus the lead coffin, of course. Everything was connected yet nothing seemed to fit.

She parked her car beside the convent and, out of nowhere, came the blinding thought that she was not looking at these elements correctly, much less making the right connections. It was also possible that there was no connection save only coincidence of time and that each element alone, if not resolved, could cause the destruction of Holy Retreat. The worst thought of all was the threat to herself and through her to Claire. And last, that her father's old respected firm, and

Hugo's too, was implicated. With her, like piggy in the middle, as the fall guy.

She was grim-faced by the time she joined the tense group in the graveyard. Mother Catherine, on one side, was in deep conversation with Dwyer; the others were variously employed. The grave diggers were filling in, rather than digging out, a grave and the JCB was busily spreading topsoil evenly over the trampled earth. As far as she could judge, there was just two or three graves left unopened. She skirted them on her way to the hut where Mike Flood, Mrs Fermoy and a nameless nun were on the point of placing a body bag in one of the empty coffins. Mike and Joan looked up at her approach and exchanged greetings. The nun turned around to face her. Tess had not met her before and stepped forward to introduce herself. It was hard to judge the nun's age. Though she wore glasses, her clear un-cosmetic-abused skin was flawless. She could have been anything from mid thirties to late forties.

'Just a couple more after this,' Mike said heartily. 'It looks as though we can wrap it all up before lunch. We'll just get this one sorted then I think we're due a cup of tea. What do you think?' He grinned at Tess as he lifted the lid off the first coffin on the fifth row. 'Could you pass a label, Tess, they're on the last row there.'

Tess went over to where they'd worked the afternoon before. 'Is this row filled already?' she asked in surprise.

'We've already done three this morning.'

'But I thought we only used the first of this row yesterday?'

'No, two.' Mrs Fermoy spoke up. 'They're both labelled.'

'Oh? My mistake. Sorry.' Tess looked at them absently and when they resumed their task she wandered casually along the fourth row checking the labels. She hesitated beside the second coffin. At first glance, it appeared exactly like all the others. The name printed in black biro: Sister Felicitas-Maria. Tess felt an icy chill run through her body. She closed her eyes and stood stock still until she regained control of herself. She ran her eye swiftly down her list and when she looked up the nun had moved a little away from the other pair. She stared straight ahead. She was extremely pale, stricken. Her eyes slithered to meet Tess's. Neither moved.

Mike Flood smoothed down the sack then screwed down the coffin lid. 'There, Sister Mary-Rose,' he said, signalling the nun's name to Tess. 'Shall we go back for the next one?'

Mary-Rose? Wasn't she the librarian? Not just that, she was also one of the trustees of the convent's financial affairs. This woman, then, knew all about the land deal *and* the library. The third most powerful woman in the convent but from Tess's point of view, the most interesting of all. She had to get her to talk. But how? Tess looked at her curiously but the nun remained silent, as if she felt more comfortable adhering to the rule, even in the present extraordinary circumstances.

'I believe your library is very beautiful.' Tess caught up with her as they were leaving the hut. At first the nun didn't answer but when she turned around and noticed Tess looking at her

387

expectantly, she touched her sleeve: 'Did you say something? Could you repeat it please? I'm deaf, you see,' she whispered courteously. Tess was struck that the nun should have chosen a life where her disability mattered so little as she repeated her question. 'Very beautiful indeed, we are blessed.' Sister Mary-Rose was evidently a skilful lip-reader. 'Mother Catherine has been waiting for you, Miss Callaway. I'll take the others for a break while you talk.' She turned on her heel giving Tess no chance to probe her further.

Tess turned to see Mother Catherine beckon. She had taken up position under a large walnut tree, sitting in a basket chair with a rug wrapped around her knees. She was even paler than she'd been earlier. She looked at Tess.

'Sister Mary-Rose found some documentation. We believe it's Sophia. Unless, unless your friend found . . . ?'

'Don't worry, Mother. There is no record of Sophia Elderson's burial in Chipping Stebton. She is neither in the church records nor in the graveyard. Her son William is there and her husband Ryland William Stebton is buried with him. But absolutely no Sophia.'

Mother Catherine's lips moved for many minutes before she said simply, 'Thank God.'

'Do you know when she died?' Tess asked gently.

'Twenty-seventh of March 1850.'

'Aaah. That explains a lot,' Tess said. *And leaves a few questions unanswered.*

'Ryland Stebton was killed in an accident in

April 1850. In Chester,' she added but the nun looked at her blankly.

'What does it explain? Has Chester some significance?'

'Well, it's not far from Holyhead and it's not long after her death. Suppose, just suppose that after her death he went over to make arrangements for her funeral in Oxford and on the way was killed,' she finished lamely. *A funeral? Are you kidding? said the little gremlin sitting on her shoulder. Try wedding. Try making an honest woman out of the second wife.* But she was not unkind enough to further complicate things for the shattered nun.

'I see.' Mother Catherine didn't look very convinced. 'It's possible. It could as easily have been bad weather, I suppose,' she added wearily. 'Nevertheless you have done us a great service. Thank you, my dear. We shall examine the lead coffin after the last exhumation, which should be in about an hour. Would you like some tea?'

'No thanks, I had some breakfast at the hotel. Sorry it took so long. Do you want me to stay while you open it?'

'If you would, please.' She smiled up at Tess. 'I'd feel easier in my mind. You don't know how I've come to depend on your good sense. Mr Dwyer and Mr Flood will stay also. Mrs Fermoy will not. I think she's probably had enough, poor woman.'

'Is Sister Mary-Rose very deaf?' Tess broke the silence.

'Profoundly so. She lost her hearing as a child. But she reads lips as accurately as we hear, you know.' She lapsed into silence. Tess took her list out of her bag and ran her eye through it. Then she read it slowly once more. She looked up as the cemetery gate opened and Sister Mary-Rose led the others back after their tea-break. She stared at Tess and inclined her head so imperceptibly that Tess almost missed the gesture. Was she imagining things? Was the deaf nun indicating that she too had noticed the odd label? That she knew Felicitas-Maria was bogus? She looked down at Mother Catherine to see if she had noticed the little by-play, but her expression was blank. She looked as though she had gone in on herself, as if her thoughts were a million miles away. She looked more than tired, she looked ill.

There was something rather despondent and jaded about the rest of the group also, as if the effort of keeping on an even keel – which they'd all achieved the day before – was proving too much. They shuffled about restlessly while the very last grave was dug. Mike Flood wandered over to her side and when he asked if she'd managed to hire in security men, she knew he was curious about why she was late. She fobbed him off.

'No, the baby wasn't well, so I haven't had time to broach it with the sisters. And anyway it just seemed one thing too many for them to cope with. I'll see what I can do later today. Thanks for, er, last evening. I think I was a bit overwrought.'

'I find it harder today, for some reason,' he replied. 'If I ever see another skeleton it'll be too soon. Which is rather a serious situation for a cemetery superintendent, wouldn't you say?' Tess felt uncomfortable with his familiarity and blamed her lapse of the evening before when she had allowed, nay, been glad of, his comforting tweed arm around her shoulder.

'Not half,' she said and stepped adroitly aside. 'I don't suppose there was any sign of the snoopers this morning?'

'Not hide nor hair. I don't expect there'll be any more trouble. They'll do the reburials in a day or so, won't they?'

'Yes, the graves are all dug. The bishop consecrated the new site last Sunday. It should be wrapped up by Friday. Poor things will be worn out.' And you don't know the half of it, she thought, and looked up to find Mother Catherine watching them.

The last coffin was complete enough to be hoisted to the surface in one piece. The grave-diggers set it carefully on the bier and trundled it over to the shed. They returned with much lighter gait, their heads thrown back as if at last they could look at the world again. One of them took a cigarette from his overalls and was about to light up when his mate jiggled his sleeve and jerked his head at the nuns who were coming towards them. The men filled in the grave quickly, gathered their tools and went to talk to the undertaker. Shortly afterwards they left. The JCB did a final sweep of the ground and then trundled off towards the new site.

Mrs Fermoy made her goodbyes a few minutes later. Tess walked her to the gate. They stood talking for a minute or two while Mrs Fermoy handed over her list and site plan. Tess rejoined the others wearily. There was a curious hiatus as they waited for their next cue, psyching themselves up for the next ordeal: discovering the identity of the body in the lead coffin.

Both nuns lowered their hoods in an almost ritual gesture and walked towards the undertaker. The action had a curious solemnity. But more, it was as if they had excluded those around them.

'Let us begin, Mr Dwyer,' Mother Catherine said with more strength than Tess had ever heard.

When excavations were carried out during the interwar years, an eighteenth-century lead coffin was discovered below the old Garden Court which had once been a churchyard. Lead protection was used because 'the deceased had been considerably disturbed in his mind before his death, from the apprehension that his body would be taken up after his death for the use of the surgeons.' Fear of body-snatchers was not uncommon at the time.

36

There was a distinct air of apprehension as they gathered around the lead coffin. In the event, identification of the remains was something of an anti-climax, or at least it was for Tess. They encircled Mr Dwyer while he solemnly prised back the damaged corner of the lead sheeting which was wrapped around the perfectly ordinary wooden coffin beneath. He ran a Stanley knife along either side and, bit by bit, pulled up the edges, as one might the foil cover of a TV dinner.

'We should be able to roll it back now, if you give me a hand, Mr Flood,' he said, as if he were asking for help with some ordinary garden chore. The two men took their positions on either side and slowly and laboriously rolled back the thin lead sheet which separated reluctantly from the wood beneath. Apart from the ugly gash where the fork of the JCB had smashed through the wood, the coffin itself was in pristine condition. There were even traces of varnish remaining in the oak grain. When they got towards the centre, Mr Dwyer looked up at the nuns. 'We're in luck, I think. I can feel the edge of a plate.' But in their excitement, the men tried to pull the lead back too quickly and it snapped, leaving a lethal jagged edge. Dwyer looked up. 'We need something stronger to prise it up. I'll see what I have in the car,' he said.

While they waited Tess stole a glance at her watch. Damn, damn, damn. It was quarter past twelve but there was nothing to be done. Sandra would have left the flat and already be on her way to their lunch date.

'All this waiting about is desperate,' Mike Flood murmured under his breath. 'Yesterday we were hard at it all day and I wasn't a bit tired, today we do nothing and I'm exhausted.' He blew his lips dolefully. 'Ah, hang on, here he comes, at last.'

Dwyer patiently tapped a two-inch chisel between the lead and the metal plate and painstakingly lifted it clear while Mike rolled it back. At first they thought the plate was blank, as one, two, then the whole six inches of tarnished metal was uncovered without any discipherable engraving. They stared at it in disbelief. Dwyer ran his rough fingers over the surface, hesitated, rubbed it and then looked up. 'I can't feel anything. Now what?'

Sister Mary-Rose had come prepared. She knelt down on the damp grass, laid a thin sheet of paper over the plate and rubbed it lightly with a soft pencil. Then she lifted it close to her eyes and examined the results with a disappointed expression.

'Anyone got a torch?' Tess asked.

'There's one in the hut,' Mike said and fetched it. They held the paper up and shone the torch behind it. Slowly, as the light moved up and down the page they began to make out faint scrolls unmarked by the pencil. But much too faint to read.

'It isn't brass, is it? I wonder if it's silver,' Dwyer said thoughtfully and Sister Rose was dispatched to find silver polish.

They were clutching at straws, all of them reluctant to suggest opening the coffin. Was it because, like Mike Flood, they'd had enough of skeletons or because they feared Sophia might not be in it? There was no talk or speculation while they waited for Sister Rose's return. Mother Catherine was transfixed, still as a statue, her eyes downcast, as if she couldn't bear to watch what was happening.

By now Tess was in a sweat of anxiety about the babysitter but couldn't think of leaving. Four or five minutes ticked by before Sister Mary-Rose came puffing across the grass with her cloak billowing out behind her.

It took ten excruciating minutes for the metal to begin to lose its blackened surface. After that, it flaked off, like a thin layer of fungus, revealing the dull silver beneath and even without burnishing, it was possible to read the spidery engraving: Sophia Stebton, née Elderson (1801–1850). Mother Catherine's eyes filled with tears. 'Thank

God,' she breathed. 'Our Founder's mother. She died in this house.'

Mr Dwyer beamed all around. 'There now, we're in luck. We know who she is,' he said. His relief was evident. 'No need at all to open it.' A collective sigh went up as the Mother Guardian fell to her knees and, as the others followed, began to recite the *De Profundis*. When she finished, the undertaker helped her gently to her feet and took charge.

'We can re-inter the poor woman immediately.' His voice was challenging, daring anyone to protest. 'I have the men over at the new site preparing a grave for her already.' When Mother Catherine began to demur he held up his hand. 'This has all been above board,' he said sternly. 'We've all witnessed that she is who you expected her to be and that she had every right to be here.' He looked around sternly. 'There were prowlers around here last night. The lock on the shed was tampered with.' He looked straight at Tess. 'You don't want mischief-makers dragging a news-paper story out of a lead coffin, do you?' he asked, inviting her support.

'No, Mr Dwyer, we do not,' Tess said deci-sively and could have kicked Mike Flood when he added, 'There was someone lurking about yester-day. And I saw a car driving past the gate last evening. Coming from this end. Miss Callaway and I checked the boundary before we went home last night.'

'I'll arrange for a security firm to patrol, if that's all right?' Tess looked to the nuns, expect-ing some sort of relieved reaction.

'No,' Mother Catherine said sharply. 'Not until

we discuss it.' She looked as though another shock would kill her. Sister Mary-Rose stood aside, eyes downcast. She was trembling.

'We shall go then, Mr Flood,' Tess said quietly. Mother Catherine looked at her bleakly as she added, 'I shall return tomorrow morning, Mother. There are things to discuss.' She turned to Mike. 'I'll take your list, the bursar would like them returned,' she fibbed blandly. 'I've already collected Mrs Fermoy's.'

He looked at her in surprise and patted his pockets. 'I must have left it in the hut,' he said. 'I'll go and get it.'

'That's all right.' Tess smiled. 'I'll do it before I leave.' He took the hint with good grace and having made his farewells, left. She waited until he went out the gate before going over to Sister Rose.

'I'll take those off your hands as well, Sister,' she said firmly and took the sheets of paper from the startled nun. 'Yours, and Mother Guardian's.' She offered no explanation. The nun glanced at Tess and then past her, pointedly, at the hut. Her breathing was uneven, her expression unfathomable. Frightened? Angry? Tess ran her eye down the lists then drew closer and stood directly in front of the deaf woman. 'There is no Felicitas, is there?' She mouthed the words without sound. 'There never was.' The nun shook her head miserably. 'Why didn't you say something?'

'I was afraid. I didn't notice the name until you did. I didn't know what to do,' the nun whispered. Her eyes were like saucers in her pale face. 'Something happ—' she started as Tess tugged her sleeve again.

'Sister Rose, you'd better tell Mother Catherine about it. And tell her I need to see her and Sister Benedicte as soon as they've re-buried Sophia Elderson. And you too, Sister Mary-Rose.'

'Sister Benedicte won't be able—'

'Just tell her it's urgent, Sister,' Tess interrupted brusquely. The nun blinked at her nervously and slowly inclined her head. She opened her mouth again as if to say something but as quickly closed it.

'I just want to make sure the hut is properly locked,' Tess said loudly for the others' benefit and stalked away.

Mike's list was exactly where she remembered him drop it. She picked it up and compared it with the others though she knew it was unnecessary. There were no discrepancies. No extra names. Therefore whatever had gone on in the hut the night before was not pre-planned. At least not by the nuns, if Sister Mary-Rose's patent terror was anything to go by. Relief surged through her. Then more to put off the moment of truth than anything else, she strode quickly along the rows of coffins checking each name against the lists. When she had finished she leaned against the wall and counted slowly to ten while she tried to compose herself.

Through the open door she watched the two nuns walk across the park towards the convent. Even from the distance of about a hundred yards, she could see their rosaries swinging from their fingers. Her eyes followed them until they disappeared around the back of the building towards the new burial ground. When she looked back she saw Dwyer and his two workmen pull away the remaining lead from Sophia's coffin and hoist it onto the bier. She did not move until they began to roll Sophia slowly over the grass towards her new resting place.

She eased the door half closed, directing a shaft of light on the fourth row, and walked hesitantly towards the Felicitas coffin. She rubbed her sweating hands against the sides of her coat and waited until they stopped trembling before she could unscrew the lid. Then forcing herself to breathe slowly, she raised it open and peered in.

She thought at first that the body was swaddled in one of the Holy Retreat cloaks, that she'd made a mistake, that it was one of the exhumed nuns. But it was not. A heavy navy-blue overcoat had been used and it completely covered the body. The empty sleeves were folded nattily over the head, concealing the face. Tess lifted the cuffs gingerly and fell back with fright. The small dark eyes were open wide, as was the contorted mouth. Tess held one hand against her pumping heart and with the other pulled the sleeve further back. The hair on the side of the head was thickly matted and the skull looked as if it was caved in. One of the eyes was cut and heavily bruised as was the mouth. She forced her hand towards the face and touched it lightly. The flesh was so profoundly, obscenely, cold, like meat from the freezer, that her hand jerked back involuntarily. How long had she been dead? Days? Hours? She shuddered as she lightly touched the matted hair and looked with horror at the faint brownish stain it left on the tip of her finger. She almost fainted then. She bent over till her swirling head almost touched her knees and waited for the dizziness to pass. When she straightened up, she replaced the sleeves over the face and gingerly unbuttoned the coat and drew it apart.

The corpse looked larger in death than in life and the awful thing was that compared to what Tess had witnessed in the graveyard over the past couple of days, the dead woman looked brutally, bloodily, *vital*. And heart-wrenchingly easy to identify. The huge, dark glasses she had used so effectively to disguise her face were gone. But she still wore the absurd tweed plus-fours and jacket. When Tess touched the front of the jacket, she found it was damp. She tried to remember when it had last rained? Friday all day. No. Only the afternoon. Mother Catherine said Friday morning was fine. It also rained on Saturday night. A little, not much. Early on Monday morning as well as the middle of the night. She looked sadly at the small podgy hands folded across the chest, the well-manicured nails frosted pink. Tess sat down with a bump. She had only glimpsed the woman once, perhaps twice, in the bookshop before the strange encounter of the previous week. But she would have bet her last shilling that the body being passed off as Sister Felicitas-Maria, the woman she'd named Mrs Plus-Fours, was in fact Jeddie Hillyard. The choice of her sister's name on the label seemed a desperate and cruel irony.

She gently pulled the sides of the coat together. It was like drawing the blankets over her sleeping child. She straightened up and took the few steps to the door then stopped. Out of the corner of her eye she caught a movement. She stood transfixed in the doorway as a crouched figure, wrapped in a nun's cape, shot out of the shadow of the hut and, using the trees and bushes as cover, ran through the park towards the cliff. As she watched, it straightened up and began to move more swiftly. The great hooded cloak looked as though it was gliding along of its own volition. It could be anyone, Tess thought. How easy it would be to move around the convent grounds unnoticed. *Inside the convent too?*

The bursar, she thought suddenly, then stopped short. In her mind's eye she saw the whole community in procession from the chapel the night before. What had Mother Catherine said? That the bursar was the first out. Tess had the impression that she was only a little taller than the rest. The fugitive she was watching was over six feet tall.

Oh God, she thought, as the figure disappeared from her sight, that's not a nun, it's a man. And without thought of the danger she dropped her bag and sprinted after him over the open ground towards the boundary hedge where she ran frantically up and down, desperately trying to find a way through the dense shrubs and under-growth. Eventually, breathless, she found the opening into the lavender field but by then she was much too late. He must have known a more direct route to the cliff gate. It had been wedged open just wide enough to get through easily. Her heart was pounding. She stopped for breath and peered over the cliff edge. She could see nothing and the pounding waves drowned out all other sound. She faltered at the top of the long steep flight of steps, scared of getting trapped halfway. Then she caught the faint crunch of footsteps on the shingle. The pebbles were deepest beneath the overhang of the cliff, and made walking difficult. He would move further out onto the beach if he wanted to make quicker progress. Had he seen her follow? Had he been watching her in the hut? Her heart pounded and pounded but her legs refused to budge.

And then, while she stood rooted with fright, she saw him come out into the open. As she recognized him, she shrank to her knees and held on to the gatepost for support. He had discarded the cloak and was casually – offensively – dressed in a dark sports-jacket and grey slacks. The back seam of the jacket had split showing a flash of white shirt. He sauntered along the shingle as if he were out for a seaside stroll. The only trick he missed was the German Shepherd. It would have completed the picture very well. Further up the beach there were several people walking with their dogs. Any one of them might have seen him, had they been nearer. But Terence Murphy-Dunne did not hesitate. As the nearest couple approached, he loitered by the water's edge and skimmed a flat stone along its surface. Mesmerized, she counted five bounces before she slowly dragged herself to her feet and began to make her way back to the cursed hut. For the first time in many years, she prayed for guidance as she ran.

She didn't know what to do or what to say. Who to tell, who to trust. Who to protect. She was not used to being on the other side of the bench. Her intellect and training were screaming one thing, her instinct the opposite: softly, softly she urged herself. Her heart was in her mouth.

She could not bring herself to step back inside the hut to collect her bag which was just inside the door. She leaned through just far enough to grab it before she steeled herself to walk past the empty graveyard once more. When she got to the gate she looked back at the deserted cemetery for the last time. Apart from the ugly hut and the great gash of bare soil which would soon be returfed, it was as it must have been since it was first laid out as parkland: peaceful, tranquil and beautiful. Innocent. She let herself out and pulled the gate behind her. As the lock clicked she went into shock and began to hyperventilate. Oh Jesus. Oh help. Oh God, oh God, oh God. He's going towards the Killiney hotel. He'll be there in a quarter of an hour. Where Claire is. Oh Claire, Claire. My baby. She backed against the door for support and squeezed her eyes shut. Her breath came in loud harsh gasps.

When she opened her eyes Hugo Boland was hobbling towards her. 'Claire, Claire,' she screamed at him. 'Hugo. Hugo. I have to get to Claire.'

He stopped short, dropped his walking stick and held up his hands. 'Stop. STOP! What's got into you? She's fine, Tess. She's fine. See for yourself.' He made a backwards motion to a taxi which was parked with its doors wide open, outside the convent entrance. Sandra was sitting on the back seat with Claire on her knee. When she saw Tess she waved cheekily. 'How'ya, Tess, thanks very much for meeting us, ha, ha. Great lunch,' she joked. Tess's knees buckled. She crouched on all fours on the gravel and wept with relief.

'Oh, I'm sorry. I'm very sorry.' Sandra jumped out of the taxi as Hugo helped her to her feet.

Tess grabbed the baby and buried her face in Claire's plump cheek. She knew if she tried to speak she would start crying again or blurt out what she'd just seen. She swallowed hard. 'I was on my way,' she murmured. 'I hoped you'd wait.'

'Didn't get a chance, did we, Claire? Mr Boland took the two of us out early and we all had lunch together,' Sandra babbled, eyeing her employer nervously. She held up her arms to the baby who gurgled at her happily. Tess felt a sharp stab of jealousy. She held on to Claire, who yielded to her passively but kept her eyes firmly on the baby-sitter.

'Tess.' Hugo was beside her. He looked terribly serious, haggard. She noticed for the first time that he was formally dressed in a dark, double-breasted pinstripe which looked rather too loose for his thin frame.

'Hugo? Why are you here?'

'We have to stay and see the Mother Guardian. The taxi will take them home.' There was no question but that she would comply.

'No,' she said fiercely. 'They must stay here. We have to stay together.' Hugo looked as though he were about to protest and then gave up.

'I can walk her up and down for a while,' Sandra said helpfully as Tess handed over Claire.

'Thanks.' Tess took a deep breath as she gathered herself together. 'Do that while I talk to Mr Boland, but keep in sight. We have to stay together,' she repeated urgently. Her eyes met Hugo's.

'Right.' Hugo held up his hand. 'Whatever you

say. Tess? What's happened? You look like death.'

'Wait. I'll be back in two ticks,' Tess said. 'Pay off the taxi. If you want to sit down, use my car.' She shoved her keys and the mobile phone into his hands. 'Ring the police and tell them Murphy-Dunne is down on Killiney Beach. Or he was a few minutes ago. I don't care what you say, Hugo, just make sure they hold him. It's urgent. They need to pick him up. At once. He's dangerous. Dark jacket, light grey flannels.'

'What? You've seen him?' he roared. 'Tess, hang on. We need to talk . . . I have . . .' But she was already striding up the steps to the convent door. The latch was released almost immediately. Tess scribbled a note as she went into the hall.

'Sister Joseph? Can you please give this to Mother Catherine? I'll be back in a few minutes. Mr Boland will be with me.' Sister Joseph-Maria made no protest. She was remarkably subdued.

'I'll do that at once,' she said. Her voice was distant.

'The baby and her sitter are with me. Have you got somewhere they can wait, please? Somewhere safe?' she asked. The nun picked up the point and urgency of her request remarkably quickly, though at the time that didn't strike her.

'Yes. There's a tiny morning room off the main parlour you could use. They'll be quite safe there. I'll see that it's prepared.'

Hugo was standing waiting for her outside the door. 'Have you rung the police?' she asked.

'They're on their way,' he replied.

'They believed you?'

'Oh, they believed me all right,' he said. He pulled a couple of envelopes from his inside pocket. 'Sinéad asked me to give you these. She thought they might be urgent.'

'You've been in the office?' Tess murmured. She glanced at the envelopes and gave a little whoop of triumph. The Companies House and Land Registry documents at last. She ripped open the first and ran her eye down the first page then looked up at Hugo. 'You'd better take a look at this,' she snorted. 'That shyster was running with the hounds as well as the hare.' As she pulled open the second document, Hugo grabbed her elbow.

'You'd better tell me what's going on.'

She couldn't yet trust herself to look at him, much less to talk. She wasn't yet sure she entirely trusted him. 'You first. What's happened?'

'I told you, Murphy-Dunne did a bunk,' he said. Tess swivelled violently.

'No. You said he resigned.'

'Well, I would, wouldn't I? He must have been in the office last evening. All sorts of files are missing. The son of a bitch has left a trail of debt. And implicated the firm. God alone knows the extent of it. He's been falsifying the accounts amongst other things. Over-billing. Mopping up inheritances. You name it, he's . . .' He glared down at the document in his hand. 'And now this. The bastard. I can't believe when that consortium was set up. Three months after he took over here. Good God.' He looked her full in the face. 'Tess, I didn't know about this. Truly. I suspected something was amiss but not this. You must believe me. I've been incredibly gullible.' His

406

voice shook. 'I should have fired him. I should . . . Oh, what's the use? I put the police on to him this morning. I should have done it long ago.'

'Which is why they reacted to your latest call?' She felt a surge of relief sweep over her.

'Yes. But I'd no idea he was dangerous. God knows what I let you in for, Tess: I was only trying to help you . . .' Hugo sounded close to tears. 'I don't know what's going on any more.'

'I do, Hugo,' Tess said quietly. 'And it's worse than you think. I'm not sure how to deal with it, that's all. But there'll be a few other charges to add to yours.' Let's hope some of them stick, she murmured to herself.

She took his arm. 'Listen, Hugo,' she began and told him everything. Well, almost everything; she didn't mention the body in the hut. Partly because her thoughts were in too much turmoil but also because Sister Mary-Rose's behaviour had her confused. At the back of her mind, Tess feared that she or one of the other nuns was involved in the murder or at the very least implicated in concealing the corpse. Silence, she reflected soberly, had its down side.

Since they are by virtue of the law judicial persons, institutes, provinces and houses have the capacity to acquire, possess, administer and alienate temporal goods, unless this capacity is excluded or limited in the constitutions.

Canon Law 634 +1 Article 3: Temporal Goods and their Administration

37

Claire was safely settled with a rather subdued Sandra in a small and bare little morning-room off the main parlour. It was decorated in the nuns' ubiquitous dingy beige and brown, but Tess didn't notice. She checked the windows were firmly locked before easing the door closed.

A nun was sitting at the table when they entered the parlour. She had her back to the door so Tess could not identify her at first, nor did she notice another figure standing to the side of, but still obscured by, the open screen. She and Hugo stood just inside the door until the nun became aware of them, rose from the chair and turned around.

'Sister, this is Mr Boland; Hugo, Sister Mary-Rose.'

The nun had taken off her heavy outdoor cloak revealing her indoor habit. The simply cut dress was a beautiful soft shade of bluish grey with a high white mandarin collar and a narrow woven black sash. She had a neat white linen cap on her head with a long, sheer, black veil over it. Tess was relieved to notice that her hair was not shorn; tiny mousy-coloured curls peeped around her ears.

She indicated two chairs on the other side of the table and waited for them to sit down before she resumed her seat. Her silence was unnerving. Every few seconds she jerked her head towards the screen. After about five minutes the Mother Guardian appeared. Literally. One moment she wasn't there, the next she was standing at the open screen. She too had left off the cloak. She hesitated, looked over her shoulder then silently took her place beside Sister Mary-Rose. Tess longed to throw herself at the screen and peer around it. She wondered if it had been opened as a ritual gesture – look, we are concealing nothing – but if it was, it didn't work. Somehow, she felt that the community might be gathered on either side of that proscenium arch; their unseen audience. Mother Catherine raised her grey-pale face and nodded to Hugo. She did not look directly at Tess.

'You have read my letter?' he asked. Tess looked at him in surprise. What letter? Hugo avoided her eye. 'Tess has just confirmed what I feared. The question now is—'

Tess stood up impatiently. It was time to stop all the pussy-footing. The important thing was the dead body, not everybody's real or imagined sensibilities.

'Where is Sister Benedicte-Maria?' she said tersely. 'She should be here.' This was greeted by a sharp intake of breath from both nuns. It took a second or two for the Guardian to collect herself enough to reply. 'Sister Benedicte is in hospital,' she replied woodenly. She looked outraged at Tess's temerity.

'Since when?'

'Since this morning. She was brutally attacked in the graveyard. She is still unconscious.'

'You didn't say.' Tess couldn't keep the hurt from her voice. 'This morning, when we talked, you didn't say.' She peered across at Mother Catherine. 'You didn't trust me, did you?' she said sadly. 'Why not?'

'You didn't trust Benedicte.' The nun sounded exhausted. 'But it is not a matter of trust, it is a matter of fear. Something happened in the grounds last night. She saw something, we don't know what. So many things have been happening, so many terrible ... We think ... we think she surprised a prowler at the hut. Vandals.'

Tess stared in disbelief at both nuns. 'Vandals? Vandals?' She laughed harshly. 'Don't you know ... Don't you know what's in there?' She directed her question at Sister Mary-Rose. Now it was Hugo's turn to stare. The nun shied back trying to avoid Tess's eye, almost as if she were pleading: give us time, we will come to it. But there wasn't time. 'You'd better come with me, Sister Mary-Rose,' Tess said. 'With your permission, Mother Catherine. There's something we need to do, now, before we say anything else.' She turned to Hugo. 'Please fill Mother Catherine in about Murphy-Dunne's antics,' she instructed, 'while we're gone. We'll be back in a few minutes.'

Sister Mary-Rose followed her without demur.

She didn't ask where they were going but headed off directly towards the graveyard. Once they were out of sight of the convent Tess caught up with the deaf nun. 'Do you know what's in the shed?' she asked. Sister Rose considered a moment before she replied, 'No.' She swallowed hard. 'Two of the nuns went out at first light to investigate but found nothing. We hoped Benedicte would come round and tell us and for a while it looked as if she might, but then just after seven o'clock she took a turn for the worse. We had to send for the ambulance.' Tears welled up in her eyes. 'We couldn't find Mother Catherine, we had to take the decision without her . . . Our life is falling apart,' she added half to herself. 'Benedicte is very, very ill. We really hadn't time to think of anything else. Poor Benedicte.' She took a deep breath. 'I went to the graveyard after the ambulance left. I was looking around the shed when the undertaker and his men arrived with Mr Flood and Mrs Fermoy. I could sense there was something amiss but until you noticed the odd label I couldn't see what it was. And I hadn't any opportunity to get back later.'

She drew herself up and glared at Tess. She was no longer the silent demure creature of the morning. 'Who is in that coffin?' she asked hoarsely, her alarm and distress palpably genuine. She beat her fists nervously against her breast. Tess was too relieved to speak, too ashamed of her suspicion that the nuns were covering up for somebody. They walked to the shelter in silence. The hundred questions Tess wanted to ask drummed away inside her head. Foremost of which was confirmation that the woman in the coffin was, in fact, Jeddie Hillyard. She found the question of why she was dead more difficult to articulate and even more so to answer.

Tess eased the lid off the coffin and pulled the coat sleeves back from the face. This time the shock of the battered face was not so great for her. But it was for the nun.

'That is Jane Stebton-Hillyard,' she said at once but so quietly Tess could barely hear. With that, Sister Mary-Rose slowly keeled over. Tess crouched beside her on the floor and pressed the nun's head downwards until she recovered then she helped her to her feet.

'Do you know who killed her?' she asked croakily.

'I think I do. But not for certain.' Tess replaced the coffin lid and gently led the nun out into the autumn sunshine.

'You sent me her notes, didn't you?' she asked. 'Why did you do that, Sister Mary-Rose?'

'I didn't trust her.' The words were harsh, angry, badly formed, slurred. As if she was too exhausted to mask her speech impediment. For the first time it was possible to tell from listening to her that she was deaf, as if shock had destroyed her control of the carefully enunciated speech. And the first time that Tess understood the effort she had to put into forming every single word.

'The enclosed life is a frail and precious thing. It cannot take alarms and excursions. It is something we work at and cherish. That woman,' she crossed herself, 'that woman brought chaos with her. Carried it inside her, thrived on it. Like a destructive child. It was like an aura around her, you could almost see it. She should never have been allowed entry to our cloister. It was wrong. Mother Catherine is too old, too trusting. She was dazzled by her family connections. She thought if the woman was related to our founder then she too must be a saint. She should have let Sister Benedicte deal with her.' She swallowed painfully and licked her dry lips.

'We have had nothing but discord since she came to Holy Retreat. I know it started before she came, that it was really because of the land. Some of us were against selling and even more so, having to move the graveyard. But somehow, the real disturbance, the bitterness, I date from the time of her arrival. I blamed her. You see, I knew from the first that she was trying to pull the wool over our eyes. She said she was a librarian, a collector of fine books . . . But she was going to sell them . . .' Her hand shot to her mouth. 'It would become known where those dreadful books came from . . .'

Tess stepped in front of the nun and looked into her face. 'Listen to me, Sister Mary-Rose. I don't think her death had anything to do with the books. But you did know she was stealing them, didn't you?'

'Not stealing. The books belonged to her branch of the family. They weren't strictly speaking our books. The Mother Founder . . . She had a right to them . . .'

'You knew about the secret library?' Tess asked. 'All of you?'

'Not all. For a long time only me,' she said and then clammed up. 'We have to get back,' she said. 'We have to get back.'

Tess grasped her arm. 'Sister Mary-Rose, why did you send me her notes?'

The nun bit her lower lip. 'I'm not sure. I didn't want her in our convent. I thought . . . I thought if she was dishonest about one thing then she would be dishonest about everything. Sister Joseph said you were asking a lot of questions about her and about the library and about who Jane Stebton-Hillyard had contact with. And then you started asking about the lavender field. Joseph felt you didn't trust her. She was quite upset because Jane was a great favourite of hers. But I was relieved. I don't know what I hoped . . . that you'd stop her selling the books? But now . . .' She drew herself upright. 'We had nothing to do with her death, if that is what is troubling you, Miss Callaway. You have my word on that.'

They were almost back at the convent when the nun stopped abruptly and turned to face Tess. 'This foundation . . . there were difficulties you know nothing about. I thought nobody did. But when I found her catalogue notes . . .' Sister Mary-Rose lowered her eyes. 'Please, Miss Call-away, let us talk about this with Mother Guardian. I should have done so earlier. There has been too much subterfuge.' Tears flowed slowly down her pale cheeks. 'I meant Jane no harm. I just wanted . . . Let us, please let us not say anything else until we are inside. I do not trust speech. I find it difficult. I'm no longer sure what I wanted. But be gentle with Mother Catherine. She is not well. Break the news gently, I beg you.'

They went back into the parlour and took their places quietly at the table. Mother Catherine looked at Tess expectantly. The room was very still, the silence dark and smothering. There was no way to be gentle. Not with the stark vision of that brutalized face so clearly in her mind. 'Jane Stebton-Hillyard is dead, Mother Catherine. Her body is in one of the coffins in the hut. Sister Mary-Rose has identified her. I believe she was murdered.' She paused. 'Perhaps that is what Sister Benedicte saw?'

The Guardian's reaction, if you could even call it that, was muted, dulled. Her face a total blank. It was as if she was already in so much shock that another blow made no impact. Her nerves were dulled to the point of . . . nothing. Had Tess said a plague had struck and all your nuns are dead, she doubted either of the nuns would react in any way. Oddly, it was Hugo who broke down. The old man just fell forward on the table and covered his despairing face with his hands. Mother Catherine rocked backwards and forwards but said nothing. Her hand fiddled with something in her lap which after a minute or two she placed on the table and pushed it, with the tip of her finger, across to Tess. She did not look up. 'Sister Albertine found this a couple of hours ago,' she mumbled. 'It was in the lavender field when she went out this morning, at the spot she'd been working all weekend. It was lying under her bucket of trimmings. She only found it when she picked the bucket up to empty it. We don't know how long it's been there. Will you kindly read it for us please, Tess.'

Monday 28.x.96, 4 a.m.
Dear Mother Catherine,
In a couple of hours a taxi will come to take me to

Dun Laoghaire for the early morning crossing to Holyhead. If you look out your window at seven you will see that great lumbering hydrofoil thundering across your beautiful bay. Yesterday I posted a letter of instruction to Mr Boland about the parcel of land I retained. I have passed it on to Holy Retreat. I want the nuns to have it. You have already paid for it dearly. You would be quite correct in assuming I am trying to buy your good opinion, I almost said your prayers. I need them. People who are clever are not always wise. I have done many foolish things in my life, for many base reasons, but my trying to outwit Terence Murphy-Dunne ranks as crass idiocy. I can match, perhaps excel, him for wit, but not for ruthlessness. He has the edge there.

My greatest foolishness was playing childish games with you, dear friend. I don't know when I first became certain that his scheme was predicated on a false assumption: that the convent would only sell their strip of land to a school. That they were only interested in the status quo. But I quickly understood that you, collectively, would have no objection to houses on the Glenadams land. I did not guess, for a long time, that you realized it was likely to happen. Did I also think then, that you knew who your actual purchaser was? That it was not the school you were selling to but a development consortium headed by your own solicitor? Was I base enough, was my sense of values distorted enough, to kid myself that you knew and did not object? Did I really think you would be able to fathom the depth of avarice of your legal adviser? Condone it? We both underestimated you. I don't suppose it ever occurred to Terence Murphy-Dunne that having made the deal, you would feel obliged to honour it unconditionally. He thought it was dependent on you not knowing that the school would be closed and the land developed for housing. More importantly so did his other partners in the

consortium. For a while so did I. Oh yes. I was in on
the deal. Indeed for a long time I really thought, poor
fool that I am, that I had the advantage of them. After
all, from their point of view I owned the critical piece
of land. No good for building but stunning for sales.
Who would not want access to the beach and a view
of that glorious bay? I had them in the palm of my
hand. I could name my price. I thought.

And then I stupidly became attracted to him. Or
perhaps it wasn't him. I think I fell in love with
everything, all at once. The country, the bay, the land,
the convent. The situation. I have never held much
power in my life; now for a brief few months I did. I
allowed myself to be wooed. For the months it took
him to persuade me not to sell the land but to join as
an equal partner he was Prince Charming himself.

I kept him dangling. I knew that as long as I
procrastinated, he was mine. So the time to sign on the
dotted line never really materialized. And all the time I
was busy playing both ends against the middle. One of
the partners, the soon-to-be-retired-headmaster of
Glenadams, was also a contender for my land, if not
my hand. Since there was plenty of room in the almost
empty school, he invited me to stay whenever I was in
Dublin. I stayed for a week last June after my visit to
you. It was he who disclosed that the third partner
was in deep financial trouble. Rather overstretched
himself in the building of a new golf-course. The
banks were about to foreclose. I already guessed that
Terence was also in a financial morass. Now I
discovered that far from being interested in me, he was
involved with the ex-wife of his senior partner. I have
few pretensions about my own looks but I did not like
being upstaged by a woman more than twenty years
my senior. No matter that his motives were other than
romance. He claimed he only did it to humiliate her
ex-husband. Which sounded absurd even to me. We
quarrelled. He was violent. I am ashamed to say I did

not leave him but felt grateful when 'he took me back'. In June he asked me to marry him. I pretended to myself that it had nothing to do with the land. But with people like Terence it is always to do with the land.

And then in July my mother became unmanageable and my situation at home untenable. I stuck it out until September then I came to Dublin to spend a week with Terence. It was not a success. I ran off to Italy to clear my head and do some research on my great-grandfather's collection. By then I'd worked through it enough to know that I had acquired the means of a life-time's dealing and my independence. I did not need to sell the land. But I still wanted Terence. By the time I arrived in Dublin a couple of weeks ago, I was in something of a dilemma about how best to proceed.

I thought I could just sail up to Holy Retreat and be sure of a welcome. I thought none of you had noticed what I'd been up to. I had planned to confess prettily that I had relieved you of the embarrassment of the erotica and that, in return, I would let you have the land. I deluded myself that you would, once more, give me a heroine's welcome. But when I called one afternoon the mute one was acting porter. At least I think it was she, I never did hear her speak much. She introduced herself as the sister librarian and said I was no longer welcome. The door opened mechanically behind me, there was nothing to do but go. I was astonished at how painful that dismissal was. How elegantly she showed me how shabby I was.

My next shock was the deterioration in Terence. He looked dissipated, ill. He said he was no longer your legal adviser but would not tell me why. He began giving me lengthy instructions about how 'I was to manage you' for the few weeks until the sale was completed. We had only to hold out until the completion date on November 7th, then we could get married. This time I think he meant it. But then he needed me to pay his debts. Was I still attracted to him? Like a rabbit to a headlight.

I kept quiet about my intentions vis-à-vis the land. I was invited to stay at the school while everyone was away for half-term. I arranged to meet Terence there one day, a week or so ago. Instead, a strange young woman turned up. She fed me some rigmarole about wanting a place for a boy in the school. She was such a hopeless liar I assumed it was Terence she was looking for – another of his damned conquests. I fobbed her off as best I could and pretended to leave the grounds. Terence showed up a few minutes later in his Land Rover. When she spotted him and came running towards him he did a terrible thing. He set the dog on her. I could see then she was running to her car and not to Terence. When she drove off he attacked me for setting him up. He seemed to think I knew who she was, that she was your new legal adviser. I eventually convinced him that this was not the case. The following night, Thursday, he called to take me out to dinner. When he arrived he said he'd had a little too much to drink and begged me to drive. I was surprised because he was quite sober. On the way we stopped for him to pick up some papers at the office. I parked just down the street. Shortly afterwards the same woman showed up and followed him into the office. Curiously she was carrying the infant I'd noticed in her car the day at Glenadams. I assumed for certain then that there was something going on between them. That his anger was a blind for my benefit.

I was wrong. He came out three or four minutes later carrying the child, which he proceeded to dump into her car. I thought it odd that he opened all the doors but odder still that he set off the alarm before he came sprinting back to the Land Rover. 'Joke,' he said. 'Drive like the clappers. That'll show her.' He looked demented. I kept my eye on the rear-view mirror as the security guard and then the woman came hurtling out of the office. The woman was out of her mind, wild, hysterical-looking. Some joke. I looked at his smiling face and knew that I too was frightened. At last.

He came to me next morning. I think mainly to make sure I still believed in him. At first I pretended, but then my anger got the better of me and I rounded on him. I stormed out. I'd made up my mind to throw myself on your mercy. I was walking towards the convent when he caught me up. When he'd finished with me I couldn't go anywhere. One eye was closed and two of my teeth smashed. I have been hiding ever since.

I should have left on Saturday but I was too ill. When I tried to get a flight home on Sunday and Monday, they were all full. I hadn't remembered the bank holiday. So the Irish Sea crossing it is. Finishing as I started. I am going back to live quietly in Oxford, where I belong. Forgive me, dear friend, Jane.

Tess carefully avoided their questioning eyes. The memory of that terrible incident was still too raw. The image of that horrible expanse of grey, grey carpet, vast and heartbreakingly empty of Claire, would never leave her.

'Tess? You all right?' Hugo asked. She nodded and bit her lip. 'Then would you mind giving it to me from the beginning? Please. I knew nothing of this woman until now. There was no letter from her this morning.'

'Mother? Please tell Hugo what Jane Stebton-Hillyard told you about the land,' she said gently. 'When she came first. Give it to him in sequence, please, Mother, if you can. It's important. We have to construct a case.'

Mother Catherine cleared her throat nervously before she replied. 'Jane said she was donating a portion of the land to Holy Retreat.' She sighed miserably. 'We knew she kept the larger part. But we didn't know what she intended to do with it and even if we had, I don't think we could have worked out the implications. But eventually we suspected she knew Mr Murphy-Dunne.'

'How?'

'One day Sister Benedicte-Maria told Mr Murphy-Dunne that we'd received a generous gift from Miss Stebton-Hillyard – she didn't mention what – and he let slip that Jane had come to see him when she was first trying to find Elderson Court. When she heard that, Sister Benedicte said, "Then we have you to thank for our lavender field." He took the credit, but he made a curious remark. "I wondered how she knew," he said.'

She looked at Tess and spoke to her directly. 'Sister Benedicte blames herself for what happened. But she is not responsible.' Her eyes filled with tears.

'What does she blame herself for?' Tess asked but was interrupted by Hugo who jogged her arm. 'Do you know what *he* meant?'

'I think so. I suspected she scouted out the land long before she came to the convent. We know from the Land Registry documents that the school had registered an Adverse Claim for the strip of land bordering theirs. She was smarter than the rest of us; she must have immediately figured out what Glenadams intended. We know from her letter, she did in fact realize *ab initio* that Murphy-Dunne was part of a consortium which had already bought the school. Or at least made an offer for it which would be sewn up once the new entrance was complete. Access from the minor road was the critical point and they could only get that from the Holy Retreat sale.'

She looked around at Hugo bitterly. 'Nice to have one's theories confirmed but I don't believe she always intended the nuns to get the land. I think she would have sailed off into the sunset with both the books and the land had things not started to fall apart. Jeddie Hillyard wasn't nobbled by old loyalties or friendship. Least of all by sentimentality. Poor fool that she was. She recognized a crook when she saw one. But still wanted him. She must have thought he was more colourful than harmful. A mistake the English often make about the Irish,' she added wryly. 'Glenadams is closing down next year, by the way. But I expect you knew that?' She looked at Hugo pointedly.

'Yes.' Hugo drew in his breath. 'I've been asking some pretty searching questions myself in the past few weeks. I feel responsible for much of this. It appears that Murphy-Dunne, the blackguard, formed his consortium prior to becoming your legal adviser. A couple of the trustees, as well as the headmaster, were in on it. I should have known.' He looked at Mother Catherine glumly. 'I take it you didn't actually notice the slight adjustment of the name on the contract? That it was *Glenadams Enterprises* not Glenadams School you were selling to?'

Nobody said anything until Mother Catherine turned to her companion: 'I wish you hadn't sent her away,' she said softly. Tess looked across at

Sister Rose whose face was flushed and miserable.

'How long have you known about the secret collection?' Tess directed her question at the librarian. It still seemed to her that Benedicte's role in the Stebton saga was being carefully obfuscated.

'Not until Jane came. I should have told the community but . . .' She hunched her shoulders and drew in a long breath. 'I could not bear to disturb the tranquillity of our house. Or besmirch our founder's name. Her name plate was on many of the books, you see.' She looked around the table and sighed deeply.

'She only came for a couple of days that first time. But long enough to get to know our timetable. I watched her discover the secret shelves. Somehow she knew exactly how to open them. She took only two volumes that first time, from the "A" shelf. I actually saw her slip them into her bag. By the time she came back I'd gone through the shelves. I was appalled when I discovered what was contained in them. But amongst the books I found a document from our foundress which seemed to show me a way of dealing with the problem. I took it away and hid it in my room.

'She stayed several times. I watched her take the books away. She went to great lengths to filch the communion boxes from the bakery. She needn't have. I would have packed the books in suitcases had she asked. But she liked her little games. She used to pretend to go to bed early. Her room was right beside the library. She worked by night, from about midnight until four or five.'

She looked at Tess. 'You've seen the books? You know where they are?'

'Yes. They were described to me. They're with a friend. They're safe.'

'Some of us were unhappy she was allowed within the cloister.' She turned her head away from the Guardian. Her voice was rougher now, stronger, as her anger once more took the upper hand and the undercurrents of dissension within the cloister surfaced. They are just like the rest of us, Tess thought with some surprise. Striving for perfection and making a hash of it. Somehow it made the nuns more human, more praiseworthy.

Sister Mary-Rose's voice quivered with emotion. 'She only ever met a few of us. Benedicte and Mother Catherine, Joseph and myself, the rest mostly stayed out of her way. It would be so in any case. We all have our own tasks to occupy us. But she was in the library so I saw her more than most. She didn't seem to realize I was deaf. But *mute* seems to indicate that she did. I don't think she appreciated that mute doesn't necessarily mean stupid or gullible. Nor did she guess how easily I lip-read. I didn't trust her, even at the beginning, so I watched her when she thought she was alone. I could even read her lips when she talked to herself.' She smiled bitterly. 'Which she did, all the time, like many people who spend time alone.'

She looked at Mother Catherine and a signal passed between them. Sister Mary-Rose went over to the cupboard beside the open screen and took something out.

'This is what I found two years ago when Jane-Edwina Stebton-Hillyard first led me to the secret library. I have allowed this matter to eat at my peace of mind. I brought it to Mother Catherine today, after we buried Sophia Elderson.' She looked across at the table and began to read aloud.

Carne Vale: *Farewell to the flesh, traditionally the last spree before the abstinence and self-restraint of Lent.*

38

The testimony of the founder of the convent of Holy Retreat

I, Adelaide Maria Stebton, founder of the convent of the Holy Retreat, do hereby state that the following document is in my hand and is the truth as I have witnessed. My mother, Sophia Maria, died, in my care, on the twenty-seventh of March 1850. My father, Ryland Stebton, was from home. He had for many years lived in Chipping Stebton in Oxfordshire but he came at once in answer to my summons. He arrived at Elderson Court the day after her death. During the days following, it was agreed between us for the reasons I shall disclose that she would be buried at his family vault in Oxfordshire where her only son, my brother William, was buried.

My mother's coffin lay waiting in the family oratory while my father went back to Oxford to arrange her interment. He promised to be back within three days but a week passed and then another without word from him. I did not know what to do. A month went by. My mother's coffin was still in the chapel. The weather had turned warm. We had to sheath it in lead for the decay.

I did not know until he died that my father had not gone to Stebton Place as he promised but to Chester where he married his common-law wife. Barely a month after leaving Elderson Court to arrange my mother's burial and but ten days after his marriage to Sarah Mulholland, he was killed in an accident from his horse. Nor did I know that his second, illegitimate son was but a year or two younger than my own dear, dead brother. That second son was, by his marriage, legitimized and therefore made the Stebton heir.

And then I understood what I had not before. That my poor mother was driven insane not only by my brother's premature death, but by my father's infidelity. I had taken his part for years and defended him against her vile accusations. I resented my enforced incarceration and blamed her for it. And God forgive me, I pitied him for what she had allowed herself to become.

I do not know why he left the books in these hidden shelves. Or why he pasted my nameplate in them. Nor could I ask him. But on one of his last visits, he said that the library would be my dowry. I thought it a cruel remark. I understood him to mean that I should be an old maid. After my mother was at last buried, I closed the bookshelves and tried to forget them but I could not enter the library without seeing them in my mind's eye. Why did I not destroy them? *Because they are Stebton, not Elderson property.* I did not know if his son would come to claim them and blame me for their loss and reveal the scandal of my father's irregular life. To be truthful, I do not know why I could not. Sometimes I am not sufficiently truthful with myself; I was afraid of scandal. Afraid that my dear companions would learn from what evil their foundation grew.

And now I discover that his other family owns a tract of land which marches our boundary as well as that of our neighbour. He bought it when there was rumour that the new railway might run along the coast one day. In the end it took another route. I have spoken to Mr Stanhope and he says there is nothing to be done. That being land-locked, it cannot be sold without right of way. I trust he is correct. I am not sure why it troubles me so, if not for ancient scandals. Someday, I know, one of his misbegotten will face us with it. Someone who will discover the books. For my sake, my sisters, let them go, or trade them off against the land. They are an abomination in the sight of God. They have weighed heavily on my mind all these years.

That is the real reason I will not destroy them. They may be our safeguard. Perhaps one day they will be discovered and sold to help us maintain this house. You will find they are worth more than you can guess. You will laugh at my foolishness and pride; I could not destroy a book. The library – the open library – was my life's blood for years. The collection was the fruit of my father's marvellous mind. He taught me to read Italian, Latin and French. I do not think his interest in the secret collection was prurient; he was not depraved in that way. He loved beautiful things and would have been amused at hoarding, in secret, such desirable objects. You see, I admire him still. He was a tender father when I was a child. Before William's death. Before he left us.

And now to a more difficult question. Why was my mother to be buried away from her own place? How could I explain why she had been kept above ground for so long? I dissemble. It was because the circumstances of her death weighed heavily on me. Not alone because of my father's flight but because I believe I was responsible for her death. I was afraid to have a public burial. Afraid of being questioned as to the manner of her death. Or have to answer for my father's long absence.

She was out of her mind for a long time and for several years before her death she had become so violent that even together with my servants, Margaret and Johnny, we could not contain her. I wonder now why I feared scandal so much. If not because deep in my heart I guessed the path my father had taken. I blamed him then, I do not blame him now. Life at Elderson Court was unsustainable for him. As it was for me when my sister Augusta married our cousin Charles and went to his plantations in Carolina. Augusta was not good with Mama. Nor would she ever more have anything to do with Elderson Court. Before she left she traded off her share of our inheritance. My father bought her out on my behalf. Poor Augusta died during General Grant's march south in the American Civil War, in 1864. With all her family, as I've been told.

The day of Mama's death, 27 March, she escaped and ran wild around the demesne in her shift. We tried everything to catch her but she was full of cunning. I did not perceive until later what she must have been about. She was trying to tire us. Margaret and I went to rest and vowed to seek her out later. She could not escape, we thought, while Johnny kept sentry. She must have watched us go. I was standing at the landing window looking out to sea when out of the corner of my eye I saw her in flight towards the cliff gate. She was crouching like an animal, swift as a fox, her long tangled hair streaming in the wind. I pounded at the window so hard it broke. She looked up at my bleeding arm and laughed. Then she curtseyed like a young girl, and gaily waved her hand.

That is how I last saw her and how I remember her. Her long white shift billowing around her in the wind she ran, not towards the gate but to the edge of the cliff. It was high tide. But the sea does not come up to the cliff. She leaped forward into space and then was gone.

I blamed myself. I do still. I should not have grown tired, I should have stayed near her but I was cowardly. The last time she escaped she broke my arm in the struggle to calm her. And so it is. I have spent my life in reparation for my sin, not for killing her, but for not loving her enough.

When the word came of my father's death, we buried her secretly in the garden, Johnny, Margaret and I. After a month it was necessary to cover the coffin. You may guess why. Johnny found some lead roof-sheeting. It made the coffin heavy but we could not bear to desecrate it in any way. The land was consecrated as a graveyard as soon as Holy Retreat was founded. She is buried twenty paces from the stone cross, on the south-west side.

Sister Mary-Rose gave a bow towards the Mother Guardian and returned to the cloister. She drew the screen doors shut behind her. They could just hear the sound of her light footsteps as she walked away. All was silence until Mother Catherine cleared her throat and began to speak. She sounded utterly weary, defeated.

'We retire at ten. Sister Benedicte is usually the last to go upstairs since it is she who makes sure the convent is secure for the night. We have been nervous in recent weeks. Until then we never saw strangers near our enclosure. Some of the nuns blame it on the sale and so for the first time that I remember we are no longer a unit, there is unhappiness for which I blame myself. Sister Mary-Rose is right, the disunity really started when I invited Jane into the enclosure.

'I should tell you that Mary-Rose was not alone in her knowledge of the library. Sister Benedicte knew of the existence of the secret library, though not its exact whereabouts, long before Jane arrived. And Benedicte knew from the moment she arrived what she had really come for. It was she who first suggested that Jane have access to the library, though I did not mark the fact at the time. You see, Benedicte is descended from Augusta's only child – a daughter who alone of her family survived the American Civil War.' She looked up at them ruefully. 'I knew nothing of this until a month or so ago when I mentioned that I was worried about Jane and Benedicte told me that she didn't think Jane would ever be back.

'Benedicte carried her burden alone for two good and noble reasons. Like Rose, she wanted to protect our founder and the good name of Holy Retreat. Also her own name. She knew the tragic history of her family better than anyone.' She looked up. 'She joined us only ten years ago. It was Benedicte who first urged us to claim the wasteland. She who mentioned it to Mr Boland when we did nothing. She was always afraid that someday, someone would turn up with the deeds. When Jane came, Benedicte knew at once what she was after. She watched her like a hawk inside the convent and got Murphy-Dunne to watch her outside. You see, unfortunately, she trusted him when, as it turns out, she would have done better to trust Jane.

'Last night as Sister Benedicte was doing her rounds, she glanced out of the chapel window and thought she saw a flashlight by the hut. She called Albertine, who was helping her, to come and investigate. Unfortunately as they were running out of the door the phone rang and Albertine stopped to answer it. Benedicte went ahead and when Albertine came out there was no sign of her. She thought she must be in the hut because the door was wide open. As she ran towards it she saw two figures in the shadows and heard a scream. Then the shorter figure fell and the other ran off into the shrubbery. Benedicte was lying on the ground groaning when Albertine got to her; she was bleeding badly on the side of the head. She had been hit by a rock which was on the ground beside her. Without thinking of her own safety, Albertine shouted for help. Sister Joseph heard her and roused the rest of us. Three of the nuns went out to help. I watched from my window.

'I could see Albertine on the ground leaning over Benedicte, stroking her face. I saw a figure creep towards them from behind the hut. I tried to shout a warning but she didn't hear me. I saw the hand raise and crash down on her head. She was saved from worse injury because just as the attack took place, the other nuns came running across the grass and the assailant made off.' Mother Catherine looked up, tears were running down her withered cheeks.

'You recognized who it was?' Tess asked gently.

'I didn't. But Albertine saw him close up. She turned her head as the stone he was holding came down. She is not badly injured, but Benedicte is. She may not recover. He took her cloak. That's why I thought . . . thought . . .'

'Would one of you kindly tell me what is going on?' Hugo interrupted sharply.

'Tess?'

'I believe Murphy-Dunne killed Jane. It must have happened sometime after she wrote that letter to Mother Catherine. He's been watching the place. He knew about the empty coffins in the hut. He hid her body in one of them and labelled it with a fictitious name. It was so easy. There was a bundle of blank labels lying about. We weren't meant to notice one extra among so many dead. But I'm afraid I did. The name didn't ring a bell and when I checked, there was no Felicitas-Maria on the list. I thought Sister Mary-Rose also knew and was, for some reason, trying to conceal the fact. That maybe she was responsible ... I'm sorry, Mother Catherine, I did her a disservice. I am so sorry.'

'Poor Jane. Poor sad, lonely woman. May God have mercy on her soul. I might have saved her. I should have realized she was in danger that day when I saw her with him. I knew in my heart, when Albertine brought her letter, that she was dead. Poor creature.'

'Poor creature?' Tess expostulated. 'A portion of what the books are worth would rebuild your walls, you know. Not to mention the convent.'

'Nothing is worth a life.' The nun spoke sadly. 'And we could never have sold those books. I keep trying to work out why the letter was in the field? He must have realized that she was trying to come to see us again. I wish ... Oh, how I wish ...'

Hugo turned to Tess. 'He always had a violent temper, you know. Ask Susan,' he said bitterly. Tess turned scarlet.

'I know,' she mumbled. 'He doesn't like being in the wrong.'

'I knew he was rotten but not until it was too late,' Hugo said ruefully. 'Then I spent my time trying to protect the practice, covering up when I should have been exposing the bas— I beg your pardon, Mother Catherine, I forget myself,' Hugo said.

'Can Sister Albertine identify her attacker?' Tess asked.

'Yes, she's seen Mr Murphy-Dunne several times. She also saw him on Friday with Jane – though she did not know who she was – while she was hoeing the lavender.'

Mother Catherine stood up. 'We will not sell the land,' she said. 'I do not know what we should do about the books. I must consult the community. We will let you know.' She smiled sadly at Tess. 'Thank you, my dear, and God bless you both.' She stood up, took a watch from a hidden pocket in her skirt and glanced at the time. 'Three fifteen,' she said. 'The police should be here by now. Will you stay and help us one more time?'

SUMMER 1997

Nunc Dimittis servum tuum: *Now lettest thou thy servant depart in peace* ...

Song of Simeon, Luke ii, 29

39

It was early May the following summer and the convent had returned to something of its former tranquillity. The sisters were collecting pebbles for the herb garden which was the delight and joy of the enclosure. Nobody could quite remember when the early morning ritual had started but for the months of May and June each year, on one day a week, they devoted an hour to collecting and sorting the stones to be used to repair the old paths or to make new.

They emerged out of the dawn mist and climbed carefully down the uneven steps to the rough sand. The first one down dragged a small laundry basket behind her and deposited its content of rejected pebbles by the bottom step. The rest carried much smaller baskets on their arms. The last through the high narrow gate turned the key in the lock and pulled the straggling hedge back in place. It may have been simply habit but it was a pointless exercise since the gate was invisible from the beach, which, in any case, appeared quite deserted.

Dawn comes early on summer mornings in

Ireland – sometimes so early there is hardly any night at all. Few take advantage of that magical twilight of sinking and rising sun. Few but the sisters of Holy Retreat. Eccentricity alone could hardly account for the hours they kept. Who else would walk at four or five o'clock?

The air was cold and they wore the hoods of their magnificent capes so far over their heads as to almost obscure their faces and kept their hands tucked well into the sleeves. Their feet were bare.

There were seven of them. They walked in single file, now and then forming pairs, banding and disbanding as they bent about their task. The pebbles on Killiney beach are of three or four distinct types: smooth grey-black sandstone, white marble, mottled Dalkey granite flecked with mica, pinkish-red sandstone. The grey are most beautiful. When still washed by the sea, they feel as sleek as sealskin. They are etched with thin white lines of quartz which trace landscapes on their smooth cool surfaces. It was these the nuns sought as they ambled silently along. When the small baskets were full they were taken back and emptied into the bigger one. One, sturdier than the rest and more vigorous in her movements, walked among the group silently directing operations. Eventually she and another sister broke away and returned to the stairway where they squatted by the laundry basket, carefully examined the stones and retained or rejected according to some imagined ideal.

The nuns made a strange silent group in their weird garb. Exotic, extraordinary, timeless. Had they set those baskets on their heads they could almost have been biblical women striding the sands of time. They walked about a mile or so along the deserted beach to where a swiftly flowing stream formed a natural boundary. Here they turned for home. By then the group had spread out. One couple ambled along together but the others remained separate for the most part, as if their way of life had entrenched a deep, unbreakable solitude. The casual observer, had there been one, might have been struck by how apart they seemed, one from the other, how uninterested. But that would be to overlook the underlying cohesion of the group. Though they did not speak there was no shortage of communication between them, the only real indication of which was the way they constantly relieved each other of the heavy baskets, taking it in turn to carry them a little of the way home.

By the time they got back the nuns who had been sorting the stones in the laundry basket had already gone back into the enclosure. Two of the younger members of the group hauled the large basket up to the top of the steps and pulled it through the gate. The others followed. The last one in turned before she went through and pulled the branches back into position. Then she banged the gate hard and turned the key in the padlock.

From beneath the overhang of the cliff, a solitary figure, dressed in the long black cape, emerged uncertainly from the shadow and dragged herself painfully across the pebbled strand. Her gait was ragged. Once or twice she toppled sideways as she made her way slowly towards the water's edge, where she went paddling into the cold sea.

On the cliff top another black-robed figure appeared, arms outstretched in supplication. Her scream was carried eerily on the wind: 'Benedicte. Benedicte, come back.'

FAREWELL

Dear Owen,

It is over. All is changed now. I have been to Holy Retreat for the last time to see Mother Catherine.

She was a truly remarkable woman. She had somehow arranged that I should be let into the enclosure and taken to her. They brought her sickbed to the library. 'I wanted you to see it, dear child. Come in,' she said when she opened her eyes and saw me standing by the mirror with Claire in my arms. 'You have been so very good to us.' There was a chair for me beside the bed. She took my hand in hers; the bones felt thin and brittle like bird bones.

A nun I'd never met was acting as porter. She was not used to visitors and found it hard to speak, too shy to enjoy her role as dear old Sister Joseph used to. She may have been rather fussed that Claire was practising her oooh-sound rather loudly as we came in. She handed me an envelope and directed me to the parlour where I found the screen door to the inner sanctum wide open. There wasn't a soul about; the silence was eerie. When I opened the envelope I found I had been thoughtfully provided with a map of the house which traced my direction to the library. From the moment we stepped into the enclosure, Claire became as overawed by her surroundings as I, and stopped warbling. She was as good as gold throughout.

I climbed the great staircase. Though everything was extraordinarily clean, it was bare, with nothing on the walls save a few religious pictures. I believe the original architect, Rothery, would have approved.

There was nothing to distract the eye from the splendour of his majestic interior. The hall is lit from above by a great cupola. Silence reigned. I saw no one on my way. The smell is exactly as I remembered from my first visit; a sort of musty sea-damp overlaid with lavender. Apart from getting the roof and gutters fixed, no work has, as yet, been carried out. Nor will it until the lodge is sold. Ten months down the line the nuns are little better off.

The library is over the chapel, I think. The entrance is down a long, narrow, barrel-vaulted corridor which is ornately panelled though I did not give it more than a cursory glance. There is a huge mirror at the end to the left of which a door leads into the library.

The bed was facing the door, its linen sheets and pillowslips were snow white, almost shining with starch. It was as narrow as a child's bunk yet Mother Catherine looked lost in it. And pale as death. She wore only a neat white lace bonnet on her head which almost covered her still dark hair. The hair was a shock, the only colour except for her dark eyes. She was very weak and could hardly speak, the cancer having destroyed her throat; her voice was almost gone. She said it was of no consequence since she did not value speech very much. She looked content, amused almost.

Her body was so wasted, beside her Claire looked obscenely healthy and robust. When she began to fret, Sister Joseph shyly appeared from nowhere, and asked if she could show the little darling to the other sisters. I was amazed at how readily Claire staggered over to her and climbed into her arms. The rules of silence do not seem to apply to small fat girls. I could hear them both chattering merrily as they went down the corridor. When I turned back to Mother Catherine, she was smiling at the sound.

'The baby has grown. Don't worry, I am glad you brought her,' she said. She could always read my thoughts. *'She brings new life and joy to us. How old is she now?'*

'Almost a year.'

'She is a beautiful child, Tess, and a credit to you, as I knew she would be. You look happier too. I am glad. I think you have resolved your future.' Her voice fell away to a hoarse whisper so that I sensed rather than heard the words.

She pointed out the secret bookshelves which lay obscured behind the Corinthian pilasters. She watched while I tried to work out how to open them and when I couldn't she indicated the middle step on the base of the upper section. I gave one corner a sharp tug and it opened smooth as silk. The interiors are no more than eight or nine inches wide and perhaps six feet tall. They are empty now, of course. The books are all gone.

She looked so pure and peaceful in her white narrow bed as if she had already embraced death, though she lingered almost a month after I saw her. I shall miss her deeply. I sat and held her hand for a little while but she didn't say much more except to ask me to pray for the repose of poor Benedicte's troubled soul. The bursar drowned a couple of months ago. She walked into the sea in early May. They do not know how she managed to get that far. Or how she had left the convent without anyone noticing. She didn't recover from her head injury. She never spoke again and could hardly walk.

One other thing. Hugo has bought the lodge for me and Claire. He didn't tell me until after Mother Catherine was dead though he says she was very pleased. The other nuns are too, it seems. There are conditions attached. It may not be sold except back to the nuns as long as Holy Retreat exists. I am overwhelmed at his generosity. I thought at first I could not accept, that I would not be able to excise the memory of Terence Murphy-Dunne from that place. But going there and seeing it all again helped. He was not picked up. Somehow, between my sighting of him and when the police overran the beach less than half an hour later, he'd evaporated. Rumours are that he's holed up in North Africa or South America or . . . The list of improbable hiding places continues to grow as does the number of charges against him.

I drove to the Chiltern escarpment the other night, the anniversary of Marcus's death. I left Claire sleeping and went out before dawn at five o'clock. I drove along the A40 to Stokenchurch then turned back onto the M40. I wanted to approach the spot as he did, through the beautiful parabolic bridge which frames the landscape so well. Oxfordshire was spread out before me as I slowly started my descent. The early morning mist had not quite cleared. It hovered above the plain with the glow of sunlight tinting it rose. It was exactly as he loved it. I remembered how he brought me out there one dawn when I asked him, 'Why Oxford?'

I drove through the cutting at a snail's pace. There was no other traffic headed in my direction though the early run to London in the opposite lane had already started. I stopped just before the turn-off to Watlington and parked on the hard shoulder. Then I walked to the B4009 sign and draped a garland of white lilies over it. They looked almost festive. I stood for a few minutes and thought of my beloved Marcus and our life together. I used to say our relationship, our 'marriage' if you like, was like Pharaoh's dream: good years followed by bad and then by good again. Now I know that my reckoning was too neat, that you cannot measure happiness in months or years, it is too fleeting. You can only say of this moment or that: 'then I was happy.' But only the moments. Marriage is a foreign language I did not take trouble enough to learn. All I claim now is that we had our moments of *ecstasy and these are what I remember. So I thought of Marcus and was grateful that I loved him. And I thought of Mother Catherine who is dead too and Jeddie, though I didn't really know her. And poor unhappy Benedicte whom I never saw, who blamed herself for everything that happened last autumn, like Adelaide before her.*

A police car pulled up beside me and two furious young policemen came over to remonstrate with me for being a fool for standing on the motorway. I knew one of them at once. He was the young sergeant who came to tell me about the accident. He recognized me in the same moment. He looked at the flowers, then back at me and held out his hand.

'A year, isn't it?' he said. He called me Mrs Rogerson. This time I didn't argue.

'Yes,' I said and felt as though I'd stepped into the sunlight. And into the future. The Veuve is in the fridge.

Love, Tess

THE END

IN THE PRESENCE OF THE ENEMY
by Elizabeth George

'The reader is in for a page-turning treat'
Sunday Times

As the editor of a popular left-wing tabloid, Dennis Luxford has made a career out of exposing scandal and destroying reputations. When he is offered the chance of breaking another government 'sleaze' story and boosting the circulation of his paper still further his hesitation seems inexplicable. But at the heart of this particular scoop lies the kidnapping of a ten-year-old girl: Luxford's daughter. To save the life of his first-born child, whom he has never even seen, Luxford must reveal the details of his brief affair with the child's mother on the front page of his newspaper. But this liaison was no ordinary one-night stand. For the woman involved is Eve Bowen, now the Undersecretary of State for the Home Office. And even when it becomes clear that her daughter Charlotte is missing, Eve refuses to involve the police, insisting that her child's disappearance is simply a ploy, however despicable, by Luxford to bring down the Tory government.

It is only when events escalate to unbearable heights that New Scotland Yard, in the guise of Detective Inspector Thomas Lynley and his partner Detective Sergeant Barbara Havers, are brought in. And as their investigations move from the heart of parliamentary London to rural Wiltshire, both Lynley and Havers discover that treachery and betrayal lie perilously close to home.

'Plenty of chill factor . . . This story is gripping from start to finish' *Daily Mail*

A Bantam Paperback
0 553 40846 1

SEXTET
by Sally Beauman

'This is a peach of a novel . . . *Sextet* is a hugely entertaining read, seriously romantic and with a terrific sense of atmosphere'
Kate Saunders, *Daily Express*

Journalist Lindsay Drummond is about to re-make her life: she plans to move out of London, change her job, and above all cure herself of her hopeless love for her unfairly handsome colleague, Rowland McGuire – but then a chance encounter teaches her that the best-laid plans can go delightfully awry . . .

In New York, actress Natasha Lawrence is also trying to rebuild her life. Pursued by a stalker for the past five years, still bound to her ex-husband, the celebrated film director Tomas Court, she retreats with her son to the precincts of the exclusive – and haunted – Conrad apartment building. But will it provide her with the security she so desperately seeks, and will she and her husband be able to lay to rest the ghosts of their past?

Lindsay's and Natasha's lives become inextricably entangled; when the cast of characters gathers for Thanksgiving at the sinister Conrad building, anything can happen, for romance and retribution, marriage and murder are in the air.

'A complex cracker of a plot with vivid characters and atmospheric locations' *Daily Mail*

A Bantam Paperback
0 553 50326 X

A SELECTION OF NOVELS
AVAILABLE FROM BANTAM BOOKS

THE PRICES SHOWN BELOW WERE CORRECT AT THE TIME OF GOING TO PRESS, HOWEVER TRANSWORLD PUBLISHERS RESERVE THE RIGHT TO SHOW NEW RETAIL PRICES ON COVERS WHICH MAY DIFFER FROM THOSE PREVIOUSLY ADVERTISED IN THE TEXT OR ELSEWHERE.

40791 0	DEATH OF A GOSSIP	M C Beaton	£3.99
40792 9	DEATH OF A CAD	M C Beaton	£3.99
50329 4	DANGER ZONES	Sally Beauman	£5.99
40727 9	LOVERS AND LIARS	Sally Beauman	£5.99
50326 X	SEXTET	Sally Beauman	£5.99
50540 8	KILLING FLOOR	Lee Child	£5.99
40922 0	THE JUROR	George Dawes Green	£5.99
40321 4	AN INCONVENIENT WOMAN	Dominick Dunne	£4.99
50611 0	THE SHIFT	George Foy	£5.99
50475 4	THE MONKEY HOUSE	John Fullerton	£5.99
40237 4	FOR THE SAKE OF ELENA	Elizabeth George	£5.99
40846 1	IN THE PRESENCE OF THE ENEMY	Elizabeth George	£5.99
40238 2	MISSING JOSEPH	Elizabeth George	£5.99
40845 3	PLAYING FOR THE ASHES	Elizabeth George	£5.99
40167 X	WELL-SCHOOLED IN MURDER	Elizabeth George	£5.99
50385 5	A DRINK BEFORE THE WAR	Dennis Lehane	£5.99
50584 X	DARKNESS, TAKE MY HAND	Dennis Lehane	£5.99
40884 4	FAST FORWARD	Judy Mercer	£5.99
50619 6	DARK SKIES	Stan Nicholls	£4.99
50438 X	MOUNT DRAGON	Lincoln Preston	£5.99
50496 7	THE RELIC	Lincoln Preston	£5.99
40933 6	TRINITIES	Nick Tosches	£4.99

All Transworld titles are available by post from:

Book Service by Post, P.O. Box 29, Douglas, Isle of Man, IM99 1BQ

Credit cards accepted. Please telephone 01624 675137, fax 01624 670923 or Internet http://www.bookpost.co.uk or e-mail: bookshop @ enterprise.net for details.

Free postage and packing in the UK. Overseas customers allow £1 per book (paperbacks) and £3 per book (hardbacks).